Inside the Whispers

(Samantha Willerby Mystery Series - Book 1)

A. J. WAINES

First published in 2016.

Re-published in 2018 by Bloodhound Books

www.bloodhoundbooks.com

Print ISBN 978-1-912604-69-2

Also by A. J. Waines

Standalones:

The Evil Beneath
Girl on a Train
Dark Place to Hide
No Longer Safe
Don't you Dare

The Samantha Willerby Mystery Series:

Lost in the Lake
Perfect Bones

Writing as Alison Waines:

The Self-Esteem Journal
Making Relationships Work

Trust is good, but control is better.

Vladimir Lenin

Chapter 1

One month earlier

I have no idea what the time is and it doesn't matter. Not anymore.

I follow the narrow winding path and, after only a few strides, the ascent begins. It isn't for the fainthearted. From now on, I'm taking a chance with every step. The rain spits, pricking my cheeks; the wind is fierce, pressing my jeans against my legs as if I'm under water. A struggle, that's what it should be.

A few times my shoes – leather, with non-grip soles – scuff the edge of the path and I stumble. But I've made the right choice of footwear. No point in cheating by coming prepared. I don't want this to be easy. I'm not expecting any concessions, any mitigation.

I lose my balance again and one foot slips off the crust of the track. I have to grab at a clump of gorse beside me. The spines send multiple stabs of pain into my palm. Good. Pain is good.

My thighs burn as I reach the crag, the highest point, and I stand to catch my breath. Under different circumstances, I might have found it bracing, exhilarating even. There is a clear view out to sea; a massive billowing curtain of white and grey filling up the horizon, making it hard to work out where the sea ends and the sky begins. Endings and beginnings.

I turn full circle and can see no one. Not a soul. No one walking, climbing or in the water. Solitude. It's better this way. No distractions.

I step over the wooden 'Keep Off' sign towards the jagged edge. I kick at the tufts of grass sprouting like bristle on an old man's chin, then gingerly slide my shoe forward another step and lean over.

My vision goes fuzzy as I look down at the spume and froth curdling around sharp rocks. Lumps of the sandy cliff have crumbled away like sponge cake. It's a sheer drop.

A white shape suddenly swoops into my field of vision. A rag? An errant sheet of newspaper? I throw up my arms instinctively to protect myself. It dives at me again, making a cawing sound this time. I almost lose my footing and stagger back from the edge. I want to laugh. How ironic it would be if this was to end with a stupid accident.

I stand tall, snap my polished shoes together, suck in the salt air through my nostrils. If I'm going to do this, I want to get it right.

I will lean forward, then stoop a little further until gravity claims me and I float off like a supple Angel of the North. I am so close to the edge. It will only take a second. I can let the empty space claim my weight.

I slide my shoe four more inches onto the grassy lip to see what it feels like. I look out towards the horizon, then down to my feet, testing the support of the turf, knowing there is a point of no return. So close. One more step. Another?

Without warning I'm forced to duck. The seagull is back, charging like a rabid dog. I flap my arms. I must be near a nest - there must be eggs only a few feet away and the gull is keeping them warm. Nature's prime instinct is to protect those it loves. The thought is too much for me; too close to home. I sink to the grass. I press my face into its coarse blades, my palms face down close to my head like someone who is praying.

Except I'm not praying; I'm not worthy enough. I've failed in every aspect. Every minute of every day since it started.

I can smell the wet juice of the grass, see each and every blade close up, like the bars of a prison. How is it that everywhere I find myself I am confined, trapped? Even in the most expansive of places.

I lift my head. The gull seems to have stopped pestering me. It must have realised I'm no threat. I get to my feet. It's now flying beneath me, the wings crossing in and out of my sight below the edge of the cliff. Taking a deep breath, I slide my feet back to the lip of long fluttering grass. The yawning space is pulling at me again, enticing me. My breath is running out. This is it. Now…

I can't decide whether to close my eyes or keep them open. How could I have failed to consider this part? My gaze trails across the far distance, seeing only choppy waves kissing swirls of clouds. I soften my view so the shapes blend away to nothing.

Go…

A speck on the horizon makes my eyes jolt into focus. It's a ship, sliding elegantly in from the right, forcing me to think new thoughts: a symbol of rescue, a new beginning, going home…

I snatch my head back from the edge. What the hell am I doing? This isn't right. It will achieve absolutely nothing. This isn't a time for giving up – I should be working it out. Planning how to turn things around. I can't duck out at this crucial moment, like a coward; I have to find a solution, once and for all. There has to be one.

I zip my anorak up to my chin and turn back.

Chapter 2

Present Day

At the sound of the doorbell I shot upright on the sofa, the book falling to the floor. My first thought was that it must be Con. The second was that something was seriously burning in the kitchen.

I rescued the pan first – brown rice, only now it was black. I tossed the whole lot in the sink and hurried to the door, but my shoulders sank. I didn't recognise the shape through the peephole. It was a woman – it certainly wasn't Con.

Cold callers had a habit of turning up at ridiculous hours in my area, so as I edged the door open, I was half expecting her to proffer some unreadable identification and then launch into a rehearsed patter about domestic products. I'm usually far too obliging for my own good in situations like this, but not tonight. It was late and my eyes felt full of sand.

'Samantha…' came the voice with a slight question-mark hooked in at the end.

I stood back, out of shock rather than courtesy and my visitor took it as an invitation to step inside.

'What are *you* doing here?' My words faded to a whisper.

Another step back. I was wearing only pyjamas and held the edges of the collar together at the neck. 'What time is it'

'Just after nine o'clock.'

'Shouldn't you be..?'

'Aren't you going to ask me in? Make me a nightcap or something?'

She was unfastening the belt on her raincoat as if she popped round like this on a regular basis.

'How did you get my address?'

I knew for a fact I'd never passed it on to my sister.

'Daddy,' she said cheerfully.

I tried to hide the click my tongue made on the roof of my mouth. My father tried to do his best, but he regularly put his foot in it.

'I pressed the buzzer downstairs, but nothing happened,' she said, 'then I realised the main door was already open.'

I nodded wearily. 'The buzzer's broken.' It was handy when Con came round, but until the landlord got around to fixing it, it also meant anyone could get right to my door.

'It's late…' I said.

'Yeah – sorry.' Taking people by surprise had always been her speciality. 'Lost track of time.'

'I thought you were still—'

'Good behaviour,' she said, laughing. 'They let me out last month. I'm called Miranda now, by the way. I'm starting a new life with a new name. Much better, don't you think?'

She did have a point. I'd never forgiven my parents for naming my older sister Mimi. It had been a curse from the start, condemning her to a life of sniggers. I'd heard every crass joke in the book at boarding school; every variation on 'Who are You-You?' or 'Come with Me-Me?' you could think of.

'Let me take your coat,' I said. It came out like the patter of a waitress in a posh restaurant. How had we got to this stage; stiff like strangers with each other? My only sister. I felt something dissolve inside my chest.

The table lamp in the hall shone a delicate beam across her pale cheek. 'Miranda' was only two years older than me – thirty-two – but deep folds in her forehead had added ten years to her looks, compounded by the way her eyes seemed to have shrunk inside her skull.

'Coffee?' I said. All I wanted was to take the bath I should have had an hour ago and sink straight into bed, but I could hardly turf my own sister out into the night without at least giving her a chance to explain herself.

'That would be nice. No milk.'

That was just as well. I still hadn't got round to buying a fresh carton.

Miranda followed me into the kitchen.

'Is everything all right?' I asked. 'What's happened?' Miranda showing up like this could only mean trouble.

'I told you,' she said, the epitome of innocence. 'They let me out. I'm on my own now. I just wanted to see how you were.'

There had to be more to it, of course there was, but I knew from past experience that pushing her wouldn't get me any closer.

I wanted to give her my full attention, but I found myself reliving a harrowing encounter at work instead. After lunch, I'd come back from a tranquil stroll along the Thames, savouring my bacon sandwich, to find ambulances backing up outside A&E. One of the paramedics told me there'd been a high-speed collision involving joyriders that had left unsuspecting pedestrians scattered like rag dolls across the pavement. On seeing the carnage spilling over the stretchers in front of me, my sandwich had made a bid to see the light of day a second time. I'd only just managed to keep it where it was.

Miranda looked bemused, waiting for me to do something: fill the kettle, ask her questions, look pleased to see her.

'Sorry Mim…Miranda, I'm a bit distracted. There was a nasty crash in central London today. We were the nearest hospital.'

'Why would they need you? You're not a paramedic,' she pointed out, leaning against the doorframe. 'Daddy said you're working with nutters now.'

I threw her a sharp glance as I held the kettle under the tap. 'I work with people who've suffered trauma,' I said. 'I was there when the casualties were brought in, that's all.'

'Oooh, you must tell me all the details,' she said brightly. She rubbed her hands together, rapt by the possible whiff of drama.

I handed her the mug of coffee and led her through to the sitting room. 'I'm really sorry, Miranda – I need a bath – I've got work tomorrow.'

'No problem,' she said, as if she was doing me a favour. 'We can talk in the morning.' She reached over and turned on the TV.

I stiffened. I wanted to protest, then spotted the bulging overnight bag she'd brought in from the hall. Had I missed something?

'I'll sleep on the sofa,' she said, then as an afterthought, 'if that's all right?'

I didn't have the energy to argue. I dragged a duvet from my wardrobe and laid it over the sofa, then piled up two pillows at one end. 'I won't be long,' I said, padding towards the bathroom.

I slid my head under the water and rested it on the bottom of the bath. I let my limbs flop, loose and heavy, closed my eyes and hoped the water would wash away the images I'd seen at lunchtime: tangles of blood and hair, severed limbs, unidentifiable faces.

Afterwards, I tried to rinse the metallic taste out of my mouth with my toothbrush, but it remained like a gritty coating on my tongue.

I was used to managing trauma up to a point – of course I was – I'd got myself some specialist training and started this job three months ago. But my everyday role was to *listen* to victims' accounts after the event, not see the sticky, gruesome mess of a tragedy first hand, like today. I didn't dare imagine what the scene of the collision had looked like; bystanders would no doubt have stood transfixed, then gone on their way carrying the most horrific images in their heads.

When I emerged from the bathroom, I'd completely forgotten Miranda was there. She was sitting on the edge of the sofa, her arms folded, as if she'd been waiting for me in that position all this time. Turning up like this was nothing short of terrible timing – dealing with her, even in the best of circumstances, had always demanded considerable alertness and sensitivity.

Her foot was tap, tap, tapping loudly on the floor and I couldn't help noticing she'd hidden something under a cushion behind her.

'Fancy a game of Scrabble?' she said, sliding out the box and bringing a tight fist to her mouth with anticipation.

Miranda's sense of judgement had always been skewed. 'No – thanks. Sorry. I'm knackered.' I was so tired every syllable required a jolt from my abdomen. Aside from the shock at lunchtime, I'd had one patient after another all day, each one struggling to come to terms with a life-shattering event.

Her look of disappointment drifted into resignation; it wasn't new for me to be a spoilsport.

'Never mind,' she said. 'I'll watch this.' She nodded at the television screen where a black and white film was just starting.

When I tiptoed towards the kitchen for a glass of water, shortly afterwards, Miranda had fallen asleep. I switched off the TV and stood over her for a few seconds, watching her eyelids flutter.

'Sweet dreams,' I whispered, wondering where she went in her sleep. In that moment I had a sudden ache to be there with her, wherever she was, holding hands and swinging our arms; laughing, like we had a special bond.

I left her in peace and shuffled back to my room, knowing that she'd brought with her a can of worms and it was only a matter of time before something unpleasant crawled out across the carpet.

Chapter 3

Miranda woke me in the morning, wearing one of my T-shirts, holding out a mug of coffee.

'I couldn't find any tea bags,' she said.

'That's because I've run out,' I replied, sitting up and accepting the unexpected offering.

'I'm going out for supplies,' she said. 'Have you got a spare key?'

This was all happening too fast. I had no idea why she'd turned up like this without warning or what she wanted. I needed to get to the bottom of it, but I wasn't sufficiently awake to handle the inevitable backlash once I started asking questions.

When I didn't respond, she turned towards the door. 'You'll just have to let me back in,' she said.

'There's one on the shelf by the front door – the nearest shop is…'

She was already out of earshot. I heard the door bang.

On mornings when the sky wasn't hurling rain, sleet or snow at me, I made my way to the hospital on my bicycle. There was no excuse that June morning, the early molten clouds were already giving way to sky the colour of forget-me-nots, when I left. It was promising to be another hot one.

London drivers don't like cyclists at the best of times and I wasn't on form after Miranda's sudden appearance, last night. A car tooted as I wobbled trying to make a flying get-away at a green light on Borough High Street, reminding me to concentrate on the road.

I'd only ever fallen off once in seven years, when an ice-cream van had pulled out in front of me without signalling. On that occasion I'd come away with fifteen bruises and a free double cornet.

Con's accident a month ago had been serious, but then he'd fallen off a motorbike. He should never have been on it in the first place. Riding pillion, drunk, at two o'clock in the morning isn't the smartest thing to do, but to fall asleep when you're meant to be holding on tight, is plain irresponsible. At first, when I got the call, I thought I'd lost him. After waiting so many years for someone like Con to come along – motorbike or not – that would have been grossly unfair.

But life could be desperately cruel, randomly picking out innocent victims like flies on a windscreen. His accident had made me remember how fragile our existence is and how we frequently don't get second chances. It made me want to make the most of my time with Con.

I still couldn't believe the impact he was having on me. I'd only known him for twelve weeks and for that entire time I'd been sizzling with an unhinged desire for him I'd never felt for anyone else before.

I passed reception and pushed open the door to my new office. During a recent re-shuffle, I'd been moved to the room nobody wanted; the one with the flickering fluorescent light and the windows that didn't open – next to the gents' loo.

As I logged onto my computer, there was a tap on the door and Debbie, who managed several units on the ground floor, staggered over the threshold carrying a heavy office chair. Debbie was blonde and barely five feet tall, with chunky limbs that were bulky with muscle rather than fat.

'I managed to pinch it for you from Dr Winkle's old office,' she said, as I rushed to help her. It was the executive sort with thick black padding. 'It's not real leather, but it's better than the one you've got.'

My current chair was plain and made of wood, with one leg slightly shorter than the others.

'You're a gem. Thank you.'

I'd warmed to Debbie the first time I met her, when I joined St Luke's, seven years ago. It was a chilly morning in January and she'd gone out of her way to bring me a decent coffee, a fan-heater (that actually worked) and a warm croissant. In return, I'd tinkered with a few wires behind her desk and managed to fix her lazy printer. Since then, we'd made a point of looking out for each other.

We set about wheeling the new chair into place, guiding one arm each, but in line with my experience with most shopping trolleys, it had a mind of its own. We both giggled as it ran into the bookcase and got jammed as we tried to reverse it.

'Oh heck, I hope it's not going to be more trouble than it's worth,' she said.

My first impression of her had been of someone who was used to having to elbow her way through a crowd to get noticed. When she told me she was the only girl in a family with four brothers, all of whom were rugby players, that made sense. With the chair finally in situ, she dusted off her hands and left me to my first patient.

Ken arrived on time at nine. He'd been in a bad way when I'd stood beside him at reception a few days earlier. Poor guy, he'd had a panic attack and had thrown up all over my shoes. He didn't look much better today and had another anxiety attack almost as soon as he sat down. Sure enough he threw up again, but on this occasion I managed to get the waste bin to him in time. I reached for the window catch, before I remembered it wouldn't budge.

After Ken, I saw another two patients, before I had to attend a 'short' meeting about data protection which overran into my lunch break. As a result, I bolted down a sandwich in the canteen instead of heading out into the sun.

On the way back for my afternoon patients, I passed a stretcher trolley parked in the corridor. I stopped when I heard a muted cry from beneath the blanket. The blonde paramedic in attendance nodded as I flashed my ID.

'We're waiting for the go-ahead from intensive care,' she said. 'This is Holly – she's eight,' she added, as she adjusted the girl's neck-brace with one hand and flipped a switch under a screen on wheels, with the other.

I swallowed hard, doing my utmost not to flinch. The blanket had come adrift revealing Holly's leg, twisted the wrong way below the knee. More worrying was that a section of metal from somewhere had lodged in her side and another paramedic, with a long blunt fringe, was holding it steady. Both professionals were wearing blue surgical gloves and were too busy with IV tubes, portable monitors and bursts of radio transmission to offer the girl any TLC. I touched her little finger gently and she turned her hand to grip mine. Hers was clammy and cold.

'Holly, you're in very safe hands,' I said to her. Her eyelashes were matted with dried blood, and I wasn't sure if she was able to see me or not. 'They're really good, here.'

'Mummy…' she whimpered, tears coating her face.

'Parents informed?' I called out to the woman who was checking Holly's blood pressure.

'On their way.'

'Mummy will be here before you know it,' I assured the girl. 'Can she have water?'

'Yeah – over there.' She pointed to a plastic bottle lying on the blanket. I tipped the water carefully to Holly's lips and she took it down in tiny gulps.

'It's so hot,' said the blonde paramedic, wiping her hairline with her forearm before leaning over to pick up a swab. She was in her early twenties, I surmised. The elastic band roughly holding back her ponytail was at odds with the fancy diamante clips above her ears. She wore heavy make-up, too, showing all the signs that she'd been snatched from her day off.

Holly stopped swallowing and starting panting and gasping. The paramedic cupped a plastic mask over her mouth.

'Okay, sweetheart, just breathe,' she said.

As Holly began to calm down, I started singing, softly. 'Feed the birds, tuppence a bag, tuppence, tuppence, tuppence a bag…'

With the familiar soothing tune, Holly's breathing started to regulate, but it was still too fast, her little chest pumping up and down.

A voice came over the radio and the blonde paramedic flicked the brake switch with her foot. 'Okay, we're cleared to go.'

'I'm going to let go of your hand, now, Holly,' I told her. 'They're going to move you on and make you more comfortable.' She didn't respond. 'You're being so brave. Everyone's going to be so proud of you.' I stood back and watched her being trundled away.

As I filled a cup at the water cooler outside my office, I noticed a young woman I didn't recognise sitting in the bank of chairs opposite. I could tell by her behaviour that she was my first patient of the afternoon; her knee was bouncing up and down at a frantic pace and her eyes were sweeping the waiting room, on high alert. Typical symptoms of Post-Traumatic Stress Disorder. My referral notes said she'd been in a fire in a restaurant and I could see pink scar tissue running from her cheek and disappearing under her collar. I wondered how severe the burn was and whether the worst part was hidden from view.

I approached her. 'Jane LaSalle?'

'Yep.' The woman jumped, then tried to hide her reaction.

We went inside. 'I'm Dr Samantha Willerby, but please, call me Sam.'

Jane sat on the edge of her seat, hugging her bag. 'We don't have to talk about what you've been through at all today, if you don't want to,' I said. 'There will never be any pressure to relive any memories of it. At any time. Only when and if you feel you can cope with it.'

Jane gulped. 'That's good. I wasn't sure I could handle going into it all again, straight away.'

I explained what the treatment would involve and how the initial six sessions might unfold. 'We'll be discussing small changes in your behaviour – seeing if you can try some new ways of dealing with situations.'

Jane nodded. She must have been in her mid-twenties, but looked like a frightened child about to make a dash for the door at any second. I was sure she hadn't blinked once since coming in.

I smiled. 'You're nervous about being here, aren't you?'

She laughed. 'Bloody terrified,' she admitted. It helped clear the air.

'That's completely normal. You've not done this before and you don't know what to expect. You've been through a terrifying experience and you're probably not sure whether talking about it is going to help or make it worse.'

Jane visibly sank into the chair, as if the puppet strings keeping her taut had snapped. Good. We were off to a promising start.

'Can I check first what symptoms you've been experiencing this week?'

I ran through a list of the common ones, asking her to rate each of them in terms of severity on a scale of one to ten. 'So, the flashbacks and nightmares are causing the most problems for you, right now.'

'Yeah. And I can't go on the Underground.'

'Okay. Would you *like* to be able to go on the Tube again – could that be a goal for us to aim towards?'

'It would make things a lot easier getting to work. I have to go miles out of my way on the bus at the moment.' She fiddled with the handle on her bag. 'I don't want to be afraid anymore.'

I made a note in her file.

She was talking again. 'I remember being trapped in the smoke. All I could see were flames closing in on me.'

She was already moving on to the difficult part. 'Just take your time,' I said.

'I fell when I got to the top of the escalator. I remember the floor was terribly hot. There was a smell of scorched oil. And the heat...it was like being in an oven.'

She stopped and looked at me, her mouth twisting from side to side as if suddenly aware she was talking about it, when she hadn't meant to.

I waited.

She went on. 'I managed to get up, but I couldn't see a thing with the black smoke. I could feel lumps around my feet – I knew they were bodies…'

I was momentarily distracted. Her referral notes must have been wrong; this didn't sound like a fire in a restaurant. But, it was a fault our end and I didn't want to interrupt her. Instead, I watched as a lone tear crept down her face, part of me trying to work out which incident she'd been involved in.

She blew her nose and straightened up. 'I was very lucky. I got out. People died. It was horrible…'

My mouth was dry. 'You've done really well to talk about it.' Whatever the disaster was, it sounded horrendous.

'How long have you been having flashbacks?' I asked.

'About ten days.'

'And when was the actual incident?'

'When I got the burns?'

'Yes.'

'About eight weeks ago.' I felt a frown fold into my forehead.

'So you didn't have any distressing flashbacks during the first seven weeks at all – just recently?'

'Oh, no.' Jane shook her head. 'The flashbacks I'm having are about the second one. More recent.'

I was confused. I rested the pen across the notes on my lap.

'We're talking about two different incidents here?' I asked.

'Yeah. I got the burns at work when the chip pan caught fire. There was a flash flame that caught me across my neck.' She turned to show me the burn I'd noticed earlier, but was dismissive about it. 'I work in Jerry's Fish Plaice. It's a restaurant on Tottenham Court Road. But I didn't seem to have any bad after-effects then. I mean, I had a few nightmares and I was anxious for a while, but it faded.'

'And the recent incident?'

'Yeah. On the Tube.' Jane looked confused herself, now. 'The weird thing is I can't remember exactly when it happened. There are loads of bits missing. But this is the one I'm so messed up about. I was okay with the restaurant fire. I went back to work there after a week or so and it was fine.'

What she said suddenly rang a bell. I'd read something about a fire at Liverpool Street Tube in the free paper about ten days ago, but it hadn't even made the national news. I hadn't realised there'd been fatalities. How unlucky for Jane that she'd been caught up in that so soon after the first fire. One at work and another a few weeks later on her way home. My heart went out to her.

I had three more patients after Jane and by the time my appointments had ended, it felt more like three in the morning, than 6pm. The sheer emotional exhaustion from hearing people relive horrific experiences – whether from a train crash, traffic collision or Tube fire – was an aspect of the job I was still struggling to come to terms with. The unexpected downside being that every time I heard a victim's story, their suffering wore away a little piece of my soul.

Trauma counselling was certainly far more intense than my mainstream work as a clinical psychologist, but having done that job for several years, I was looking for a change of focus. I suppose I wanted to make more of an impact. Now, I was helping people through that terrible wasteland in the weeks following a devastating incident, when a barrage of disturbing symptoms often took hold.

I could always go back to mainstream therapy, if it turned out the job wasn't for me. I was going to give it three more months and see.

When I got home, Miranda had left an 'enlightening' note on the mat, stating merely: *Gone Out*. I took a step into the sitting room and stopped. It looked like the aftermath of the party to end all parties. Whatever Miranda had been doing all day, it had involved scattering a wide selection of food substances everywhere. I found scrambled egg plastered to the sitting room wall, cereal crunched into the carpet, ground almonds in the bathroom plug-hole. She'd also had a go at painting, but in the absence of a canvas she'd chosen a corner of my bedroom to start a decidedly erotic mural.

I'd called the care home earlier and it turned out everything my sister had said was above board. She was out. For good. Let loose in the big wide world over a month ago.

I tried Con's number, but his phone went to voicemail and I'd left enough messages already. I didn't want to pester him, but we needed to talk. There was one issue between us that we needed to iron out. Unfortunately, he had a habit of disappearing when I most wanted to speak to him.

I heated up a tin of spaghetti and spent the rest of the evening vacuuming and rubbing frantically at the wallpaper, inhaling white spirit that made me dizzy.

When I finally went to bed, I had no idea whether Miranda had come back or not.

Chapter 4

Morning broke to the throbbing chorus of *Knowing Me, Knowing You* from the sitting room.

'Can you turn it down?' I groaned, dragging myself out into the light, thrashing the belt of my dressing gown around my waist. 'You'll disturb people.'

'A bit of Abba never hurt anyone,' Miranda retorted.

'It's early.' A broad yawn made my point.

My sister stood by the window with her arms folded and I noticed her eyes were puffy.

'You okay?' I said, taking a step closer. She winced and shrank back as if I'd tried to strike her. 'What's going on?' I said, as softly as I could. 'Have you been crying?'

'Don't be silly.' She sniffed and walked away.

I followed her into the kitchen. She stepped around two cardboard boxes with pan handles sticking out of the top. 'Just moved in?'

'No. I've been here over a year.' I waved vaguely at the boxes. 'I haven't got around to sorting everything out yet.'

Ever since I moved here I felt the place would 'do for now'. Situated on the first floor of a Victorian house, it was only five minutes' walk from Clapham Junction railway station. The bumf from the letting agent said it was 'ideally located for local shops and amenities' and for once it was an understatement. The area had everything: wine bars and restaurants galore, delis, a fresh organic bakers, an apartment store, takeaways, a library, a gym and vast expanses of parkland.

I hadn't done much to it, because in spite of the great location, I kept thinking I wouldn't be here for long. The flat itself was cramped and shabby, in need of serious refurbishment. The shower leaked and the kitchen sink kept clogging up and there were patches of damp in the bedroom I'd turned a blind eye to. I saw it as a stepping stone to the next, better phase of my life when I was more established, more sorted. Whenever that might be.

Nevertheless, I liked to think I'd made the place cosy and put my stamp on it. I'd made bookshelves from old planks of wood and bricks; the coffee table was carved by my father from a storm-felled tree. The shape reminded me of a map of Cyprus and was speckled with knots, impeccably sanded down so that the surface was as smooth as glass. Sometimes I sat beside it and skimmed my fingers over the surface. It was oddly soothing.

The flat came furnished with the basics, so I'd draped throws over beaten-up old chairs and put down rugs in pastel shades over worn patches in the carpet. All in all, the place had grown on me.

'What's that?' Miranda was pointing inside a cupboard I'd just opened. A green lava lamp from the sixties. I'd bought it at a car-boot sale about ten years ago. 'I love it!' Miranda was stroking the base. She'd never seen it.

I caught my breath as a memory shot into my mind. It was the earliest one I could recall of the two of us one summer when we were at the seaside. Mimi was seven and I was five. A man was jogging across the beach carrying a surfboard towards the water. He was in a hurry.

Mimi ran in front of him chasing a beach ball and the man turned sharply, swinging the board round straight into her. I remembered the snapping sound and the wide gash as her forehead cracked open. Copious amounts of blood rolled down Mimi's face and her look of bewilderment before the tears came will be forever imprinted on my mind. I'd never seen so much blood. I thought the man had killed her. It sent a gooey sick taste into my mouth even now.

Miranda turned and I saw the thin scar from that day catch the light. Hard to imagine she was the same person. So much had happened to her since then.

She pointed to the old-style Trim phone. 'Hey – we used to play with one of these when we were little! Do you remember?' She was like a child in a sweet shop.

I nodded with a transient smile. I had done my best to forget most of our shared childhood memories.

I wanted to ask why she was here – but I couldn't think of a way to broach the subject that didn't sound unwelcoming. I knew if I bided my time, she'd tell me eventually.

'Is this your boyfriend?' she said, stroking a photograph on the fridge of Con and his son, Justin. We'd been on Hampstead Heath. The picture was slightly blurred; a gust of wind had yanked a clump of Con's curly hair across his eyes just as I'd taken it.

'Kind of,' I said. Miranda had caused havoc with my boyfriends in the past. I didn't want her getting her sticky fingers into this relationship. Con was too special.

'Married?' she asked, pointing to Justin.

'Not now,' I replied. 'His ex-wife has custody of his son. Con's away a lot.'

'Wedding bells?'

'Hell, no – it's only been about three months,' I said. Three divine and delicious months.

'Good-looking,' she said wistfully. 'Why is his arm in a sling?'

'He came off his motorbike,' I said.

I remembered Justin's fascination after it happened. 'Dad's shoulder nearly came right off,' he'd said, with a nine-year-old's innocent pride. 'The doctor said they might have to pull the skin off Dad's bottom and stick it onto his arm.' Justin had been laughing. 'How funny would that be?'

Miranda straightened up, clearly bored with this line of questioning.

'Didn't you get my letter?' she said.

'Letter? No. When was that?'

'Last week.' Miranda had stopped examining everything and stood in the centre of the space, looking terribly fragile. I noticed her mousy hair was thinning, turning grey at the temples. She seemed to have lost her train of thought.

'Do you want cereal?' I asked with warmth. I wanted to reach forward and stroke her arm, but my heels stayed pressed into the floor.

'No. No cereal.' There was a poignant silence. 'I've changed,' she said. She looked at me, her thin smile seeking acknowledgement.

'Okay…' It was one of those statements that could imply either a minor alteration or a turnaround of enormous proportions. I wasn't sure how far down the road towards personal transformation Miranda was talking about – or was capable of, for that matter. 'The letter?' I said.

'Oh that. It was asking if I could come and live with you.'

I dropped the butter knife. 'Live with me?'

'Yeah. Not for long. Just until I get myself back on my feet.'

Miranda was twirling a clump of hair around her finger non-stop. 'I bet you rang Linden Manor,' she snapped accusingly.

'Yes, actually,' I sniffed. 'I needed to check, that's all.'

She pulled the knot of hair across her mouth and started chewing it. 'They said I can try living in the community. Properly, you know, but the place they lined up for me was awful. I had to leave. They're sorting something else out for me – somewhere better.'

'When? Where?'

'I'm not sure, yet.'

'Sit down,' I said evenly. This wasn't the kind of conversation we could have standing up. She plopped down in one single movement.

'Tell me how you've been, Mimi.'

I was struggling to hide how unsettled I was by this unexpected announcement. I needed to slow things down.

'It's *Miranda*. I'm not that person, anymore.'

'Okay. Sorry.' I handed her a glass of orange.

'I'm much better. Obviously.' She laughed, nervously. 'If I could—'

I didn't want this sliding away from me. I needed to get things straight right from the start.

'You can't live here, Mim—' I stopped myself. 'It's a one-bedroom flat, Miranda. There isn't room.'

She got up. 'Yes, there is.'

She went into the sitting room. I watched her spin around with a look of approval, like a satisfied buyer about to put in an offer.

'It's not meant for two,' I called out from the kitchen.

She stood at the door, a sulk dragging at the corner of her mouth. She'd never been a proper older sister. Never been a proper *sister* – full stop. But it was easy to forget that none of this was her fault. Her mental health problems had been diagnosed a long time ago, although Mum had always maintained that Miranda was just plain 'difficult'.

I drained my glass of orange and left it where it was, resting my heavy head on my hand. Before I knew it, Miranda was refilling my glass.

I tried to grab her arm. 'No – it's okay, I—' The glass tipped over and juice splattered across the table making a little waterfall onto the floor. She grabbed a blouse from the clothes horse, squatted down and draped it over the puddle forming on the lino. 'No, don't use my—'

I sat back.

There was no way I could cope having my sister to stay. She'd been here less than thirty-six hours and already I was tearing my hair out. She seemed to be in every room at once; beside me, behind me and standing in my way.

Almost instantly, an unwelcome vision of the alternative jumped into my head; Miranda wandering out into the street, trailing her coat on the ground behind her, staring straight ahead, following a distant light only she could see. Easy prey.

'Listen, you can stay for a few days – but that's all.'

'Fabulous!' She reached out and scooped me into a firm embrace. My arms turned to lead. I couldn't lift them. I tried, but

I couldn't move. I couldn't even press my cheek into her shoulder. She drew back, pretending not to notice.

I wanted to say something kind and hospitable, but it felt like all my emotions were squashed inside a washing machine – tumbling around, mixed up, choked. I asked instead if she wanted toast.

'Only if you've got Marmite,' she replied.

Now that the arrangement for her to stay a few days was settled, we moved on to other subjects. Safe subjects: London, fashion, cooking. She told me she'd been working at an art project in Camden.

'You've got a job?'

'Selling art materials and covering a few shifts at the café. They're letting me have gallery space to see if I can sell some of my own work. There's a workshop, so I paint there, too.'

Perhaps she really had moved on.

Our words came and went; a robotic conversation. *How will I get to Camden from here? Plenty of trains every hour. Yes – it would only be for a few days.*

'I've got access to a van, now and again,' she said. 'It's not mine – but we can book it through the project.'

'You drive?' It was hard to regard my sister as an adult, doing things that normal adults did.

'I'm not incapable, you know,' she retorted. The strain of keeping up with this new version of Mimi was giving me a headache.

As I cleaned my teeth before heading off to work, she let out a squeal from the cupboard in the hall. 'You've kept it!' She appeared at the doorway. 'My lovely trench coat…' She hugged it tight against her, as though someone was inside it. 'You still wear it?' She rubbed the wide floppy collar against her cheek.

'Now and again.'

That was a lie. I wore it all the time. Miranda had given it to me the last time I'd seen her. Was it really more than four years ago? It was expensive and she'd loved it, so I'd always suspected the gift had been an aberration; a moment of rash camaraderie. It was the only physical connection I'd had to her apart from a handful of photos. I didn't want her to know just yet how much the coat meant to me.

A sudden ache warned me she might want it back.

'What happened to me – it can happen to anyone, Sam,' she said, as she hung it back on the hanger. 'It's not about being weak.'

I nodded. It was the most grown-up thing she'd said since she'd arrived.

Chapter 5

One month earlier

There's no reason to come here. It's simply where I got off the bus, unable to carry on. I couldn't sit there any longer with normal people around me. I couldn't breathe.

I close my eyes and rest my elbows on the top of the fence. I need to stride out across open spaces, feel a sense of freedom, feel in touch with the bigger scheme of things. I start walking across the common but it's no good. I can't escape.

It hits me like this – fresh each time, as if I didn't know about it. I'll be going about my day and suddenly I'll plummet into a massive pit that opens up in front of me. I can't help returning to the pain of it; scratching it, prodding it, making it worse.

Why is it coming at me again and again? It's not like it happened last week. I should be used to the horror of it by now.

Heading out to the clifftop the other day was a mistake. Thinking about it now, I feel stupid, pathetic. What I need is something constructive – to confront this. Something to combat these constant feelings of helplessness.

But, I still haven't worked out what that's going to be.

I've tried everything I can think of to fight back, but there are too many obstacles. The whole thing is too big, insurmountable. The worst part is feeling powerless. I'm left with this terrible resentment, too, that my world has been blighted. Bitterness that this has to happen to me, when I've done nothing whatsoever to deserve it. It's so unfair!

I've got to take matters into my own hands now – before I run out of time.

Chapter 6

Present Day

After my first session of the morning, I had a call from a nurse in intensive care to tell me a patient had been asking for me. I thought it must be Holly, the little girl I'd spoken to in the corridor, but I was led to a man's bedside in the adult section instead.

The man was Asian, around twenty, banked up on high pillows gingerly holding his chest, as if worried it might burst open at any moment. I recognised his eyes – bold and almost black – with light creases scoring his tall forehead.

'I'm Aaqil Jabour,' he said, his voice hoarse. A tube had been fitted between his ribs attached to a suction device. 'Thank you for finding me. I thought after what you did for me, I'd feel able to speak to you.'

I'd first met Aaqil after a racist attack, last week. The ambulance carrying him drew up alongside me as I was walking over to the bike shed at the end of the day. I'd moved to get out of everyone's way, but a nurse beckoned me over to his trolley as he was wheeled on to the tarmac.

'Punctured lung – he's unconscious,' she'd whispered, easing a ventilator tube out from under his head. 'Someone stabbed him on the way back from his uncle's funeral. He asked me for words from the Koran,' she said, gritting her teeth, 'but I couldn't help.'

It was essential in my work to have meaningful words of solace to hand, but I knew only one part of the Koran by heart. I leant close to his ear and gently asked if a few lines from Fussilat, verse forty-one, would be okay. He showed no signs of having heard, but I carried on anyway:

'Do not fear and do not grieve but receive good tidings of Paradise, which you were promised…'

His eyes had flickered and opened briefly, then he'd extended a limp hand towards me and squeezed my thumb. Running on adrenalin, I went on reciting, drawing out the words from the far corners of my memory. He'd slipped back into unconsciousness by then, but the grooves in his forehead had softened.

Now, seven days on, he was lying here smiling at me.

'I wasn't sure you'd heard me that day,' I said, looking down at him with tenderness. 'I'm glad it helped a little.' I pulled the curtain around his bed; the rings rattling along the pole like someone dropping a handful of coins.

'I thought I was going to die,' he said, 'but hearing those words, I felt I could have met Allah with peace in my heart.' I pulled up a chair and sat beside him. 'They said you are a therapist, that I could come and see you.' He continued to hold his chest.

'Most of my appointments get booked months in advance, but I always keep some for emergencies,' I said. 'I'd be very happy to work with you.'

I meant it. It's rare for members of the Asian community to seek help beyond their extended family; going 'outside' to see a professional is often considered taboo. He must have felt a genuine connection with me.

'When can I start?' he asked. He tried to laugh, but it turned into a guttural splutter instead.

'You'll need to feel a bit stronger, first. Also, when you're still in shock, it's hard to see if there are going to be any long-term issues.'

'I'll speak to the doctor and get my name on your list straight away,' he rasped. 'It's cognitive, right?'

'Mostly, yes. We'd explore your feelings first, sort it all out in your head and look at managing some of the immediate symptoms.' I talked him briefly through the procedure and asked about his sleeping, any intrusive thoughts and flashbacks. He complained of nightmares, being afraid to fall sleep, being jumpy at the slightest noise – just as I'd expect.

I got up to go; already he was looking grey with the exertion of talking to me.

'I'll see you soon,' he said. 'It will help, I'm sure of it.'

He tried to sit forward and wavered, needing me to catch him before he toppled sideways. He clutched his chest and I guided him back down again while I called for help. Dr Boyd didn't take long to make an assessment and within two minutes Aaqil was being wheeled away for emergency surgery.

I felt sick after he'd gone. He was clearly not yet out of danger.

Before my next patient, I made my way to the A&E main desk.

'There was a little girl called Holly,' I said, holding up the ID badge hanging around my neck. 'She had a broken leg and internal injuries…'

'Oh yeah, I remember – coach accident,' said the receptionist, flicking through sheets in a file. 'Here she is. Holly Farnbury. Eight years old.'

'Which ward is she in? I thought I might pop in to see how she's doing.' I could picture Holly's pale, bewildered face; the pleading grip of her small fingers.

The woman turned a few more sheets, then moved over to the computer screen.

She straightened up. Her voice dropped. 'I'm so sorry…'

I nodded and took a step back, unable to speak.

I was going to need a thicker skin for this job than I'd thought.

As soon as I returned to my office, there was a tap on the door and my next patient, Terry Masters, came in. He was in his early twenties; a tall, gangly man who looked like he was going through a turbulent, but misplaced, adolescence. He had all-encompassing acne, lank greasy hair and an inability to look me in the eye. He sat on the edge of the chair, leant forward on his knees and stared at the floor. This was his second session. He'd fallen off scaffolding six weeks earlier and had needed surgery on his arm.

Like many of my patients he was troubled by nightmares and now his sleep was out of kilter, he was having difficulty during the daytime too.

'I can't get interested in nuffin',' he muttered. 'Can't even be bothered to see my mates.' He rubbed his eyes. 'What's weird is I can't feel nuffin' – you know? I see the images in my head, like watchin' a movie or sommat – and it's like it's not me. Like I was there, but I wasn't.' He shook his head. 'I dunno how to explain it.'

'That's a totally normal reaction,' I said. 'It really is. People tend to cut off because it makes what happened seem less scary. You don't *want* it to be real.'

'I find it hard going out. Every time I leave the house, I think this is it. I'm gonna die. This car is gonna leave the road and run me over. This bloke is gonna come at me with a knife.' He grabbed at his hair. 'I feel like I'm goin' mad.'

I spent most of the session, just like his first one, trying to help him normalise his experience. Just before the end, he said something that made my ears prick up.

'You said the traumatic experience happened about ten days ago,' I said. I ran my finger down my notes. 'But it says here you sustained your injuries *six weeks* ago. Have we got that wrong?'

'No, that's about right.'

'So there were *two* incidents; the one where you fell off the scaffolding at work and needed a skin graft for your elbow and—'

'Yeah – that's right. The bad stuff is about the recent one. I was shocked by the fall, obviously, but it was just one of them things. I shoulda been more careful. But the fire…on the Underground…'

'At Liverpool Street?'

He bit his lip. 'I don't even remember gettin' down there. I don't know where I was going. All I can remember is bein' trapped on the Tube. We came to a sudden stop and the lights went out and people fell all over the place, grabbin' on to each other. They were hammering on the doors trying to prise 'em open. Someone said they could smell smoke and we thought there'd been a bomb. Everyone was just desperate to get out, but there was nowhere to go. It got hot, like effin' fast – and this dreadful stench of scorched oil was everywhere…'

It all came tumbling out. He started to hyperventilate.

'Okay, Terry, purse your lips like I showed you last time, like you're going to whistle.' He did as I said. 'Now count to three on the in, and three on the out breath…easy…good…and again, count to four, this time…that's it…now five…'

I handed him a glass of water, but he waved it away and insisted on continuing. 'I wanted to help, you know, but I was scared. No – that's not true. I *didn't* wanna help. I just wanted to get out. I didn't care about anyone else. I managed to get through the connecting door into the next carriage. And then the next. I didn't stop. People were cryin' out, holdin' out their hands. I shoulda stopped, but I stepped over 'em until I got to a door that was open. It was the only part of the train by the platform, the other carriages were still inside the tunnel. It was a crazy stampede, man.'

He froze, staring ahead of him as if the events were unfolding right here in the room.

'On the stairs, before I got out, the lights flashed on and there was this little kid wearing a red coat. She was cryin' for her Mam – and I just pushed past her, knocked her over…' He dropped his head, drew in a thick, gluey sniff. 'I was a bastard. I can't forgive myself for that,' he said.

I let out a deep breath. 'It takes a lot of courage to admit to that,' I said.

'I feel like fuckin' shit,' he replied.

Once my consultations were over, I walked along the Thames path to the Royal Festival Hall. I bought myself a gin and tonic, taking it down to the riverside so I could stand and watch the water roll and break.

As the river lashed the wall beneath me, I began to see the depth of psychological wounds I was up against in this job and it didn't fill me with enthusiasm. It also brought up disturbing questions I imagined no one ever wants to answer.

Would I have done anything differently? Terry said, in the frantic bid to save his own life, he'd knocked down a little girl. I'd like to think – wouldn't we all? – that I would have stopped to help, but in the terror of the moment, would I really? I took a sip of my drink, letting the fizz sizzle on my tongue.

Terry, like Jane, had been involved in the fire on the Underground I'd read about, but it must have been much worse than I'd thought, at the time.

It was always sensible to know what patients had gone through, so I pulled my laptop from my briefcase and set it up on a small table on the edge of the outdoor café area.

Before long, I had all the details from several news sources in front of me. The fire had started in an office below ground on the Central line at Liverpool Street on May 28th, causing huge amounts of smoke and loss of visibility. There was something odd, however. All the reports shared one important factor; there'd been no fatalities and only around ten casualties, with minor scrapes and bruises.

That wasn't the way Jane and Terry had described the incident at all. I must have got things mixed up.

I took another sup of gin, hoping the alcohol would take the sting out of my confusion. I wasn't ready to head straight home for the weekend. Not yet. I couldn't face dealing with Miranda, for a start. I was trained to spot emotional imbalance and there was definitely something troubling her. Getting to the truth, however, would take more energy and cunning coercion than I had to hand right now.

Besides, the idea of her unfettered autonomy, of my sister's life having the potential to overlap with mine was too huge for me to absorb straight away. I wanted to leave the notion of her being back in my life on a shelf somewhere and return to it bit by bit, when I wasn't so drained and could consider the impact it would have.

I put my laptop away and thought of Aaqil Jabour. He hadn't booked in for his session so far, but I wanted to live with the hope that he was still alive. A list of fatalities went up daily on our staff website, but after what had happened to Holly, I couldn't bring myself to look.

More survivors from the Tube fire would presumably come through to me shortly. I'd have to brace myself.

Chapter 7

I woke with a start on Monday. Panting. I'd been dreaming about my sister. For one panicky moment I thought Miranda was there in the room, sitting on the end of the bed. Then I remembered she'd gone. Her new Camden friends were helping her move into her new place later that day.

I sat upright, dragging myself back into reality. A jabbing pain cut into my shoulder, as if I'd been running all night with a heavy bag around my neck. Wisps of disturbing dreams flitted around inside my head – something to do with trying to find Miranda. Racing through endless, dark tunnels on the Underground looking everywhere for her. Calling for her until my throat was burning. Her face was her own one minute, then it became Holly's. It took me a moment to remember that the little girl had died.

I got out of bed and made a strong coffee, trying to take stock of the day ahead. A full diary of appointments, supporting patients reliving their traumas. I laid out my outfit for the day on the bed, then flopped back down beside it. What I wanted more than anything was just one more hour in bed; pure dreamless sleep to cleanse away the tormenting nocturnal images. Instead, I made my way in a fuggy daze to the bathroom and set the day in motion.

As soon as I swung open the door to my office, I managed to snap into professional mode. The morning started with three fairly straightforward sessions, then before lunch, Jake Stowe came in. That was the point when everything started to tip slowly sideways.

'I get these terrible flashbacks about climbing up the steps,' he said.

It was Jake's first session and we were thirty minutes in to the hour. He was twenty-five, a respectable-looking guy, in a navy suit that was a little too tight around the chest and an inch or so too short in the leg. His eyelids were raw from crying and teardrops were pooling on his patent leather shoes.

'One minute I'm talking to a client about his expense allowance and the next, I freeze. All I can see are people crashing into me, everyone pushing, screaming,' he sniffled. 'There was this massive suck of wind and a flash, then this fireball comes from nowhere. The tiles were burning through the soles of my shoes, there was black smoke like an engine in flames, a stink of scorched oil. People were *on fire* all around me in the ticket hall. Their coats, their arms.'

People on fire? If this was the incident at Liverpool Street Tube, hadn't there been only minor injuries – a few cuts and bruises?

I took my eyes swiftly down to my notes. There didn't appear to be a record of Jake suffering any burns.

'You said there were people on fire right beside you.' I said gently. 'You didn't get burnt yourself?'

He squeezed his temples. 'No. I don't know how I managed it, but I got moving. I had to tread on people to get out, but eventually I was running and I could see a light in the distance.' He dropped his head. 'I made it, but people died. I heard them. Felt them.'

His gaze raced around the room, unable to settle on any one spot. 'There was this one woman with a bundle of shopping bags lying on the floor. She grabbed my leg and pleaded with me to get a message to her son.' He straightened his cuff. 'You know what I did?' He looked up, giving me an imploring stare through streaming eyes. 'I kicked her hand away to get past.' His body sank. 'Can you believe that? Good people don't do that kind of thing, do they?'

I saw Jake Stowe again, by accident, later that day. He was walking towards me, his head down, using his mobile and we nearly collided in the corridor. He'd come for a check-up. Several weeks ago he'd torn his left ear in a car accident. He hesitated after our awkward greeting and I could see he wanted to say more.

'I can give you a minute,' I said. I followed as he backed into an alcove away from the earshot of passers-by.

'Since our session things've got worse,' he said, 'I can't get those images out of my head.' He leant against the wall, half his shirt hanging out, taking heavy breaths. Add to that the effort he was making just to get his eyelids to part and I could see he was suffering from an acute lack of sleep.

'That's common, I'm afraid,' I said. 'People with Post-Traumatic Stress often find that certain images just won't go away. But they *will* – with time and special techniques – we've only had one session.'

'I thought it might help if I drew what I could remember.' He started pulling crumpled sheets out of his pockets. 'You know – get it out of my head onto paper.'

'That's a really good idea.'

He handed me a bundle of pencil sketches. Some were crude line drawings of distorted bodies, others showed the layout of the Tube station, detailed sections of maps with escalators, corridors and exits marked.

'I was trying to work out exactly what happened.' He slapped his palm into his forehead. 'I can't remember it properly.'

'This is good, Jake – but don't force it. Our brains try to protect us by blocking things out, but sometimes they wipe out more than they need to.' I looked down at the pile of pages he'd given me. 'Can I keep one?'

'Sure. I've got loads of them.'

I took a sheet showing the layout of the ticket hall, with escalators and lifts.

'I'll see you soon,' I said, as he drifted towards the seating area.

I'm not sure why I asked for the drawing. I just had a weird feeling.

Something, somewhere didn't add up.

***

On the way home, I stopped off at a chemist's for some over-the-counter sleeping tablets. I couldn't cope with another night like the last one. Since starting my new role, my sleep had got incrementally worse. It wasn't just the hard-hitting nature of the job. I was still giddy after hooking up with Con, plus Miranda's unexpected appearance had knocked me sideways.

As I wheeled my bike the last few hundred yards from the shops, a black cab pulled up at the kerb beside me and a woman in a long velvet gown got out and leant through the open window to pay the driver. It transported me straight back to the day Con and I first met.

It was after the final curtain of a West-End play when my friend, Hannah, insisted we loiter at the stage door. I picked him out straight away. He'd played the 'rugged villain' and had been formidable on stage, but appeared even more so, out of character. His hair was a metallic black and untamed, and he stood like a warrior. He was good-looking in such an obvious way, I wondered why there wasn't a harem of women drooling over him.

To my astonishment, he caught my eye and beckoned us over. I glanced behind me, certain there must be a staggeringly beautiful woman by my shoulder, but there wasn't. He invited us both backstage for drinks and swilled the red wine around in the glass, as if to check it was up to scratch, before handing it to me. It was embarrassingly obvious which one of us he was most interested in.

I'd always been enthralled by actors, but had never known any personally. They fascinated me; their ability to take on another persona, to walk, talk and breathe like a different person. I could never do it. I could *hide* my true self, but I could never stand up under scrutiny and transform myself into a monarch, a lawyer, a murderer.

Our first few dates were magical – a drink, another West-End play, the cinema. After that first film, he taught me popcorn-racing. Apparently, it was one of his son's favourite games, but not in the way we played it. We started out – just the two of us – blowing the puffed-up little pieces along the kitchen table with a straw.

We raced them across the carpet, tried to flip them into shoes, then Con got me to lie flat on my back. He tugged my blouse out of my jeans and unbuttoned it, then rolled a piece down my chest aiming for my belly-button. Then he placed his lips around the popcorn and ate it.

We stripped off and took it in turns to explore the ridges and hollows in each other's bare skin using no hands, eating each piece of popcorn wherever it came to a halt. Since then, if anyone mentions popcorn, Con and I exchange knowing glances.

Con was funny and intelligent. Being with him was like stepping inside a labyrinth; there were so many places to go, so many sides to him, so many mysteries. I was hungry to find all the hidden selves and most of all – to find the *real* man behind all the masks. I was in a dreamy state most of that time, walking on cushioned air, waiting for those enchanting moments spent with him. We sent raunchy text messages to each other and he left saucy voicemails that made my toes curl.

I couldn't work out how I'd been so lucky.

I stopped the memory right there, not wanting to sour it with recent concerns that had come to light in our relationship, and climbed the stairs to my flat. I needed a quick shower, a light meal, then I was off to the theatre. I'd nearly squealed with joy when Con had finally rung me at lunchtime to say he'd got free tickets for a play at the Haymarket that evening. I just had to make sure I got there on time, looked effortlessly sexy and stayed awake. No mean feat.

As I approached the front door, I could see a figure lurking outside. I quickened my step, then slowed down as I recognised the jacket.

'Miranda?'

'I'm back. I've got a place in a hostel, but it's not ready. They're going to ring me.'

'Right,' I said, unlocking the door.

'I thought you still had a key,' I said.

'I think I lost it. Sorry.'

Miranda stood, immobile, with her fingers touching her lips, her suitcase leaning against her bare leg as if tied by string. She looked like a refugee left behind at a railway station.

'The rest of my stuff is being sent on to the hostel,' she said. I glanced down at the large case. 'It's only for one night. Two at the most. Then I'll be out of your hair.'

We stepped inside. I noticed her tremble as she dragged her belongings into the hall. 'I'll try not to be a bother,' she said plaintively.

Yeah. I'd heard that one before.

'Listen – I'm going out tonight – so you'll have some peace,' I said. I couldn't help wondering what kind of state I'd return to, but there was no way I was changing my plans.

Miranda came through into the kitchen and presented me with the flowers. 'These are for you,' she said.

I forced a smile. I'd never liked chrysanthemums. I couldn't expect Miranda to remember. They looked like they'd been out of water for a long time, their heads already drooping and the foliage in a sorry state. Nevertheless, she'd made an effort and I didn't want to spoil any chance of getting our relationship onto a better footing.

'You shouldn't have,' I said. 'Thank you. I'll get a vase.'

'You look wrecked,' said Miranda.

I turned away. 'I'm fine.' I took a breath. 'We must go out for dinner some time. Sit down together without any distractions and catch up properly.'

'But you're going out.' She took the vase and filled it noisily.

'I don't mean tonight. I'm sorry. I'm going to see a play,' I said. 'There is a pie in the freezer – are you able to manage that sort of thing?'

'I do cook for myself, you know,' she said in a flash of hostility.

'Fine. Or there's a fish and chip shop on the corner.'

'I'll have soup,' she said, still holding the vase of sad flowers. We stood at opposite ends of the kitchen. Prim and gloomy, like two people at a wake who'd only just met.

'Just help yourself if you want a hot drink.'

'I don't expect you to wait on me.' She handed me the vase, pushed past me and reached down to her shoulder bag. 'I've got a flask left over from lunch.'

I followed her into the sitting room and moved some books so that I could put her flowers on the side table. One of the volumes fell to the floor. Miranda picked it up.

'*New Directions in Counselling*,' she read. 'Your chapter on ethical practice in here?'

'Who told you that?' I reached out for the book and took it from her.

'Daddy. We've been emailing each other.'

I smiled to myself. I bet Mum didn't know about that.

'Didn't get a publisher for your own book proposal, then?' she said, twisting her mouth to one side.

So Dad had told her about that, too. What else had he said?

'No – that didn't work out.' I was still holding the book. She looked warily at it, as though it was a weapon.

'Bummer,' she said.

I shrugged.

'Mummy doesn't approve, by the way,' she went on, giggling like a naughty child. 'About not having your *own* book out by now.' I didn't respond, didn't rise to the bait. 'You know Mummy – careers and advancement at all costs. She thinks you should be making a name for yourself in print, working your way up whatever ladder it is that psychologists climb, instead of writing the odd chapter here and there.' She pulled on the cuff of her blouse. 'That's what Daddy said, anyway.'

'I've got to get ready,' I said, backing away. I wasn't sure if Miranda was trying to provoke me or simply reminding me that the parental pressure had been there for both of us growing up. That was the problem with Miranda – I never quite knew what she was thinking. Or what she was going to do next.

I went into the bedroom to find something to wear.

'It must have been a big step,' I replied. 'Leaving Linden Manor for good. It'll take some getting used to, I should think.'

I had an unwelcome vision of Miranda at twenty, being dragged screaming from the local library, naked, her own faeces in her mouth. That was the first time she'd been sectioned.

The first of many.

'I haven't been on Mars, Sam,' she snapped. 'I know a little bit about what's been going on in the real world.'

'Of course you do,' I said. 'Sorry.'

Miranda had been diagnosed with schizophrenia shortly after that outburst in the library, but since becoming a psychologist, I was convinced that was only part of the picture.

I really needed a shower, but I was running out of time. I pulled on my best jeans instead.

'I just thought it might be harder than it looks,' I said, my back to the door, fastening my bra. 'You know…coming back, joining in with everything again…it must be—'

Suddenly she was right behind me. I felt her hot breath on my bare shoulder.

'Well – I'm back – and now it's my turn,' she said, her voice raspy. 'Everything was easy for you. When *I* was born, Mum had a clear idea of the sort of child she wanted – and it wasn't me. I was "a rebellious artist" with a "mind of my own" and I didn't come up to scratch. She saw me as nothing more than defiant and uncontrollable. That's why she packed me off to boarding school as soon as she could.'

'I was sent away to Ryland's, too,' I said, twirling the tongs to put some life into my dark flat hair.

She folded her arms. 'You were okay. You were the academic one who towed the line. You got your PhD, then headed down the psychology route. Dad was sweet, but he was on her side – he wanted us both to be clones of them. Can you see me as a barrister? Or a university professor?'

Miranda had a point.

'We were both under enormous pressure.'

I turned away from the mirror and Miranda looked me up and down. 'I thought you were going to the theatre.'

'I am.'

'In jeans?'

I looked down at my legs. I wasn't used to Miranda acting like the older sister. It felt all wrong. Like she was playing a part, trying out the role to see if she could get away with it. I had spent years mothering Miranda, because our actual mum had abdicated all responsibility and Dad had faffed about on the side-lines not knowing what to do.

'Let me do your hair,' Miranda said, coming towards me. 'You're pretty – but I could make you look gorgeous.' She reached for the tongs.

'I haven't time,' I said, swiftly unplugging them.

Once I was making headway in psychology, I'd made several attempts to 'fix' Miranda. I think, deep down, it was the reason I'd become a therapist in the first place. My attempts were totally useless and inappropriate, of course. All that happened was that Miranda got nasty and lashed out, verbally and physically. And I stepped further away. Ultimately, I'd given up on her and shut her out altogether.

I turned back towards the wardrobe. Perhaps Miranda was right. I needed to look my best. I wanted Con to open his eyes wide and stand back when he saw me. I wrenched off the jeans and pulled on a slinky black dress with a lacy bodice instead. I'd bought it for a TV awards show I never went to.

'That's better,' said Miranda. I gave her a peck on the cheek and left.

On the way down the stairs, I opened my purse to check I had enough money for the taxi and found a scrunched-up piece of paper. It was the map Jake had given me earlier that day. I'd put it in there and forgotten all about it.

I went over to the window ledge by the communal front door and pressed out the creases. Jake had drawn the ticket barriers, the position of the escalators and stairs at Liverpool Street Underground station. It was clear and precise.

I tried to picture the last time I'd been there, but I couldn't remember it in sufficient detail. Nevertheless an uneasy feeling broke through.

I was sure of it. There was something in Jake's drawing that didn't make sense.

When I got back from the theatre, I could hear a tap running and found Miranda in the bathroom. She was rubbing at a woollen jumper in a basin already overflowing with billowing suds. Her bare feet were wet as the rising tide of warm water was gradually swamping the floor.

'Careful…' I said gratuitously.

I reached across her to turn off the tap and went for a mop. As I passed the bedroom, I noticed that in my absence, she'd opened all my cupboards and dumped every item of clothing I had in a heap on my bed.

'What's going on?' I said, fighting to stay calm, knowing that my irrepressible craving to go straight to bed would have to be put on hold once again.

She dabbed a blob of froth on my nose. 'Don't be such a boring old fart. You need some new clothes. Your outfits are ancient.'

If I'd been under any illusion that Miranda had changed, I was wrong. Having her back in my life was going to be far from easy.

Chapter 8

My nine o'clock appointment on Wednesday had been cancelled, so I took the opportunity to head over to Liverpool Street on the Tube. I needed to see for myself. I organised my journey so I arrived via the Central line, where the fire had started. Part of the platform was still cordoned off and there were smudged sooty patches on the walls. A man in overalls with a bucket and long-armed brush was swilling sections down.

The adverts blurred past at my side as I stood on the escalator. There was a smell of emulsion and tattered 'wet paint' signs were still stuck with masking tape to billboards. Once I was through the barrier at the top, I walked over to one of the ticket booths. The official jerked his chin in lieu of asking what I wanted.

'Were you here the day of the fire at the end of May?' I asked.

'Why, what's the trouble?'

'I just wondered what it was like. How crowded it was. If there was a mass panic.'

'You press or something?'

'No – I work at St Luke's Hospital. With trauma victims.' I showed him my ID card which seemed to do the trick.

He shrugged. 'It wasn't bad, to be honest. The fire started in one of the admin offices down on platform four on the Central line. Electrical fault. The guys down there couldn't get the extinguishers to work. There was a lot of smoke; it billowed up through the corridors so fast and everyone was disoriented. It was 6.30pm, so right in the middle of rush hour, but we did everything we could.' He pointed to the barriers. 'We opened the gates. One of the escalators was out of order, so it got a bit manic.' His blinking became fast and pronounced. 'I mean, it was congested, but it didn't turn into a stampede or anything and we gave out announcements on the PA system.'

'Which escalator was out of order?'

'The one coming up from the Central line. It was only for a couple of hours.'

'So, anyone leaving a train on the Central line would have had to walk up the escalator?'

'Yeah. We've got lifts as well, but we have to shut those down during an evacuation.'

'How far did the fire spread? Were any passengers up here caught in the flames?'

He snorted. 'Up here? Oh, no. The smoke damage only went as far as thc bottom of the escalator.'

As I thanked him, I glanced at his lapel badge and noted the name, *Perry*. I had a feeling I might be needing to speak to him again.

I took out Jake's sketch and I wandered around the ticket hall, noting the position of the escalators and lifts and comparing the layout to his map. I turned it around one way, then the other. I went back down to platform four and followed thc same route Jake said he'd taken to get out. By now, it was clear that the map didn't fit at all.

Then I headed round to the Transport Police.

The officer at the desk was busy tracing a line on a maze puzzle in front of him. It took him a moment to register I was waiting and he hurriedly squashed the booklet under the counter.

'Hi – is it possible to see someone who was involved with the fire on May 28th?'

'And why might that be?' He rattled the biro between his teeth.

I used the same approach as I had with Perry, adding that I was counselling survivors and needed to check some facts. He disappeared through the back and a woman returned in his place.

'DS Patrick. How can I help?'

I gave her the background. 'Were you actually at the station when it happened?' I asked.

'Yeah. I was here with a team before the fire brigade arrived.'

'Can you tell me about the fire itself? Did it spread far?'

'Only from the admin office as far as the first strip light in the ceiling.'

'So the main problem was the crush of people getting up the stalled escalator, and the thick smoke?'

'I'm afraid so.'

'Do you have a record of the injuries?'

'Hang on.' She disappeared and came back holding a file. 'I've got the initial report here.' She flicked through several pages. 'Yep. There were a handful of casualties who suffered smoke inhalation and some minor injuries caused by the overcrowding.'

'Any fatalities?'

'Oh no, nothing like that.'

'Were there any reports of people – their clothes – being on fire?'

She drew back her chin. 'What? No.' She shook her head adamantly.

'Not in the ticket hall?'

'Oh, definitely not up on the surface. The fire got nowhere near there.'

I thanked her and left, my brow crinkled into a tight frown. I knew for certain: Jake's account was all wrong.

I felt numb as I wandered to the outside of the station and caught the bus to the hospital. My next session with Jake wasn't until next week, but I was agitated, eager to find out what was going on. Had he simply been confused? Was his memory playing tricks on him? Surely, that *had* to be it.

I went straight to the Burns and Plastic Surgery Unit when I arrived. When I'd seen Jake on Monday, his check-up had been cancelled. Luckily, he was due in that day at 11.30. I made a mental note to come back.

I headed over to the canteen, desperate for a real coffee, not one from the vending machine where you had to chew the powdered milk. I was hoping the caffeine might jolt my mind into making sense of what was happening.

The rush before appointments was worse than usual and the place was packed. I collected a drink and was trying to work out in which direction the queue was heading, when someone with a stacked tray barged straight into me.

My cup and saucer hit the floor. There was a sudden hush before the inevitable cheer.

'A little less haste and a bit more focus on the task in hand,' said the owner of the tray. Without waiting for a response, he glided past me like a Ferrari might pass a pedestrian who had foolishly stepped off the curb.

I swallowed my impulse to swear. 'You took a step back,' I snapped. 'You walked into *me*.'

'Never argue with a man holding a knife,' he called out over his shoulder, without humour. 'Especially when he's a surgeon.'

He continued to walk away.

Damn nerve!

A woman with a sly smile on her face passed by, right behind him. It was Lian Moore, a PA in the Burns and Plastic Surgery Unit. I'd seen her several times in the ladies' toilet applying lipstick in a garish shade of fuchsia. She had a wild tornado of naturally orange hair and someone should have told her that this particular lip colour didn't suit her.

An older woman who had appeared with a mop and tin bucket nudged me out of the way.

'That's Dr Hansson,' she said. 'Isn't he something?' She shifted her gaze to look wistfully at Lian. 'She's so lucky working for him.' She leant her cheek against the wooden pole and I watched her moony eyes follow him as he found a seat. 'And he's Swedish,' she added, as if that gave him special rights.

To me, he looked the sort who flounced his self-appointed superiority around at every opportunity. Wearing his hair long over his collar and, no doubt, regularly touching it up with blonde highlights, he struck me as a man in his fifties trying his best to look thirty-something. He might have women drooling over his designer suit and Palm Beach tan, but he didn't fool me. There was nothing the least bit attractive about him. The skin around his jaw sagged and he looked like he was carrying cushions in the plump bags under his eyes. I was deeply unimpressed and joined the back of the queue, empty-handed, for another go.

I'm ashamed to admit I was running on autopilot for my first patients. I was keen not to miss Jake. At 11.40, I phoned the unit and found out he'd arrived and was still in the consultation room. Shortly afterwards, I sauntered past the waiting area and spotted him nodding to the receptionist, accepting a small card for his next check-up. He saw me and gave a weak smile. I asked if we could have a private word in my office.

I offered him a seat in front of my desk and he sat on his hands looking like a schoolboy hauled up for smoking behind the bike sheds.

'I know we have another session soon, but I just wanted to check a few details about the fire. I don't want to ask you anything that might be upsetting, but are you okay to run through a few simple points?'

He looked surprised. 'Okay…'

'I've been looking at your map,' I smoothed it out in front of him. 'And I notice here you've marked stairs and here you've got the escalators.'

'Yeah, that's right – and there are two lifts around here.'

'When you came off the train and left the platform, were you on a stationary escalator or steps? Can you remember?'

'Definitely steps,' he said. 'I don't like walking up escalators when they've stopped, I always think they're going to suddenly start up again or go too fast…'

'But, in the rush to get out, could it be that you didn't notice you were climbing a static escalator?'

He thought for a second. 'No – because I went past the escalators, see here?' he pointed to the map. 'I saw everyone was crammed onto them and got to the staircase.'

'Okay…' My mouth was dry.

'You said there were flames in the ticket hall – are you absolutely sure about that?'

He responded immediately. 'God, yeah. I told you, people's coats were on fire. It was definitely in the hall, because I remember the barriers themselves were burning.' He started to shake.

'It's okay – we'll stop there. Are you all right?'

He muttered something I couldn't hear.

'Let's take a few minutes.' I talked him through a simple grounding process to help him re-orientate himself: *What day is it? What are you going to do next?* Simple questions. He looked confused, but fully recovered by the time he left.

As he shut the door, I plopped down into my chair.

I knew now for certain. Jake sounded so genuine and yet his story didn't make sense. He'd told me he'd climbed up from the Central Line to the ticket hall using the steps. But, there *were* no steps from the platforms to the ticket hall, coming in from either east or west. I'd checked the area twice and there was access by escalators and lifts, but no steps until you want to leave the ticket hall to reach the mainline concourse.

Another part of his story didn't add up either. He said people were on fire around him in the ticket hall, whereas the police were emphatic that the flames never got anywhere near there.

I thought about two other patients, Jane and Terry. They, too, had talked about the Tube fire and described fatalities; I had it written down in my notes. I'd need to ask them some direct questions about it if they came back, but in the meantime, one thing was clear. For some reason, Jake was lying.

Chapter 9

As soon as I got home after work, I knew all was not well. Glancing up, I could see from the street that my kitchen window was wide open.

Miranda was still here. I left my bike in the hall downstairs and followed the aroma of spicy chicken all the way to my flat.

Before I found my key, she opened the door and waited for my response. 'Don't you like it?' she asked.

Miranda's hair was now a striking, but not brassy, blonde in a short pixie style. It was a complete transformation.

'It's just…so different.' It had taken years off her face and made her look cute and sexy. 'I like it,' I exclaimed. 'It really suits you.'

In a strange twist of time-travel, I instantly felt like the older sister – drab, and on the shelf at thirty. For the first time in my life, I looked at Miranda and felt a twinge of jealousy.

'Cold drink – or tea?' she asked. She took my briefcase from me, leaving it in the hall as if I was the guest.

'Just water, thanks.'

'Ice?'

I nodded.

'What brought this on?' I said, still taking in her new look.

'Fresh start,' she said, passing me to get to the kitchen where she sprinkled a handful of herbs into a pan.

'I thought you didn't have any money.'

'Someone at the project did it – she's an apprentice.' She handed me a glass of water, tinkling with ice-cubes, a big smile igniting her face. She'd been out and back in again during my absence, so must have found her 'lost' key.

I sat down at the table, pushing aside a batch of pencils and a sketch. The new French cookbook Con had lent me was open on the table. I couldn't deny that whatever chicken dish she was cooking smelt extremely tasty. She was wearing my old fashioned frilly apron, like she was on the film set of *Downton Abbey.*

'Problems?' I said, referring to the fact that she was supposed to be settling into new accommodation by now.

'No – it's coming along nicely.' She lifted off one of the pan lids and sniffed. Then she went to the window and leant out, drawing in loud lungsful of air. 'So bloody hot…' she said.

Miranda had set napkins folded into origami swans on the table. There were fresh flowers in the centre. Roses this time. They wouldn't last long in this heat, but she was certainly trying her best.

'No, I meant…I didn't expect you…to be here,' I said, wondering for a moment if Miranda had forgotten all about the fact she was supposed to be somewhere else.

'Oh. Yeah. Sorry about that. The room wasn't ready after all.' She shot me a worried look. 'Is that going to make things difficult?'

'How long?'

'Just a day or so.' She bit her lip. 'Is it okay? Can I stay?'

It would have been churlish to suggest otherwise after she'd gone to so much trouble. Nevertheless, Miranda was a landscape of liability I could have done without.

'Just a day or so,' I stressed. 'Seriously. This flat really isn't big enough.'

She smiled. 'Okay.'

She put two empty wine glasses beside the plates on the table.

'Before you protest, I know it's a week night and you won't be drinking, but I thought the fizzy water would look nicer in these.' She picked up a glass and twirled it round by the stem.

'You've done the ironing,' I said, noticing the empty clothes horse folded up in the corner.

'I had a few minutes when I got back from the studio. You must come and see my pictures some time. I sold one today.'

She clapped her hands together. 'I sold one last week, but I found out it was Daddy. But this one's a proper buyer.'

'That's great. Yeah, I'll bring Con – he'll be interested.'

'Things okay between you two?'

I turned away. 'Who said otherwise?'

'Just picked things up, that's all. You've been checking your phone a lot, for a start.'

'Everything's fine.'

I didn't tell her that during the evening at the theatre, Con and I had had a bit of a disagreement. The problem wasn't exactly new – it had emerged around five weeks after we'd first met. The fun-loving, smart, sexually responsive Con wasn't quite the entire picture. There was one little blip. As we started to get to know each other and peeled away the layers, I came across Con's possessive side.

'Careful!' Miranda yelped, diving forward to prevent me from creasing a drawing. I pulled it out of Miranda's reach to take a look at it, just as she caught hold of the corner. There was a splitting sound and the sheet ripped right down the middle.

'*Now* look what you've done!' she yelled. She was almost in tears.

'I'm sorry,' I said, holding up the two halves. 'Was it important?'

'Of course it was important. It was *mine*, for a start.'

'We can mend it with sticky tape.'

She snatched it away and instantly ripped it into tiny pieces. 'Of course, we can't mend it with sticky tape,' she hissed. 'It's ruined.' She tossed the pieces in the air and the kitchen became the inside of a Christmas snow globe. Only without the magic and good cheer.

'Even when I was *well*, you hated me,' she snapped.

I stared at the white scraps scattered on the lino. 'That's not true.'

She buried her fists in the pockets of the apron. 'I couldn't help it,' she whispered.

'It was never-ending, Miranda. The havoc you left behind. We all had to pick up the pieces.' I kicked a layer of torn scraps under my foot as if to demonstrate my point.

'I'm sorry,' she said.

'You stole my things. You cut the hair off my dolls. Ripped pages out of my books. Smashed my CDs…'

'I was ill.'

'That's true – but you've never acknowledged all the upset you caused me.'

'It was an *illness*,' she insisted – the perennial windbreak she'd always hidden behind.

'I know,' I relented, 'but you weren't diagnosed until you were twenty. We had years before that dealing with a wayward, unmanageable child. No one knew why. It wasn't easy.'

'I didn't *want* to be like that. I didn't *want* to push everyone away. It was like there was someone else inside my body running my life for me, right from when I was little. I couldn't breathe or think for myself. I just reacted all the time. I was scared. I didn't understand anything.'

I looked at my sister's face; lost and vacant. The face I remembered when we were growing up.

Being with Miranda was like being forced to step off dry land onto a plank floating on choppy water and having to keep my balance. I felt I was about to be tipped off into the rapids at any moment. It had been like that every single day I'd lived with her. How could I possibly explain that to her?

'You don't know the whole story,' she said ominously.

'Well, tell me then.' I looked up to see her face, but she was staring at her nails.

I'd always had the feeling my parents had hidden a great deal about Miranda's past from me. The day after she'd been sent permanently into care I'd had a row with my mother about the decision they'd made. I was eighteen at the time.

'You have no idea what a nightmare she is,' my mother had barked. 'Your father is useless at keeping her in check. Useless! He's all for hugs, pandering to her and second chances. That sort of approach doesn't teach anybody anything. He's never taken charge of the situation – it's always been down to *me*.'

I'd rarely seen my mother so enraged. 'Someone has to step in and prevent Mimi from destroying our lives,' she yelled. 'I am the only one with enough guts around here. She's going into a home and that's that.'

It was a long time ago, but I still winced at the memory of my mother's fierce words punching the air.

Miranda leant over me, placing the knives and forks beside the plates with painstaking symmetry.

'I want to get married one day,' she said casually, as if the squabble over the drawing had never happened. 'I liked a guy at Linden Manor, but I couldn't cope with his depression.'

She returned to the hob and had her back to me, stirring the stew. 'Well – you never know,' I said, trying to make my words sound light.

Miranda turned, sucking on the spoon. 'I'd like children, as well – you know, one day.'

I opened my mouth and closed it again.

She started humming and poked the potatoes in the pan with a fork.

'You said I don't know the whole story, so why don't you tell me?' I asked, keeping my voice soft.

She acted like she hadn't heard me, so I checked my phone again. Nothing. I thought Con might have called. We needed to resolve the friction between us, get it out in the open and find a way through it. It was one small graze in the skin of our relationship that I didn't want turning into a gaping wound. Problem was, Con couldn't see there was an issue at all.

I knew actors could be insecure, but Con's attitude around other men seemed extreme. When we were on our own he was brilliant, but as soon as we were in public, he could get tetchy, controlling. It became clear that every social event was to be followed by a gruelling postmortem. Instead of a cosy nightcap and the delight of being alone with each other, I'd be in for a grilling. *Who was I talking to? Why had I spent so long with the guy?* I'd tried to discuss it with him, but every time Con claimed he didn't know what I was talking about.

The evening at the theatre had started well. We stayed for a drink in the bar afterwards and Con suggested our first 'holiday' together – a weekend in Brighton. I wanted to throw out my arms and scream *YES!* but managed to curb myself.

When he went to buy another round of drinks, a man sitting on the next table turned round and asked me what I'd thought of the performance. We were still discussing the third act when Con came back.

I knew before he sat down. Con's face was set in a scowl and his eyes flickered like he was seeing flames. The other guy nodded and turned away; even *he* was picking up the vibes. Then the interrogation started. *Who was he? Did I know him? Why had I spoken to him? What did he say?*

I answered calmly, but without showing any signs I'd done anything wrong. *He was just a friendly guy. He'd seen the same play. We were just talking.* I felt like I was falling from a tall building, waiting for the awful crash when I hit the ground. Shortly afterwards, Con took a call on his mobile and said he had to go. Just like that, he was gone.

Miranda clunked the pan lid down on the draining board bringing me abruptly back to the kitchen. She started serving the meal.

'I'm not all bad, am I?' she said, as she sat down, as though our conversation had been carrying on inside her head. I fastened on her sad eyes for as long as she'd let me.

'Why don't you tell me everything,' I said evenly. 'Tell me your side of things.'

'*My* side of things?' She stiffened. 'Like that wouldn't be the truth – just my version that I've made up.'

'No – I didn't mean—'

She dropped her knife and fork so they clanged loudly against the plate, snatched the apron from her waist and flung it at me. 'I'll go tomorrow,' she said.

'Look, Miranda, you don't have to—'

She spun round. 'I'm in charge of my life now. I can do what I want.'

Her hands were shaking. I had a sudden panic that she might have stopped taking her medication. She pushed past me, grabbed her jacket and stormed out of the flat.

Chapter 10

One week earlier

I'm outside the church behind St Pancras. I don't know why I've come here again. This place has no significance for me.

I go inside the gate and start walking. Why is everything so difficult? I'm trying my best – I really am. Can't people see that? Why can't some greater force come and resolve this. I'm sick of struggling with it all by myself.

I sit down on the nearest bench, scaring the pigeons away. I've gone past the point of no return. I'm in it for the long haul, now.

A rush of air rips into my lungs and races back out again, gaining in speed and intensity – faster, deeper – taking me with it. Don't lose control, whatever you do. Hold it. You must contain this. Don't let the anger get the better of you. USE it instead. That's what my therapist said.

I had to do something – that was clear. I couldn't let it go. Every action has a reaction. I admit I've made mistakes, but other people have committed far greater sins right under my nose.

I flex my fingers and feel a bolt of energy charge through them. There's a pulsing under the surface of my skin, bubbling, determined to get out. In that moment, I feel like I could crush a man's head with my bare hands.

I've taken all the steps I could, but I'm swimming against the tide and feel acutely alone. No one knows the truth and it's obvious now that no one is going to step in and stop the worst from happening. No one.

Chapter 11

Present Day

Miranda had got up early; I found her laying out all her tubes of oil paint on the kitchen table. She was wearing a bikini and nothing else.

'What are you doing?' I asked lightly, as I poured myself a glass of juice. I thought she was leaving today; I'd expected to see her bags packed.

'I'm thinking of doing some body painting.'

I blinked fast. 'What, here?'

'Don't be silly!' she sniggered, 'I'm looking for the right colours.' She took the cap off the cadmium yellow and sniffed it.

'Only, I thought…' I glanced down at her bare flesh, already bronzed with the good start to summer.

'Oh, I see. The bikini.' She wafted her hand in front of her. 'It's so warm, don't you think?' She sniffed the air. 'It's going to rain later though – I'd enjoy it while you can.' She leant forward and squeezed my nose like I was a toddler. 'Don't worry, I'll be gone by the time you come back.' She wandered into the bathroom and shut the door.

I finished my toast and as I tossed a thin burnt crust into the bin I thought about Jake, and his story about the Tube fire. Not for the first time, I wondered about Jane and Terry, too. They both said they'd been there.

I'd never come across a patient faking it before and wanted to know more. I'd heard something about false witness claims connected to 9/11, but I didn't know the details. Miranda, however, had taken my laptop and was sitting on the edge of the bath glued to YouTube and I couldn't face the hassle of asking for it back.

I left sooner than I needed to, once again dreading what I was going to come home to.

Miranda was right about the weather. The temperature felt close to boiling point when I got outside. It was like stepping into the kitchen of a busy restaurant. Perfect for lolling on the grass in a park somewhere, but not ideal for cycling. As soon as I set off, heat seemed to seek out all the folds of my skin: my eyelids, under my arms, behind my knees. Before long I was bordering on meltdown, with bands of dark sweat seeping through my T-shirt. I decided to dismount and walk the last part alongside the Thames. A couple walked past me; one was holding an ice-cream cornet and the other was trying to knock it out of her hand. I thought of Con and just then my phone buzzed.

'Morning, gorgeous – at work?'

'Not quite. I got off my bike. It's too hot.'

'Fancy meeting for lunch?'

'I'd love to.' He seemed to have forgotten all about his outburst at the theatre. I scrolled through that day's appointments. 'I've got a gap between one and two o'clock – any good?'

'Not long enough – but I'll take it. How about I meet you at Hebdon Street and we go to that old pub under the arches.' Before I could answer, two lads on skateboards came out of nowhere, hurtling towards me. I was forced to take the phone away from my ear to steer my bike out of their way.

'…talk about it, then,' he said.

'Sorry – I didn't catch that.'

'See you later.' He'd gone.

I had no option but to take a quick shower at work in the few spare minutes before my patients arrived, but as soon as my morning appointments were over, I logged on to my computer, my mind on Jake. Why would he pretend to be involved in a terrible disaster? Was it a cheap dare with his mates…or a sign of mental illness?

I found the references to fake survivors from 9/11 straight away. A woman had told her poignant and distressing story for years until it became clear she hadn't even been in New York at the time. Gradual inconsistencies in her reports had emerged and it was strangely comforting to read that she'd even fooled her own therapist.

I pulled my copy of DSM-V from the shelf behind me. *The Diagnostic and Statistical Manual of Mental Disorders* is the psychologists' bible. I found that neither pathological lying nor compulsive lying were listed as distinct disorders. My training had led me to believe that compulsive liars tended to lie habitually, about everything. They don't deliberately try to mislead, but find the intrusiveness of the truth too much for them. They lie because it feels safer. Pathological liars, however, are a different kettle of fish. They tend to lie to manipulate with cunning forethought and often have a Borderline Personality Disorder – close to, but not quite, psychotic.

Having spoken to Jake, he didn't appear to be a compulsive liar, but I didn't know him well enough yet to know whether he showed other symptoms of BPD. I needed to know more about his history.

It was usual practice with a new referral to get a medical report sent over from a GP, but I hadn't received any such documents for my recent patients. I made a quick call to reception to request Jake's as a matter of urgency.

I had to work out what I was going to do about him. Jake's next appointment would come around soon and I needed to be clear about how to handle it. It could be that faking his involvement was an extreme form of seeking attention. He hadn't done so yet, but if this was the case, I would expect him to start making out he was 'special', having been 'chosen' to survive. Until I'd digested the notes about his history, I wouldn't know what other issues might be pertinent.

I could be wrong about him, of course, Jake might simply have got himself terribly mixed up after the trauma, confused about where he'd been and what he'd drawn on his little scraps of paper.

Just as I was setting out to meet Con my phone buzzed with a text.

Really sorry, lunch is off. Got to see Agent. Will call later. xx

This tended to happen with Con. I had a string of broken dates with him crossed out in my diary. I was beginning to wonder if this was simple disorganisation, or whether there was something more underhand going on. Apart from anything else, I'd been looking forward to a tasty pork pie and chips.

I dropped into my office chair and pondered my choices. I didn't fancy either the canteen food or the long queue to get to it, so I left the hospital, found the nearest sandwich bar and sat on a wall soaking up the sun.

By the time my final consultation finished at 6pm, the weather had completely shifted and it was pelting down. Hard, violent rain that was intent on boring holes in everything. It struck my head and arms like stabbing needles as I ran to the bike shed. I knew exactly where all my waterproof gear was – hanging behind the bathroom door at home. Miranda had said it might rain and I'd ignored her. Since when had my sister ever been a reliable source of information?

Already soaked, I clipped on my helmet and hauled myself onto the saddle. The tyres made a squelching sound as I pushed against the pedals. I had to press down hard to make progress and the wheels felt laboured and heavy. When I got to the gate, I realised why. The metal rim of the front one was grating against the tarmac. I'd got a puncture. I got off, avoiding the row of drivers, dry and cosy inside their cars, and wheeled it back to the shed.

My first thought was that I was glad I hadn't arranged to meet Con straight after work. *I had a flat tyre* sounded like one of those feeble and unimaginative excuses no one ever believed.

My alternative plan was to head for the train station. Without an umbrella. I loitered for a few minutes under the shelter of the corrugated roof, the rain making it rattle and shake. It was verging on hailstones and wouldn't ease off anytime soon. It was early summer, but one of those inhospitable days that could have belonged to any other season. I'd just have to make a run for it.

I bolted towards the gate, dodging the queue of vehicles waiting to leave. Without warning, in a bid to jump the queue, an impatient driver shot out of the line just ahead of me. I couldn't avoid the car in time and the side of the bumper rammed straight into my knee, then screeched to a halt with a jerk.

'Oh, my God, I'm so sorry…'

I recognised the slight foreign edge to the voice. It was Dr Hansson. He was out of the car in a flash, bending over me.

'Are you okay?' He seemed genuinely concerned.

The car had knocked me off balance rather than run me over and I was left sitting in a puddle, more shocked and mortified than injured.

I rubbed my knee, but knew instantly that the worst I could expect were a few bruises. There was no blood; I hadn't even broken the skin. Dr Hansson's reactions controlling the brakes had been incredibly fast.

He helped me to my feet and I feigned a limp just to make him feel guilty.

'Let me take a look.' He glanced up at the sky and the row of vehicles behind us. 'Why don't you get in the car? Can you manage that? Or do I need to call an ambulance?'

I almost sniggered at his suggestion, but played it cool. 'I think I'll be okay,' I replied, with a wince.

A horn tooted behind us, then another and Dr Hansson waved his hand by way of apology. He guided me towards the car – a navy Jaguar saloon, I noticed – and opened the passenger door. I was soaked by now, but there comes a point when you're so wet that you barely notice anymore. I was, however, secretly pleased to see from his dripping hair and speckled shirt, that the doctor was wet, too.

He eased me inside the car, water flying everywhere: over the pale blue leather upholstery, the dashboard, the handbrake. A Beethoven symphony was playing on the radio. He hurried round to the driver's side and we pulled out of everyone's way, heading towards the spaces reserved for taxis. He stopped and switched off the engine.

'Can I take a look at your leg?' He sounded genuinely polite and respectful.

I played along and rolled up the leg of my trousers, sucking in a sharp breath for good measure when he touched my knee cap. His fingers were warm and supple, well-practised at exploring skin. After various tender prods and strokes that felt more pleasant than I'd anticipated, he looked up and smiled.

'All good,' he said. 'Take it easy for a few days, you'll have a few bruises.'

I laughed. 'Are you content with knocking a coffee out of my hands and trying to run me over – or can I expect anything else?'

I was certain he wouldn't remember, but he surprised me.

He grimaced. 'I know. I'm sorry. I was rude in the canteen. I'd had a hellish early start in surgery. The air-conditioning wasn't working and one of my nurses collapsed during a tricky operation to reattach an amputated thumb.' He shook his head. 'But that's no excuse.'

'Oh…' I was tempted to offer words of consolation, but I didn't want to let him off the hook so easily.

He started the engine. 'Where can I take you, Sam?'

He knew my name.

'Oh, just to the nearest Tube – London Bridge,' I said. 'I'll be fine.'

'Let me take you further than that. Please. Where are you going?'

'I live at Clapham Junction,' I said. 'But the nearest Tube is fine.'

'How about a compromise – a wine bar by London Bridge?'

A wine bar? His proposition startled me. Prickles exploded on my arms and I shivered, rubbing my arms instinctively. 'There's a blanket on the back seat. I should pull it on, if I were you. Don't want you catching pneumonia as well.'

I dragged the tartan blanket through the gap between the seats and wrapped it around me, like I was tucking up a baby in a pram. I felt better inside the woollen cocoon. Not just warmer, but safer, somehow. Neither of us said anything and he continued driving. I wasn't sure what we'd decided, where we were heading.

'You'll be doing me a favour, to be honest,' he said. 'It's my daughter's birthday soon and I don't know what to get her. The place I have in mind has jewellery stalls and knickknacks outside. Maybe you can help me find something?' He glanced across at me, an imploring look in his eyes.

'Yeah – sure. I can do that, but not for long.'

'Thank you.'

Why was he asking me – a complete stranger? But, having accepted the lift, I felt obliged to follow through.

'How old is your daughter?'

'Nineteen.'

We pulled into a small square that looked like it was reserved for private parking and stopped. He slid a large umbrella out from behind his seat and hurried round to help me out.

'You okay walking?'

'Yes. Honestly, I'm fine.' I'd done enough playacting and walked on without the limp.

'This way – I know a short-cut,' he said.

It was warm under cover of the glass barrel-vaulted roof, but he insisted on giving me his jacket. I wrapped it dubiously around my shoulders, aware of the subtle smell of expensive cloth and something else that reminded me of Turkish Delight.

We wandered around the stalls.

'What sort of thing are you looking for?' I asked.

'A silver or gold necklace. Petite. Understated. Nothing too garish.'

'Does that describe your daughter?'

He ran his finger along his chin. 'I suppose it does, yes.'

He picked up a silver chain with a cat on the end of it. 'How about this?' he said.

'No,' I said. 'Too 'young'. You want something more sophisticated.'

'You're right. Elegant, delicate.'

Dr Hansson was assiduous in his task, carefully vetting every section of the well-stocked stalls. It was hard to imagine either of my parents ever spending this amount of time choosing a present for me. They'd always given me money on special occasions. Even as a young child I was handed a padded envelope at Christmas and birthdays, neatly wrapped in sparkly paper and a ribbon. Like it was a surprise.

'So you can get exactly what you want, dear,' my mother used to say, patting me on the head.

So you don't have to bother to find out what I'd like, I didn't say in response.

I called Dr Hansson over. 'How about this?' I pointed to a necklace hanging inside a glass case. The silver pendant was twisted into a loose knot, with an opal set in the centre.

As he looked at it, I found myself scrutinising his face, trying to judge his response.

His wistful stare lasted several seconds, then he nipped his lips together. 'It's perfect,' he said, something catching in his throat. He spoke to the vendor, pulled out a credit card and paid. I was surprised by the tender way he took the bundle of tissue paper.

Having done him the favour, I turned towards the exit. He nudged my elbow. 'Come on.' He indicated a small bar at the far end of the market. 'This place is new – let's give it a try – then I'll take you home, I promise.'

I took a moment to consider it. Our encounter felt a million miles away from the one in the canteen and he'd given me a plausible reason for that. Besides, it was still pouring down.

We found seats by the window with a view of the Thames. The skin of the river was ragged and torn with the ferocity of the rain.

'Thank you for choosing the necklace. That has set my mind at rest. What can I get you? Is it okay to call you Sam, by the way?'

'If you like. I'll have a small brandy, please.'

'Good choice,' he said. 'Me too.'

He came back with the drinks and sat opposite me on a small stool. 'Let's drink to…family,' he said. 'And I'm Leo, okay?'

'To family,' I said quietly. In the light of my current situation with Miranda, his choice of toast struck me as ironic. We chinked glasses. I glanced down at the broad ring on his wedding finger. I wondered why he'd asked me, and not his wife, to choose a gift for his daughter.

He took another sip of brandy. I followed suit and felt the heat as the alcohol trickled down my throat and entered my bloodstream. I felt like I was slipping into a warm bath. I was practically dry now, self-conscious however, that my hair remained plastered to my head like seaweed. To anyone looking over, Dr Hansson probably looked like a rich pervert who had picked up a down-and-out from cardboard city. I smiled at how deceptive appearances could be.

'What's funny?' he asked. There was a little spark of challenge in his eyes.

'I was thinking what a pair we must look.' I looked down at the oversized jacket still wrapped around me. 'Well – me, actually.'

'You're dressed in Gucci – you should be honoured.'

I rubbed the cloth between my fingers. 'Very nice. I'm hardly doing it justice.'

My phone came to life just as someone turned the music up. It was Con.

'Sorry – better get this.'

Leo tapped my shoulder, mimed holding a glass and disappeared to the bar.

'Where are you?' said Con, in a flat tone.

'Er – on my way home.'

'It sounds like there's a party going on…'

'It's pouring down. Someone gave me a lift. We…stopped off for a quick drink.'

I knew exactly what was coming next. *Who was I with? A Man? Who was he? Who else was there?* The usual twenty questions. I took a deep breath and stumbled my way through them. By the time I got to the end I realised the phone was dead.

'Bad news?' said Leo.

I pulled a face at him and switched the phone off. 'Do you have to go?' he added with concern.

'No,' I answered straight away. I was staying exactly where I was. I'd done nothing wrong and I was finding Leo's company strangely comforting.

We went on to talk about the hospital, about psychology and his interest in research. We finished our drinks and he asked if I wanted another. 'I know I said we'd leave,' he said, 'but do we have to?'

I caught myself realising that this out-of-hours version of Leo was surprisingly engaging. His approach was personal without being intrusive; he asked me difficult questions that made me think. And he listened and evaluated my responses. I liked that. So much better than the idle chit-chat I often had with colleagues.

'I've probably got time for a coffee,' I said, taking my purse from my handbag.

'I'm rather enjoying myself. And it's nice to have company.' He tapped his lip, toying with the idea of saying something. 'By the way, I saw you looking at my wedding ring. My wife isn't at home waiting for me, in case you're wondering.'

'Right…' I didn't know what to say.

'She's in St Luke's, as it happens. Acute lymphocytic leukaemia.'

'Oh – I'm so sorry.'

His eyes fell down to his empty glass and he twirled it in his hand. I could see he didn't want to talk about it.

I got up. 'I'll get the coffees.'

The music got louder and the place filled up. Before long, we decided to share a Mediterranean platter: hummus, vine leaves, olives and pitta breads. I couldn't believe it when he said it was nearly ten-thirty. We got in the car and he drove me all the way to my front gate.

As I handed back his jacket, I realised I'd seen no trace of arrogance in him, this evening. Not once. Instead, under his impressive exterior, there was something damaged and out of reach. It was hard to say what exactly, but it was familiar. There was a tender spot inside me that was just the same.

Surprise, surprise – I got back to find Miranda sprawled on the sofa with her shoes on, watching what looked like a horror film. My eyes ran a hasty scan around the place, looking for signs of disruption.

'Nice evening?' she said, as I dropped my bag on the comfy chair. 'Someone got soaking wet.'

I hadn't looked in a mirror all evening and slid in front of the one outside the bathroom.

'Bloody hell!' I said, lifting up clumps of my rats-tail hair. How on earth had Leo taken me seriously?

'Bad enough to scare pets and small children,' sniggered Miranda.

'You need talk. What's this?' A green monster, dripping in a glutinous substance, lurched towards the camera. 'Should you be watching this sort of thing?'

'Will it turn me into a raving lunatic again, do you mean?'

'No – just that…' I sniffed. 'Sorry.'

'Can I get you anything?' she said stretching.

'I'm okay, thanks.'

'Con okay?'

'Why do you ask?'

'Only, he rang…'

The hairs shot up on the back of my neck. 'What did he say?'

'Not much.' It must have been before he tried my mobile.

The credits began to roll at the end of the film. 'Who was it?' she said, sitting up.

'Who was who?'

She arched an eyebrow. 'The guy I know you were with tonight.'

Chapter 12

Stepping off the train at Brighton station felt like I was gliding through a magical curtain into another life. I was no longer Dr Samantha Willerby, the dedicated and scrupulous clinical psychologist. I was a woman in the throes of passion and I was planning on abandoning myself to it for the entire weekend.

Once we'd left our bags at the hotel, Con and I headed straight down to the beach. It wasn't cold in the least, but the wind buffeting across the great expanse of sea gave us an excuse to huddle together and wrap our arms around each other. He was just the right height for my head to nestle onto his shoulder. I shut my eyes and listened to the seagulls.

'I hate the noise they make,' I said. 'They sound so distressed.'

'You spend too much time with messed-up people,' he said. 'When did you last have a decent break?'

I didn't need to think about it. 'It's been ages.'

'You see – you need to come away with me more often. Every month or so, from now on.' My heart did a little skip at the way he was including me in his future.

A group of noisy gulls swooped across our path. They dived at clumps of seaweed, taking strands of it with them.

'What do you want to do tonight?' he said, his mass of hair tossed back by the breeze. I could have listened to his deep, chocolaty voice for hours; with our bodies pressed together, it resonated inside my breastbone.

'A nice meal somewhere?' I suggested.

'It has to be expensive – I want to treat you.'

Was this by way of an apology for being so suspicious recently? If so, he didn't say. 'Then an early night, I think.' He raised an eyebrow.

He stopped, held my hands together against my blouse and slowly dropped his head, drifting towards me. His lips brushed mine, then he pressed harder, letting his tongue meet mine. It was delivered with a tenderness I'd barely experienced before, yet also with an undercurrent of greed. A heady mix of sensitivity and raw desire. Whenever I was with him, I had this same tight feeling of anticipation, aching for the moment when I could fully lose myself in him.

Over dinner, we spent a while simply catching up.

'Got anyone yet for the flat?' I asked. Con's last flatmate had been a nightmare. A total slob who used to leave his dirty socks on the draining board. He'd left Con in a hurry, owing rent.

'Got a couple of possibles,' he said. 'People linked to the Young Vic. It's always a risk when you don't know someone.' He held his fork a few inches from his mouth and looked at me, pointedly.

'I've got my own place, Con. I love it.' I tore a chunk from my roll. 'Besides – it's too soon.' I chewed it and smiled. 'Maybe one day…'

'Is that a promise?'

I tipped my head on one side and didn't answer.

'How's your arm?' I said, after I saw him fiddle with the dressing under his sleeve.

He held it out. He still couldn't fully straighten it. 'Okay. The specialist says I definitely won't need a skin graft.'

'Justin will be disappointed,' I said grinning.

'You remembered.' He reached under the table and stroked my bare knee. As it happened, there was barely any bruising after getting knocked over in the carpark. I hadn't told Con about it, and as he hadn't mentioned his call to me in the wine-bar, neither had I.

'Will you be okay when you start filming?'

'We'll be in space suits the whole time,' he said, 'so no one will see the scar.'

'Any more news on the dates?'

'We start in four weeks. It's called *Machine on Mars* – a kind of dystopian sci-fi movie.' There was a pause, then he added, 'I'll be in Arizona.'

I'd known we'd be apart, but only now did it fully hit home.

'How long?' I said, reaching out to grip his fingers.

'The first stint is about two months.'

'Ouch.'

He looked at me longingly. 'Why don't you come with me?' he whispered, lifting my fingers to his lips and gently biting my nail.

I thought he was joking at first, then he froze, waiting for me to answer. 'I can't. Not with work.' He must have felt me stiffen because he let my hand drop.

'Can't you take extended leave? Come out with me for a month. You *never* take leave.' His face was hard, his eyes boring into mine.

'It's a new job. I can't just walk away. In any case, I've built up relationships with my patients. I wouldn't want to leave them in the lurch.'

'So you're the only one who can possibly help them?' he tutted. A woman on the next table turned round at the sound of his raised voice.

'No, I'm not saying that.' I wanted to say I didn't *want* to leave them, especially with so many questions involving the patients from the Tube incident, but I stopped myself. 'It's a new job, Con. It's difficult.'

He dropped his chin and ate the rest of his *pâté au fruits de mer* in silence.

The wind had dropped, but it was cool when we got outside and Con pulled me close. We ambled through the back streets, laughing at some of the terrible jokes Justin had passed on to Con from school. He seemed to have forgotten our little rift.

Once inside our room, he lifted me off my feet and carried me to the bed. Every moment after that was pure bliss. Dreamy, warm and delicious. In the early hours, he rolled me over and wanted to start again. In my sleepy state, I gave myself to him, wishing all the clocks would stop so we could stay right where we were for ever.

Morning came too soon; I felt like our bodies had only just drifted apart, a sheen of honeyed sweat coating my skin.

Con yawned and sat upright, leant over and deliberately held my hands out across the rumpled sheets. He looked like he was going to say something. It felt like it was going to be something big – definitive and show-stopping. But, if it was, he must have changed his mind. He took a breath and shook his head, smiling.

'You're just so gorgeous,' he said. 'I'm sorry – I can't leave you alone.'

We rolled into a hug and I hid my face in his hair.

I don't know how I would have responded, if he'd popped the big question. Con was amazing, but it was too soon. We barely knew each other. And there was the issue of his possessiveness. We'd have to sort that out. Would there be a good time to address it while we were in Brighton? The idea filled me with dread; I didn't want to spoil our special time – and I was in no doubt that by dredging it up, our weekend would be ruined.

Nevertheless, I felt uneasy.

Things didn't go well after that, in any case. Con took a call during breakfast and turned to me grim-faced.

'I've got to go – I'm really sorry.'

I nearly choked on my mackerel. 'Go? Go where?'

'It's the theatre – I need to sort something out. I hate doing this, but…' He didn't finish the end of his sentence.

He got to his feet, his hands on his hips.

I dropped my napkin on the table, rising to join him. 'I'm a bit confused, Con. One minute you're all over me, the next—'

'It's not you, honestly.' He grabbed me round the waist and squeezed too hard. His face was too close, his grip too tight. I had to push him away. 'Really, it isn't,' he said. 'You've got to believe me.'

His eyes seemed to grow to twice their normal size, imploring me to understand. Understand what? It didn't feel right.

'Well – we'd better start packing,' I said with a sigh.

Monday morning found me sitting in my office staring at a painting on the wall of a girl with a parasol, swaying effortlessly on a swing hanging from a tree. I wanted to be there. I wanted to be her.

Con had rung me on Sunday evening. He apologised for dragging me back from Brighton so soon, but the rest of the call was stilted and difficult, with neither of us really saying anything. Something was out of kilter, in spite of how well things went on Saturday.

Then there was Miranda. She was still at the flat when I got back on Sunday. I knew I was going to have to say something. I didn't want her to think that the longer she stayed the more I'd get used to it. One week – one month – then in for the duration. Being around her wound me up before she'd even opened her mouth. The place wasn't my own and I couldn't relax. I knew I was being unreasonable, but that was the effect she had on me.

Calling her by her new name took some getting used to, for a start. For Miranda it was easy; she seemed able to snap from one persona to another in the same way anyone else might jump on and off buses. But for me it was hard to reframe my memories of an unruly girl called Mimi into this new identity. Somehow, it made her more of a stranger.

I felt guilty for being so uptight with her. I wanted more than anything to trust her – but I couldn't. Even on medication, she did impulsive, reckless things – often involving wet paint. When I was in Brighton, she'd invited fellow artists over without asking and traces of green glitter were now embedded in the carpet. She'd also seen fit to rearrange all the furniture in the sitting room. 'Looks bigger this way,' she said, waiting for some expression of gratitude. Every time I queried or challenged what she'd done, she snapped and slammed doors in my face. It kept me constantly treading on egg-shells.

I didn't have a patient until later and intent on getting a hefty backlog of admin out of the way, I was surprised when there was a gentle tap on my door.

A man wearing a white short-sleeved shirt, so crisp it looked as if it was straight from the packet, stood expectantly in front of me. Perhaps I did have a patient after all.

'Come in…I'm Dr Willerby.' He was fresh-faced with vibrant blue eyes.

'I'm not sure if this is the right place,' he said, faltering.

'You're not here for psychotherapy?'

'Tempting,' he said, a grin creeping across his face, 'but actually no. I'm Dr Lester Graham.' He held out his hand. 'I'm here for the neurology briefing. Not that an hour telling you my troubles wouldn't be very beneficial, I'm sure.' His voice was verging on aristocratic with slow rounded vowels; he sounded straight out of Eton.

He looked down at the sheet of paper he was holding. 'I'm new here – as you've probably guessed by now.'

'Ah. Where's the briefing? This is the Mental Health Unit.'

'Room 212.'

'Next floor up.'

He gave me a winning smile and left.

I left my office in search of caffeine and on the way over to the coffee machine, I noticed a message on the white board outside the Burns and Plastic Surgery Unit: *Dr Hansson's patients delayed this morning by 65 minutes.* Audrey, one of the nurses I'd met recently in the lift, caught me looking at it.

'Are you waiting for him?' she said.

'No…is he okay?'

She drew closer and lowered her voice. 'He's struggling to keep up this morning. Been here all night with his wife; she's not got long to live, apparently. He adores her – she's only in her forties.'

I squeezed her arm and slipped away.

***

At lunchtime, I bumped into Leo on the way to the canteen. Before he said a word his stomach growled and he patted it.

'Sounds like you're keeping a dog tied up in there,' I said.

'Pardon me – I don't think Fido got fed this morning.' He fell into step alongside me and took a quick look at his watch. 'Got time for a quick snack? I'm due back in theatre in twenty-five minutes.' He grimaced. 'I've had a cancellation – thank goodness.'

'Well – I wouldn't want to have to report you for animal neglect.' He laughed and squashed his hands into his pockets.

I couldn't believe how easy-going he seemed; he must have been crumbling inside over his wife. Maybe the only way he could survive was to soldier on as if nothing was happening. Thinking about it, I tended to do the same.

We found a small table in the canteen. 'How are things?' I said, focusing directly into his eyes. It was an invitation for him to refer to his wife if he wanted to. I'd found out she was called Helena and was in a ward where the patients only ever emerged with white sheets over their faces.

'I've just found out I'm a useless father,' he said flippantly.

'What do you mean?'

'I had a call this morning,' he said. 'From the police. About a young woman arrested for shoplifting. I thought it must be a wrong number.' He crumpled the wrapper covering his salad into a tight ball and tossed it onto his tray. 'The young woman was Kim, my daughter.' He shook his head. 'The first thing I wanted to know was what she'd stolen. For some reason I felt it was important to know.'

I remembered the beautiful necklace we'd bought and wondered if Kim was the one it was intended for.

'Toothpaste,' he said.

'Toothpaste?'

'What was she thinking?'

'It must have been a mistake, surely?'

'No. No mistake. I told the officer she's not thinking straight with what's happening with her mother, but Kim told them she knew exactly what she was doing. And it hadn't been the first time.' He scraped a slice of blackened tomato to the edge of his plate. 'The world is turning into a Punch and Judy show,' he said. 'Toothpaste, for goodness sake.'

'What did you say to her?'

'I offered to pay any costs, but Kim wouldn't have it. "You think you can fix everything if you throw money at it," she said. I accused her of throwing her life away – she's training to be a vet – and she said, "Yeah – well, whose dreams are they, Dad? Whose dreams are they, really?"'

I was taken aback by his frankness. He chased a radish around his plate half-heartedly, then put down his knife and fork.

'Kim said my wife had carried the family single-handedly. She accused me of being a mere mechanical provider all her life. She plans to drop out of Edinburgh and join a whale conservation project in Mozambique.'

'She's confused. She's angry. She's taking out what's happening to her mother on you, because you're safe and she can get away with it.' He nodded and I could tell he knew all this, but he still needed to hear it. 'Very common symptoms,' I said reassuringly. 'Shoplifting, too. She's crying out in the only way she can.'

He smiled, getting up to go. 'So, it's not the end of the world?' He looked into my eyes, from one to the other, taking his time. For a second, we were both caught off guard, as if each of us knew far more about the other than we made out.

'I should keep on taking the tablets, should I, doctor?' he said, looking away. There was a strain in his voice, the lines at the side of his eyes reluctant to unfold. I was disconcerted by how deeply he seemed to affect me.

It was my turn to smile. I wanted nothing more than to reach out to him, show him I knew he was in pain, but this wasn't the right time or place. 'Maybe you could spend some quality time with your daughter?' I said, snapping back into professional mode. 'Show an interest in the Mozambique project. Read up on it and tell her something she doesn't know. Talk to her. That would be my prescription.'

He nodded slowly. 'You're right, of course.'

A note on my desk told me that my first afternoon appointment had been cancelled. Typical. It was due to be Jake Stowe. Perhaps I should have seen it coming. Maybe Jake had already twigged that I'd sussed him out.

It was stiflingly hot in my office again and the fan I'd ordered still hadn't arrived. I went to track down someone to look into it. Stan, one of the technicians, dragged a spare out of a cupboard and handed it to me.

'It might rattle a bit, but it'll tide you over.'

Back in my office I was struggling to find a spare socket to plug it in. There seemed to be only one behind my desk and the lead from the fan wouldn't reach that far. Reluctantly, I went back to Stan to ask for an extension lead. He followed me to my room, convinced I'd missed a socket.

'There's often one tucked away at waist level,' he said, moving towards the shelves beside my desk. 'May I?'

I helped him shift books aside. 'You know about this already!' he said, 'You've been using it.' He held out a black lead plugged into the wall. There was nothing attached to the end of it.

'No – I…this isn't mine,' I said, staring at the cable. Stan pulled it out and handed it to me. He plugged in the fan instead and stood it on the edge of my desk.

'There you are,' he said smiling. 'Perfect.'

I thanked him absently, holding the cable in my hand. It looked like a lead for a computer or television, but the space on the shelf was too small. Perhaps someone had popped into my room to boil a kettle?

I didn't like the idea of people coming in when I wasn't there. I had the trust of vulnerable people and their confidential files were in my care. From now on, my office was going to be under lock and key whenever I left it.

***

I was coming back from a team meeting, mid-afternoon, when Lian drew alongside me.

'You okay?' she said.

'Sure, why?' I'd been miles away, thinking about Con.

'Must be upsetting when it's one of yours.'

'One of my what?' I had visions of my bike having been stolen or files going missing.

'Didn't anyone tell you? Your two o'clock appointment.'

'Oh, yeah – I know – he cancelled.'

She pulled me towards an empty waiting area. 'It's not quite as simple as that,' she cautioned.

I felt my forehead crumple into a frown.

'He…committed suicide,' she said.

I didn't say anything. There must have been a mistake. Jake had been faking it. He simply hadn't shown up. That was all.

'That can't be right…'

'Debbie took the call just now from the police,' Lian continued. 'They might want to talk to you.'

I must have looked as if I hadn't heard. I took hold of the back of a chair, allowing her words to register.

'Do you know how it…how he…?' I asked, my voice distant, as if carried away by a sudden breeze.

'He jumped from the Holborn Viaduct. At lunchtime.'

I flopped into a seat and stared at the floor.

'Are you all right?' she said. I found myself shaking my head and saying *Yes* at the same time. 'I'm sorry, I've got to go,' she said. 'Debbie might know more.' She brushed the top of my shoulder with her hand and disappeared down the corridor.

I ran straight to Debbie's office. She was chatting as I approached, but stopped abruptly as soon as she saw me and wiped her palms down her skirt.

'Lian's just told me,' I said. I felt unsteady on my feet. 'What happened?'

Debbie led me to a quiet corner of the office. The rest of the staff buried their heads in a staged 'busyness'.

'The police said he jumped in front of a bus from the Holborn Viaduct,' she whispered. 'That was about all they said, except that they need to speak to you. He had his appointment with you written on a note in his pocket.'

I spun away from Debbie and perched on the edge of a desk. He'd been on his way over to see me, but instead had gone to a bridge in Holborn and killed himself.

'You okay?'

'It's never happened to me before,' I said gasping. 'One of my patients…'

Debbie side-stepped towards the water cooler and filled a plastic cup, then pressed it into my trembling hands. She stood beside me, but seemed unsure about whether to touch me or not. I slowly leant against her, so that my head met her shoulder.

'He seemed okay,' I said, 'when I last saw him. He wasn't all he appeared to be, but he didn't seem to be at risk.' I stared into space. 'I completely missed it.'

'No one's going to blame you,' Debbie concluded.

I squeezed the cup absently and it crackled like a log on a campfire as it buckled. I should have seen it coming. I should have been more sensitive, more understanding. I'd been side-tracked into finding holes in Jake's story and hadn't paid enough attention to his mental state.

'The police said a female officer, PC Lockley, will need to talk to you this afternoon,' Debbie said gently. 'Do you want me to cancel the rest of your appointments?'

'No,' I said immediately. I couldn't let anyone else down. I was here to help people, not crumple at the first sign of distress. 'I'll see my patients until the officer arrives.' I straightened up and briefly gripped Debbie's hand. 'Thank you. I'll be in my office.'

'Just to warn you, Professor Schneider wants to see you, but he's not in this afternoon. Some family crisis, I think.'

I'd met the professor only once since I'd joined the hospital and wasn't sure what to make of him. Staff from various ranks described him as one of the 'top dogs', but they also said he'd been snappy and, in recent months, increasingly fierce. He spent half his time as a consultant cardiologist at St Luke's, but no one was altogether sure what he did with the other half. He'd taken it upon himself to oversee certain members of staff in psychology for some reason, including me, although he was never around when I had a query. The phrase 'he's unavailable' was bandied about a lot, but various admin staff were now replacing it with a blunt 'he's disappeared'.

I was dreading what he was going to say when he finally caught up with me.

At around 5pm, there was a sharp rap on my office door. I let PC Lockley in and invited her to sit down.

'How long had you known Mr Stowe?' she asked, a small notebook in her hand.

I sat upright in my seat trying to look like I was a hardened professional eminently capable of handling this, but my voice cracked as soon as I spoke. 'I...only had one session with him. And bumped into him a couple of times in the corridor.'

The fan ticked loudly every other second and made a moaning sound when it changed direction.

'And how was his state of mind?'

'Well – like all my PTSD patients, he was upset, but I ran through my usual procedure with him about suicide. Like a large proportion of the population, the idea of suicide had "crossed his mind" at some stage in his life, but he assured me he wasn't about to act on it.'

PC Lockley looked up accusingly. 'He *mentioned* suicide?'

'It was me who mentioned it. I have to,' I continued, 'and I always make an agreement with patients that they will call a friend, *The Samaritans* or their GP if they're having suicidal thoughts and are in fear of acting on them. It's standard procedure. Without that agreement, I can't work with them.'

I sounded professional and assured, but inside I was floundering hopelessly.

'So you didn't think Mr Stowe was at risk?'

'No.'

'He said he *wasn't* suicidal?'

'That's right.'

'Do you tape your sessions, Dr Willerby?'

'Some of them, but not that first one with Jake.'

I told the officer the gist of what Jake and I had discussed.

'There was one thing,' I added, 'something that bothered me about him.'

She looked up from her notebook, her eyes wide, waiting.

'I had reason to believe that Jake hadn't actually been present at the incident he described.'

'What do you mean?'

'He claimed to be a survivor of the fire a few weeks ago at Liverpool Street Tube Station, but I checked with the transport police and his story didn't match the facts. I don't think he can have been there.'

She blew hair out of her eyes. 'A time-waster?'

'I don't know. I'm waiting for his medical records to see if they can shed any more light.' She made a note. No doubt the police would want to see his records, too.

'What made you think he was lying?'

'Three inconsistencies. He said he escaped the area using the steps, but there are none on that particular platform at Liverpool Street Station. He said people were "on fire" in the ticket hall, except the fire never reached the top of the escalator and no one was burned. And Jake had no injuries, no burns or problems with smoke inhalation. Anyone who had gone through what he described would have had something to show for it.'

Her nod betrayed a hint of reluctant respect. She got up. 'Who knows what's going on in people's heads when they do this kind of thing?' She moved towards the door. 'Maybe he had a bet on with his pals…'

'Or perhaps, he was just very sick,' I said.

She pressed her pen into a slot on the side of her waistcoat. 'Thank you for your time.' She gave a smile that was half a shrug, and left.

Chapter 13

Three days earlier

A thin fly lands on the page I'm reading and creates a comma where there shouldn't be one. It means the sentence no longer makes sense. I try to blow it away, but it holds fast, stubborn, refusing to budge. I'm tempted to snap the book shut, but don't want a comma to be forever stuck in the wrong place.

Not that it matters, anyway. I've read the same passage three times and it still doesn't make sense. None of it makes sense. I can include life in its entirety in that conclusion. I lay the open book down on the table beside me. Let the insect take its chances.

I glance around the room, at the corduroy sofa and tasselled cushions. Everything feels fake, temporary. Like I'm on a film set waiting to get the final scenes over and done with.

I'm doing my level best to make things work, but I'm making a real hash of it. I'm resorting to behaviour no one would ever believe possible and there's no going back. Can't people see how hard this is? Isn't it in capital letters carved into my forehead?

I had to act, I had to go out on a limb and now everything's at boiling point. I only hope it's worth it. No one really understands what it's been like. All the waiting, not knowing. I tried my very best to sort it out in the right way, but nothing is working in my favour.

Now I have a terrible secret. I don't know if it's going to break me. My grip is starting to slip away. I'm clutching at straws and I don't have a good feeling about where this is going to end up.

Chapter 14

Present Day

I was an hour late for the open evening at the Camden Community Art Project and it was in full swing when I arrived. I'd invited Con at the last minute, thinking he wouldn't be able to make it, but he'd already arrived and introduced himself to Miranda without waiting for me. I spotted them sharing a joke by the fire exit. Justin was in front of them, sipping a glass of orange juice.

I didn't approach them straight away. I watched the easy way Miranda was chatting to Con – full of smiles, fluttering her eyelashes, flicking her fingers through her newly styled hair. They looked like old friends.

The team had put on a good show; there was plenty of white space between the pictures and sharp spotlights. Someone behind the scenes was taking this very seriously. Shame my mind was in a mess; I couldn't take it all in.

I stopped in front of a canvas and allowed my eyes to travel over the images. If I'd been asked to find one word to describe the painting, I would have said *grotesque*. It was abstract and garish, with shapes that depicted something between a cow and a human foetus. I glanced at the title: *Home*. Then I saw the name of the artist. I took a faltering step backwards. It had been painted by my sister.

Suddenly the room felt cramped and airless. I fanned myself with the programme, torn between slipping away before I was spotted and a morbid interest to see more. Scanning the walls, I came across further works in a similar style; swirling browns and purples – one with a huge pair of leering lips, another with what looked like a breast sliced in half.

I had no idea Miranda was producing work like this. On the one hand it looked bold and striking, but on the other it was abhorrent. Was this a true reflection of what was going on inside my sister's head?

I tried to remember a time when I hadn't been afraid of her, a time before the outbursts had started to define her. There must have been periods when we'd been a relaxed and harmonious family. Before my world became taut; before that continual feeling that I was living on a knife-edge. Gradually, insidiously over time, we'd closed ranks and shut Miranda out. My mother was ashamed, my father was bewildered, but I was just plain scared.

She was my *sister* – we shared the same DNA. From as far back as I could remember, my unspoken mission had been to hold on tight to my sanity and never be like her. It was hard to love someone when so much fear got in the way. Hard to get close when all my instincts told me to keep my distance.

'You've barely mentioned your sister since I've known you,' said Con, stepping to my side. 'I didn't know she was so gifted.'

'I didn't know this was what she was producing,' I retorted.

'She's sold three tonight already.' He gave me a hug. 'I'm sorry about the weekend.'

'Did you manage to sort things out at the theatre?'

A tiny hesitation. 'Yeah, yeah…it was…yeah.'

Over his shoulder, I was half-watching Miranda and Justin. She was showing him something in the brochure and he was looking interested and holding her hand. Justin saw me and dragged Miranda in our direction.

'What do you think of the exhibition?' Miranda asked.

I felt all their eyes on me. I was trying to figure out the right thing to say.

'They're challenging Sam's comfort zone, I think,' said Con. I couldn't work out if he was having a go at me, or trying to make things easier.

'What's that?' said Justin, attracted by a mobile twirling in the air by the window. Miranda followed him.

'She told me her creativity is her reason for living,' Con said pensively. 'She said it saved her life when she was ill.'

'She told you that?' I said, staring at him. I felt a hole rip open inside. I couldn't imagine Miranda ever confiding anything like this to me.

'We had a chat on the phone the other night – when you weren't in. She told me all sorts of things.'

'Did she now?' I felt my shoulders rising.

'You're not close?'

'Did she tell you that?'

'She said you had a lot of catching up to do. That she'd been in an institution for twelve years.'

I nodded, impressed by Miranda's frankness. 'It's difficult. She's wonderful – bright, funny, eccentric – but she's…'

'She told me she couldn't cope with normal existence, with the responsibilities and pressures when she was younger.' He looked over at her; she was making Justin laugh, finding coins behind his ears. 'She had to break free, that's all.'

'She told you all this?'

He shrugged.

'Listen, I dearly love my sister – I really do…' I was misty-eyed now; hurt, angry and upset with everything the day had brought me. 'But she's got a whole universe of demons and dragons inside her.' I held my arm out towards the nearest picture as if to rest my case.

'Yeah – she said as much.'

I brought my hands to my hips. 'Did she tell you that at the age of nine, she went manic in the supermarket, ran down the aisles knocking boxes and tins off the shelves, yelping like a hyena? That at twelve, she emptied five wheelie bins of rubbish over the neighbour's lawn? That at fifteen, she set fire to her own hair at one of my parents' posh dinner parties? That at eighteen, for their silver wedding anniversary, she tried to bring a horse – yes, a two-year-old stallion – into the conservatory?'

I wasn't sure what had sparked off this tirade. I'd turned up tonight to genuinely support Miranda, but it was starting to feel like a mistake.

'She told me about that time in her life,' he said. 'Miranda's sorted now. She's on medication.'

'*That time*? You make it sound like it lasted a couple of days. You weren't there.'

'It's over now. Look at her – she's better.'

'How do you know? Are you some great psychiatric expert all of a sudden?'

I admired Con's optimism, but right now it felt not only naïve, but reckless. 'You don't know what people are capable of, Con. One minute they're acting perfectly normally, the next they're…' I knew I wasn't talking about Miranda any more. Since the shock of Jake's suicide my mind had flooded with self-doubt and fears of incompetence. 'It doesn't matter. I've got to leave.'

Con grabbed my arm. 'Don't let this spoil things…for us,' he said.

'I'm sorry.' I let him pull me towards him. 'I've had a terrible day. One of my patients killed himself. I feel like shit.' My anger was melting into exhaustion.

Con held me close. 'You should have said. We could have come another night.'

'I didn't want to disappoint Miranda.'

Con interlocked his fingers with mine. 'She would have understood.'

'I think I need to go,' I muttered.

He stroked a strand of hair out of my eyes. 'Shall we come with you?'

'No. Justin is enjoying himself,' I said. 'I'll get some fresh air and have an early night. Say goodbye to them for me.' I gave him a warm, lingering kiss on the lips and he watched me go.

On the bus home I felt numb. I tried to put Jake out of my mind and I thought about Con and Miranda instead. About how quickly he seemed to have got to know her and how little he seemed to know me. Was that my fault? Was I too preoccupied with work?

The bus pulled away from the next stop and a man carrying an old television sat down in the seat next to me. I shivered when I remembered the spare lead Stan had found in my office that afternoon. I remembered looking up and seeing the books tumble into the space when he unplugged it.

Then one of the PC's questions came to mind and sparked a query of my own. She'd asked if I'd taped my sessions. Now I was wondering if someone *else* had.

Jake Stowe's parents were waiting for me when I arrived at the hospital the next day. They looked like they'd had about as much sleep as I had.

'They said you were the last person to see him,' said Mrs Stowe accusingly. She was tall and wiry like Jake. 'He was due to get married in the autumn,' she added, as if I'd deliberately ruined his future. She buried her face in a man's handkerchief. Patients sitting in the nearby waiting area were starting to crane their necks. I had no option but to invite the couple into my office.

'We just want to know why,' said Jake's father, as they took adjacent seats. He was clutching his wife's hand as if they were on a particularly hair-raising fairground ride.

I cleared my throat. 'I only had one consultation with Jake, I'm afraid. I didn't know very much about him. He gave no indication – no indication whatsoever – about what he was going to do.'

'But he must have been upset. I'm mean – that's why he was here in the first place, wasn't it?' said Mrs Stowe, tipping the chair forward onto two legs.

'I see patients who have Post-Traumatic Stress,' I said. 'Yes – they're all having problems coping after some horrific experiences. Did he talk to you about what had happened to him at all?'

'The car accident?'

I hesitated. 'Or anything else that might have been worrying him?'

'No – we…he's always been a quiet boy. We thought it was a good idea when he finally decided to come and see…a professional.' Mrs Stowe looked up with disgust as she said the final word.

'He didn't mention an incident on the Tube?'

'What incident?'

'The fire at Liverpool Street.'

Mr and Mrs Stowe looked at each other. 'No. Are you sure you're talking about our Jake?' said his father.

'It's a bit of a mystery, I'm afraid, but Jake definitely talked about being involved in an incident on the Underground.'

'It's news to us,' said Mrs Stowe.

'I think Jake could have been confused,' I said. I didn't want to come straight out and accuse their son of an obvious lie. I still hadn't seen Jake's medical history, so I had to tread carefully. 'Was he prone to periods of depression?'

'He was a bit low after the car accident, if that's what you mean?'

'And *before* the accident?'

She looked at her husband and they shook their heads. Now wasn't the right time for these sorts of questions. I'd have to wait for Jake's notes.

'I'm so very sorry…' I finished feebly.

I opened the door for them and watched as they shuffled along the corridor in a daze, like they were making their way through thick fog.

I needed an urgent fix of caffeine after that, so I hurried to the canteen for an espresso. When I returned to my office, I found Professor Schneider standing inside.

He was portly but tall, with receding dark hair swept back as if he was constantly battling a fierce wind. He had his hands in his pocket like he was hiding something.

'I wanted to speak to you and your phone…was engaged,' he said, not quite looking at me. 'So I thought I'd drop by, instead.'

I walked over and lifted the receiver to be greeted by a healthy dial tone. 'I don't know what the problem is,' I said.

He rocked from one foot to the other. 'Just wanted to check you were okay…after the…terrible business.'

'It's been a nasty shock,' I said.

He nodded, his thumb under his chin, his finger on his lip.

'What does your supervisor have to say about it?'

'I'm still waiting to have a new one sorted out…after Dr Derriman left…if you remember?'

Professor Schneider knew I'd been without a clinical supervisor for weeks. He was the one who was supposed to be setting up a new one.

'Ah, yes, we need to get that fixed up.'

There was an awkward silence.

'I'll leave you to it, then,' he said. 'Let me know if there's anything…' He tailed off. Our eyes met and I caught a glimpse of hostility, not concern.

'Thank you,' I said, trying to mask my confusion.

Once he'd left, I stood by the door – the key in my hand.

What had Professor Schneider been doing alone in my office? With icy realisation, I was suddenly certain about one thing. When I'd left the room a few moments ago, I'd definitely locked the door.

I had back-to-back patients for the rest of the day. I was exhausted by the end of it, but glad to focus on other people's emotional turmoil instead of my own.

'You're working late.' Leo Hansson loomed out of the shadows, making me jump.

The canteen had long since closed and we had both chosen to risk the vending machine for a coffee. It was about as close to the real thing as Bucks' Fizz is to champagne, but it gave the illusion of a caffeine hit.

'I've got a report to do for the police.' I glanced at my watch. 'What's your excuse?'

I knew he was behind with his patients again today. One of his colleagues had told me he'd been at his wife's bedside again for most of the previous night.

Leo ignored my question. 'The suicide?'

'You heard,' I said, nodding.

'Are you okay? He was one of yours, I understand.'

'Yeah, although we'd only had one proper session.'

He stirred the murky mixture. 'We can't work miracles.'

'He was obviously very mixed up…you know…' I caught a drip from the bottom of my cup. 'But it's still a horrible shock.'

'People are unpredictable – you should know that by now.' He walked with me down the corridor, but his steps were crisp and stiff, putting me on edge. 'Kim was right, you know, the other day,' he continued. 'I've been busy providing for her and Felicity, her sister, giving them what I thought they wanted, but I haven't *been* there at all.'

I turned to him, forced him to stop. 'People show love in different ways,' I said. 'Women often use words, or show love with physical affection, but men often *do* things – they take action to show their love.'

There was a taut silence. I could tell my argument wasn't holding any water.

'Nice try,' he said. 'I'm taking your advice and seeing them both soon, anyway. It's a start.'

'Good.'

'I think I've been overcompensating for my own childhood,' he said. 'Sorry, I shouldn't be telling you this.'

'Don't apologise…go on…I'm a good listener…or at least, I'm supposed to be.'

'It's true, you are. But, perhaps we should leave it there. You've got enough patients to cope with in your day job, you don't need any more, after hours.' He smiled and turned to go.

I touched his arm. 'Not at all…I'll let you into a secret. I can't bear small talk and idle banter. Besides, I can tell you're someone who thinks and reflects deeply on things. I find that very…' I was going to say 'attractive', but rapidly changed it to 'interesting'.

I stayed still, waiting for his response. 'You really want to know?'

'It's a problem we therapists have,' I said. 'We're inveterate nosy parkers.'

He pulled a face. 'You asked for it. Shall we sit?'

He indicated a bank of empty chairs in an unlit waiting area ahead of us. Instinctively, we turned our chairs towards each other.

'My mother was a successful historian,' he began, 'she was always hidden away in her study. The first words I ever learnt to read were *Do Not Disturb* from a notice hanging on her door. I remember her drifting like a ghost from room to room; passing through, but never stopping to speak to me. As an only child in a large house cut off from neighbours, I learnt to occupy myself with reading, studying and playing with the anatomical skeleton that belonged to my father. My best friend became an old set of encyclopaedias I found in the cellar.'

I nodded. I knew the feeling; with Miranda off the rails and Mum and Dad preoccupied with their careers, I too had sought friendships in books.

'One of my earliest memories is of a fishing trip with my father…' he went on. 'I'd managed to fill a plastic box with writhing three-spined sticklebacks. Then I'd hooked a brown trout. The fish was wily, I was inexperienced and lost it. My father didn't say a word. He took my plastic box and threw all the fish I'd caught back into the river. Then he made me crouch down as he ducked my head under the water and told me to start again.'

I swallowed hard.

'Seems rather sad to have to admit that this is my most vivid childhood recollection. I'd have preferred a special occasion, brimming with love and sunshine. I thought I'd learnt my lesson, thought I could avoid the imbalance of my own upbringing. Now I realise, of course, that I'd got it all wrong.' He found my eyes and didn't let them go. 'I thought the most important thing for any child was to have a good relationship with its mother. I'd really missed out on that when I was young, so I guess I stood back and let Helena do all the work. I didn't play enough part in the family myself.'

I was shocked by his candour. And deeply touched.

'You did what you thought was best at the time,' I said. 'That's all any of us can do.'

For a second I wondered why Con and I had never had conversations like this. It was hard to explain, but Leo and I seemed to be made of the same emotional fabric. I looked at him and saw a reflection of myself: outwardly strong and self-assured, but confused and lost underneath.

We shared an unspoken look that signalled we still had work to do and stood up. Our footsteps echoed in the dim corridors until we reached my office.

'I bet you were all exemplary in your family, weren't you?' he said.

'What makes you say that?'

'You seem composed, well-adjusted, as they say. Refreshingly on top of things.'

'I wish. It might surprise you to know that my sister is schizophrenic.'

'Ahhh,' he said, drawing out the sound. 'Sorry. I've really put my foot in it. But you seem so unruffled. You're obviously well-practised at looking like everything's fine.'

I unlocked the door. 'I'm not the only one, am I?'

He gave me a sad smile and disappeared back into the shadows.

Chapter 15

The next couple of days slid past in a blur. Miranda finally moved out – she'd yet to give me the details – and quiet sacrosanct evenings to myself were possible again.

So, when I heard loud music one evening as I climbed the stairs, I was decidedly put out. It wasn't like my elderly neighbour, Mrs Willow, to have her radio turned up high. It was even less likely that she'd be listening to *Get this Party Started* by Pink. As I got to the landing I stopped sharply. A strip of light was shining under the door to *my* flat, not hers.

My first thought was that I had a burglar. A rather overconfident one judging by the volume of the music. There was, of course, a more obvious explanation.

I slid the key into the lock and as an after-thought, rang the doorbell.

They were sitting on the sofa playing cards. Miranda, Con and Justin. Justin cheered when I came in.

'You scared the life out of me,' I said, pressing my hand to my chest. 'What's going on?' I was trying to maintain a degree of levity, but I was furious, not just at the scare, but at the intrusion.

'I came back for the rest of my things,' said Miranda. 'Don't you remember?'

'Snap!' said Con, slapping a card down next to Justin's six of hearts. 'Got you.' Con looked up and gave me a cheery smile.

'I thought you'd left your key,' I said to Miranda, still stunned.

She didn't answer. I stood and watched them. There were smells of cooking coming from the kitchen. They had put my music on and opened a bottle of my wine. It felt like I was the one who didn't belong. They looked like a happy family I was observing from behind a glass partition.

Con got up and came towards me as Miranda shuffled the cards expertly to impress Justin.

'I dropped by on the off-chance,' said Con, helping himself to a packet of jammy dodgers that I hadn't noticed before, open on the coffee table. 'Miranda let me in. We've been getting to know each other. We've—'

'I've been showing Conrad some of my drawings,' interrupted Miranda.

'At the project?'

'No – the ones I did here.'

She pointed to a large folder, open in the corner of the sitting room.

'You didn't show me,' I said.

'You saw…one of them…'

I knew she meant the one we'd torn in half in the kitchen. After that, I wasn't sure either of us had felt like looking at any others.

Miranda emptied her glass in one gulp.

'Should you be drinking?' I said.

'It's fine. It's only a little bit and I've been great lately.'

I was disconcerted. I felt like something was going on. My estranged sister and my boyfriend were in my flat making themselves at home without me.

I went into the kitchen to gather my thoughts and noticed my green lava lamp had been installed on the ledge over the radiator. Miranda must have seen fit to bring it out of the cupboard and switch it on. Globules floated up from the base and collected at the top like a deep ocean landscape. It was meant to be soothing, but right now it merely irritated me.

I poured myself a drink as no one else was bothering to offer. Con came in as I was about to take a large sip.

'All right?' he asked cheerily.

'Tired, that's all.' I snatched my much-needed slug of wine, then put the glass down and let the hit of alcohol swill through my veins. He came up behind me, pulled me hard into his thighs. He didn't ask about the suicide. It seemed like he'd forgotten. There was a hollow silence. 'What's up?' he asked.

I stepped away. 'It's been a difficult week, Con. I need an early night and I come home to find a party in full swing.' He tucked his thumbs into the pockets of his jeans and leant against the table.

'Do we need to talk?'

'What do you mean?'

He made a sucking sound with his teeth. 'Miranda told me.'

'Told you what?'

'The other night you were with a bloke in a bar somewhere.'

I stretched my eyes wide. 'It wasn't like that. He's a surgeon at the hospital. His wife is dying.' Con was waiting for more. 'You get so jumpy when I just *talk* to other blokes – I feel like I can't breathe sometimes.'

The kitchen door opened and Miranda's head popped round, a quizzical look on her face. She swiftly retreated when she caught my expression.

Con screwed his face up. 'I can read the signs, Sam.'

'What signs? What are you talking about?'

He broke into a singsong voice. 'For God's sake Sam, just admit it.'

I was aghast. 'Admit what?'

'There's someone else, isn't there?'

I felt like I was being charged at by an angry bull. I had to sit down. 'There isn't, Con. Honestly.'

All of a sudden, the world was in league against me. 'You're the one who's been mysteriously disappearing.'

Con opened his mouth to say something when Miranda burst in again.

'Sorry, love-birds – but the pie is going to burn.' She slung on the padded gloves and opened the oven door. Justin wandered in.

'Smells great,' he said, making himself at home at the kitchen table. He stared at his empty plate, standing his knife and fork on end. 'I love shepherds' pie.'

The meal was delicious in spite of the tension, and afterwards Justin talked me into a few rounds of Charades. Con was brilliant, of course. Amusing and clever. Miranda was surprisingly unselfconscious, but I was nervous and dithery, mixing up my books with my films and breaking words down into too many syllables.

At around nine-thirty Justin started yawning. I was tempted to suggest it was getting late for him, but didn't want to get into an argument. I was glad when Miranda was the first to make a move to go. She gathered up all her remaining belongings and said goodbye to Con and Justin.

'By the way, I've got a room in a shared flat,' she said, as I opened the door to see her out. Not the hostel, then. I didn't ask. 'I'll let you have the address once I'm settled, but you can always reach me on my mobile.'

She turned and held up the door key, before leaving it, like a payment, on the window ledge by the front door.

Justin was busy tying his shoelaces when Con took me to one side.

'I'll see you over the weekend?' he said. I was standing on the mat, fiddling with the security chain.

I took hold of his hand. 'Sounds good.'

He hesitated. 'I've got someone in doing the decorating, so I'll come to you,' he said. 'Don't bother to cook – I'll bring something.'

'That would be lovely. Just the two of us.'

He pressed his lips into my hair and I held the door open as he led Justin out.

'You're crap at party games, by the way,' Con shouted up at me as they disappeared down the stairs.

Jane LaSalle was just as nervous as she'd been in her previous sessions. She came into my office before lunch, pressing her bag to her stomach as if it was her only possession. She sat down and brushed her fingers nervously against her lips. I cut straight to her mental state. After what had happened to Jake, I needed to highlight the suicide issue with every patient.

'I ask everybody this on a regular basis, so please don't be alarmed. I know you've been having disturbing thoughts and flashbacks, but have you had any suicidal thoughts since I saw you last?'

Her head dipped down and back up a fraction, but she didn't say anything.

'It's perfectly normal, especially after a very distressing experience. Can you say – on a scale of one to ten – how you would score your feelings about suicide? If one means it barely crosses your mind and ten is that you've got a plan all thought through?'

'I don't know.' She stared at her trainers.

'Have a try.'

She curled a strand of hair around her finger. 'About seven.'

Alarm bells. That was high. That was in the red-flag zone. My heart rate shot up a couple of notches.

Tread carefully. 'And can you tell me what kind of plan you've got in mind?'

'I don't know yet.'

She didn't know – a good sign. Either that, or she didn't want to tell me, which was definitely a bad sign. Once again, I hadn't been given Jane's full notes to show her medical and mental-health history, but the form from her admission session gave me no cause for alarm. No history of self-harm, no history of depression, no medication.

'What sort of thoughts have you had? Can you say?'

'I…er…it feels weird talking about it.'

'I know – but it's important. We need to make sure those kinds of thoughts are taken very seriously.'

She froze, her mouth tight, looking like she wasn't going to utter one more word.

'Shall we come back to it before we finish today?' I asked.

She nodded. I also asked if she was comfortable with me recording the session and when she agreed, I switched on the microphone.

'Did you want to tell me how you've been coping?'

She watched her fingers as she nipped the fabric of her jeans into little folds. 'I keep remembering weird bits of it. Silly things like looking down and seeing I was wearing open-toed sandals and my feet were wet with the rain. Everyone had wet umbrellas pressing against my legs. I could feel the rubber rail under my hand and the picture boards as I climbed the static escalator. There were a lot for that musical, *The Lion King*. I can't get the images out of my head.'

I could see sweat forming a silky sheen on her forehead.

'I keep feeling the bodies around my feet at the top of the escalator, people clawing at me. I was trampling on them in the crush, shaking them off, trying to stay on my feet. I knew if I fell, I'd get suffocated. I had to hoist myself up to get over the barrier. There were flames everywhere. Someone grabbed me to shove me out of the way and I nearly fell down. I managed to pull myself free. I could see the daylight then and I was out.'

She said it all in one breath, then sucked in air as if she'd been trapped underground there and then. 'I didn't deserve to survive.'

I wanted to ask questions about the fire itself – how there could have been flames by the barriers, how the barriers could have been shut – but didn't want to commit the therapist's worst sin of taking over.

'You were terrified – you wanted to get out,' I said, reflecting back her experience, instead. 'You did what anyone else would have done.'

'No – you're wrong. I should have helped people. I could have pulled people to their feet. There was a little black boy, about six. I remembered he was holding his mother's hand on the step behind me on the escalator.' A sob sent a shudder through her shoulders. 'All the lights went out and I could hear him crying. People were rushing past me and he was pushed, he ended up at my feet. I could have picked him up, carried him.' Her voice tailed off to a whimper. 'I didn't – I pulled away.'

'You're ashamed?'

'I was a coward. I should have a "story to tell" about how I helped someone. Instead I'm just…worthless.'

She seemed to be in a genuinely tormented state. It went against all my instincts to question her version of events.

'You need to remember that you weren't to blame for what happened,' I said. 'You were completely innocent, caught up in a horrible situation.' She was staring with her mouth open. 'You're prepared to come to me and talk about it – admit how you feel. That's not the act of a coward.'

She made a small squeaking sound.

I looked down. 'It says here you gave blood last week. That's about going out of your way to help save someone's life.'

She shrugged, unimpressed. 'It's a bit late now, isn't it?'

At the end of the session, I checked Jane's suicidal intent again. It was now between five and six on the rating scale. Better, but not out of the woods. She was still unable to discuss a plan with me.

'Can you be honest with me, Jane?' I said softly.

'I'll try.' She fiddled with a loose thread on the hem of her T-shirt.

'Do you think you might hurt yourself?'

Her eyes were dry, but there was strain in her forehead. 'I don't want to,' she said. 'But I'm not sure I deserve to be here.'

Unless you're convinced a person is about to take their own life, you're limited in the precautions you can put in place. You can't section them just because they have suicidal thoughts.

With Jane's permission, I rang her flatmate and asked her to keep an eye on Jane and make sure there were no stockpiles of painkillers in the bathroom cabinet. I managed to get Jane to agree to ring me, every day, on my mobile and promise to call me or a friend, if she found herself starting to take steps towards harming herself. Then I got in touch with her GP. It was all I could do without stalking her.

'See you next week,' I said, as she left.

I sat back in the silence, running over what she'd told me, then clicked on the audio file we'd just recorded to play it back from the start.

Alarm bells were ringing loudly inside my mind as I listened.

When I'd taken the trip over to Liverpool Street, a shop-owner and newspaper seller had both confirmed it had been a fine, sunny evening on May 28th. There was no rain. So why had Jane described wet umbrellas?

I picked up my phone and rang through to Liverpool Street Underground and asked to speak to Perry again. He was just about to go off duty, but agreed to talk to me.

As he answered my questions, another piece of the picture twisted out of shape. He told me the billboards beside the escalators hadn't advertised *The Lion King* since March 28th. Two months before the fire. When I'd been over there myself, the advertising was for *Mamma Mia.* It had stayed in my mind, because the same poster was repeated beside the full length of the escalator.

There was one further point. Jane described having to climb over the ticket barriers at the exit. Perry assured me categorically that as soon as the fire was discovered the barriers were opened. They remained open until 9pm.

Jane hadn't been there either. She was faking it, too.

Chapter 16

Present Day

I'm on automatic pilot. How long can I function like this? I laugh and smile, but the cracks are starting to show and I don't know if I've got enough strength to hold it all together.

I have people around me, but no real friends. No one to talk to. What I'm involved in is hardly a subject I can drop into conversation at the dinner table. People would be disgusted – even though it's not really my fault. They wouldn't see it that way – they'd find me repulsive.

I think about the people I've been mixing with and I know I should keep my dark secrets hidden under the table. I can't talk to anyone – not about this kind of thing.

Not a soul.

Just as well, really. If I start opening up, the truth might come spilling out. Then all hell will break loose. What's happened is certainly not something to be proud of.

Chapter 17

I needed to get some air. Thankfully, it was lunchtime, so I hastily left the building, half ran along Tooley Street and cut through Hay's Galleria to reach the water's edge. I was desperate for a sense of space. Everyone was outside enjoying the dazzling summer's day. I heard the clink of dishes, watched waiters bow their heads at tables, smelt wafts of fresh fish and minted potatoes.

Tourists were lifting their wine glasses and pressing cheek against cheek, taking selfies. I wished I could share their sense of carefree abandon. I wished my greatest concern was whether to choose the salmon or the cod.

In spite of the sunshine, it was a breezy day and the water was choppy. I leant against the railing and tried to think.

What was going on?

Everything was starting to feel surreal. Now a *second* patient was taking me for a ride. Two pathological liars in the same week, how common was that? Perhaps I needed to check some statistics.

I pulled out my sandwich and took a bite, then took in the view. The breeze caught my hair and I rolled my shoulders, trying to ease away the tension that had gripped me as Jane had left.

As I scanned the path, people-watching, I spotted a group pointing to the river, jumping and shouting. I followed the direction of their arms and saw something bobbing in the water alongside HMS Belfast.

Had a dog jumped in? Had someone lost their rucksack?

The tide was swiftly going out and the shape was picking up speed in the water, heading towards Tower Bridge. Someone screamed and one or two members of the group were racing up and down, horror on their faces. Instinctively I broke into a run, dropping my sandwich. As I got closer, I heard snatches of shouts.

'He's drowning – I'm sure of it.'

'I saw him jump – from London Bridge.'

'Someone should go in.'

A man started stripping off his jacket and shoes. 'I can't get down,' he said. He was darting back and forth trying to find a way to reach the water.

'Don't risk it. The tide's too dangerous.'

'We've called the river police – they're getting a boat over there.'

I slowed my step and for a moment was torn about pulling away. I didn't need this. I was working with trauma all day long – I didn't need an extra dose of it during my lunch break. This had nothing to do with me. Other professionals trained for this would be here any minute.

A police officer appeared and started talking into his radio.

'It's a girl,' someone shouted. He was holding binoculars. 'She's gone under.'

I couldn't turn back. I stood staring, the railings pressing into my chest. A yellow and blue checked police boat came from upstream, spewing white spray. It swung round, holding position, but the shape in the water was moving fast. I couldn't see the girl's head any more. Two divers flopped backwards into the water. A huge crowd had gathered on the walkway by now, some of them concerned, but most excited by the impromptu entertainment.

'They've got her,' came the cry from the man with the binoculars.

I saw a distant shape being hauled into the boat.

'They're giving her CPR.'

Shapes hovered over the bundle and the boat starting moving. The nearest jetty on the south side of the river was about fifty metres away and I could see the telltale blue flashes in the distance, as emergency vehicles were gathering. I starting running again. Others were running too. As we all gathered around the ambulance, two police officers tried to hold us back and an

Alsatian dog started barking. I strode up to an officer and flashed my hospital ID, hoping she wouldn't bother with the small print.

'I might be able to help,' I said.

I couldn't go back to work without knowing more. I gritted my teeth, digging my nails into the apple left uneaten in my pocket.

The officer let me through, just as the boat pulled up at the jetty. As soon as I saw the green T-shirt I knew, but I needed to see her face, just to be certain. The diver had stopped punching down on her chest and one of the officers on the boat was shaking his head.

The sodden body was carefully lifted onto a stretcher and taken up the ramp towards the ambulance. The stretcher was dripping as it passed me and lumps of mud slopped to the ground. An arm was flapping over the edge – the nails delicate and pearly-pink. I wanted to take hold of her hand, but it was too late. Her eyes had a strange film over them, like raw egg white, but the rest of her face was finally at peace. A paramedic pulled the blanket over her head.

'I know the victim,' I said, my voice breaking. 'It's Jane LaSalle.'

'It isn't your fault,' said Con for the tenth time. He was out of his depth, pacing up and down beside my bedside.

The last few hours had been a blur. I'd spoken to police and given a statement, had a debriefing and was given the once-over by the team psychiatrist. Professor Schneider asked to speak to me, but he could see I was too upset to give precise details. I'm sure staff were starting to worry about my mental health and they had every reason. I couldn't stop crying.

I'd sat in my office with the blinds down, holding a mug of cold tea, unable to move. I don't know how long I'd stared into space. At some point, a nurse came in and put a blanket around my shoulders. She told me to go home. In the end, Con had to come for me in a taxi. He half carried me up the stairs to my flat.

I was exhausted. A deep, racking fatigue that dragged every ounce of energy from my body. I kept going over and over it in my mind. I thought we'd had a productive session a matter of minutes before Jane had decided to take her own life. *I'd let her down. I'd missed something obvious. What the hell was I doing? I was a disgrace. I should be struck off.*

I clutched my damp forehead. 'I'm killing people, for God's sake.'

The psychiatrist had given me a sedative and by now my bedroom was shifting around. I felt like I'd been cast adrift at sea. I wanted the world to stop bobbing up and down.

'You need to take a break,' said Con, wiping my forehead with a cold flannel. 'This girl – she must have been psycho.' I didn't have the energy to argue with him.

I thought again about Jake taking his own life a matter of days ago – and now this.

'You need to come with me to Arizona,' said Con. 'Think about finding another job when you get back.'

I blinked hard in disbelief. 'I can't just walk away,' I croaked, anger swiftly rising to boiling point inside me. He got up to make yet another cup of tea.

I slept fitfully after that and woke up to find Miranda kneeling by my bed. She was stroking my hair.

'Con's been great,' she said. 'He's just done a massive supermarket shop. He's even bought you some of those herbal teas you like. I should hang on to him, if I were you. He's a gem.'

'Yeah…yeah…'

'One of us will be here until you feel better.'

I didn't care about me.

'I can't see Jane's parents – not yet. I can't cope with that.'

I could already hear the cries of Mr and Mrs LaSalle: *What the hell happened? What did you say to her, for God's sake?*

'Shush. No one's going to bother you. Just stay here where you're safe and sound.'

'I should have done something.'

'You can't rescue everyone, Sam.' She looked at me. A look that said she knew I'd spent my life devoted to saving others, because I could never save her.

I took her hand, but before I could say anything more, I slipped away from her into drug-induced slumber.

The next few days came and went in snatches. It was like listening to a radio that kept sliding off the station for hours at a time, but then suddenly came back loud and clear. Miranda left Con and me together; she was right about his kindness. He was a consummate nurse: attentive and patient. Nothing was too much bother for him.

By the third day, I felt like I was finally waking up and as I climbed out of the shower, the doorbell rang. Con had gone out after I'd mentioned a craving for chocolate mousse, so I answered the door in my dressing gown.

'I brought this,' he said, producing a small canvas from behind his back. 'I thought it would last longer than flowers.'

'Crikey, Leo – it's gorgeous.' It was a painting of an empty rowing boat floating on shimmering water. It sent tingles up the back of my neck.

'He paints lots of Venetian landscapes,' Leo said, without telling me who *he* was.

I backed up so he could come inside. 'What are you *doing* here?'

Then it clicked. A surge of dread made me stagger back; he must have heard I'm about to be fired and has decided to break the news to me gently, in person.

'The department has managed to fend off Jane's parents. They won't be bothering you.'

'That's a relief.'

Our eyes met. There was no point beating about the bush. 'Have I still got a job?'

He laughed. 'Of course.' He waved me away down the hall. 'I hope you've booked plenty of sick leave,' he said.

I scoffed. 'No way. I can't just hide away. I've got to face this.'

'Fair enough,' he said smiling.

I offered him coffee and he stood with his hands behind his back appraising items in the sitting room as I went to boil the kettle. As I brought in the drinks, he pointed to a painting Miranda had insisted I hang up to cover a crack in the wall.

'Yours?' he asked.

'No – my sister's.'

'The one with schizophrenia?'

I nodded.

He continued to scrutinise the picture. 'Mmm…interesting.'

I offered him a seat, aware his eyes were now following my every move.

'When did your sister first start showing symptoms?' he asked without a preamble. It was a big question and I was shocked by its directness. Admittedly, he'd been very frank with me recently.

'My parents were ambitious and self-obsessed. They sent Mimi – that's her original name – to boarding school when she was eight. I followed suit two years later. Tidy the children away.'

I tugged my dressing gown around me, closely.

'But she'd been volatile before that,' I continued, perching beside him. 'She was chaotic a lot of the time, both at school and in the holidays. Everyone thought it was attention-seeking. It got to the point where any social event became fraught. Will Mimi behave herself? Will Mimi have an outburst? Dinner parties… Christmas.'

Leo leaned forward so he could see me better, listening. I could smell his expensive aftershave – a seductive musky smell, with hints of cedar and vanilla.

'She took her A levels a year early, because she was actually very bright, but failed them all,' I said. 'The following year, after terrible pressure from my parents, she retook them and scraped through. She got a place at university to study Medieval History, but then she failed her first-year exams and my mother humiliated her by burning all her course notes so she couldn't do the re-sits. She dropped out when she was twenty and a few months later she was in a psychiatric ward. I think my mother's actions in destroying her files were the final straw and that's when the full-blown symptoms became undeniable.'

He gave me a sympathetic nod. 'Like Superman bursting out of a phone box – only the person who emerged wasn't someone you were pleased to see.'

'Exactly. From that day, instead of trying to help or understand, my mother disowned her and Dad went along with it. They completely cut her off.'

I hadn't intended to tell him any of this, but here I was, practically giving him my life story. Maybe it was because all my emotions were tripping over themselves after what had happened at work. But it wasn't just that. There was something about Leo that made me want to open up. I'd felt it before with him; like there was an instant understanding between us. Then I put my finger on it – he made me feel safe.

At that moment, my phone chimed. It was a text from Con saying 'something' had come up and the chocolate mousse was on hold. I was relieved he wasn't coming back. I didn't feel strong enough for any fuss and nonsense over Leo's unexpected visit.

Leo waited for me to put down the phone. 'Okay?'

'Yes,' I said, with a sigh.

'Carry on,' he said, 'what was Miranda like?'

Now I'd started telling him the whole story, I couldn't stop. 'Well, there were hallucinations, delusions, the voices she talked to and the periods of lucidity. Miranda was in and out of hospital and care homes. She ran away twice in her early twenties – hitch-hiked her way to the East End, stopped taking her medication, ended up homeless and disoriented. A stranger would pick her up, get in touch with my father who would collect her and the cycle would begin again.'

'And you?' he said. 'What effect did this have on you?'

I hesitated. 'I got tough. I cut Miranda off like everyone else did. I was no better than they were. I could never relax if I was around her, always waiting for the next thing to smash, the next person to scream.'

'You were scared?'

'Yes – scared of *her* – she was so unpredictable.'

He narrowed his eyes, taking time before he spoke. 'But scared in other ways, too?'

He was spot on. He *knew*.

'Yes,' I said. I stared at my fingers, coiled in my lap. 'My worst fear was that I might become like her.'

As I spoke, a prickle crept across my scalp. I'd never admitted this to a soul. The words came tumbling out, as though Leo had opened a hidden valve inside me that I knew nothing about.

'If I spent time with her,' I said, 'I'd be "infected", so I had to steer clear of her. And of course, I had good reason to be afraid – as her sibling, there's a seven to nine per cent chance of developing schizophrenia myself. I'm still *terrified* by that. Always on the lookout for signs.'

'So you let her go.'

I nodded. 'I dreaded my visits to the first care home she was in. Every time I was due to go, I threw up the night before. When I actually came face to face with her, it was like talking to a hostile stranger.

'After a few months, we'd set up a pattern where half the visiting time was spent in silence. Not just an awkward silence, but one saturated with accusations and guilt on both our parts. Eventually, she asked me to stop coming. I think she found my visits just as painful as I did. I wrote to her instead for a while, but she never wrote back. She told me she wasn't ready. Ready to do what, I'm not quite sure. I waited and waited, but it never happened.

'The last time I saw her in care was four years ago when I went with Dad at Christmas. Two years ago, she moved to a new place, but I'm ashamed to say in all that time I've never been. Then a couple of weeks ago she turned up on my doorstep.'

To my dismay, I felt a tear tickle down my cheek. Why hadn't I told Con any of this? Was it just because he hadn't asked the right questions?

'Perhaps we can learn to face our regrets about the past together,' he said softly.

***

Con brought over a wine-and-dine meal for two, the following Saturday. Only hours before, I'd been tempted to cancel and opt for a night alone with *The Grand Budapest Hotel,* but I knew time was running out before he started filming.

He looked ravishingly handsome as he stood in the doorway; his thick hair freshly washed. Breathing in his smell of leather and coconut, the tragedies of Jake and Jane folded themselves away at the back of my mind.

I don't remember many details of what we ate – one minute I was spooning out horseradish sauce, the next Con was pulling my top over my head. We used our tongues, lips, fingertips to get to know each other all over again – grabbing each other's flesh. Our love-making was frantic, verging on ferocious.

Afterwards, we took the dregs of the wine bottle to bed and listened to Adele, curled around each other.

I plumped up my pillow and was about to say something when I realised that Con had fallen asleep. I was too wide-awake to join him, so I read for a while.

As I reached over to put out the light, I stopped and propped myself up on one elbow, watching him. His eyelids quivered and he let out intermittent groans, then every so often he'd say a word. Most people mutter in their sleep, but with Con the words came out crisp and precise as if he was reciting poetry. Sometimes his words woke me with a jolt and with such clarity that I was able to scribble down what he said. In the morning, when I told him about the surreal little Haikus he'd produced during the night, he never believed me.

'Rubbish,' he'd say. 'No one recites poetry in their sleep.'

I got up shortly afterwards for a glass of water. When I climbed back into bed, I felt the prickle of an unpleasant realisation. It wasn't just Con's possessive streak that made things difficult between us, there was another underlying problem. Lust had made me so blind, I hadn't even spotted it. It was about the level at which we connected. Even though I wanted to share my deepest feelings with him, he didn't give me enough space to do it. He swept over my emotions and made his own mind up about what I was going through, before I'd even opened my mouth.

Even when he *did* listen, he didn't seem able to grasp the finer points of what I was trying to explain. It sent a wave of deep disappointment through me.

The following morning, Con left early. He bolted down the stairs pulling his jacket on, gripping a slice of toast between his teeth. He said he needed to get back to let the decorator in.

As I was tidying up, I discovered his watch on the floor. It was Sunday, so I didn't need to rush off anywhere. I decided to drop it off for him in Balham and buy fresh fruit on the way back.

He took a while to answer the door.

'Oh – I wasn't expecting you,' he said. His voice carried surprise rather than the delight I'd anticipated, but he softened it with a smile.

I dangled his watch. 'Thought you might be needing this. I found it under the television.'

'Can't imagine how it got there,' he crooned, pulling me close by the lapels of my jacket. We were still standing on the front door mat.

'Aren't you going to invite me in?' I asked.

He tucked his shirt in. 'Fancy going out for some decent coffee?'

I could smell paint and remembered Con had said he'd got decorators in.

'Okay,' I said shrugging. 'But we can stay here if you like. I don't mind the smell of emulsion.'

There was a shadow moving behind Con and I adjusted my eyes. The figure came up behind Con's shoulder.

'Well – this is cosy,' she drawled, a paintbrush in her hand.

'Miranda! What are *you* doing here?' I said, my mouth tight.

They both looked at each other. *Why do they look so guilty?* No, not guilty, more like smug. I felt the way I had the other evening when I'd found them in my flat. Like they were colluding against me. Like they had a secret and were using it as a weapon.

'I meant to tell you last night…' said Con, kicking at the mat with his bare foot.

'I'm Con's new flatmate,' said Miranda. 'Coffee?'

She turned away.

My eyes pinged wide open. 'Flatmate?'

He scratched his nose.

'Did you think I wouldn't find out?' I said, once Miranda was out of earshot.

'Of course not, I was trying to find the right time to tell you.'

'And the whole of last night wasn't enough for you? How long does it take to say "By the way, your sister has moved in with me?"'

'You make it sound like I was trying to hide it.'

'Why didn't you check with me first?'

'I didn't think I had to ask your permission,' he shot back.

I felt like storming off, but I didn't want a row hanging over us. Instead, I took a step inside. Con walked ahead of me into the sitting room, running his hands through his hair in agitation.

'I'll stop for a coffee,' I said. 'But not for long.'

'Good,' said Con firmly, although I wasn't sure which part of what I'd said he was glad about. He left me in the sitting room and joined Miranda in the kitchen.

As I sat down, I noticed that two of Miranda's paintings had already found their way onto the walls. I recognised trinkets and books that belonged to my sister on the shelves and ledges. She hadn't taken long to make herself at home.

The kitchen door was ajar and I watched them from the sofa. Miranda was pouring the coffees and Con was laying biscuits on a plate. I didn't want to get caught up with any silly jealousy about the two of them. It was all above board. I was sure of that. The only reason Con hadn't said anything was because he knew I'd react badly, due to Miranda's turbulent history.

As I watched her, a memory flickered on the edges of my vision and then came out into the open. It had been kicking around inside my head for so long, I wasn't sure if it was a memory or a dream. We were young; Miranda must have been about eight. She came out of my parents' bedroom one morning, her thumb in her mouth, trailing a towel behind her. The look on her face said she'd been smacked, but the towel hid her legs. Dad always left his mark. Although Mum was the disciplinarian, it was usually Dad who was railroaded into dishing out the final punishment.

I remember I was sitting on the landing and Miranda walked straight past me with a fixed stare.

I don't know why that particular scene had lodged itself in my mind. Maybe it was the blank look on her face that I'd found so disturbing. Maybe her illness had been taking hold, even then.

I heard Miranda laugh and looked up. She and Con appeared to be sharing a joke. I wondered if I'd spent most of my adult life feeling not only afraid, but sub-consciously jealous of Miranda. Not of her artistic skills per se, but of her unfettered ability to express herself.

I stayed for coffee but the strain was palpable. Invisible strands of barbed wire crisscrossed the room with every comment we made to each other. After twenty minutes, I made a hasty and somewhat inelegant exit.

Chapter 18

In spite of my sleeping tablets, Monday morning broke early, at 5am, with fierce, driving rain that thrashed against the windows, declaring war. I gave in and caught the bus to the hospital.

The harsh reality of Jake and Jane's deaths hit me again as I entered the building. I'd kept calm over the weekend, remembering Miranda's words – I couldn't save everyone. But here I couldn't escape reality.

Leo spotted me in the corridor on his way to theatre.

'How are you coping?' he said, with concern.

'So-so,' I said.

'I didn't expect to see you back so soon.'

'I can't just disappear. There are other patients at risk.'

'Are you going to section them all?' he said, with a wry smile. He didn't look like he expected a response. He squeezed my shoulder. 'Ask if you need anything,' he added.

That evening, Con invited me to join him and Miranda for supper. He met me outside the hospital and we caught the Tube to Balham. I could see what he was doing; trying to get us all onto a better footing. There was an unspoken brittle edge between the three of us now, which would take more than a few helpings of coq au vin to sort out, but I admired him for his intentions.

It was clear as soon as I arrived that Miranda was making a supreme effort, too. She'd bought a bottle of my favourite wine (she must have asked Con). She'd put Norah Jones on the hi-fi (again, no doubt after consultation) and the pair of them served up an exquisite three-course meal. Being the guest felt altogether different this time.

Con's mobile rang just as he was about to start the washing up. He left the room to take the call and came back seconds later with his jacket on.

'Sorry – got to go,' he said, grabbing his keys from the stand by the door.

'Is it Justin?' I said, getting up.

'No.' There was nothing else. No further explanation. 'I'll try not to be too long.' He pulled me towards him, buried a kiss in my hair and waved to Miranda.

'What's that all about?' I asked, after the door slammed.

She made a dismissive grunt. 'Probably the theatre,' she said. 'He often rushes off at short notice.'

A frown crept across my forehead as I went to fill the washing up bowl. Then as Miranda made coffee, I asked to take a closer look at the pictures she'd brought to the flat and thought no more of it. I realised that I hadn't done justice to the ones I'd seen at the opening in Camden. I stood before each canvas in turn. The wine helped, but I found the tormented images just as disturbing.

'I don't make them up,' came a voice behind me. 'It's just what I see inside my head.'

'I think I'm starting to understand that now.'

'Painting helps to clear them out,' said Miranda, a tea-towel slung over one shoulder. 'It's like a catharsis and confession all in one.'

'Confession?' I couldn't imagine what Miranda meant by that.

She didn't answer. Instead, she blew dust off the frame of the next picture and started plumping up cushions. I knew she'd heard me. I didn't push it. I tried to imagine what it must be like to have these images – not here, safely on the wall, but roaming loose and untamed inside one's own head.

All of a sudden I needed to know the answer to a question.

'Can I ask you something before Con comes back? It's been on my mind.' I felt the back of my throat tighten.

'What?' Her eyes were locked onto mine, steely with fear and defiance, trying to read what I was going to say. There was no going back.

'Have you ever tried to…commit suicide?'

'Oh, that,' she said, casually, flopping onto the sofa. 'Yes – just once. Shortly after I was put away. I cut my wrists.'

She turned her hands over and I saw pale scars running across the veins under her plaited bracelets. I cleared my throat, trying to hide my horror. I was surprised and ashamed that I'd never noticed them before. My own sister.

I couldn't string the right words together. 'I'm sorry…I should…I wish…'

'Oh, come on – you're not going to stand there apologising all night, are you?' She rubbed my arm. 'It's over.' She was trying to sound flippant, but she didn't convince me.

'Is it over?' I asked. 'For good?' I stood over her so she had to look at me. 'Do you ever go back to those dark feelings?'

She took her time, staring blankly over my shoulder. 'You want the truth?'

'Of course – these paintings…they're recent. Something is definitely not right,' I said gently, not daring to move.

Her next words came from a distant place. 'The truth is – it's never over.'

I stayed perfectly still and when she didn't say more, I spoke again. 'I'm sorry I've been so hard on you.'

She stretched out her foot and pointed and flexed her toes, like a child. 'I know it must have been tough – I was insufferable at times.'

'You *can* talk to me, you know…tell me what's going on.'

She shrugged me off. 'I'll explain, one day.'

With that, she shut me out, flicking on the television and humming out of tune.

She slipped out for a pint of milk shortly afterwards and in the meantime Con returned. He looked grim until he realised I was watching him, then he kissed my cheek hard with a loud *mwah* sound.

'Everything okay?' I said, with concern.

He slipped into a blasé tone. 'Yeah, yeah. All sorted.' He threw his jacket over a chair. 'Any coffee going?'

I poured him a mug. 'Miranda's gone to get milk. She won't be long.'

I tried to read his face; tried to work out what was going on. Were all these sudden disappearing acts about the theatre? He obviously wasn't going to volunteer anything and I was too tired to risk a heated discussion about it.

'Is it working out with Miranda at the flat? Has she been okay?' I asked, instead.

He laughed and clapped his hands together. 'Actually, she's a great flatmate. She insists on cooking all the time and doing the cleaning. I've landed on my feet.'

'I'm a bit worried about her,' I said. 'Something's not right – it's as if she's trying too hard – covering something up.'

Con gave it some thought. 'Na – you're seeing things.' His eyes rolled slightly, with fatigue. 'You spend too much time with head cases. She's doing fine.'

Con insisted that I stay over. Even though I had work the next day, I agreed. I felt our relationship could do with some extra consolidating. I wanted so much for him to be right for me, but something was always just slightly off.

During the night, Con started his sleepy monologue again. A noise downstairs disturbed me or I might not have heard him. I went to the bathroom and, too awake by then to seamlessly slide back into the flow of sleep, I took a pen and wrote down his words. They might provide some light relief over toast in the morning.

'Blocked,' he said. Then, 'busy…crowd.' He turned over, churning up the duvet, raising his voice, 'Stuck…' His leg jerked and he huffed. 'Dark…faster.'

It didn't take long for the novelty to wear off and for me to wonder how long this sleep-talking episode was likely to go on for. I needed my rest, especially as I had patients first thing in the morning.

Con grunted facedown, then a low wail came from his mouth, muffled by the pillow. I noticed beads of sweat breaking out on the back of his neck. 'Run!' he said. 'Get out…' He thrashed his arm, narrowly missing my notebook. I put it down and put my hand on his back. He was boiling.

'Con, it's okay,' I said, stroking his shoulders.

He barked something at me. It sounded like 'doorway… narrow…can't get through.' Then he broke into a loud shout and sat up, 'Got to get OUT…what the—'

He was awake. 'Bloody hell,' he said, wiping the sweat with his palm into his hairline. 'I thought I was done for.' He pulled his knees towards his chest and rested his head on them, panting.

'It's okay – it was just a nightmare.'

'I haven't had one of those in years.'

I definitely couldn't remember a time when he'd been distressed in the night like this before.

He got up and I heard him running water in the bathroom. He came back wiping his face with a towel. 'Sorry, I woke you,' he said. He stretched out over me pinning me to the mattress. 'Now that we're both awake, however…'

He started nibbling my ear and my neck, but we didn't get far. His breathing got heavier, his movements slowed to a stop and I could tell he'd fallen back to sleep. I eased his weight gently to one side of me and pressed my face into his hair to fill myself with the smell of him. Then I put out the light.

Con didn't mention the disturbance over breakfast and neither did I. It was a one-off. With any luck he'd forgotten all about it.

When I got to the hospital that morning, Debbie told me Professor Schneider wanted to see me.

'So does that new doctor. What's his name?' She clicked her fingers. 'Dr Graham.'

'Dr Graham?' The man who had got the wrong floor and ended up in my office. 'What did *he* want?'

'I don't know. He was hovering near your door earlier. I told him you weren't in yet.'

I shrugged and made my way to the stairs. Dr Graham was going to have to wait.

I found the professor in his room pacing back and forth, talking on speaker-phone. He didn't look well. His hair was tossed awry and there was an untamed look in his bloodshot eyes. I hadn't been looking forward to this meeting. No doubt I was about to be hauled over the coals for sitting by while two of my patients killed themselves.

'Come in,' he said absently, as he switched the phone back to the handset, still on his feet.

I tumbled into the seat in front of his desk and waited. I thought about Jake. What sort of inner torment had he gone through before he ended up on the Holborn Viaduct? And Jane – what had happened to send her straight down to the river to drown herself, right after our session? They had rarely been out of my mind.

The professor ended the call and straightened up. I decided to jump in first.

'This is the second one,' I said. 'Something is terribly wrong and I don't know what to do.'

He put up his hand wearily in an effort to get me to calm down. I took no notice and ploughed on, telling him it was now clear that both Jane and Jake had fabricated stories about being involved in the Tube fire. He leant his elbow on the filing cabinet, watching me. Confusion twisted the already grim expression on his face.

'You're sure about this?'

I explained all the areas where their stories didn't add up.

'You've done your research,' he said, sounding exasperated. 'Who knows why people do these things.' There was a tremble in his voice when he spoke. 'We've had our fair share of suicides before you joined us, believe me, it's nothing new.' He was trying to reassure me, but not making a very good job of it.

'But – so close together? Both seeing the same therapist? Both lying about the same incident? Jane rushed off to kill herself the moment after I'd spoken to her.'

I pressed my fist into my mouth. I didn't want to cry again. I needed to be strong to face this, sort it out.

He was unnerving me, standing there. Finally, he sat down. 'It isn't the first time we've had a glut of suicides,' he said.

A glut? How many more was he anticipating?

'I've looked into their records,' he continued. 'Apparently, Jane LaSalle had taken anti-depressants in her late teens and Jake Stowe had made an attempt before – three years ago.'

'Really?' My gaze was glued to his face. 'I asked Jake if he'd ever considered suicide and he assured me he hadn't.' Another lie. 'I'm sure his parents didn't know about it.' I glanced down at the batch of files on his desk. 'Why didn't these records come through to me?'

'They're here.'

'Yes – I can see that. But I requested them. I should have had them from the start.'

'And you requested them through the correct channels?'

I hesitated. 'Well…I think so.'

He straightened his tie and I had the distinct impression he was trying to create some kind of smokescreen, letting the blame hover over me for not following the right procedures with hospital records, rather than admitting to a failure in the system.

He spread his hands on the desk and leaned towards me. 'Don't worry, we'll all back you to the hilt.' He drew a loud breath. 'But…what we need to do is make sure that the hospital is covered at every turn. We can't afford for this to escalate into a media witch-hunt or for people to start claiming we were negligent.'

'I see,' I said. So his concern was more for the hospital's reputation than for the victims.

'You just need to learn to say "no comment" whenever anyone asks you any questions – understand?'

I nodded. 'Is there going to be some kind of investigation?'

'The police will want to cover all the usual ground, but it's nothing to worry about.'

He took off his glasses and rubbed his eyes. At that moment his phone rang and he snatched up the receiver. I wasn't sure whether I should leave, but he stuck out his arm and beckoned, when I started to get up.

I sat back and waited.

'Yes…I know that already…yes, you did…no, that's not what I said…' he hissed into the receiver. I pretended not to listen and let my gaze roam around the room instead.

On the wall by the door hung an over-sized photograph: a group of four in soft-focus, presumably his family. The professor, looking dignified, was at the centre, a distinguished woman stood by his side and two boys of university age knelt at the front. I'd heard, however, that this epitome of domestic bliss no longer told the full story. Perhaps the person he currently didn't sound too pleased to hear from was his wife?

Beside the photo was a framed certificate from several years ago, awarding the professor *The Jeffersen Prize* for medical advances. I'd heard through the grapevine it was for improvements in pacemakers, although various colleagues had joked that he was building his wife a kinder heart.

He ended the call abruptly and blew out his cheeks.

'Where were we?' he said.

'The files. Can I have them now?'

He considered it. 'Yes – I think that's appropriate under the circumstances.'

'I need to find out if there's a link between Jane and Jake. Maybe they knew each other. Perhaps it was some kind of pact. We need to know.'

For a second, he looked like a rabbit caught in headlights, before he turned his response into a shrug. 'That's not our concern.'

I thought I'd misheard him at first. *Not our concern?* Who was he trying to kid?

'But shouldn't we be finding out exactly what's going on? We could track the two of them down on social networking sites – see if they were in contact.'

He was shaking his head. 'You're not a detective, Dr Willerby. If the police want to do that, it's their business – it certainly isn't ours.'

I couldn't let him do this. Couldn't let him fob me off. 'But – we need to find out what this is all about.'

'Find out how? We can't climb inside their heads, Dr Willerby – dead or alive.' He laughed. He *dared* to laugh and I nearly stormed out there and then. I grabbed the arm of the seat, squeezing it hard, forcing myself to stay within the bounds of professionalism.

'Claiming to be a survivor, telling a therapist, then taking your own life – it's an extraordinary series of events,' I insisted. 'And for it to happen *twice*—'

'Just leave it!' he roared. He slammed both palms down on his desk in an emphatic gesture.

I got up, snatched the files, grabbed the door handle with slippery fingers and left, even more certain that there was something weird going on.

Why was the professor so guarded about finding out the truth? I wasn't going to rest until I got to the bottom of it.

As I stormed along the corridor, I remembered the time he'd appeared in my office without my permission and I thought about the lead that had been hidden in my bookshelves. Had he been recording my sessions? Why on earth would he do that without my knowledge?

I had a cancellation that afternoon and took the opportunity to look through all the medical records the professor had reluctantly handed over. Apart from the three patients who had given the Tube fire as their reason for seeing me, there were notes from Mandy, who'd lost relatives in a coach crash, and Steve, who had watched helplessly as his best friend was decapitated in an industrial accident.

My office was stuffy following the muggy weather and I lit my fragrance burner. It had two functions – together with the fan, it helped refresh the room and when I added a few drops of rosemary or peppermint oil, it kept me alert.

I found nothing in the files to worry me. In a few cases, there was a history of depression or anxiety and one patient had stayed briefly in a psychiatric ward, but there were no records showing any suicide attempts apart from Jake's.

I double-checked Jane and Jake's files in detail, turned to my computer and ran their names through the main social networking sites, but couldn't find anything to suggest they had any connection to each other.

I didn't tape all my patients, but I did keep meticulous notes, taken by hand during appointments and transferred later to the computer. It was important to remember details – get the slightest point wrong with a patient – call their cat *she*, say, when it's a *he* and it can instantly break any established trust. It tells the patient you haven't been paying enough attention.

I went through my notes from Jake's first session and a tape of Jane's second, searching for any links, but drew a blank.

I didn't know what I was looking for, I just had a feeling I'd know when I found it. The strongest sense I had was that there was *something* to find. This wasn't over – I was sure of it.

I had a meeting arranged for 3pm, but I cancelled it and carried on. If I went off to do other things, I'd lose my train of thought. There was a clue here in these notes, in these tapes; there had to be.

By 4.30pm, my brain was saturated. I took off the headphones, stood up and did a full body stretch. I was going to have to leave it. Go home. Perhaps I'd been wrong. Maybe what happened to Jane and Jake was just some weird and tragic coincidence.

I went to my desk and blew out the candle beneath my burner. The instant the flame went out, a neuron exploded inside my head.

I'd got it.

Chapter 19

Present Day

It's all going wrong.

I keep thinking people are looking at me, sizing me up, wondering how stable I am. Perhaps I should confess everything in full. Get it all out in the open. Over and done with. But where? In a church? With my therapist? I really need to tell someone the truth – otherwise it's going to suffocate me. I'm tempted to spill it all, spit it out – the truth – but as soon as I start imagining what words I'd use to explain myself, the whole idea feels too risky. By far.

I carry on with my daily routine pretending I'm on top of things. I smile, I laugh, but it's all fake. It's like the elephant in the room I can't talk about. Any normal, sane person would be shocked and horrified by my part in this. There's no way they could understand and I can't trust their reactions. Before I know it, I'd be led away and locked up.

Something's got a fierce grip on me – it's like being poisoned – a venom getting to me from the inside. Seeping from one cell to the next, contaminating every inch of me with so much pain and shame. If people knew, a grim scandal would erupt. I feel desperately guilty – of course I do – about the mess it's making, but it was never my fault. I've got to keep hold of that. I am NOT to blame.

Chapter 20

It was the tiny whiff of black smoke that touched my nostrils as I blew out the candle, that did it. *Black smoke* – the *smell* of it.

I'd been about to go home, but I stayed where I was. I sat down abruptly and allowed the buzzing in my head to run its course. This was really important. How could I be certain I'd got it right?

I turned again to my computer and checked all the online reports of the Liverpool Street fire from the local press, the Metro and Evening Standard. None of them had printed the words I was looking for. The police hadn't used them, none of the quoted witnesses had either.

It meant only one thing.

It was right there on the tape and in my notes. Jane and Jake's accounts shared one particular phrase that was identical. Remembering the black smoke, they had both described the smell as *scorched oil.* Exactly the same words. It was very specific. Too specific, it seemed to me, for two patients who had never actually met.

But Jane and Jake weren't the only ones who had used that particular description. There was someone else.

I tried Leo's number, but Lian answered.

'He's with his wife,' she stated curtly. 'Can I help?'

I muttered an apology and put down the phone.

When I found Leo the following morning, he wasn't the epitome of calm I was expecting. He didn't appear to hear me when I knocked. I gingerly pushed open his office door to see if he was there, and found him kneeling on the floor looking as though he was trying to build himself a life-raft with a pile of A4 paper.

'I went to see the professor,' I said.

'I'm sorry, I'm really busy,' he said, without looking up.

I glanced down at the overlapping papers on the floor. Some appeared to be photocopies from medical journals, others looked like print outs from the Internet. He began frantically scooping them together.

'Leo – listen. I think I've got another faker – another patient who's claiming to be a survivor from Liverpool Street – and who wasn't there.'

Leo appeared to be counting pages. 'Have you told Professor Schneider?'

'No…' I wasn't sure how much I could trust the professor any more.

I explained about the connection between the three stories. 'This guy, Terry Masters, had inconsistencies in his story, too. He talked about stairs when I know there aren't any. He insisted that the lights on the Tube went out. He said it was one of the main reasons for the escalating panic; no one could see a thing. Except they could. I called the transport police earlier and they categorically stated that the lights in the train itself never went out. All the police witness accounts state the same. Terry wasn't there, either.'

I slapped my hands against my thighs. 'I'm worried about him.'

Leo was breathing heavily; the knot of his normally pristine tie was swinging at half-mast below his unfastened top button. There were damp patches under his arms.

'I'm not sure I can help you,' he said distractedly. 'I don't know what to suggest.'

'But don't you think the whole thing is really odd – more than that – suspicious? Three people lying about the same incident – two of whom have committed suicide?' My voice was starting to squeak. 'I'm scared Terry might be about to join them.'

Leo let out a thinly disguised moan. I'd never seen him like this. Dr Hansson seemed the most composed and self-controlled person I'd ever met.

There was a sound behind me. Lian rushed in.

'Oh, it's you,' she said sharply. 'Dr Hansson isn't feeling well.' She gave me a fierce stare that was clearly more than an invitation to leave. She ushered me into her office, next door.

'It's not a good time,' she whispered. 'His wife has taken a turn for the worse. They think she's got only hours left to live.'

'Oh, no…how awful,' I muttered, hovering by her desk.

She gave his door a concerned glance and pulled it shut. 'He's insisting on seeing his patients, but I'm going to get someone to take over from him.'

'Can I have his home address?' She drew her chin back. 'So I can send him a card,' I assured her.

She spun the old-school Rolodex on her desk and scribbled a few lines on a sticky note.

'I'll see if I can persuade him to take a few days off,' she said. She flicked her hands in my direction to shoo me away like she was herding chickens.

I was on my own.

Back-to-back patients for most of the day prevented me from doing anything further. Then, it turned out my brain was needed on another matter altogether. A matter I'd completely forgotten about until a colleague happened to wish me luck on my way back from the canteen. I was booked to give an important paper at a conference in Cambridge on Thursday and hadn't yet written a word of it. I urgently needed to throw some last-minute ideas together or I'd be in real trouble. As a result, I spent the next two hours with my head down poring over reference books.

I locked my office and was about to leave, when I heard Debbie arguing with a burly looking man at reception. I hung around nearby, in case she needed some back up.

'I've already told you, the professor's not *here*. Perhaps you can see someone else.' Debbie tapped the computer vigorously as the disgruntled man leant over the counter trying to see what she was doing. She looked at the screen, then tentatively back up at him. 'Er – we don't seem to have you registered. Can you spell your name again?'

'I can't believe this,' he roared. 'We had an agreement and—'

'If you could just tell me your name again,' Debbie said, cutting across him.

'It's a *private* matter,' he hissed, between clenched teeth. 'I'm not on any of your sodding lists.' With that he stormed off.

Debbie slammed her pen down on the desk and dropped her head into her hands.

'You okay?' I said, approaching the desk.

'It's just mayhem,' she said, looking up in despair. 'Professor Schneider had loads of commitments this afternoon and he's disappeared again. No one can reach him.' She dropped her voice. 'I know he's been having some domestic problems. Karen, in the office, said she overheard him on the phone having a nasty argument with his bank.' She scratched her scalp. 'I don't know what's going on – and I certainly don't know what *that* was all about.'

I wanted to be sympathetic, but with everything I had to cope with right now, I couldn't think of anything to say. I patted her on the arm and headed home.

I rang Con as soon as I got in; I just wanted to hear his voice. When the call went to voicemail I tried my best friend, Hannah, instead. She'd been away, so I hadn't spoken to her in a while.

We were at University together. She'd gone on to set up a private practice in Harley Street, but just a few months later her brother had died suddenly from anaphylactic shock. Her world was blown apart. Friends rallied round her at first, but then they gradually dropped off. She told me I was the only one who had stayed the course, although I did little more than sit quietly with her and make cups of tea.

The last time I'd seen her, she'd decided it was time to claw her way back into life again and she'd booked a holiday to Rome with her mother. It looked, from the photos she'd posted on Facebook, that the bubbly character I remembered from the past had come through the worst of it. Her freckly skin was a soft shade of peach instead of ghostly white, her long coppery hair had soft waves in it.

Hannah answered quickly and I could tell from her rapid breathing that she was on the move.

'Hi there, Sammie, get my postcard?' There was a roar of traffic in the background.

'I did, thanks. How did it go?'

'It was just what I needed. I'm so glad you talked me into it.'

'Did I? Well – you'll have to tell me all the details soon, but for now, if you've got a moment, can I ask a favour? I need to pick your brains – it's not very pleasant, I'm afraid.'

She laughed. I could picture Hannah striding fast, swinging her arms. She was always involved in what was going on around her, never watching where she was heading.

'Come on, Sammie – I owe you a zillion favours.' She hadn't sounded so sparky in ages. I cheered inwardly.

Hannah had a sharp brain and keen insight. For her, getting a first in psychology had merely been a matter of turning up. She was also the kind of person who changed the energy in the room when she walked in, as if someone had switched on a light.

I told her about Jane, Jake and Terry and the loopholes that were bothering me; the question I most needed an answer to was *why. Why would patients go to such extreme lengths?* Hannah would know.

'I haven't a clue,' she said. I waited for more. 'Why did they come to you in the first place?'

'Good question. They all seemed emotionally cut up.'

'Not faking the PTSD?'

I considered her question. 'I don't think so – that's the odd thing. They seemed genuinely distressed. They'd have to be amazing actors to fake the symptoms. It's one thing to spin a story, it's another to make yourself tremble the whole session…'

'Mmm,' she considered, 'it's a bit odd that they'd go to all that effort to get attention and then end it all.'

'One person might do that,' I said, 'but two following the same pattern, with a possible third waiting in the wings?'

I heard the regular click of her heels on the pavement. 'Could they be talking about a different fire? *Not* the one at Liverpool Street?'

'I've thought of that. I checked with the police and they said there've been no similar incidents on underground trains anywhere in Europe in the last nine months.'

'I've never heard of anything like this,' she said.

'You don't have any ideas?'

I could imagine her now, using her free hand when she spoke, creating little semaphore patterns in the air like she always did. 'Sorry. That's psychology for you. It's all about people doing wacky things, for wacky reasons.'

I had to laugh. 'Thanks for that, Hannah.'

It was only once I'd ended the call that I realised something I hadn't seen before. Talking to Hannah had given me a new angle after all. The patients hadn't just lied about being involved, each of them spoke about someone they didn't help during the incident. The little girl, the young boy, the old lady.

I felt goosebumps prickling my spine.

Jake, Jane and Terry had been faking the *same* emotions – they were each pretending to be riddled with *guilt*.

Chapter 21

Con turned up unannounced late that evening. He fell in as I opened the door, looking dishevelled as if he'd been on the streets for hours.

'What's happened?' I was practically holding him up. He staggered towards the sofa.

'Oh God,' he said, as he sank down holding his head in his hands.

I suddenly had a bad feeling. 'Oh Lord, what has she done?'

Images sprang into my head of Miranda trashing Con's flat or someone having to break in because she'd left her keys somewhere.

'No – it's not your sister.' He hunched forward on the sofa and I noticed he was dressed for the middle of winter, with a thick scarf and heavy boots. I looked down at my T-shirt; one of us had got it wrong. 'I've been having terrible flashbacks.'

'To the motorbike accident?'

'No – something far worse. It's all terribly patchy.' He swung his head back, exhausted. My mind backtracked to his disturbed sleep, two nights ago. 'I need a brandy,' he said. I wasn't sure that was a good idea, so I made a coffee and added a small tipple.

I knelt in front of him. 'These flashbacks – what are they about? Can you tell me?'

His eyes popped wide. 'Like I say, it's patchy, but I was on the Tube…'

'The Tube?' My stomach rolled into a tight ball. 'Where?'

'I'm not sure.' He hit his head with his fist. 'Can't blinkin' remember.' I gripped his hand and noticed his knuckles were scuffed and bleeding. 'There was smoke and…then I was in a tunnel…running…'

A ghastly déjà-vu was descending on me. I could barely get the words out. 'When was this?'

He put his hand over his mouth, shaking his head. 'I can't remember. Yesterday? The day before? I can't say exactly…it—'

I interrupted him. 'No, Con, this isn't right.'

He looked at me, curiously.

'What are you talking about, Sam – this was *real.* I was caught up in the middle of something. There was a terrible panic. It was pitch black and then there were these orange flames – like a blasting fireball – that came from nowhere. And the smell, God…' he started coughing. 'This thick acrid smell of…'

'…scorched oil,' I said, finishing his sentence for him.

He stared at me, like a child trying to solve a magic trick performed before his very eyes.

'How did…?'

'Hold on,' I said. I went to get the notebook where I'd recorded the words Con had spoken in his sleep. I started reading, 'Blocked…busy…crowd…dark…run…get out…'

'Yes – that's it,' he said, he shuffled to the edge of the seat, agitated. 'I was in the ticket hall, surrounded by all these people and there was mayhem. There'd been a huge crowd coming up the escalators and a stampede because we were blocked by the barriers. People were scrambling over them and falling and getting trampled. There were people at my feet. I was standing on them.' He started to weep, swinging backwards and forwards clutching his head. 'I stood on people's arms and legs trying to escape… trying to find the way out…'

'Oh – my God, Con – it's happening to you!' I took hold of him, not knowing what to do – just knowing I had to protect him.

He was gasping, grabbing my hand, digging his nails into my skin. Reliving it.

'Listen, Con – this *didn't* happen to you.' I gave him time to let my words sink in.

'Why are you—?' He was about to lose his rag.

'Okay – where were you at six-thirty in the evening on Monday, May 28th?' I wasn't going to let this get the better of him. I had to make him see.

He looked dazed. 'That's ages ago. I've no idea.'

'You don't have a diary?'

He shook his head.

'How do you remember appointments?'

'I just remember them, or I write them on my hand.' He held up his fist, which had a smudged black doodle on it I couldn't make out. I reached into my bag for my diary and flicked through the pages. He hadn't been with me at that time.

'Do you remember going to Liverpool Street?'

'No.' His response was immediate. 'Why would I go there?'

'That's where the fire you're describing took place. On May 28th.'

He scratched his head. 'Did it? It can't be that, then – this was just recently.'

I sighed loudly.

His forehead crumpled and his eyebrows dipped together. 'You think I'm…I'm…making it up?' he stammered.

I faltered. 'No. I don't know what's going on.'

He looked deflated, lost.

'Have you never heard the names Jake Stowe, Terry Masters or Jane LaSalle?'

He pulled a face. 'No. Who are *they*?'

'Patients,' I said. I didn't tell him that two of them were dead. 'One's an accountant, one's a builder. Have you ever been to Jerry's Fish Plaice on Tottenham Court Road?' That was the café where Jane used to work.

'No way – you know I hate the smell of fish.'

'When did you last go on the Underground?'

'Earlier this week, with you.'

'You're sure that was the last time?'

He nodded.

I remembered it. He'd met me after work on Monday and we'd caught the Underground to his flat. He'd been his usual self.

No hesitation about going down the escalator, no problems getting on a train. Even a person with nerves of steel would show *some* signs of trepidation having been through the incident Con had described.

I bit my lip. I wasn't getting anywhere.

What had happened to him? I *knew* Con. He was a fine actor, but he wasn't into stupid make-believe like this.

'Can I stay here, tonight?' he said. 'I know Miranda's back at my place, but she's been a bit cranky lately and I don't want to be alone – if you know what I mean.'

'Yes,' I said. 'You must stay here.' After what had happened to Jane and Jake, I didn't want him out of my sight.

I went straight to the kitchen and grabbed all the knives from the wooden block, rolled them in a tea towel and stuffed them in a drawer. Scissors? How many pairs were there in the flat? I found one pair under the sink, another in the cutlery drawer.

I pictured the sitting room and bedroom – what other sharp objects were lying innocently around the place? Everything had become a potential weapon. Con hadn't said anything about feeling suicidal, but it was the first thing I thought of. I couldn't take any risks.

As Con brushed his teeth, I did a flying cull of the flat, tipping everything I could find that might cause any damage in a bag at the bottom of my wardrobe. I pulled the cord from my dressing gown, scoured the cupboards and hid away all the tablets. Was all this necessary? I didn't care – who knew which way Con's brain would turn? I had to keep him safe.

After he'd got into bed I went back to the kitchen. I switched the light off and stuck my head out of the window, willing the balmy night air to take all this madness away. It couldn't be happening. Not to Con.

A waft of wisteria from the guttering below drifted up to me. Down on the street, a taxi honked its horn at a cyclist cutting the corner. It was never truly dark in the city – too many bright lights.

A shudder took hold of my entire body. I couldn't lose Con. I'd got it all wrong. His jealous outbursts were bold statements of his love for me – that's all. They showed he cared who I was with and what I was up to. They showed he wanted me for himself. I could live with them, couldn't I? He couldn't leave me now. I wouldn't let him. No way.

I peeled off the grime on the window ledge; moss and twigs that had fallen from the gutter above. I dropped it over the edge and waited to hear the patter as it hit the patio below.

It sounded like Con was reliving the same horror as the others, but how was that possible? He recognised the smell when I said *scorched oil*. He seemed utterly convinced that he'd been involved.

There had to be another explanation. A cloud slid away from the moon and in that split second, a realisation hit home. They hadn't been lying. They *weren't* faking it. Jane, Jake and Terry, like Con, wholeheartedly *believed* they'd been there.

The following day, I was up at six-thirty, printing out notes and running through the PowerPoint presentation I was due to give that lunchtime. I'd slept fitfully, finding myself looking at the clock almost every hour. I'd given up the sleeping tablets. With Con potentially suicidal, I was prepared to stay awake all night if I had to. With so little sleep, I was feeling woozy, as if everything had a sheet of cling film over it.

When I came out of the bathroom, I had second thoughts about going. How could I leave Con and swan off to Cambridge?

I waited until eight-thirty, then called a friend of Con's from the Young Vic.

'I'm sorry it's so early,' I said. 'I'm concerned about Con.'

'Yeah,' said Danny. 'He was really weird when I saw him yesterday. Jumpy as hell. I've never seen him like that.'

'Listen – are you busy today?'

'Got a performance tonight, but largely faffing until then.'

'This is going to sound crazy, but can you…look after him? Stay with him.'

'I don't see why not.'

'Don't let him out of your sight. He's really not himself. Some patients I've seen at the hospital have had something similar and they've ended up…in a very bad way.'

'Is it some kind of virus?'

'I really don't know. It's got me totally flummoxed, I can tell you.'

'Where is Con now?'

'At my place.' I gave him the address.

'How is he?'

'Asleep right now, but he was very upset when he came over last night.'

'He was talking about a fire when he was with me yesterday, at the theatre. It was bizarre…I couldn't work out what he was on about.'

'I know…I felt the same. Can you come straight away?' I checked my watch. 'I've got to catch a train.'

'I'll be right over.'

Danny arrived looking like I'd dragged him away from Ascot, wearing shiny grey trousers, a checked jacket and waistcoat. A pink cravat was nestling inside his open-necked shirt, but it wasn't unusual. Most times I'd seen him, he was incredibly well turned out. Con said it was because, when he was ten, he was plucked from obscurity on Oxford Street by a talent scout, to play a key part in *Home Alone 3* and was always primed in case it happened again.

I pointed out the kettle, bread and biscuits.

'Anything sharp, like the bread-knife, is hidden away,' I told him, nodding towards the drawers in the kitchen.

'Sure,' he said, taking it all in his stride.

I liked Danny. He was intense, but gentle. I didn't want to burden him, but I couldn't leave Con on his own. After what had happened at the hospital, I had to give this lecture; I couldn't afford to appear negligent in any other area of my work.

Con had spent another troubled night moaning, throwing himself around, clawing at the pillow, calling out. He was still asleep by the time I left, but it wouldn't be for long.

I made Danny promise not to let Con fob him off and go walkabout.

On the way to the station, I took the radical step of looking up Terry's number and giving him a call. He was booked in to see me next week, but I persuaded him to meet me at the weekend to try something I had in mind.

At the conference, I stumbled through my presentation, hoping there was no one important in the audience, my mind still firmly on Con. My plan was to escape as soon as I'd finished, but a professor from Oxford University, who claimed he'd read my research paper on separation anxiety, cornered me, insisting I stayed to have lunch with him.

Professor Monkton reminded me of a turtle, in his old-fashioned seaweed-green waistcoat. He had ginger sideburns the texture of scouring pads. I think he was bluffing about reading my work. I think he'd just glanced at my profile in the conference brochure and fancied some female company.

I picked at the salad, making trite small talk, checking my watch more often than was polite. He told me about the research he was doing. I was only half-listening – something about monkeys on an island.

After we'd finished, I took the opportunity to ask if he'd come across any recent papers on brainwashing or covert forms of coercion.

'Not really…it doesn't ring a bell.' He scratched his blubbery cheek. 'But you're at St Luke's aren't you?'

I nodded as we stood up, ready to leave.

'Well, have you spoken to Professor Schneider?'

'Er, not directly.' I tried to hide a shudder.

'He might know,' he said. 'He's been taking some diversions into neurology lately, I believe.'

I avoided his eyes. 'Really?'

'Anton Schneider's a good friend of mine. I'm sure he wouldn't mind talking to you about it. I can mention it, if you like.'

'N-no, no – it's okay,' I stammered, as he held up my jacket for me. 'Please don't bother the professor,' I insisted. 'I can speak to him myself.'

When I finally managed to extricate myself and was on the train home, something about what Professor Monkton had said began to niggle at me. I wished I'd paid more attention. I flipped through the list of delegates in the brochure to find his name and the title of his latest research paper: *The Hundredth Monkey and the Collective Unconscious.* I read the abstract. It was based on the theory that an idea or skill can jump instantaneously from one portion of the population to another once a critical number is reached.

I leant against the window, my head jostling as the train rattled over points on the track. Could this be in any way related to what was happening with these four 'survivors'? Was some sort of sinister idea being passed around that certain vulnerable people believed to be true? Was there some kind of cult involved?

I tried to remember what each of my patients had told me about their personal lives. Not much. I thought about Con. What groups did he belong to? The theatre was his life – was that the connection?

Con was asleep again when I got home. Danny was looking bored, doing a jigsaw at the kitchen table.

'I haven't had any trouble,' he said. 'He's been in bed most of the time.'

I thanked him and offered to make him an early tea, but he wanted to get to the theatre.

While Con continued to sleep, I opened my laptop and looked for more information on the theory Professor Monkton had been working on. The concept wasn't new; research had begun in the 1970s. The more I tried to apply it to the Tube incident, the more I was pulled towards the question of *how*. How had four people picked up the idea that they had been involved in a serious incident when they hadn't been there?

It wasn't long before I realised that the starting point wasn't my biggest concern. It was how it was going to *end* that I should be focusing on. It was obvious now that all four of them had been genuinely traumatised by the scenes they believed they had witnessed, but there was a more significant factor. They all seemed to be suffering from extreme guilt. Was it *this* that was sending them over the brink, making them take their own lives? Terry Masters was still affected. Now Con seemed to be having the same experience. It was like a runaway train. I had no power to stop it.

I slammed my laptop shut.

I had to explain to Con the full story about the suicides. He had to know he was in grave danger.

Chapter 22

I dragged Con halfway across London on Saturday morning without telling him what it was about. Terry Masters joined us outside Liverpool Street shopping mall at 10am. What I had arranged was highly unorthodox, but it was the only idea I could come up with.

I thanked Terry for turning up and introduced him to Con, watching to see if there was any glimmer of recognition between them. I saw nothing.

'Is this that exposure therapy thingy?' asked Terry. 'Where you have to face what's scarin' you?'

'Not quite,' I said. 'I'm not going to ask either of you to do anything you're not comfortable with.'

I led them past the flower stall until they could see the underground ticket hall, closely observing their reactions.

Terry looked edgy. 'I'm not goin' down there,' he said.

I reassured him. 'We're staying right here. I'm not suggesting you go anywhere.'

Con turned to me, confused and rapidly running out of patience. 'What's going on? Why have you dragged us both out here?'

I addressed both of them. 'Does this look like one of your flashbacks. Is this the ticket hall you keep seeing in your nightmares?'

'I'm still squeamish about goin' anywhere on the underground,' said Terry straight away. 'But I can tell you for sure. It wasn't 'ere.' He jerked his head in all directions. 'Nah. The ticket office was on the other side and there weren't as many barriers.'

'He's right,' Con agreed. 'This isn't the place.'

I led them to the nearest café, finding a secluded table near the back, and explained that the only fire on a Tube in London in the last nine months had occurred here on the Central line on May 28th.

They looked at each other.

I also explained that two of my patients had described exactly the same kind of flashbacks. There was a chilling silence. Then I told them those patients had committed suicide.

There was an even chillier hush around the table.

Terry stared at me blankly. He had what looked like smudges of charcoal coating the sunken skin under both his eyes and he was using his elbows to prop his head up on the table.

'That's bollocks,' he said. 'You sayin' I'm makin' it all up?' Despite being angry, his body looked too heavy for him to drag it out of the chair and leave.

'No – I think you sincerely *believe* you were involved. You've all had extremely vivid memories of it. That's part of the problem. It feels *so* real that you're having difficulty coping with it.'

'Okay,' said Con, 'What were we involved in then, if it *wasn't* that fire at the end of May? It must have been somewhere else.'

'That's the issue – there hasn't been any other incident – nothing remotely like the one you've all described. So – I thought if you two shared your stories, we might see a link somewhere.'

'Won't that just prove we were both there? Wherever it was?' said Con.

'We'll see,' I said. 'You might have both been involved in something else that could be at the heart of this.'

'Okay,' said Con, looking like he was anxious to get it over with. He turned to me, his lips tight. 'Before we start – what exactly happened to the others?'

I took a breath. I didn't want to influence their accounts by saying too much. 'I'll tell you later.'

Terry swore under his breath. His knee hadn't stopped bouncing up and down since he took a seat. Con started rattling his nails on the table.

I asked if they felt comfortable speaking about it in each other's presence and they both nodded reluctantly. I also asked if either of them were taking recreational drugs or medication of any sort.

'Headache tablets,' Terry admitted. 'Nuffin' else.'

Con shook his head. I'd certainly never seen any signs he might be using drugs.

'Okay – when you're ready, I'd like you to explain your experiences in turn, in as much detail as possible.'

I knew exactly what I was looking for. It was *how* they told the story that was of most interest to me.

They both gave me permission to tape them, so I set my phone to record and placed it in the centre of the table. Con went first. He was articulate and his story flowed.

'It was like this dark sea of faces. Hands reaching out to me, cries for help,' he said. 'At one point a guy broke through the smoke and his hair was on fire, his jacket, his arms. I ducked away from him.' Con put his hands over his ears. 'His screams were terrible. I should have tried to get him to the floor to beat out the flames with my coat. But I was scared I'd catch fire too. I turned away, I left him. Left them all. To die.'

His final words resonated in the space around us. But his theatrical skills were useful; he wasn't afraid to turn it into a performance and I could see that was helping Terry to validate his own version of events. Terry nodded several times and his eyes glazed over as if he was seeing everything Con was describing inside his own head. He then followed with his version.

Terry's account was stilted and more emotional, but their stories were remarkably similar. It was no surprise to me that both of them used the words *scorched oil* to describe the smell they'd encountered.

I asked them again if they knew where and when the incident took place. They both looked blank. I put the crumpled map Jake had drawn on the table.

'Is this the layout you remember?' I didn't explain where the map had come from.

'Yeah, yeah – that's it!' said Terry. He stabbed at points on the sketch. 'Barriers 'ere, escalators there – steps round 'ere.'

Con couldn't take his eyes off it. 'God – yeah – this is what I remember, too.'

'Where's this, then?' said Terry.

'I don't know, but it's not Liverpool Street.'

They both looked at each other.

'The next bit is a bit more difficult,' I said, my voice catching in my throat. 'I'm not going to beat about the bush here – I need to know how you're feeling about suicide. I'm not saying either of you are going to do anything like the others – but we do need to address it.'

'You're reading too much into it,' said Con. 'I'm not going to top myself – that's ridiculous.'

'Jake said the same,' I said. 'He's the one who drew this. He was dead a few days later.'

'Shhhhit,' said Con. It was like a little explosion.

'How?' asked Terry.

I kept my voice even. It was only fair to tell them. 'One jumped in front of a bus, the other jumped into the Thames.'

Terry shuddered. Con groaned.

'I'm not trying to scare you,' I said. 'I'm trying to let you know that these overwhelming feelings might come on very suddenly…'

'What – like just sorta take over?' said Terry.

'Exactly. It's as though the guilt becomes so extreme, it totally blocks out anything else.'

'And these others couldn't live with themselves anymore?' said Con, trying to sound matter of fact. It sounded like the truth of the situation was starting to sink in.

I felt a drip of sweat trickle past my ear. I was struggling now, fighting to stay professional when my insides were churning with dread for them both, especially Con.

Terry had talked about the little girl in a red coat. About how awful he still felt that he'd knocked her down in order to get to an exit. Con said he'd been in the ticket hall, too, and had leapt over the exit barriers. He said he knew he was treading on hands and legs, desperate to get out.

Con admitted he'd woken the previous night with those same images and couldn't get back to sleep. 'Those have been my darkest hours, so far. And yes,' he didn't look up, 'I did think for a split second about not being here anymore.'

'Toppin' yourself?' asked Terry, his eyes shifting constantly, unable to focus on one thing.

Con nodded. 'For me, it was more like knowing I shouldn't be here,' he replied. 'I knew I'd only got out because I'd forced my way ahead of others. Like some grotesque queue-jump.'

'Yeah – I feel like that, too,' said Terry, picking at a solid drip of candle wax on the table. 'It's like I need to be punished for what I did. I've got this feelin' like I'm worthless most of the time.'

I studied their faces. They both had the same blank, lost look. I needed to get my message across, but they were both so close to the edge. The last thing I wanted was to make things worse.

'You're both going to have to be extremely vigilant about your mental state from now on,' I said, switching from one to the other.

I managed to get Terry to agree to phone me every day, morning and night, with an update on how he was coping. I gave him an open invitation – more like an instruction – to call me immediately if he experienced any suicidal impulses. He also agreed to allow himself to be supervised – to tell friends and family – and to make sure he wasn't alone over the next few days. We agreed to meet again and review the situation in two days' time.

After Terry had gone, Con reached out and held me close.

'Thank you,' he said stiffly.

'You won't be thanking me when I have you tailed like a Mafia gangster from now on.' I said, attempting a smile. I knew my response was flippant, but it was either that or let myself drown in an all-consuming panic.

He pulled a face. 'I won't mind if it's you.'

'Whenever possible, it will be.' I trailed my finger down his cheek. 'Not for the rest of today, though. And I suggest you don't arrange to see Justin for the time being. Not until we find out more about this.' He turned away, unhappy. 'It's not safe,' I said, tugging him back to face me.

I rang Miranda. 'Can you be at my place this afternoon?' I said. 'I need someone to keep an eye on Con.'

'Why? What's wrong with him?'

I gave her only the essential details. She wasn't an ideal choice by any means, but there was no one else I could call on at such short notice – and at least they knew each other.

'I'm not his babysitter,' she complained.

'*Please* do this for me. Don't let him out of your sight. Seriously, for one minute.'

'What if he goes off somewhere?'

'Go with him. I'll take over as soon as I've had a meeting with someone.'

'Can't you just give him a sedative or something?'

'Drugs aren't always the answer, Miranda. You should know that.' I grimaced as soon as I said it.

'You always have to make it personal,' she said and hung up.

Con and I caught a bus back to Clapham. On the way, I began typing a transcript of the tape I'd just made. I wanted to be sure of the exact words Con and Terry had used to describe their flashbacks.

Miranda arrived and made it clear through hissed whispers just how much my request had ruined her day.

'Miranda, I wouldn't ask this if it wasn't really serious.' I held her wrists, shook her a little to make her look at me. 'Don't let him out of your sight, okay?'

She rolled her eyes and put the TV on. I joined Con in the hall. I hated leaving him, but I had to start making headway before it was too late.

On the train over to Waterloo, I finished off the transcript. As I did so, a further revelation broke through to the surface.

When I'd spoken to Terry and Con, I'd held the notes from my sessions with Jane and Jake out of sight on my lap. Now I examined them all together, I hit on an extraordinary discovery. I could see it right in front of my eyes, in black and white. It was more than the one phrase, *scorched oil,* that all four victims used to recount their experiences – there were *other* duplicated expressions using the exact same words. It was a break through that left me completely baffled.

It was as though they'd each learnt their accounts from a script.

Chapter 23

Dr Imogen Reiss was waiting inside the Royal Festival Hall by the gift shop. Without hesitation, I threw my arms around her, almost knocking her over.

'I heard about the suicides…through the grapevine,' she said. 'I was going to call you.'

Imogen had been my tutor during my psychology training and we'd kept in touch ever since. She wouldn't let me down. Tears flooded my eyes as I realised she was the only person I could say that about, right now.

'Sorry,' I said, sniffling into a tissue.

'It's okay,' she said, scooping one of my tears away gently with her thumb. 'You've got every reason to be upset.' She held my shoulders. 'What support are you getting at work? Who's your supervisor?'

'Good question. Professor Schneider was supposed to find a new one for me ages ago.'

She grunted. 'He's hopeless. What's wrong with him? You need to make a fuss about it, Sam.'

Imogen was the sort of person you'd want leading your team, whatever you were undertaking. She took charge without being bossy and always made sure the quietest voice was heard. She also knew when to lighten up. Her wicked humour always broke any tension and continued to take me by surprise.

We climbed the stairs to the celebrated restaurant overlooking the Thames. I wanted to treat her for taking time out of her busy weekend schedule at Guy's Hospital, plus there were spectacular views of the water through the wall-to-wall glass panels. Not that I took the opportunity to enjoy any of it. I had too many questions.

We clinked together our glasses of mineral water and I filled her in on the situation.

'Under what circumstances might someone believe something fictional is real?' I asked. 'Supposing they don't have mental health issues or aren't taking mind-altering substances.'

Imogen's field was human motivation; I was certain she'd know about forms of coercion. She stared out over the water pensively. 'What have you considered already?'

'The obvious one is subliminal messages,' I said. 'Could these individuals have accidentally picked up a hidden message from an advert? A TV programme? Could they all have seen the same YouTube video or listened to the same CD?'

'Possibly, but all the research I've read suggests that the effects, if any, are minimal and short-lived.' She twirled the stem of the glass as she spoke. 'Conscious persuasion has much more impact.'

'What about hidden triggers; words or images that could cause people to act in certain ways?'

She shook her head. 'They don't have much effect. There was an interesting experiment on a television show, in the late fifties, where the message "telephone now" was flashed up three-hundred and fifty times over half an hour, but there was no notable increase in calls. Things haven't moved on much since then. Covert messages generally only nudge people to do things they were already intending to do.' She shrugged. 'You can buy tapes if you want to stop smoking, say, but they only work if you want to give up.'

'What about false memory syndrome? I know psychoanalysis came in for a lot of stick in the nineties when that label came on the scene.'

'Well – patients can have an apparent recollection of an event that didn't actually happen, usually after hypnosis or relaxation therapy.' She picked up a crouton from her plate and nibbled it. 'But, even under hypnosis the patient is always in control, always able to "come back" to being fully awake, if they want to.'

I nodded. We'd covered all this at university.

'And hypnosis can't make you do anything you *don't* want to do – like killing yourself,' I concluded, feeling like we were getting nowhere.

Imogen gave me a sad shrug. 'Exactly.'

She tucked into her Caesar salad. I hadn't touched my risotto. A persistent fluttering in my stomach stopped me from picking up my fork and the more I looked at the mushrooms, the more they turned into slugs embedded in wet concrete in my mind.

'How's Con?' she said, changing the subject. 'How's his arm?'

'Oh, that's on the mend,' I said. I paused, waiting for her to finish her mouthful. 'Actually, Con's been affected by this too, he's one of the people I'm talking about.' I told her what had happened.

She snatched a breath and leant forward. 'I'm so sorry. I had no idea. No wonder you're so worried.' She put down her knife and fork. 'I'm not sure I see a link between the flashbacks and the suicides per se,' she said. 'Are you certain the patients have no previous mental health issues?'

'One of them had made an attempt before,' I said.

'There you are then. It doesn't mean Con will. How much do you know about *his* medical history?'

'He's flagged up difficult times in his past, but it doesn't sound like he's ever had any mental health issues. I've never been worried by anything.'

It wasn't the sort of thing you necessarily delved into when you were getting to know someone: *Hi, I'm Sam – by the way, have you ever tried to kill yourself?*

She shrugged. 'That's a good sign.'

'How can I find out where Con and the others got these images from? Was it the same place, do you think?'

Imogen sat back. 'Are you sure you've got this right? You're going headlong down this brainwashing tack. It started after that fire at Liverpool Street, didn't it? Couldn't they have simply exaggerated what happened to them?'

'None of them were there – I'm sure of it.'

'Are you absolutely certain?'

'What they said…the layout of the station…their experiences, their injuries – or lack of them – don't match what happened at Liverpool Street.'

'Okay,' she said, 'let's try a different tack. Let's suppose there *was* something sinister going on. What do these four people have in common?'

'I've racked my brains but I can't find anything. They have totally different professions, live in different parts of London, they're different ages, have different interests.' I stared at my untouched meal. '*I'm* a common factor – they all know *me*.'

'But this problem didn't *originate* with you.'

I thought again. Then it hit me. I didn't know how I'd missed it.

'There *is* a connection,' I said, sending my eyes sharply to her face, my mouth gaping.

Before I'd spoken to Imogen, I'd been aware that St Luke's Hospital was a common link between the three patients I'd been seeing for PTSD, but I hadn't been able to work out how Con fitted in. It was only after I reflected on Imogen's earlier question about Con that I realised where I'd been going wrong. It was his arm. Con had been given over a dozen stitches after he'd fallen off his motorbike two months ago. He'd been seen at St Luke's.

The hospital was the one concrete link between all four of them.

Fluttering on the edge of my mind, something else was bothering me. Something I couldn't put my finger on.

When I got home, Miranda was furious.

'So you trot out *to lunch* – Con told me – for the whole bloody afternoon and leave me to do your nannying for you?' She was pulling on her jacket.

'I wasn't socialising,' I said. 'I was meeting an expert on motivational psychology.'

She sneered at me. 'I'm off.'

'Where is he?'

'In the bath.' She flung open the front door and slammed it so hard, my post flew off the windowsill.

In spite of her reservations about my line of questioning, Imogen had promised to email me some recent research on mind-control and I intended to spend the rest of the day scouring the articles, while keeping Con occupied with some DVDs and a Chinese takeaway.

I put the kettle on and opened up my laptop. I could hear the radio playing from the bathroom; an old song, *Vienna* by Ultravox, and decided to leave Con in peace. He liked to sing in the bath and I expected him to break into song any moment. Once the kettle had boiled, I waited for his voice, then when I couldn't even make out any splashes of water, I crept closer to the closed door. The only sounds were the sultry tones of Amy Winehouse now, hissing away, slightly off station.

How long had Con been in there?

A shaft of dread shot down my breastbone.

'Con? CON? Are you okay?'

I tried the handle, but the door didn't budge. I hammered on the wood.

Standing back, I considered whether I'd have enough strength to break down the door. I thumped it again with my fist and pressed my ear to it. No sound except the DJ. I took a deep breath, turned sideways and positioned my shoulder in front of the door. I was about to launch myself at it when there was a tiny click and the door opened. Con was bleary-eyed, one of my towels wrapped around his waist.

'I fell asleep,' he muttered. 'Has she gone?'

I nodded.

'There's something I've just remembered,' he said, leaning against the door frame, still dripping. 'Oh God, this is really bad. It just hit me when I got out of the bath…'

'What is it?' I said, half holding him up.

'There was a woman with a baby. Wrapped in a blanket...just ahead of me on the escalator. I'd forgotten until now. It was before the massive fireball filled the ticket hall. There was billowing smoke and everyone was freaking out, pushing and shoving to get out.' He ran his hand through his hair and shuddered. I reached past him to grab my dressing gown.

'The woman with the baby broke into a run, but someone caught her on the arm and she fell. Within seconds, the fireball exploded in the hall. I knew the baby must have landed on the floor. I could hear the mother screaming right near me, but I kept going. I didn't stop to help.'

He melted into sobs. 'I didn't stop. What kind of man am I?'

I held him, his body twitching and shuddering with remorse.

'Listen – there was never any record of this,' I said, with authority. 'I know for a fact that no one was killed in the fire. The baby didn't die, Con.'

His sobs grew louder, hearing me perhaps, but unable to believe what I was saying. He was doubled over, howling like a wounded bear.

'So you...keep telling me. But, it was so *real*. And in any case, I'd do the same – if it happened again. I know I would.'

'You don't know that,' I said firmly.

He shook his head, spraying water over me, 'Why is this happening to me?'

'I don't know...'

He stood staring at me as if I had the answer.

'Put this on,' I instructed, holding out his T-shirt. He looked bemused as if he wasn't sure what to do with it, then lifted his arms at my instruction and allowed me to pull it over his head. It was like dressing a child.

His weeping gradually subsided and he stood around while I made hot drinks. He was mopey, but less agitated.

The chicken chow mein arrived later and we sat with platefuls of it tumbling over onto our laps, staring blankly at the television screen. Neither of us were hungry. I was keeping an eye on the clock, aware that I'd asked Terry to call me at nine to check in. I didn't want to miss him.

I left Con on the sofa and scrabbled around in the bottom of my briefcase for the memory stick with copies of all my case-notes and plugged it into my laptop. I sat in the chair opposite to keep an eye on him and, with my handwritten notes on the chair arm, I started to go through everything line by line.

The answer was here right before my eyes, I was certain.

Chapter 24

While Con watched a Woody Allen DVD, I ran through every word of the accounts and transcripts of the fire, looking, not for the facts this time, but in detail at every emotional shift. A picture started to emerge. The same dominant feelings were cropping up in each account, based around guilt, shame and remorse.

Each of the victims had been suffering not just unpleasant flashbacks, but a tremendous emotional charge. They not only seemed to have false memories, but feelings of overwhelming guilt for not helping others. So much so, that two of them had committed suicide.

I switched to looking up online information on brainwashing and its history; how it was done, how effective it was. I trawled through page after page, and read about various techniques used during the Korean War in the 1950s, to persuade prisoners of war to defect. It turned out afterwards, though, that most of the prisoners had simply gone along with the indoctrination methods to make escape more likely, they hadn't seriously been taken in by it.

I moved on to articles about mind-control and found reports of torture techniques where individuals were kept in drug-induced comas for weeks and given electric shocks. I knew for a fact that nothing like that had happened to Con recently.

It was all too extreme. It all sounded a bit old-fashioned, too. What about more modern methods of programming people's minds? Perhaps I should be researching illusionists or TV hypnotists?

When the film ended Con got up, looking a little more animated and asked if I wanted to play a game of cards.

'Sorry, Con. Not now.'

'Coffee?' he volunteered.

'Go on, then.'

He smiled, but it faded quickly. He leant against the doorframe. 'Am I going mad?' he said.

'No. Of course not.'

'I can't get the fire out of my head. Why does it seem so real…? How can…?' His questions dried up.

'I don't know.' I cleared my throat. 'I think you might have been involved in some weird brainwashing process.'

'Oh, come on…'

'I know it sounds crazy, but it's as though you believe something bad has happened with every fibre of your body – and it hasn't.'

'But why would anyone want to cause something like this?' He put his hands over his eyes.

'Beats me,' I sighed. 'Did you have any extra tests at St Luke's? Anything out of the ordinary you wouldn't expect? Did you take part in any experiments?' He shook his head vigorously.

'Have you done any research for any hospital or university, at all – ever?'

'No.'

'Have you been in any groups experimenting with drugs or—?'

'Bloody hell, Sam – you're beginning to sound like an SS officer.' He stomped off to the kitchen. I went after him.

'It's really important, Con.'

'No – no way. Not drugs. I'm not into any of that.'

I grabbed his hand and tugged him towards me. 'The main thing is to keep you safe until we know what to do about it.'

Con returned to the television and I noticed the time: 9.50pm. Terry should have rung by now. I grabbed the phone and called his number. No reply. His phone wasn't even switched on. This wasn't good.

'I'm going over to his flat,' I said.

'Oh for God's sake, Sam, he's probably in the pub and just forgotten.'

'I can't take that risk.' I got straight on the phone to Miranda.

'I'm already in bed,' she grunted.

'I'm sorry,' I said. 'I'm bringing Con back to Balham – can you keep an eye on him?'

'What again? I was nearly asleep.'

I squeezed my eyes shut willing her to help me. 'Terry hasn't phoned – something's wrong – I'll bring Con right over in a taxi.'

I heard her swear before putting the phone down.

Miranda opened the door to Con's flat twenty minutes later, in skimpy baby-doll pyjamas.

'Why don't you call the police?' she said, as she kicked the door shut with her bare foot. 'This is getting completely out of hand.'

'The police can't do anything. There's no crime. There's no real evidence of anything.'

'Well – maybe you're overreacting. Have you thought of that?'

I didn't have time to wrestle with her. Terry might be about to do something stupid at any moment. Con gave a loud sigh and sloped off to his bedroom.

'Listen,' I said firmly, 'just make sure you watch him the whole time.'

'Are you serious?'

'Just do it.' I softened my voice as much as I could. 'Please.'

I gave her a peck on the cheek and ran.

There was no answer at Terry's address in Brixton. I'd tried his phone several times, but it was still switched off. I stood outside for a while, not knowing what else to do. Perhaps Con was right and Terry had gone to his local for a drink.

I crossed the road and walked past a cluster of shops until I came to the nearest pub. It was rowdy inside and no one looked particularly friendly. I did a quick scan of the place and made a hasty exit. I tried several more in the area. No joy.

I was walking back to the bus stop, when my phone rang.

'I don't know how it happened,' came a breathy voice. 'One minute he was sitting there, the next he…'

'Miranda, slow down.'

'Con's given me the slip,' she whimpered. 'I only turned my back for ten seconds…and his jacket's gone…'

Shit! I fought the white noise inside my head. 'Okay, okay – stay put.'

I flagged down a taxi and got straight on the phone to Danny.

'No – he's not here,' he said.

'Let me know straight away if he turns up or gets in touch, will you? Can you put some feelers out in the theatre crowd?'

'Will do,' he promised.

I tried several other numbers, but continued to draw a blank. Everything around me felt like it was sinking under water.

When I got back to Balham, Miranda was pacing up and down, an empty glass of whisky in her hand.

I blocked her path to the bottle. 'That's not going to help,' I said bluntly.

She reached round me and snatched it up. 'You haven't got a clue, have you?'

'What do you mean? Clue about what?'

'Oh – forget it,' she groaned, turning away.

'What happened to Con?' I said. She was having trouble focusing and swayed slightly when she tried to stand still. This was all I needed.

'After you left, I made him a hot chocolate – I'd really woken up by then.' She hiccupped and carried on. 'The kitchen bin was full so I went down to take the rubbish out. Honestly, Sam, I was only gone for a—'

'Then what?' I said, grabbing her wrist.

'Ow – you're hurting me.' I let her go. 'He must have been waiting for the chance to get out. I didn't hear anything. By the time I came back he'd gone.' She looked up, her eyes rolling all over the place.

'Go to bed,' I said, fighting to curb my anger. 'And get yourself a bucket.'

It was late. Terry and Con had both gone AWOL on 'suicide watch'. They could be anywhere. I rang Con's phone again, but it went straight to voicemail.

Panic was fizzing inside my head. I tried Danny once more, but he had nothing to report. I'd called the police as soon as Con disappeared, but I knew they wouldn't act until more time had gone by. There was nothing else to do, except go home.

I couldn't sleep that night. I didn't dare take sleeping tablets in case I missed the phone. I couldn't get comfortable in bed. I kept swallowing hard, feeling like I was about to choke. I'd been furious at first when Con had given Miranda the slip, but my rage had curdled into an acute sense of foreboding. I stared for hours at the changing shadows on the ceiling, primed at any moment for a phone call from the police to break the unwieldy silence.

I'm afraid we've found him – but…

I couldn't bear it any longer; the sound of the clock was boring into my head like an interminable drip, drip, drip and my body was twitching, ready to get on with something. I got up and padded into the sitting room. My laptop was where I'd left it, still switched on.

I leant over the screen, my blurry nocturnal vision turning the text into meaningless words. As I stuffed a cushion behind me on the comfy chair, I found myself humming the song I'd heard earlier on the radio when Con was in the bath.

…this means nothing to me…

Suddenly, I was sitting upright, my hand over my mouth. My pulse was throbbing through my fingers.

I entered the words that had been swirling around in my mind for days into the search bar and pressed go. Nearly two million hits came up – far too many.

I narrowed it down, adding the words, *Tube, fire, tunnel* and *fatalities.* Just like the song – it meant nothing to *me*, but…

I scrolled down the list and there it was.

Chapter 25

I've been sitting, staring at the floor for nearly an hour. Something big is going to happen, I can feel it in the air.

It's escalating, mushrooming right in front of my eyes. Any minute this catastrophe is going to blow up in my face and my life won't be worth living. I don't know how much more I can take. I've never felt so claustrophobic; it's as if my whole body is too small for me and my bones are getting crushed inside my own skin. I need to escape, but ultimately, there's nowhere to go.

People are starting to put the pieces together and before long they're going to have the full picture. There's no point in regrets now. It's gone too far. I should have known that no matter how hard I tried, I couldn't contain this.

No one knows the truth and it's got to stay that way. I've got to hold my nerve and carry on as if nothing has happened and hope I can cover my tracks.

Needless to say, I'm genuinely sorry for the distress I've caused. But the damage is done. It's gone too far – it's too late. It will have to run its course and we'll all have to cope with the backlash.

That's the problem; innocent bystanders always get hurt.

Chapter 26

As soon as I heard the world outside my window coming to life the next morning, I rang Con. His mobile went to voicemail, then Miranda answered his landline with a grunt.

'No, he isn't…' she groaned, before putting the phone down.

I tore over to Piccadilly, trying his mobile every few minutes. I tried Terry's too – still nothing.

The bookshop didn't open until eleven-thirty – I'd forgotten today was Sunday. I don't know how many times I walked to Green Park and back, before someone finally came to open the doors.

My Kindle was on the blink and after about thirty tries last night, it wouldn't download the book I'd found online. *Terror Underground* – a novel by Dexter Beaumont. Published earlier that year, it was about a group of tourists trapped on the Tube during a London terrorist campaign. Hundreds of online reviewers had given it five stars for realism.

I rushed through to the crime fiction department and started scouring the shelves.

A…B…Ba…Be…I flipped the spines to one side as I went, out of breath as though I'd been running. Bennett, Brontë – no, I must have gone past it. I tracked back, names turning into black smudges as I jumped from spine to spine too quickly. I stood back from the shelf in dismay. It wasn't there. I was about to pounce on an assistant, when I spotted a book lying on its side above the Cs. *Got it.*

I took the novel to a nearby table and opened it at the first page. There was no prologue; it began with a scene describing a man in prison. I flicked through passages set in an airport, a lowlife bar in Soho, a lift in a tower block, looking for specific words and phrases. I reached the end of chapter seven and found nothing, then as I turned the page my pulse gathered momentum.

I spotted the word *smoke*. I slowed down and read properly. Sure enough, the next chapter opened with passengers trapped in a Tube station; a bomb had been detonated, the train had moved off and the smoke was starting to mushroom into the corridors.

I read two more pages before I had to stop and take a slow breath. The words, the phrases were uncannily familiar: passengers scrambling up the escalators, the ticket hall suddenly engulfed in flames, the crush at the barriers, coats on fire, people blinded by smokescreens and flames, not knowing how to get out.

I laid out my handwritten session notes and the transcript of the tape from Liverpool Street alongside the novel, crisscrossing back and forth between them. The similarities were astonishing. Identical in some cases: the heat through the floor, the screams and hysteria. Then, there it was – final proof of an undisputable connection.

Characters in the book spoke of the terrible burning smell and the words *scorched oil* flashed up at me from the page. Two of the key words I'd put into the search engine last night. This was no coincidence. I could almost hear Jane's plaintive tones, Jake's nervous croak. It seemed as if my patients had read these passages from the book and then relived them as nightmares.

I stared at the open pages, transfixed. This was the 'script' I'd begun to imagine might actually exist. I was dumbfounded. But how did it become brainwashing material? And why would anyone want to do that?

I knew then that this was no random accident. It was coordinated, somehow. It could only indicate one thing. What was happening to these people had to be deliberate. The same story, the nightmares, the feelings of guilt – they had all been manufactured.

This discovery was far worse than presuming the victims had been lying. This was pernicious and venomous, and somewhere behind the scenes, a mystery person was pulling the strings. Someone who was controlling this entire macabre dance.

I went straight to the cash desk and bought the book. I asked the assistant how many copies had been sold, but as soon as I said it, I knew it was a futile question. She told me they'd sold over four hundred copies from that branch in the last month. I thought of all the bookshops in London and all the online outlets and knew there could be tens of thousands of readers, all around the world. The four victims I knew about might only be the tip of the iceberg.

I wandered outside, pressing the book to my chest as if it was a wad of banknotes. I needed to get a grip. This was only one piece in a complex puzzle. You don't suddenly start believing you've been through terrifying fictional experiences just by reading a novel!

I tried to take stock. I'd discovered what could be the source material, but what now? *How* had the 'mind-twister' managed to persuade normal healthy individuals that they had lived through this fictional disaster? Who'd had the audacity to perform such a trick?

On the way home, I looked up Dexter Beaumont on my phone. He lived in Manchester and had started writing after he attended a short course on crime fiction. Nothing about his website mentioned neurology or connections to a hospital; he'd previously been a history teacher at a secondary school in Moss Side. Nevertheless, I sent him a message through his website, asking him to contact me with the answer to several questions.

Next, I began a major ring-round of all the people I could think of who knew Con, starting with the theatre. Danny and another friend, Kadir, gave me a handful of numbers and it snowballed from there. I spoke to voicemails, got wrong numbers, got passed from pillar to post, but I kept calling. I asked if they knew anything about the book or about any unusual hypnosis groups or events.

When I got back, I looked up Con's Facebook profile and gathered names from there. By mid-afternoon, I'd pressed my phone against my right ear so tightly, it was red raw.

***

Back at work on Monday morning, the first thing I did was ask Debbie for the admission data for all four patients.

While she was printing out the details I tried calling Con and Terry, but still couldn't reach either of them. As soon as they reappeared, I was going to thrust the Dexter Beaumont novel in front of them both, in turn. I had high hopes they'd remember more once they saw the cover and read passages from it. That's if they were still alive.

Debbie handed me the sheets and left me at her desk while she answered a colleague's phone. I ran my finger down the first page. Jane LaSalle had been the first patient, ten weeks earlier, with burns after the chip pan fire. Then Con had needed stitches in the gash in his arm. Terry Masters was next, needing a skin graft for his elbow after falling from scaffolding at work, and finally Jake had been admitted with a torn ear after the car crash.

So they'd all had injuries requiring surgery.

I felt a weight press against my chest. All the injuries were the sort Leo might deal with. I took the printout to my office and logged on to the computer, then ran down the list of specialists at St Luke's in reconstructive and cosmetic surgery. There were seventeen consultants at the hospital. Leo wasn't the only one.

I hurried back to Debbie and asked for the consultation records for each patient. I needed to see exactly what appointments they'd had at the hospital. She gave me a batch of photocopied sheets.

'Help yourself,' she said, 'you can keep those.'

I checked the name of the consultant beside each one. Leo Hansson was listed beside Jane and Jake. I moved further down, hardly daring to breathe. Then I found Con's name. Leo was the surgeon who had treated him, too. I'd never thought to ask. It gave me a nasty stab of shock.

I moved down to Terry Masters and let out a little whimper of relief. There was a different consultant beside all his entries. My mouth twisted to one side.

It meant Leo *wasn't* the common denominator.

On the way back to my office, I spotted Professor Schneider, wheeling a trolley with what looked like an EEG monitor on it towards the lift. My mind did a double-take. Was there a serious shortage of hospital porters? Otherwise, what was a cardiac surgeon doing with a device that records brainwave data?

I remembered what Professor Monkton had told me in Cambridge about Schneider taking 'diversions into neurology' and made a snap decision to follow him. I saw him press the 'up' button on the lift, so I headed straight for the stairs.

I dodged out of the stairwell on the next floor, only to see the arrow still flashing beside the lift, so I ran up another flight.

I heard the high-pitched squeak of the trolley before I saw him and immediately side-stepped into an open doorway as he came past. Fortunately, the office was empty. The trolley trundled by and I followed at a distance, around two more corners, by a drinks' machine, a stack of blankets and an abandoned wheelchair. It looked like Professor Schneider was taking the equipment to his own office. I hung back as I saw him disappear inside, then waited a moment before getting closer. The door was slightly ajar.

A few scraps of conversation floated my way. I could hear the professor's guttural tones, 'No…I'm not having this…' His voice lowered. '…there has to be another way.'

'No – listen, Anton, it can't be as bad as that…' came another male voice. This second voice sounded vaguely familiar, but I couldn't place it. There seemed to be just two of them.

I didn't catch the next part. Then there was arguing. I was trying to tune in to what they were saying, but my mind was side-tracked into figuring out what I'd do if one them shot out suddenly and caught me loitering.

'…well – re-check the results!' yelled the professor, suddenly raising his voice.

I spun towards the noticeboard and pretended to read a flyer just as he strode out into the corridor. He came so close to me that the air in his wake sent the hairs prickling on the back of my neck. I dreaded hearing the footsteps stop short and the sound of my name being called, but he seemed to keep moving. I made myself wait until he'd turned the corner before I scuttled back to the stairs. I had no idea whether he'd seen me or not.

Just before I got back to my own office, Debbie came out of nowhere, charging towards me.

'I've just had a phone call,' she said, out of breath, her face puckered.

'No – no – please…' I muttered, begging her not to tell me what I felt for certain was coming.

She winced, gritting her teeth, seemingly not knowing where to start.

'Is it Conrad Noble?' I said, snatching her arm.

She shook her head. 'No – not him,' she said, her shoulders lifting and falling fast.

I pressed my palms together. 'Terry Masters?' I said, putting her out of her misery.

'I'm afraid so…' She sighed. 'You knew…?'

'It's following a very nasty pattern,' I said. 'What happened?'

Debbie clutched her forehead. 'He was found in an industrial waste bin in Soho, he'd—'

I didn't hear the rest of it. I had to race along the corridor and only just made it to the bathroom. I threw up over the sink inside the door. Thankfully there was no one else in there. I slammed open a cubicle door with my foot, lowered the toilet seat and sat on it, my hands holding my head.

Moments later I heard the sound of footsteps and a creaky hinge.

'Sam? It's Debbie – you okay?'

'No – not really,' I moaned.

She tapped the door and it swung towards me. 'You have to know this isn't your fault,' she said, squatting down in front of me. 'I spoke to Professor Schneider and he said this happens sometimes. Clusters of people all in one place do this kind of thing from time to time. He said there's a village in Wales where, in just over a year, seventeen teenagers killed themselves – they blamed it on social networking sites…'

She was doing her best and I was grateful to her for trying.

'Yeah,' I said, getting to my feet with a wobble.

I realised my physical reaction had been as much to do with relief that it wasn't Con they'd found, as the horror of Terry ending his life in a rubbish bin.

'What a place to die,' I said. It sounded stupid, as if anywhere was a good place.

'Do you need to go home?' she said quietly.

'No,' I hissed, splashing water roughly on my face. I was angry and fired up. 'Was it definitely suicide?'

'An overdose. That's what the police said, but I imagine there'll be a postmortem and so on.'

'No doubt they'll want to speak to me again.'

I rested my arms on the sink and stared at my reflection in the mirror. 'I can't believe it – another one.' I scrubbed my face dry with the paper towel and hurled it in the bin.

I'd had enough of this madness. 'Where's Leo Hansson?'

Before I reached his office I tried Miranda again. Con still hadn't shown up. I made no headway on his mobile, either.

'Dr Hansson is not seeing anyone,' Lian called out from her desk, as she spotted me bursting through the doors of the Burns and Plastic Surgery Unit.

'I don't care. I need to speak to him.'

She rose ready to block my path, but didn't advance when she saw how determined I was. I stormed past her and flung open Leo's door. There was no sound or movement and it took me a few seconds to get accustomed to the darkness. Only then did I realise Leo was sitting behind his desk. Without any lights on and the blinds down, he'd become nothing but a sketchy charcoal shadow.

'What are you doing?' I cried out. I leant forward and switched on his desk lamp. As soon as the space around him was flooded with light, I realised he was holding a picture frame. He propped it on the desk facing away from me, but I knew from my previous visit what it was. A photograph of his dying wife.

'Leo – I'm sorry to intrude, but—'

'It's okay,' he said graciously. 'It must be important.'

'It is,' I blurted. 'Another one of my patients has just killed himself. The one I told you about.'

'No…what happened?' he said, taking his hand to his forehead.

'I don't know the details, but he was found this morning in a waste bin, in Soho.'

'Oh Lord,' he said, getting to his feet. In the lamplight the creases in his forehead looked like savage cuts.

'I don't know what to do. My patients are killing themselves! And now my boyfriend is—'

He came to the front of his desk and perched against it. 'I'm as perplexed as you are.'

'Are you?' I said. I took a seat without waiting for an offer. 'We've got a dire situation here and I desperately need your help.' I fought the urge to reach out and grab his hand. 'I think this is about mind-control, some kind of brainwashing.'

He looked lost for words.

I went on to explain. 'I think someone has forced these four patients to believe they were involved in scenes from a book.'

I took the paperback out of my bag, but hid it behind my back. I wanted to watch his face. I felt an undoubted attachment to Leo, but with so many unanswered questions darting around in my brain, I wasn't ruling anyone out.

'*Terror Underground*,' I said. 'Have you read it?' I brought the book out into the light to show him the cover, scanning his features for a reaction. He seemed genuinely baffled.

'I don't understand…' he whispered.

'The experiences of three of my patients: Jane, Jake and Terry *exactly* replicate sections from this book,' I said, tapping the cover. 'I can show you the pages. You can see for yourself.'

He puffed out his cheeks. I flicked through to the appropriate section and held the book out to him. 'I think they were deliberately led to believe they were involved in this incident and as a result they're seriously traumatised. Read it.'

I watched him scan the words and turn the page. His perplexed expression didn't shift. When he didn't speak, I carried on. 'I'm convinced they must have been put through some mind-altering experience in the last few weeks.'

His eyes flashed wide. 'What kind of experience?'

'I've no idea, but it's something very clever – and deadly.' He handed back the book looking vacant.

I expected him to tell me I was being ridiculous and order me to calm down, but he didn't, so I carried on.

'There's a link between all four of them,' I affirmed. 'They all had injuries and needed treatment in this hospital. Three of them came to see you.'

I banged my fist down on his desk in exasperation.

'Was there anything unusual about their visits at all? Can you remember? When did you last see them?'

'You said there were *four* of them.'

'Yes – there's one we haven't discussed. Con –Conrad Noble – he's my boyfriend.'

'Okay…let me check.'

Leo went behind his desk and pulled out a drawer in the filing cabinet, managing to find the files he wanted in spite of the limited light. He started rifling through.

'I saw all of them in the last few weeks – except Terry of course – he was never my patient. We had the usual consultations.' He tapped the page. 'None of them required further treatment.'

'Who could be doing this, Leo? You've been at the hospital for years, now. Who might it be?' He stared at me as if I'd asked him to recite a poem in Russian.

'But it's not my field—' he muttered, looking lost.

'Is there anyone we can speak to who knows about mind-control?' I asked urgently. 'You must know people.'

'Right. Okay,' he said, shaking himself into action. 'I'll get on to it straight away. Leave it with me.'

'This is my mobile number,' I said. 'Please call me as soon as you find something.'

My jaw clenched. 'There's something else.' I didn't want to hear myself say the ill-fated words. 'Con has disappeared.'

'Disappeared?'

'Yes – I've had him more or less under house arrest since he started getting flashbacks, but he's slipped through the net and I can't find him.' I stood up, but my legs didn't feel strong enough to support me. Tears burned behind my eyes. He leapt towards me. There was an awkward moment when he looked like he was going to wrap himself around me, but he gently guided me back into the chair, instead.

'We'll find him…we'll find him.'

'But, even if we find him, what can we do? We don't know what we're up against.'

'I'll find out. I'll call people. Experts. Leave it to me.'

He walked behind my seat and laid his hands on my shoulders sending a wild shiver right to the base of the spine, as if his touch had magical powers. He proceeded to rub his thumbs into the knots in my muscles, finding exactly the right spot, making me gasp.

I sank back. Leo was going to help. It was as though his fingers were pressing reassurances deep into my skin. He'd know what to do. He'd know where to look, who to ask and he'd help me save Con. Everything was going to be all right.

'I'd better go,' I said breaking away, acutely conscious of the intimacy between us.

Lian happened to be paying an inordinate amount of attention to the parlour palm just inside her open door, as I passed by. She watched me leave like a hungry cat watches a bird on the garden fence.

Chapter 27

I had two consultations left before I could find the other person I urgently needed to see. I tracked him down, tucked away on his own in a diner-style booth in the canteen. He was slumped in a corner with a newspaper resting in a tent over his head. I slid into the space opposite him.

He lifted the paper up an inch to see who it was and winced at the burst of light. 'I'm off-duty,' said Professor Schneider.

'Are you okay?'

'Blinding headache. I thought I'd be safer hiding here than in my office. Is it important?'

I asked him what clinical experiments were going on at the hospital. I claimed I was interested in getting funding for a project.

'Haven't you got enough on your plate?' He looked at me out of the corner of his eye as though turning his head would hurt. 'Haven't you just lost another one?'

'Yes – I know. Terry Masters, it's awful.' I dropped my head.

'So you're bothering me – with research? Now?'

'I meant…later…for professional development.'

It sounded not only inappropriate, but completely heartless to pursue this, but I had my reasons. Hours earlier, I'd checked in-house records and bulletins detailing research at St Luke's and there was nothing about brainwashing or false memories. I wanted to ask the elusive professor certain oblique questions and see if I could judge from his reactions whether he was hiding anything.

He straightened up and put the paper down, resigned to engaging with me. 'Just before you joined us, we had our funding cut, so we're largely limited to high-profile projects: anaesthetics, HIV, cancer and strokes, mostly. We're not putting resources into many areas of psychology. The Institute of Psychiatry is the place for that.'

'Are there any psychological or neurology research programmes on the go, here?'

He shook his head. 'Sadly not.'

'Would someone like me be able to set something up?'

'What have you got in mind?' His eyes settled on mine, unnerving me.

I looked away. 'I'm not sure yet. But, if I wanted to, could I get access to all the high-tech equipment?'

He yawned. 'Not without winning an external award or getting financial backing from a university.'

'Even if I set up a project myself? As long as it's all signed for, can anyone here hire lab equipment?'

He snorted and for one horrible moment I thought he was going to pat me on the head. 'You can't just start lining up volunteers and run a hundred volts through them to see what happens. You'd need an authorised proposal, assured funding and supervision in place, before you ever set foot inside a lab. Every aspect needs to be accounted for – all the drug formulas, the technical equipment, the samples that go for testing – down to the very last test-tube – we run a tight ship here, you know.' He loosened his belt a notch. 'Let me have your proposal,' he said, 'then we'll see.'

What I really wanted to ask was what the professor had been doing wheeling EEG equipment into his office, but I couldn't find an indirect way to ask.

I thanked him in a faltering fashion and left him in peace.

On my way back to my unit, I tried Con's numbers again, but got nowhere.

As I approached the main office, I spotted Debbie standing just inside and drew her away from the others.

'How would I find out about any off-the-record research programmes at St Luke's?'

She looked blank. 'Sorry, Sam, I've got no idea. Is it about these awful deaths?'

I nodded and lowered my voice. 'Do you know if Professor Schneider might be involved in any behind-the-scenes research at all?'

She shook her head. 'No idea…'

I showed her the Dexter Beaumont novel and asked if it rang any bells. More head shaking.

'You could ask in neurology,' she suggested.

I didn't tell her I'd already thought of that. The problem was I had no business there and didn't know how to poke around surreptitiously. No one was going to admit to anything up front.

The police turned up shortly afterwards to grill me about Terry.

On my way home, I found myself noticing subliminal messages everywhere. On billboards, the sides of buses and taxis, in flashing coloured lights on the walls of buildings. I was becoming totally obsessed.

Miranda turned up at my flat, looking sheepish, shortly after I got back.

'Any sign of Con?' she asked.

'No. Nothing.'

She made us both coffee and sat cross-legged at my feet, in front of the sofa.

'I'm sorry I let you down.'

I let the words hang in the air.

'Are you staying for supper?' I asked, more as a straight question than an invitation. 'It won't be much.'

'If you'll have me.' She looked sunken-eyed and her skin was puffy.

We looked at each other and I felt a bleak weariness descend on me.

'Another patient died.' I dropped my head. 'It was another suicide.'

She snatched a sharp breath, but didn't say anything. I tried to keep the tremor out of my voice. 'The third one in as many weeks.'

I got to my feet, stepping over her. 'I feel so helpless and I'm terrified about Con. I don't know where to look…'

She followed me out to the kitchen. 'Could he have gone to see Justin?'

'I've already phoned Con's ex-wife, but she hasn't heard from him.' I flung my head back. 'It's *so* irresponsible. He *knew* how worried I was about him. He knew how serious this had become.'

'Perhaps he needed breathing space.'

'Obviously,' I growled. 'Nice bloody timing, Con.'

'What about his sister? Have you tried her?'

'Fiona hasn't heard from him since his motorbike accident.'

'Any other siblings?' she asked.

'No, that's it.' I glanced at my watch. 'All this hanging about, I can't bear it.'

She put her arms around me and, for once, I let my arms fold around her waist and held her tightly in return. It felt both wonderful and strange.

'I'm sorry I snapped, before,' I said, resting my hand on her shoulder. 'And I'm sorry I've been so pre-occupied.' I looked into her face. 'Are you okay? You've seemed jumpy and out of sorts lately.'

She took a step back and leant against the oven. 'My paintings have brought up a lot of stuff…'

'From the past?'

She laughed. 'You could say that.'

'Want to talk about it?'

'No – you've got enough on your mind.'

I stroked her arm. 'I've still got time for you.'

She looked down.

I gripped her arm. 'You *can* talk to me, you know. I *am* here for you.' I knew it didn't sound entirely convincing. I wanted to be there for her, but any attempts to foster the bond between us had got completely sidelined amidst the current situation.

She wriggled free. 'It's okay. I'll go back to Balham after we've eaten. Con could show up at any minute and at least I can make sure you know straight away.'

I nodded.

'I left him a huge sign in capital letters on the fridge, by the way, telling him to ring you when he got back.'

'Thank you.'

Neither of us wanted much to eat, so I opened a can of beans to have with toast. As I poured them into a pan she asked a question.

'How do you remember me as a kid?'

'What do you mean?' Miranda's questions were often off the wall.

'Do you ever remember me being normal when we were growing up? Not mentally screwed up?'

I wiped my fingers on the tea-towel. 'I remember you always wanted to do things your way and bend the rules. A bit of a fire-cracker…' I looked up with a smile.

'Ever in a good way?'

'Oh yes – of course. You were creative, bright, intuitive, imaginative. You were always rehearsing little songs and plays for Mum and Dad, making pretty things from shells and feathers, dancing about…much more than me. I was a real stick-in-the-mud.' I sniffed. 'Still am.'

'That's true,' she said with a giggle, laying out the plates.

As soon as she left, I rang Leo to see if he had come up with anything. He was still at the hospital and sounded hot and bothered, but assured me he was doing his best.

I couldn't face my own thoughts, so I phoned Imogen again.

'I'm in Berlin,' she said. 'Didn't I tell you? I'm here for ten days at a conference.'

'Ten days…?'

'It's two days really, but I'm tagging a holiday onto the end.'

'Good for you,' I said. I didn't mean it. I really meant it was *no good at all* her being out of the country at a time like this. 'I'll be quick,' I said.

I told her Con was missing.

'No! Sam, what's going on? Is he still having those flashbacks?'

'Yes – it's got worse.'

I wanted to give in to a tsunami of self-pity and tears, but I had to keep my nerve.

'Have you heard of any research into mind-control by Professor Schneider?' I asked.

'He's a cardiac surgeon, isn't he?'

'Yeah, but I'm looking at any links he might have elsewhere.'

'You still on with the brainwashing idea?'

'Another patient with the same nightmares has killed himself, Imogen – there's something really weird going on. Two is a terrible coincidence. Three is highly suspicious.'

'Shit – I see what you mean.' She ran his name through her mental databank. 'Schneider? No...doesn't ring any bells in psychology,' she said.

'I've looked up the research files at St Luke's to see who's been doing what and found nothing remotely related to mind-control,' I told her. 'But perhaps the reason we can't find anything is because it's all very new.'

'I've got a pile of recent journals you can look at, if that might help, but I won't be back for another eight days.' I heard roars and horns blasting in the background. It sounded like she was at Berlin's version of Piccadilly Circus. 'You'll know most of them anyway: *British Journal of Clinical Psychology*, *Journal of Psychology*, *Journal of Social Psychology* – the usual. If anyone's done any recent research it will be in there, somewhere.'

I was ashamed to realise I hadn't opened any of those journals since my student days.

'One further thought,' Imogen said, sounding sombre. 'I'm not sure – but there's something about all this that sounds very *theatrical*.'

I stiffened. 'You mean it might have nothing to do with the hospital?'

'The victims were all patients there, but it doesn't mean whatever they went through actually happened there.'

There was an awkward silence. 'When you say theatrical, do you—'

She cut me off. 'I'm not saying Con's involved, but…'

I was aghast. 'Con's been targeted. It can't be *him*.' But suddenly, all the times Con had rushed off claiming there was some emergency came tumbling into my mind. I felt a wave of dizziness and said I'd get back to her.

By morning there was still no sign of Con. It was nearly sixty hours since anyone had seen him. Was he in some ditch somewhere… floating face down in Regent's canal? Or, as Imogen suggested, could he be madly trying to undo whatever he'd got himself mixed up in?

I felt sick, only managing to push down half a slice of toast. At 8am, I called the police and they gave me the same line I'd heard before: 'We're doing all we can, Dr Willerby.'

I'd had rather too much contact with them in the past few weeks, having given my third statement about Terry's death only yesterday. The situation was not only tragic, but starting to get embarrassing.

I sat hunched on the sofa in my dressing gown and rang three hospitals to see if Con had been admitted to A&E, but there was no record of him. Then I rang St Luke's to cancel my morning patients.

I had an early call from Miranda.

'Is he back?' I gasped, hoarse with anticipation.

'Sorry, no.'

I waited.

'I know this is a bad time, but I'm going over to see Daddy, today,' she continued.

'Now?' Once again, Miranda's timing was second to none.

'Mum's away on a retreat so he'll be on his own. She's due back tomorrow, though, so it has to be today.'

My parents live in a small village in Kent. I imagined the picturesque setting; the gable-fronted house, the pretty summer house, the back lawn always in classic stripes.

'Well – if you have to,' I said. 'You sure Mum won't be there?' I knew Miranda hadn't seen our mother in twelve years and wanted to keep it that way.

'No way – he promised it's just him.'

'Okay. Fine.' I said flatly, deeply disappointed that Miranda was going to waltz off during my hour of need.

I called Leo. He'd consulted various experts, he said, and was looking into what might have caused the flashbacks.

'I've got some ideas about how we might be able to approach this,' he said.

'Really?'

'But we can't go any further without Con.'

I had to find him.

I threw on jeans and a T-shirt and made more follow-up calls, getting on people's nerves by now. It didn't get me anywhere. I paced about aimlessly, muttering under my breath. The flat was shrinking with every step and I had no option but to take my phone and get out. I took a walk along to the expanse of grass at Clapham Common to try to distract myself, but it didn't work.

I saw a man tickling a young boy by the swings and thought of Con and Justin. I turned away to walk beside the pond and spotted a man pulling a woman towards him in an embrace and thought of Con in my arms. He was everywhere inside my head, but not where I wanted him to be.

In a bid to cheer myself up, I bought a bunch of flowers on the way home. As soon as I closed the communal front door, I heard my mainline phone ringing and bolted up the stairs.

'Hello?'

'Something terrible has happened…' It was my father. He was on the move, I could hear the roar of traffic. 'We're on the way to the hospital.'

'What?! What's going on?'

'I'm not exactly sure. Moira came back a day early—'

'Oh hell…'

'Mimi attacked her.' He snatched a breath. 'They were in the hall and there was a bit of an altercation. As far as I could see, your mother tried to touch Mimi, but the next minute Moira was clutching her cheek and there was blood all over the place…'

'She *bit* me…' came a distant wail.

'There's something badly wrong with Mimi,' Dad went on. 'She's here too. Just staring ahead of her, her thumb in her mouth. The paramedic said she's in a catatonic state. She hasn't said a word since it happened.'

'What about Mum?'

'Well – it looks like she's going to need stitches. There's a nasty wound on her face.' His voice cracked. 'It's all my fault. I told Mimi – promised her that Moira wouldn't be here, then she turned up out of the blue just as we were sitting down for lunch and—'

'It's not your fault, Dad. There's no way you could have known this was going to happen.'

'Mimi's been so much better…and now this…I can't believe it.'

'Which hospital are you heading for?'

'They're taking us to the William Harvey.'

I was in the middle of offering soothing words of comfort when my mobile buzzed in my pocket. I recognized Danny's number.

'Sorry, Dad – I've got to go. I'll call you back.' All fingers and thumbs, I switched phones. 'Danny? Danny? I can't hear you.'

There were crackles and pops on the line.

'We've got Con. He's blind drunk – but he's okay.'

'Thank God! Where are you?'

'Dartford police station. The police picked him up. They found him on the M25.'

He gave me the details. 'I'll be right there,' I said.

Chapter 28

I didn't recognize Con. He looked like a tramp, with a thickening beard spreading across his chin and various mysterious substances in his hair: glue? vomit? Cornish pasty? He was sitting on a metal bench in the police station with his head in his hands. At least he was alive.

I sat beside him and he took my hand.

'Oh, Con. What happened?'

'Not sure, to be honest.' Each word rolled into the next; his breath smelt of sick and alcohol. I slid a few inches away from him.

Danny answered for him. He was wearing a stripy Fedora hat cocked to one side, like a gangster. 'The police found him playing "crisscross" near the Dartford Tunnel.'

'That wasn't me,' said Con, slurring his words. I could tell I wasn't going to get any sense out of him in this condition.

I rang Leo.

'Thank God,' he said. 'Where is he?'

'At Dartford Police station.'

'Can't think of a better place,' he said.

'Will you be able to help him?'

'I'll be honest. I'm not sure yet. I spent most of the night looking into the concept of implanting false memories. It's a complex field – I've got stacks of notes and printouts here.'

'*Implanting false memories*? My God, what the hell's that?'

'I'll explain, but I've got more work to do. Call me tomorrow.'

A police officer approached us. 'We're placing Mr Noble in police custody until he's sober, I'm afraid,' he said.

It was music to my ears. At least he'd be safely locked up in a cell. I took the officer to one side.

'I'm a clinical psychologist and I need to tell you that Mr Noble is having some…psychiatric problems at the moment. I need to stress that he be put on suicide watch the entire time.'

The officer nodded. 'We had a doctor take a look at him earlier and she recommended it too, after his antics on the motorway. These guys…I don't know…' He looked across at Con, rubbing the line where his cap met his forehead. 'He seems really smart. Well-off. What gets into them?'

'If only we knew,' I said pointedly.

As soon as Danny and I were outside, I rang my father. Danny opened the passenger door to his old Corsa and let me in. I mouthed an apology to him for being on the phone.

'Your mother's fine,' Dad told me. 'She's had stitches. She's furious – so she's obviously on the mend. We're still at A&E waiting for Ted to pick us up.'

'I'm sorry I can't be there, but I can't leave just now.'

The silence hung between us.

'It's okay. Mim…Miranda said something when she first got to the house about your boyfriend being depressed. Bad business.' I could imagine him shaking his head.

'It's a bit more complicated than that – but…'

'It's your sister I'm worried about – she's been seen by the psychiatrist.'

'And?'

'They want to keep her in for observation. The way she went for your mother. I can't understand it…'

'Has she been taking her medication?'

'She says she has.' His voice almost petered out. 'Your mother wants to press charges.'

'Bloody hell!'

'I'm doing my best to stop her, but she won't listen to me.'

'Is Mum there?' I asked.

'Hold on…'

I heard footsteps before a huffing sound.

'How are you doing?' I asked.

'That girl!' she snapped. 'She's gone too far this time. She's completely disfigured me.' There was an abrasive tremor in her voice and I was glad I wasn't my father, having to sit with her while she was like this. 'She has to be punished. She's not going to get away with it. She's a public menace.'

'Mum – Miranda wouldn't do something like this without… something must have—'

'Mimi has always needed an iron will to bend her into submission. I did everything I could to try to bring her into line – but some creatures are born wild and there's nothing you can do to tame them.'

'Miranda's not an animal, Mum.'

'Wait until you see what she's done to my face! Then tell me it wasn't done by a crazy, rabid creature.'

Dad came back on the line, but he didn't have much more to say. I put down the phone knowing there would be one big question on all our lips: *Was it starting again?*

Already the day had been far too long, but I still had things to do. Danny had a performance that evening, but he took the time to drop me off at St Luke's on his way.

When I opened my office door, three figures turned to face me; two were in police uniform.

'What's going on?' I said. I wasn't expecting company, besides, my room had been locked.

'And you are?' asked the man in plain clothes.

'Dr Sam Willerby.'

He extended his hand. 'Detective Inspector Casper and two of my team; Sergeant Wallis and Sergeant Hwang.' He flashed an ID card at me. 'We're investigating the deaths of three patients from this unit. I know you've been interviewed by my officers already, but we—'

'Do you have a warrant to search my office?'

'The coroner has requested all medical records relating to the cases of Jane LaSalle, Jake Stowe and Terry Masters.'

'On what grounds?'

'Standard procedure when we have a series of deaths like this. We'll be talking to all the professionals here who treated the victims.'

'You'll have to sign for the notes,' I pointed out. 'I need to know exactly what you've got.'

'Of course,' said DI Casper. 'We need access to your work computer and your own notes, too.'

'My briefcase and laptop are at home.'

My mouth was dry. Everything was going to be under the spotlight. I gave DI Casper the password for my computer and left them to it while I made a quick call to Leo from the corridor. Much as I wanted to get to the truth about the suicides, I didn't want it all coming out *now* – not when Con was in so much danger.

'The police will be hovering around you any minute,' I warned Leo. 'They're seeing everyone who had contact with Jane, Jake and Terry. I don't want them knowing anything about the false memory angle. If they get their hands on your notes about it, they'll know there's an altogether different side to this. They'll confiscate all your material before Con—'

'That's okay,' he said. 'I'll leave the building and take all the relevant files with me.'

As I hung around near the reception desk, waiting for the police to finish poking about in my office, a man in a white coat came hurtling through the double doors straight into me. It was Dr Graham.

'Sorry,' he said, as the files he was carrying went flying. 'Wrong floor.'

'No broken bones,' I said, rubbing my shoulder. I bent down to help.

'I'll do it,' he said.

I ignored him, scooping the pages together.

'I said, I'll do it,' he said, more forcefully.

I straightened up. 'Sorry…'

As I handed over the sheets of loose paper, I spotted his name followed by the title: 'Neurologist'.

'Everything all right?' he said. He was looking over my shoulder towards my office.

'Police,' I said. 'We've had suicides.'

'Really?' he said, although, in fact, he didn't sound at all surprised. He looked like he was going to say something else, but then took off without another word. I stood dazed for a second.

As it happened, he didn't need to say any more. He'd said just enough for me to register his sophisticated accent and work out that he was the one Professor Schneider had been arguing with in the Prof's office the previous day.

Before the family drama and Con's reappearance had taken over, I'd been meaning to check something. Imogen had suggested I trawl through a stack of psychology journals, but there was another resource I could try first.

I borrowed Debbie's computer and looked up Dr Graham's personal profile online and scrolled down to his neurology research, just in case there was anything missing from the main list I'd already seen. Past papers included new findings relating to the spinal cord, head trauma and stereotactic surgery. I checked for current subjects: epilepsy – that was all. No further details.

I checked Professor Schneider's record again, too. All his published papers related to cardiology and were from several years ago. There was nothing connected to the brain and nothing at all listed in the last two years.

I needed to take stock. I was dashing off in all directions and it was far too speculative. My suspicions about both Dr Graham and Professor Schneider were completely tenuous. Dr Graham happened to be a neurologist and the professor was believed to be interested in the subject. I'd heard them arguing together and it so happened there was a brainwave machine in the room at the time! That was it. I had nothing the least bit conclusive and I couldn't afford to throw myself into a line of enquiry that was going to take me up a blind alley.

The problem was I didn't really know what I was looking for.

Chapter 29

I didn't mean it to happen like this. Will anyone believe that? It wasn't a lashing out on my part. It was never meant to be a punishment although, to be fair, certain individuals have acted very badly.

Now there is a price to pay. Everyone is seeing me differently. Moving away with grave, suspicious faces. I know what they're thinking – I'm a lost cause.

No more self-pity. Instead, I'm going to fight back. Show them what I'm made of. But first, I must recuperate, make myself whole again. I'm sliding around searching for footholds, trying to get a grip so I can claw my way back to some kind of normality. But it's hard – time isn't my friend. It puts weights in my pockets and attaches itself to the end of my feet, dragging me down.

The endless hours feel like empty shells cracking open one after another.

Chapter 30

Danny brought Con over from the police cell to my place first thing. He went straight to bed with a sore head and Danny had a quick coffee before dashing off.

I didn't go to work. I had a call from Debbie to say Professor Schneider had seen fit to cancel all my appointments and transfer my patients elsewhere for the time being. I was pleased on the one hand – it gave me more time to look deeper into the brainwashing – but a part of me was also outraged. So much for backing me to the hilt! I rang Leo but kept getting his answerphone.

The police had come home with me the day before and copied my audio files and relevant notes onto a USB stick. They also took away my handwritten notes from sessions with Jane, Jake and Terry. I didn't tell them about all the extra notes I'd made and the transcripts from my meeting with Con and Terry at Liverpool Street. Thankfully, their warrant didn't extend to the laptop itself.

I didn't tell them about the novel either. It would only kick-start a line of enquiry I was sure would lead to Leo and involve confiscating his notes about the reversal procedure. Without them, Con was going to end up like Jane, Jake and Terry. I couldn't risk it.

With Con fast asleep and snoring, I sat next to the bed and logged on. An email from Dexter Beaumont was waiting for me, stating he had no background in neurology, not in any other area of medicine. He claimed he was 'somewhat baffled' by my questions about brainwashing and suggested I may be mixing him up with another author.

I moved on to the psychology journals Imogen had identified, searching for anything connected to mind-control. My access was limited, though, as most of the journals required professional membership. I'd need to get to a specialist library to find out more.

Con snuffled in his sleep and opened his eyes. 'Come here,' he said, when he saw me.

I leaned closer, but didn't touch him.

'I'm sorry I skipped off like that,' he said. 'I couldn't breathe with all this…fuss.' He must have had a shower at the police station – he smelt almost presentable. I sat on the edge of the bed, still at a distance.

'You didn't answer the phone. You didn't even leave a message, Con.' I was trying to remember that he wasn't in his right mind, but I still found myself simmering with rage over what he'd done. 'I was worried sick.'

He reached out for me, but I wasn't ready for a big all-is-forgiven hug. 'Terry, the guy you met – he killed himself on Monday.'

So much had happened since then, the start of the week seemed a very long time ago.

'Shit – he seemed…'

'Yeah – well – you seemed…*normal, together, sane* – whatever words you want to use. But then they found you dashing in front of cars on a bloody motorway!' I threw a punch at the duvet and he shifted his leg.

'I don't know how I got there.' He rubbed his forehead. 'I don't remember any of it.'

'What *do* you remember?'

'Needing space. Getting on the bus. Going to…' He shook his head. 'I don't know. I was on the streets for one night, I think, in Brixton. I had those terrible flashbacks again…'

'I told you it was serious, Con. You *must* stay put this time. Be with someone all the time.'

He held out his wrists. 'Handcuff me to the bed, if you have to.' He narrowed his eyes and gave me a dirty smile.

I ignored him. 'This is serious, Con. You could have been killed. You didn't know what you were doing.'

'I know.' He looked down. 'I'm sorry.'

I toyed with a loose thread on the duvet cover. 'At the theatre…' I said, hesitantly, 'have they run any experimental workshops or introduced any avant-garde acting methods, that you know of?'

He scrunched up his face. 'What d'you mean?'

'I read that method acting can be dangerous to some actors who immerse themselves too deeply in their roles.' I avoided his eyes.

'Oh – so you think this wacky brainwashing thing is about the theatre?'

'I don't know,' I replied. 'I just can't work out where it's come from. I'm questioning everything.' I felt a tremor of discomfort. 'And you *have* taken off all of a sudden several times when we've been together, saying it was something to do with the theatre…'

He laughed and leant forward, pulling me to him. 'Don't be silly.'

He brushed me off with a kiss, but there was definitely something he wasn't telling me.

I watched him for a moment, then went into the next room. As I'd done with Leo, I came back with the Dexter Beaumont book hidden behind my back.

'What's that you've got?' he said grinning, thinking I had a present for him.

I held it up. 'Do you recognise this?'

'*Terror Underground*, what's that?' He sounded disappointed.

I read out the synopsis from the back cover and watched his face. He sighed with boredom.

'Have you read it?' I asked.

'You're joking, aren't you?' He looked confused. 'You know I don't read stuff like that.'

It's true; I'd only ever heard Con enthuse about literary novels. I was about to hand it to him when I thought better of it. If he read the sections that echoed his flashbacks, wasn't it likely to set off another suicidal episode? I couldn't take the risk. I needed to keep him as unruffled as possible.

'Never mind.' I said. I sat beside him and surreptitiously slipped the book under the bed. 'Anyway,' I said, drawing upright. 'I think we might have a way to sort this out.'

'How?'

'Dr Hansson – you remember him from the hospital?'

'The plastic surgeon?'

'He's been working really hard trying to find a way to help you. He knows the right people.'

'Woah – hang on. You're talking about a *plastic surgeon*, here. He sews limbs back together. He's not tinkering with my *mind*. There has to be someone else.'

I got to my feet. I was exhausted and exasperated and didn't have time for this. 'Well – there *isn't*!' My face was on fire. 'At this point in time, he's the only chance you've got. If I make it known what I think has happened to you – and to the others – there'll be a massive investigation. We don't have *time* for that.' I jammed my hands into my hipbones, my nostrils flaring at him. 'I can have you followed around every minute of the day, but sometime soon you're going to find a way to kill yourself – I guarantee it, you *will*. This isn't a game, Con. You *have* to see him.'

Con played with the tassel on the corner of the duvet. 'I get the impression you've been seeing quite a bit of him, yourself,' he said sarcastically.

'What? Oh, come on!' I stood glaring down at him.

He threw back the covers and stood up to face me, his expression wild. 'You and the swanky plastic surgeon.'

I took a step back. 'Look – you can drop this right now,' I snapped.

'Are you seeing him?' His tone had changed, to a snide and accusing whine. He grabbed my shoulders and shook me slightly.

'Listen…' I tried to wriggle free, but he held me tighter. 'I've never—'

'You haven't answered my question,' he hissed, cutting across me. His hands had made their way to my neck and he was starting to squeeze.

'This is ridiculous, I…Con – let go of me – you're *hurting*!' I wrenched his hands from my neck and stood back, stunned.

He flopped back onto the bed. 'I notice you're not denying it,' he said in a sullen voice.

'Con – this is stupid. Dr Hansson thinks he can help. We're going to see him.'

'I'm not going anywhere,' he said, folding his arms.

The doorbell rang. It wasn't even 10am. My father came in with Miranda looking gloomy, right behind him. She was heavily sedated and could barely walk in a straight line.

'She's going back to Linden Manor in an hour or so,' said my father. 'It's clear she can't cope on her own.' He gave me a sad smile. 'She just wanted to say goodbye.'

We sat and drank tea in the kitchen. Con joined us, but he was still in a mood. We were like a dysfunctional community. My sister had *bitten* our own mother, my boyfriend was on the verge of suicide and my position at the hospital was looking decidedly wobbly. The situation would have been laughable if it hadn't been so tragic and so real. I didn't dare think about what the next few days might bring.

Miranda was staring at the oven, her eyelids drooping as if they were made of heavy-duty rubber. Con was trying to make an origami butterfly out of a torn envelope, but it ended up looking like a squashed frog. Dad was upset and didn't know what to say. Eventually, he went into the sitting room and hid behind the paper.

Before long, Con went for a lie down on my bed.

'I know – I'll keep the door open,' he said in a singsong voice, before I suggested it myself.

Miranda and I were left together. Her hair hadn't been combed and her teeth were chattering.

'Have you taken your tablets?' I asked.

'I wish everyone would stop asking me that!' She screwed up her eyes and started picking at the skin around her nails.

'I gather you nearly bit her nose off,' I said. She looked up and giggled. I laughed too. I knew we shouldn't, but I was on the verge of hysteria. The whole scenario was ludicrous.

She got up and started walking around the room with exaggerated grace, extending her arms like a child pretending to be a ballerina.

'Is it happening again, Miranda?'

'Why are you calling me that?' she said, in a dazed, distant voice. 'My name is Mimi.'

I wanted to cry. After all the steps she'd taken, all the progress she'd made, she was back where she started. Everything she'd achieved had fallen away like one of those precarious wooden bridges spanning a gorge in the jungle. She was left on the wrong side. And the bridge had collapsed.

I left her humming to herself absently, all too reminiscent of unstable times in her past and went to check on Con, popping my head into the bedroom and coming straight out when I saw him asleep. A string of disturbed nights had taken its toll on him.

I joined my father in the sitting room and sat on the arm of the sofa. He folded the paper carefully.

'Two body-blows in one week,' he said, with a sigh.

'I know.' I squeezed his shoulder.

'I can't believe we're losing Miranda…Mimi…ha, I don't even know my own daughter's name any more.'

I kissed the top of his head. 'I'm sure she'll be back before long.'

He let out a little groan that suggested he wasn't convinced.

'How's Mum?' I asked.

'Still furious. I've managed to persuade her to drop the charges, so that's something.'

Miranda appeared in the doorway.

'You will come and see me, won't you?' she said.

'Yes,' I said.

Things would be different this time. I'd shut Miranda out all those years ago and, once in care, she'd done the same to me.

Back then, in our own ways neither of us could cope, but having her in my life once again had reminded me of the gap her absence had created. She was annoying and unmanageable at times, but there'd been moments recently when I realised I'd genuinely missed her. This was only a minor setback; I wasn't going to give up on her again.

I met her eyes. 'If you'll let me.'

I was back at St Luke's Hospital by early afternoon. Con was still adamant about not seeing Leo and I'd had to rope Danny in to keep an eye on him for the rest of the day. They were going to spend most of it at rehearsals, so I knew at least Con wouldn't go stir-crazy. One day at a time.

Before they left together, I took Danny to one side. 'Make sure he doesn't run off – don't let him distract you.'

A pause. Poor bloke. It was a tall order. 'I'll do my best,' he said, 'but he's not the kind of guy to sit still for long.'

'I know. Just try to keep him busy with other people if you can.'

He let out a despondent moan that I took to be: 'I'll try'.

I also asked him the same question I'd asked Con about any unusual acting methods they used at the theatre.

'You're joking,' he said. 'Too busy learning lines and getting the lights to come on at the right time for any fancy stuff.'

I laughed and felt a shadow lift.

It didn't last long.

Chapter 31

Leo looked like he'd been in a fight when I found him in his office. Papers were strewn everywhere. He had a stubbly beard emerging and his eyes seemed to have shrivelled into glistening raisins.

Lian grabbed my wrist from behind before I could go inside.

'Leave him be,' she hissed, pulling me close.

'I can't – I don't think you realise how important—'

'His wife died last night.'

My mouth fell open. *Oh, no.*

I was about to back straight out, but Leo spotted me and called me inside. Lian gave me the kind of look that could burn off eyebrows.

'Is Con with you?' he said, looking behind me.

'No.' I stayed in the doorway. 'I've just heard. I'm so sorry.'

'It might be better to get an independent expert in,' he said, ignoring my sympathy. 'I can't think straight anymore.'

He was pacing around the room, blindly trampling on the sheets that had fallen to the carpet. 'I'm no use to you – not now.'

'Leo, no, you can't give up.' I took a step into the room.

'I've had it,' he said.

I stood closer to him. 'I know it's terrible to ask you at a time like this,' I said. 'But, if you give up now, it will set us back days. Someone else will have to start from scratch.' I put my hand firmly on his arm. 'I'm not sure Con will last that long.'

He sank into his chair. It looked like his body was shrinking before my eyes.

'I'm sorry,' I said faintly, backing off. 'I'd better go…'

He put his arm out. 'No. Stop. Don't leave.' He patted the chair beside him. 'Talk to me. I don't want to be alone.' He rubbed the indentation marks from his specs on the bridge of his nose.

I pushed the door shut and sat down. 'Can I help? Is there anything I can do?'

'Lian is ringing people. I've been prepared for this for a while.'

He closed his eyes for a moment. 'Talk to me about anything…'

I said the first thing that came into my head. 'My sister's gone back to the psychiatric facility.'

He leaned forward. 'Why? I thought she was doing well.'

'She bit my mother's face in an unprovoked attack.'

He stared at me with startled eyes. 'Bit her? That's serious.'

'I say it was unprovoked, but…' I tried to imagine them in the hall of my parents' house. What had happened to make Miranda so angry?

'You're not convinced?' He folded his arms. He sounded slightly less distraught now we were talking. Perhaps, like me, he found dealing with other people's problems removed him temporarily from his own. 'Have you ever considered that Miranda might be broken inside?'

'Broken?'

There was a drawn-out silence. 'That someone…damaged her?'

'I think she cracked under terrible pressure at home – pressure to be the golden girl and make our parents proud, if that's what you mean.'

'I meant something more…sinister.'

I shook my head vigorously. 'I know what you mean. I've thought about that. Of course I have. I know sexual abuse is one factor that can trigger schizophrenic psychosis. But, I've *never* had that concern.'

Leo made a bridge with his fingers.

'Honestly,' I insisted, 'I know reports say that fifty per cent of adults abused as children never report it, but I know what to look for. I've thought about all the people we came into contact with when we were young and I can't think of a time when anyone beyond the immediate family was alone with either me or Miranda – certainly not on a regular basis. When relatives came over it was usually for rather formal lunches, followed by a game of cards or badminton on the lawn. It was always a group thing. I don't ever remember us being taken on trips or even to the park by outsiders.'

'Mmm,' he said.

'It's difficult to see Miranda's situation with a professional eye when she's my sister, but I'd like to believe she would have told me by now…if there was anything to tell.'

He looked as if he was thinking about how best to phrase what he had to say next.

'Have you asked her?'

I stroked a patch of dry skin on the back of my hand. Had I asked her? Had I ever asked her directly? Had I ever sincerely encouraged her to explain what really happened to turn her from a fun-loving, cheeky child into a wild, untameable creature?

'No,' I said, shamefacedly. 'And I think it's time I did something about that. But I'll have to be really careful. I don't want to plant seeds inside her head, put words into her mouth. It could create terrible havoc.'

'You're a psychologist.' He smiled. 'You know how to tread carefully.'

He was right, I *should* know how to get to the truth. I'd done enough work with patients over the years to know how to gently and subtly instil trust and help people to tell their story, in ways which were safe for them. I could do it with my own sister, couldn't I?

'She paints, doesn't she?' he added.

I'd forgotten Leo had seen one of Miranda's pictures in my flat.

He sat back with his fingers interlocked across his abdomen. 'Maybe the answer's there.'

I pictured the garish paintings I'd recoiled from, but hadn't explored properly. 'You might have a point.' I wanted to hug him. 'Thank you, Leo. You've helped me more than you can possibly know.'

He shrugged it off, then stood up breaking the intimacy. 'I'm sorry. I don't want to let you and Con down, but…'

I got to my feet, but faced him and stood my ground, biting my lip. 'I know this is the worst time in the world to ask this of you, but there's no one else…and I can't save Con on my own.' I hated putting pressure on him like this, but I couldn't walk away without a fight.

He looked down at his hands, shook his head sadly, then straightened up, seemingly imbued with a little more energy. 'Okay. I'll try, but you'll have to give me a hand.'

'Of course.' I glanced down at the jumble of papers on his desk and picked up the loose sheets from the floor. 'Dare I ask how you're getting on?'

He patted the nearest pile of papers. 'We don't know, of course, how the false memories were first implanted, but my theory is laid out here. I've spoken to a number of experts and this seems to be the general consensus.' He shuffled through various sheets and put them in a pile. 'The blue file contains my assumptions about the false memory process – the green file has everything for the reversal.'

I returned to the seat beside him, again.

'Let me show you.' He rested his hand on the green file. 'This is the "antidote". The important file. I've spoken to memory experts, and a Professor Hune, in Illinois, thinks whoever did this had some kind of script – like the book you found, using very specific words and phrases guiding patients through the experience – the sounds, smells, visual images, the heat, being touched and so on.'

'Why would anyone do this?'

He shrugged. 'Maybe it was research that went wrong.'

'Maybe…' I hesitated. 'Hold on…I don't know if it's relevant, but I saw Professor Schneider with an EEG machine the other day.'

Leo drew back his chin. 'I'm not sure why he would he need one…he's a cardio specialist.'

'That's what I thought.'

We let it go for the time being. I knew we couldn't spend time speculating on why this cruel procedure had been carried out, or by whom. Our priority was to work out how to reverse the effects.

'Hune told me he's worked with patients to encode memories in the brain by manipulating individual neurons.'

'Really? That's so scary.'

'This isn't hypnosis,' he said, with an ironic chuckle. 'It's way beyond that. It's memory implantation – it's about neurons in the brain and the right drugs.'

'Go on.'

'According to experts, both false and genuine memories rely on the same brain mechanisms. Hune and another expert, Dr Clara Warner from Sidney, both used a technique known as optogenetics, which allows the fine control of individual brain cells in the hippocampus. Are you still with me?'

'More or less.'

'The process brings about a false association between what the patients have in their mind and what is actually happening to them.'

He went on to describe a procedure involving electrodes, transcranial magnetic stimulation and electrical scalp signatures. Most of it went straight over my head.

He tapped his notes with a pen. 'All the experts I've spoken to agree this is how the process could have been implemented and if we can set it up correctly, there is a way we can reverse it.'

I swallowed with a loud gulp. 'So, we can somehow isolate Con's rogue memories and wipe them out?'

He put up his hand. 'In theory. There are no guarantees and it's complicated.'

'You managed to find all this out?'

He nodded with resignation. 'I have some very good friends and it's been a useful distraction, you know, from my wife…' He glanced over at her gentle smiling face in the photograph.

I'd almost forgotten.

I put my hand over his. 'Thank you for doing this,' I said earnestly. 'I'd like to come to the funeral, if that would be okay.'

'That would be good,' he said simply.

He drew his finger halfway down one of the sheets. 'This is how we could make it work.'

He took me through the stages in the process – how we'd have to get Con into a relaxed state, then administer a selective amnesia drug while Con focussed on the disturbing images in his mind with all his might.

'The drug will act on the hippocampus in the brain and interrupt the way those particular memories were stored,' he said.

'And doing this to Con is going to be safe?' I asked, gripping the edge of the desk. 'It will only wipe out the distressing false memories?'

He frowned. 'Well, before we get to that question, there is a problem.'

'What's that?'

'I've ordered the drug we need from America, *tronocept*, and it hasn't arrived yet.' He showed me a sheet at the front of the green file with the name of the drug, the exact dosage and the source in Seattle.

I let out a loud sigh. 'And this is the only way the reversal will work?'

He looked at the floor and grimaced. 'I checked with everyone I could get to speak to me. They all said the same thing. Without this exact compound at the correct dose, we could cause more harm than good. We need this particular drug.' He sat back. 'I'll let you know as soon as it arrives.'

I thanked him profusely, much to his embarrassment, but nevertheless, I left downhearted. We were still stuck.

The door felt unaccountably heavy as I opened it. We'd got so far, but without the right drug all the information we'd discovered was useless.

Chapter 32

Over the next few days, Leo waited for the drug to arrive and worked on the reversal process, while I watched Con like a hawk. At least he was reasonably compliant by now and didn't fuss about being constantly supervised. Danny took turns with me, so he was never left alone. Meanwhile Miranda went back to Linden Manor and I dropped in to St Luke's only for essential meetings.

As promised, I went to the funeral for Leo's wife the following week in a quiet little chapel in Holland Park. The place was packed with mourners, many standing, squeezed in at the back. I was happy to be one of them, but Leo insisted I join his pew. I felt honoured, but self-conscious, sitting alongside close family friends and relatives. We all stood for the coffin, which trailed white roses and ivy, and there was a rush of air as Helena glided past, almost brushing against my shoulder.

I didn't recognise any of the hymns, nor it seemed did Leo, by the vacant look on his face. The vicar must have slipped in a few of his own favourites or maybe Leo knew only Swedish ones. His voice faltered, not helped by the fact that the organ was out of tune.

Leo's daughters, Felicity and Kim, stood either side of him at first, but I couldn't hear either of them singing. Kim held a handkerchief over her mouth the whole time, as if there were poisonous fumes in the air, and Felicity stared at the coffin as if she was trying to work out who was inside. I saw Leo reach out to hold their hands when the vicar started his eulogy, but after a cursory squeeze, they both let go at the same time.

Kim went up to do a reading and returned to sit alongside Felicity, so I was bunched up right next to Leo. I could feel the warmth of his arm radiating into mine.

Next, Helena's sister, Elizabeth, gave a moving tribute.

'I couldn't get up to speak,' Leo whispered, as we stood for the last hymn. Thin trails of tears ran down his face, splashing every so often onto his open hymn book.

'I haven't brought a handkerchief,' he sniffed. 'How stupid is that?'

I pushed a spare tissue into his hand and he squeezed my fingers before letting go.

After the hymn, there was a hiatus as all eyes drifted up to the organ loft.

'Helena never complained,' Leo muttered, as rustles and thuds indicated an effort by the organist to prepare the right music and pull out the correct stops before proceeding. 'She understood that my role was to provide for them all. We wanted Kim to have her horse and Felicity to have her skiing lessons. I couldn't possibly have furnished those luxury extras *and* been around for bedtime stories and egg and spoon races. Helena understood.' He touched his lip. 'Or I thought she did. Maybe she *didn't.* Maybe she complained and I didn't hear, or wasn't listening…'

We sat in silence as the organist stumbled through a short solo piece by Schubert. Felicity was tugging at his sleeve and I realised the vicar had asked us all to stand again and Leo and I were still sitting down.

Afterwards, I put in an appearance at the wake at Elizabeth's house, but I felt like a gate-crasher at a stranger's party. I was working out how to put an iced doughnut back on the buffet table, when I spotted Leo slipping out through the French windows and hurrying across the lawn like a burglar.

He'd left Felicity and Kim in the lurch.

I left soon after and within half an hour Leo rang me. 'I'm sorry I ran off like that,' he said. 'I just couldn't handle the mass of people trying to…' There was a short silence. 'You know… people's sympathy…I'm not very good…'

'Are you all right?'

'Still alive, still breathing…'

'It's Kim and Felicity you should be ringing, not me.'

'I know. I should have talked to them, not just at the wake, but all through Helena's illness. I should have prepared them for the worst.'

'They are more or less adults, but they still need you at a time like this.'

'You're right, of course. I know they'll see it as yet another example of my ineptitude as a father – and they're right,' Leo sighed deeply. 'To be honest, I've always been an understudy as a parent, standing in the wings, out of sight, never knowing quite what to do if I was called upon. I think my failings might have gone past the point of no return by now. But I'll call them,' he said, unconvincingly.

As I made my way to the hospital, I wondered why Leo felt he could talk to me on such a personal level. Was it because I'd already shown trust in him with my own confidences? Or did he feel his family had given up on him after too many perceived parental shortcomings?

I spent the rest of the day in my unit at Debbie's request, sorting outstanding admin and trying to avoid people. I'd already had 'the look' from various nurses on my floor. The look that said *you might not be with us for much longer.*

When I got home, Danny had left a message to say Con was staying at his place that night. I have to say it came as a great relief; I needed a night off from the stress of watching Con's every move.

I took a long bath, rang for a takeaway and watched the original version of *The Hunger Games* for the nth time, curled up on the sofa in my dressing gown. I crawled into bed and was fast asleep by ten o'clock.

At some unearthly hour, I woke up. I was panting and sweating. My head was filled with terrifying images: people running, darkness and screaming. It was all wrapped up within a pervasive sense of dread. I rushed to the toilet and threw up.

Clutching the bowl, I pressed my forehead against the cool porcelain. I'd had trouble sleeping since I'd started the new job, but I'd never suffered a nightmare like this one. Was it the stress of the last few weeks catching up with me?

I went into the kitchen and boiled a kettle. It was five-thirty in the morning; too early to be up and about, but I was scared to go back to bed. I desperately wanted to sleep, to have soft, floaty, reassuring dreams. I couldn't face re-entering the gruesome world I'd just escaped from.

I lifted my hot mug and put it straight down again. I was seized by a shattering burst of horror. I'd never experienced anything like it before; it had me doubled over. I couldn't pinpoint exactly what I was seeing inside my head, I felt like I was caught up in a human stampede. Blind panic, desperation, the sound of bones snapping, bodies stacking up, not being able to breathe. I sank to the floor, holding my chest, wondering if I was dying.

I focused on the items in the kitchen; solid, domestic, homely things – the table, the waste bin, the fridge. I tried to remind myself that I was safe, that nothing bad was happening. I pressed my hands into the lino – cold, firm, secure.

Then the thought struck me. *No! It's happening to ME.*

I scrambled to my feet. *This is just like what happened to the others. I'm affected too…*

I leant over the sink and splashed cold water on to my face. *What was going on? Had someone used the false memory method on me without me knowing?*

I thought about it again. I'd read through sections of Leo's notes, hadn't I? I'd read Beaumont's novel. Was that all it took? Had I been indoctrinated by these horrifying images, just like that?

I stared at my image in the mirror, sweat glistening like melted butter on my forehead, my flickering eyes trying to focus. *No – I'm overreacting – this couldn't possibly be the result of having just read the book. If that was the case, suicides would have escalated astronomically all around the country.*

I ran to my bedroom and flung on my jeans and a sweatshirt.

By 6am I had Lian's sticky note in my hand, with three lines of an address, and was on my way to Leo's.

Rain was pounding against the roof and pouring down the windows of the taxi. I jumped out and stood, sodden, on the front step, pressing the bell and keeping my finger on it. Leo hurried to the door in his dressing gown.

'You've got to help me,' I said, stumbling inside.

He guided me through to the kitchen. In his sleepy state, he tried to offer me a cup of tea, but I gabbled away at him about the nightmare I'd just had, the terrible experience I'd just gone through in my kitchen.

'They're the same flashbacks, Leo. I've got something just like those false memories.'

He made me sit down. 'Where did you go yesterday – after the funeral?'

'I was sorting admin in my office and then I went home.'

'Did you see anyone?'

'No. I spoke briefly to Debbie – but to no one else, except a few people on the phone.'

'Let me see your arms.'

I rolled up my sleeves.

'No – it can't have happened – you'd have needle marks,' he said.

'But what if it's been *transmitted* to me, because I've heard the story time and time again, in detail? Through my patients, Con, the notes you had?'

'No.' He cut the air with his hands. 'It doesn't work like that. It's more likely to be a case of secondary PTSD – you must have heard of that…'

'Of course, but this is different.'

'It's common with carers and counsellors,' he insisted. 'When you deal with other people's pain every single day, you can pick up some of their distress.'

'Yes, yes, I know,' I snapped. I felt unaccountably hot. 'But these feel *real*, like specific flashbacks, Leo.' My throat was dry and prickled as if I'd swallowed a writhing beetle.

He cupped his hands around mine. 'It's *not* the same. It can't be.'

I didn't like the sound of those last three words. Or the way he narrowed his eyes. He wasn't sure. After all – he wasn't an expert.

'We've got to get the reversal sorted out now, Leo. I can't bear this.'

'I'll have to see if the *tronocept* comes through today from the States.'

'Use it on me, first – do a trial run.'

'No – you haven't had the false memories implanted.'

I got to my feet, breathless, unable to sit still. 'But I freaked out in the kitchen with the most terrifying images.'

'Of the fire?'

I hesitated. 'No, not exactly, but—'

'There you are. This is acute anxiety, because of what you've been dealing with. An occupational hazard. It's not the same.' He was sticking to his guns.

I glared at him. 'I'm still not convinced.'

When I left his cottage, the world was still only starting to wake up. Coffee shops were opening and the smell of fresh beans wafted across the pavement. Normally I would have savoured the aroma, but that morning I walked quickly past and kept my head down. In spite of Leo's assurances, I was terrified and my mind kept creeping to the idea of suicide. *Had I been having any thoughts about it lately? Was I at risk? Had it slipped on to my radar while my back was turned?*

A van tooted me long and hard as I crossed the busy road without looking properly. It brought me abruptly to my senses. *Just focus on the job in hand.*

As I climbed the stairs to my flat, I saw two figures on the landing.

'I've been calling you,' said Con.

I pulled the phone from my bag. 'Sorry, I must have switched it off.'

Danny raised his hand in a meek *Hi* and took a step back.

Con tapped his watch face. 'It's seven-thirty in the morning! Where the hell have you been at this hour?' He hesitated, resting his finger on his lip. 'Oh, I get it.' He turned and grabbed the banister. 'Tell me you haven't just come from his place.'

I couldn't think fast enough to avoid Con's wrath. My brain was still woolly with lack of sleep. 'It's not what you think,' I said, pushing past them to put the key in the lock.

'I came here to tell you I'd do it,' he said. 'That I'd see that plastic surgeon and try his dodgy little experiment, but now I don't know what the two of you have cooked up for me.'

'Con, listen.'

'I'll leave you to it,' said Danny meekly, edging towards the stairs.

'Why can't you just admit it?' yelled Con, pushing his screwed-up face into mine. 'It's been this plastic bloody surgeon all along…'

Before I could say anything, he took off down the stairs after Danny. I didn't have the energy to chase after him. I wanted to put Con's paranoia down to the effects of the false memories, but I knew I was kidding myself. I went inside and made a strong coffee. Ten minutes later, I rang Danny.

'We're on our way to the theatre,' he said. 'Con says he'll spend the day with me again.'

'Are you okay with that?'

'He's going to have a go at directing rehearsals. Gives me a break, to be honest – as well as keeping his mind off things.'

'You're amazing – thank you.'

I waited until after eight o'clock, then called Imogen, hoping she wouldn't mind being disturbed so early. She was at the airport on her way back. She said much the same as Leo about my nightmares and the panic attack in the kitchen. She didn't think I could have picked up any sort of mind-control by proxy.

'How's Con? Have you found him?' she asked.

'Yes – he turned up, thank God, but he's still a liability. He's playing ball for the time being and allowing round the clock supervision.'

'Nightmares are perfectly normal, you know. They tend to repeat, because we wake up before the frightening emotional issues we're grappling with have been resolved,' she said. 'I've been thinking that Con's experiences might be a delayed reaction to his motorbike crash – or poor sleep, a slight fever, worry about his new film, a reaction to certain foods...he's probably suffering one or more of those factors. You, too.'

I wasn't convinced. The effects were too extreme.

Leo had consultations and surgery most of the day, but I managed to catch him in the canteen during a short lunch break.

'Can we go outside?' I said. I didn't want anyone eavesdropping on our conversation.

He hastily dropped a sandwich and an apple onto his tray and followed me.

We sat on a bench overlooking a flowerbed in the courtyard. Turmoil had brought us together, forcing us to spend our entire time problem-solving, but I was aware of another dynamic brewing for me in the background – a cocktail of profound respect and the tiniest trace of suppressed desire. I wondered if he felt it too. In that instant, sitting there with Leo, I felt the yawning gap between Con and me splitting even wider.

'I was going to ring you,' he said. 'The drug should be here tomorrow, first thing.' He scrunched up his sandwich wrapper.

'At last!' I snatched a fresh breath and blew it out sharply. 'What time shall I bring Con in?'

'Get him to my unit by eight-thirty. We'll make an early start before my usual appointments. It should take about forty-five minutes.'

'I'll get Danny to persuade him,' I said. 'We've got to do this.' Forty-five minutes to bring Con back. I couldn't wait for that glorious moment.

'What about me?'

'Let's see how it goes with Con, first. I'm loath to risk it on you when I'm not the least bit convinced you have the same condition.'

I let it go for now. Once Con was safe, then maybe I'd be able to think straight again.

He looked at his watch. 'I've got to go. Skin graft on an ankle to sort out.'

I watched him stride back inside. I couldn't imagine what pressure he must be under. Struggling with the loss of his wife, strained relations with his daughters, performing meticulous operations right through the day *and* spending hours of his own time planning how to save Con. He was a rare find indeed.

Debbie insisted I stay and catch up with emails that afternoon.

'You have every right to be here,' she insisted. 'You've done nothing wrong.'

I squeezed her arm in appreciation and she slipped a small packet of *Twiglets* into my bag. 'You're not eating, are you?'

I gave her a weak smile and thanked her.

When I closed my office door, an unnerving thought crossed my mind. If I *hadn't* been caught under the spell of Leo's notes in a kind of proxy transference, and my nightmares were down to secondary PTSD, it still wasn't good news. Maybe I wasn't cut out for this kind of work. Perhaps hearing people recounting their traumas was too much for me. I'd only been in this role a few months. I felt pathetic.

I shut the blinds and sat at my desk, staring at the carpet. Not for the first time, I thought of Miranda…Mimi – whoever she wanted to be – and wondered if I had the same fault-lines inside my brain. Were my nightmares early symptoms of mental illness? Was I heading in the same direction? Was it a matter of days before I, too, starting stripping off in the supermarket and flinging bags of frozen peas at innocent shoppers?

Whichever way I turned, things didn't look good. I made a decision. I was going to book in to see my own therapist again. If now wasn't the right time, when was?

Chapter 33

By 7pm, outpatients had long gone at the hospital and the empty spaces echoed with the rumble of the odd trolley. Being here after hours was like being left alone in the London Underground. Endless lines of dim, yellow corridors unfolded in every direction, on and on, like they were caught in infinity mirrors.

Whilst I still had every right to be at St Luke's, nevertheless there were plenty of places inside where I didn't have authorised access. There were so many departments; a warren of hiding places – and one place in particular I'd been planning to snoop around in, for days.

I climbed two flights of stairs and waited until the corridor was clear before slipping through the double doors into the cardiology unit. A strip-light was flickering in the waiting room, but most of the others were turned off.

Professor Schneider's office was dark, but a thin band of light seeped under the door of his secretary's office. *Damn.* I'd met Pauline a couple of times in the canteen and didn't have her down as the conscientious type.

Pauline's blinds were drawn so I had no way of knowing whether she was inside or not. Perhaps she'd just forgotten to switch off the light. I had to think fast.

I found a phone inside an empty office nearby and called the hospital operator.

'Er...can I speak to Pauline Lessinger, Professor Schneider's secretary, please?'

'Putting you through...'

Seconds later, the phone behind Pauline's closed door burst into life and after two rings, someone picked up.

'Pauline Lessinger…' came the response.

I squeezed my eyes shut for a second, willing this spur-of-the-moment plan to work.

'Pauline, hi. It's Suzanne from the car park. What make of car do you have?'

'A Ford Focus, why?'

'Dark green?'

I hadn't remembered the make, but I did recall the colour from one time she'd driven past me when I was on my bike.

'Yes – why – what's happened?'

'The driver's window has been smashed. Did you have any valuables inside?'

'Oh, bloody hell. Hold on. I'm coming down…'

Seconds later the door flew open and Pauline dashed out. Once her footsteps had receded, there were no other sounds, although the cleaners would be here any minute.

My hand trembled as I tried the professor's door. It didn't budge. That didn't surprise me; he was a fastidious man. My original plan was to cajole a cleaner into letting me in, but now I had another option.

I slipped inside Pauline's office and approached her desk. It was covered in typewritten sheets, including one headed 'Pauline Lessinger – CV'.

That explained it. Applying for another job are we, Pauline? Don't worry, I won't tell.

I patted the pages, feeling for a key, but found nothing except an opened packet of chewing gum. I hoped in the rush to get to her car that Pauline hadn't bothered to lock her desk. Sure enough, the drawer beside her chair slid open. I scrabbled around and found a stapler, a hole punch, a pile of paper clips and, tucked at the side, a bunch of keys.

I went back to Professor Schneider's door and fumbled with one key after another trying to find the right one. At last, I made it inside and pressed the door almost shut, listening intently for footsteps. My own breathing was so loud I couldn't be sure if Pauline was on her way back or not, but I didn't have time to waste.

I shut the door, checked the blinds were closed and flipped on the desk lamp. I turned full circle. Filing cabinets, desk drawers, book shelves – too many possibilities.

I began with the shelves. There were books on every imaginable field of cardiology: coronary artery disease, pacemakers, diseases of the aorta. Everything you'd expect.

I returned to the desk and used the keys to get into the drawer. It was deep, with two ring-binders and several manila folders inside. I pulled them all out. There were pages of figures and photographs; close-ups of the heart, valves, operations – none of it what I was looking for.

I tried the filing cabinet and lifted out a batch of around ten journals from the bottom drawer and piled them on the desk, trying not to make any noise. Leo's investigations pointed to some radical new advances in memory research, so it was likely there'd be published papers on it. If the professor was involved in some way, he may have kept the details.

I flicked through the first few magazines, but they were all about cardiology. By now my fingers were leaving little smudges of sweat on every page as I flipped them over. I didn't dare check how long I'd been here, but it felt like ages.

Then my luck changed. At the bottom of the pile were two journals on neurology. I ran down the list of contents in the first, spotting an article on personality disorders and memory, but on reading the abstract, I could see it wasn't relevant.

Why would the professor keep these journals at the bottom of his filing cabinet? It was common knowledge that he was only spending half his time in cardiology and he certainly appeared to have more than a passing acquaintance with the new neurologist, Dr Graham, given the heated argument I'd overheard. Was he dabbling in the workings of the brain? Did this explain the EEG machine?

I'd got halfway down the list of articles in the next periodical when I heard the abrupt swing of a nearby door and footsteps. I lunged forward and quickly switched off the desk lamp, just as the steps came to a halt. I stood still, not daring to breathe, peering under the door waiting for shifting shadows, but everything was still.

Pauline would be in a foul mood after the prank call about her car and if she burst in on me I would have no defence. I'd be suspended right there and then, if not fired for good, but I couldn't give up now.

I stood at the blind and carefully tweaked two slats apart. The corridor was empty, so I put the lamp back on and went back to the list, skipping over the next few titles: *Molecules and Short-term Memory*, *Amnesia and the Stages of Forgetting*. Then there it was: *New Strides in Memory Implantation.* Someone had marked it with a highlighter pen. It was dated February of *this* year and described how seventy-three percent of students taking part in a particular experiment had been led to believe that a parrot had entered their bedroom during the night. Certain key words leapt out at me:

optogenetics…brain cells…neurons in the hippocampus…false memories…

My mouth fell open. This was exactly what I'd been looking for. I went back to the top for the important part – the name of the person who had carried out the research – and let out a sigh. It was blank. I scanned the text before noticing a statement in small print at the end:

*Author's name withheld by Editor**

I frantically flicked through the pages to find an explanation for the asterisk and eventually found it in the appendix:

**Research paper submitted for the annual UK Jeffersen Prize. Author's name withheld in accordance with panel's selection process.*

I had to stop myself from letting out an exasperated howl. Somewhere in the UK there *was* an expert in implanting false memories – that part was clear – but I was barely any closer than I had been before. The article was in Professor Schneider's office, but there was no proof it was written by him. I glanced up at the framed certificate for *The Jeffersen Prize* – also right here in his office. Was it him? Had he entered again with this research, this year?

I put the journal in my bag and bundled the others back into the filing cabinet, then switched off the lamp. I eased open the door a fraction and waited. All was quiet. Then I heard the slam of a drawer from Pauline's room.

I locked Schneider's office, cringing when the bolt made a loud clunk as it settled into the slot. I swallowed with a gulp and tapped on her door, the keys behind my back.

'Who is it?' she snapped.

'Hi,' I said, going in, trying to keep my tone breezy. 'Someone said you were still here. You should be getting off home.'

'Oh, yeah, still at it.' She went back to her typing. 'Sam, isn't it?'

'Yep. Mental Health,' I said casually, strolling towards her desk, deliberately not looking at any of her papers. She glanced at me over the rim of her glasses, looking edgy.

'Anyway, you're busy,' I said. 'Sorry. I'll leave you to it.' I was doing my utmost to sound casual, but I could barely get my mouth to work; my jaw felt like it was tied up with wire.

As I backed up, I looked down and made a noise as if I'd trodden on something.

'What's this?' I said, reaching down and coming up holding a bunch of keys.

'Strewth!' she said. 'The professor would kill me. They should be in my drawer.' She took them.

'Is he really that bad?' I asked, loitering.

'Absolutely. He's a stickler, I can tell you.'

There was a pile of forms and letters beside her computer. This was my chance. 'Is he keeping you late with his typing?' I asked innocently.

She glanced at the screen, then away again. 'Oh, you know – it never stops.'

'I bet you even have to type his research papers.'

'I shouldn't – but I do.'

'Did you type his latest one, about the parrot…in the students' bedrooms…?

She looked confused. 'Parrot?'

Either she was a very good actress or she didn't have a clue what I was talking about.

'I must have got it wrong.' I said, retreating to the doorway. 'You don't know of anyone else here, do you, who's prepared to type up research papers?'

'You need a typist?' She pulled a face. 'Don't you have any in mental health?'

I went along with her. 'I'm looking for someone reliable – who's been recommended.'

'Not me!' she scoffed. 'Too busy. Ask around.' She held up the keys. 'Look, I need to check everything's locked up.'

'Sure. I'll leave you to it.'

I wanted this tortuous performance over with and turned too abruptly, catching my knee on the corner of a stack of cardboard boxes. The stack tottered, then a loose ring-binder and a couple of paperbacks slipped off the top, narrowly missing me.

'Sorry,' I muttered as I bent down to retrieve them. Pauline sighed with impatience, but tried to pretend she was just clearing her throat.

My stomach jolted as I saw the cover of one of the books. I straightened up slowly, holding it up, my eyes latching onto her face ready to catch any signs of alarm.

'*Terror Underground* by Dexter Beaumont,' I read aloud, my hands shaking. 'Any good?'

There was no lowering of her eyes, no muscles kicking into a twitch near her mouth. She shrugged. 'I haven't read it.'

I glanced inside the front cover, half-heartedly, so she wouldn't know I was looking for a scribbled name. The front sheets were blank.

'It looks like it's been read, though,' I said, 'the spine is creased.'

'Someone lent it to me.' She put out her hand waiting for me to give it back.

'So there are f-fans of crime fiction here...?' I said, cringing inwardly. I was so startled at seeing the book, I could barely string two sensible words together.

'Looks like it.' She was keen for me to leave now, jangling her keys at me like they were a talisman she was using to ward me off. But, I couldn't leave it there. I needed to know who had given her the novel – the poisonous script behind the suicides.

'I quite like this genre, actually,' I said. 'Who gave it to you?'

'Oh – er...' She sounded side-tracked now. My hands squeezed up into fists. *Don't say you can't remember.*

'Er – Dr Graham,' she said offhandedly, holding the door open for me and shuffling me out.

I muttered some sort of hybrid between an apology and a thank you – and left.

Imogen wasn't answering her phone. She was probably fed up with my interruptions. It was a long shot anyway. Was Imogen really likely to know who might have written an anonymous article?

And now there was another copy of *the book*; the sinister source of the terrible flashbacks on the Underground. Was Pauline lying? Had she read it? Was she involved?

If Dr Graham had any connection with the mind-controlling text, why would he openly pass it on to someone else in the hospital? Wasn't that a bit risky? If you'd used the text to achieve such terrible outcomes, wouldn't you drop it in a wheelie bin miles away, or burn it?

There was another explanation, of course. People read books every day. It could be an innocent coincidence.

If I could find out if anyone had been using the specific neurology equipment Leo had told me about, it might throw more light on the situation. Problem was, everything was locked up now: the labs, most admin offices. Nevertheless, as I wandered towards the exit, I felt a strong sense of conviction. I was getting closer. Whoever had been messing with people's minds, I was going to bring them out into the open any day now. It was only a matter of time.

Chapter 34

From the moment I chucked half my supper in the bin, I was dreading bedtime. I phoned Danny and at least Con was safe. He agreed to make sure Con was at the hospital early the next morning for his off-the-record appointment with Leo.

But it wasn't only Con's procedure I was worried about; I was terrified that once I got to sleep I'd start having the nightmares again. The sleeping tablets didn't seem to be working their magic any more. I normally looked forward to sinking my head into my pillow, but not tonight. I kept thinking ahead to what I might face, which demons were lining up ready to burst out at me.

I stayed up as late as I could, hoping I'd be so tired that sleep would claim me and carry me straight off to a tranquil place. At half-past midnight, I crept into bed a jittering wreck, feeling like I was about five years old. The weather didn't help. The scene was ripe for nightmares; heavy rain was battering my bedroom windows. Roars of wind came in fierce waves, wrapping around the aerials and satellite dishes as if trying to wrench them off. I couldn't believe June had turned so wet.

I switched off the light and there was an immediate flash of lightning, splitting the room down the middle. A loud crackle of thunder was close on its heels, chasing it across the sky. I pulled the duvet up to my chin and realised I was shivering, even though it was a muggy night. I wished Con was there. Or Miranda. Anybody.

I will never know if any nightmares were brewing, because I was in the middle of a curious dream about Peter Pan, when a loud bell cut across my consciousness. At first it sounded like sleigh bells, then a 1950's ambulance. Then it made sense. The phone. In my bleary state, I wondered what Miranda had done now.

It was Danny.

'Con's on the roof.'

'What? What time is it?' I still had one foot in Neverland.

'Nearly three.'

I shot up, his words starting to sink in. 'Call the police.'

'They're on their way.'

I got out of bed, pulling on my jeans with one hand. 'What's he doing?'

'He's drunk and waving his arms around, shouting that he's going to jump.'

'Oh shit. I'll be right over.'

Leo answered on the second ring. 'Con's climbed onto a roof – you've got to get over there now.'

Danny lived with three others near Waterloo Station in the top flat of a Victorian house. He was pacing around outside without an umbrella, squinting up into the rain. With the stripes of his pyjama bottoms showing between his anorak and his unlaced hiking boots, he looked like an escaped convict.

A small group of people – Danny's flatmates, intrigued neighbours and a couple of late-night passers-by – were staring up at the roof. Con was sitting near the chimney pots. He stood up when he saw me and his left leg slithered down the wet slates, almost forcing him into the splits.

'For God's sake, Con, stay where you are,' I bellowed. He managed to drag his leg back and appeared to be squatting.

'How the hell did he get up there?' I asked, turning to Danny.

'He went out onto the fire escape, then he must have climbed up the drainpipe. I only realised when a gale starting blowing through the open window and all the doors in the flat were slamming.'

I heard the gate clunk and Leo came charging towards us under a large golf umbrella.

I grabbed his arm and gave him an imploring look.

'This is Leo. He's a…doctor.' Somehow, *plastic surgeon* didn't sound the least bit appropriate. 'When did you call the police, Danny?' I added.

'They should be here by now.' He checked the time on his phone. 'About twenty minutes ago. I'll call them again,' he said, turning and pulling his mobile from the pocket of his anorak.

Leo held his umbrella over my head. For a fleeting second, it was like being inside a little capsule; rain dripping off the edges creating a silver-beaded curtain. I wished that an extra-terrestrial force would beam us up together, to a place far away from this absurd ordeal. A private, secret spot – for just the two of us.

Instantly, a shudder of guilt gripped me for having a thought like this when Con was in such acute danger.

'They're on their way,' broke in Danny.

Con had stood up again. He was shouting, waving his arms, his bare feet sliding around on the dripping tiles.

'We've got to get to the nearest window,' urged Danny. 'We've got to talk him down.'

Leo turned to him. 'Can you get together mattresses, sofa cushions, anything that'll give him a soft landing. Start laying them on the ground around the edges of the building.' Leo took a few steps to one side, extending his arm to keep the umbrella over my head, and looked towards the back of the house. 'Front, back and side.'

'Sure – yeah,' said Danny, jamming his hand into his hair and inadvertently creating a Tintin quiff. His flatmates were soon struggling in and out of the house, trailing their bedding through the deepening puddles.

I grabbed Danny's sleeve. 'How close can we get to him?'

'Follow me.' Danny led us into the house, up to a window in the kitchen on the top floor. 'This is where he got out. If you lean back you can see the roof.'

With the help of a chair, I backed out of the window. Leo held my arms and I got on to the narrow and slippery ledge.

I straightened up, leaning into the bricks. It wasn't a place you'd want to be loitering for any length of time. There was an outdoor fire escape to my right. I reached out to the handrail and shuffled towards the platform.

I hoisted myself over the railing and stood looking up at the roof. Leo took no time to follow in my footsteps. The angle was tight, but I could see Con's arm from time to time. Then he saw us and shuffled a few steps in our direction, losing his balance for a moment and swinging his arms like windmill blades to compensate.

'Welcome to the party! Aren't you coming up?' His whisky-soaked words bled into one another.

'I think the party's over, Con,' I barked at him. 'It's time to come down.'

'What did you bring *him* for?'

'Leo's here to help.'

'Cradle snatcher…' he snarled at Leo.

'I need to get closer to him,' said Leo.

Before I realised what he was doing, Leo was climbing up onto the handrail of the fire escape. 'Give me your hand,' he insisted.

His spectacles looked like the inside of a bubbly glass paperweight. 'No, Leo, this is madness. You mustn't go up there.' I tried to block him, but he was reaching for the drainpipe. He checked it was secure and managed to hoist his weight against the wall, holding the pipe and using the brackets as footholds.

'I know about your clandestine meetings,' continued Con.

Leo heaved himself up and scrambled over the gutter onto the roof. The rain made a sound like tiny pebbles spitting at the tiles. It gushed down the drainpipes.

'I want to help you,' said Leo. He was wearing trainers, but the water on the slates had turned the roof into a sloping ice rink. I hoped he wouldn't try to stand up. I didn't want him getting any closer to Con.

'Stay low, Leo,' I shouted. 'Please, *be careful*.'

Con was drunk, angry and still under the influence of the false memories, plus he had nearly twenty years' advantage over Leo and was far fitter. I didn't fancy Leo's chances in a head-to-head. More worryingly, Con was about as far from his right mind as he could get. I could lose them both.

'You've been seeing each other, haven't you?' Con yelled. 'Don't try and deny it.'

'This is ridiculous,' I cried, but my voice was dragged away by the wind. 'Stop playing games and come back to the fire escape – both of you – and get down.'

'Come on – what's the point?' cried Con. 'Why don't you admit that you and my girlfriend are having a sordid little affair.'

'No…that's not how it is…' Leo's denial sounded pathetic even to my ears.

Con shook his head in disgust. Then he suddenly dropped down onto all fours and started crawling towards Leo. He seemed to have something in his hand. They looked like two bedraggled lions, prowling before they pounced on one another.

Then Con lunged at Leo with some sort of wire fork. Leo covered his head, curling into a ball.

I shouted the first thing that came into my head. 'Drop that, Con. RIGHT NOW. Get down – both of you.'

They were too far away from me by now, on the front slope of the roof. I ducked down towards Danny who was poking his head out of the kitchen window.

'I'm coming down,' I shouted. 'Get everyone to drag all the mattresses round to the front. Someone's going to fall.'

I scrambled down the steps of the fire escape and began helping the volunteers to adjust the padding to make sure it was all beneath the slope of the roof. There was a line of dense privet in front of the downstairs window, which might have helped to break a fall, but we couldn't count on it. I called on onlookers standing by the gate to come inside and hold a duvet stretched out tightly above the ground. If a body fell from the sky, we'd need to be ready to catch it.

'Where the hell are the emergency services?' I called to Danny. He pulled out his phone and redialled.

The sky was flinging down water like it had some big point to prove. My face was getting battered and my neck was aching from looking up the whole time.

Con was leaning over, hitting Leo with what I now realised was a piece of television aerial. Even though he was drunk, Con seemed more able to keep his balance. Maybe the alcohol had dampened his fear. Leo was covering his glasses, as the jabs rained down on his scalp and hands.

A flash of lightning splintered across the sky, followed by a hollow roar, giving form to the turmoil I was feeling inside. Con reared up and flung the aerial into the sky, then sank down onto his backside and started slapping the water with his palms. He looked like a toddler in a paddling pool. He seemed to be enjoying himself.

Leo crouched on his haunches. 'I can help with the flashbacks,' I heard him call out.

'That's what Sam said,' Con sneered.

'Well – how about it?'

Con was on the move again. All of a sudden, he sounded like he was crying. 'Oh God, the fire…I should have helped people. I shouldn't have walked away,' he blubbered.

It was hard to imagine this was the same man I'd been attracted to. The mind-games he'd been subjected to had turned him into a maniac one minute and a drivelling child the next.

'Wipe your eyes,' shouted Leo, 'You won't be able to see properly.'

'What does it matter? I'm a shitty person.' Con used his hands and feet to walk himself crab-style towards the front edge of the roof.

'Con! Keep away from the edge,' I yelled. 'Look at Leo. Focus on Leo.'

The group holding the duvet appeared to shrink together.

'The fire never happened,' called Leo. 'The nightmares are false.'

'I'm not sure it matters anymore.' I heard the despair in Con's voice and watched him slide closer to the gutter. He was trying to stand up again.

'Sit down!' shouted Leo. A cluster of blue lights were flickering in my peripheral vision. A fire-engine and an ambulance. About time.

In a calculated pounce, Leo grabbed Con's legs and forced him to fall backwards away from the edge. Con landed on his backside, looking up at the sky, surprised. Leo, however, had ended up spread-eagled across the guttering.

I cried out.

Suddenly Leo's legs were dangling down and his elbows were tucked inside the gutter. The muscles in his shoulders must have been burning with the strain. He couldn't hang on much longer.

I directed the dozen or so people holding the duvet to stand underneath Leo's hanging body. The fabric was saturated with the rain. 'Get a firm grip!' I shouted at the volunteers. 'Keep it taut!' I grabbed a corner, muttering snatches of prayers, pleading with Leo to hold on, while Con was motionless, still flat on his back.

Leo tried to heave himself up, but the guttering was starting to peel away. Doors banged and the fire-crew were heading inside the gate at last. They'd have ladders. They'd reach him. *Come on! Hurry up!*

There was a snapping sound and two of the plastic brackets gave way. Then another. I sucked in a bucket-full of air and held tight to the sodden duvet.

Leo wasn't holding on any more.

He made no sound as he fell.

Chapter 35

Leo's fall seemed to happen in slow-motion. The group congregating below whooped in one high-pitched gasp. Then there was a dull thud as Leo plummeted into the duvet. As he landed, several hands snapped away with the sudden weight and Leo hit the ground.

I felt like all my internal organs had exploded.

I bent over him and frantically searched for his pulse. There was a faint tremble, but his eyes were closed.

'Leo…?'

Someone helped me get him into the recovery position. I laid a sleeping bag over him, grabbed a blanket that had been draped over the hedge and rolled it to put under his head. Everything was soaking wet. His glasses were lying, smashed, beside his head. Rain dribbled down my cheeks into his open mouth. I used my coat to shelter him, keeping him warm, tenderly stroking his face.

A paramedic was kneeling beside me. Then another.

'Leave this to us, love. Are you a relative?'

I stood back shaking my head and watched them check his vital signs again. They lifted him onto a stretcher and put their own dry blanket over him. I wanted to go with him, but they wouldn't let me.

I watched firemen climb up onto the roof. Before long, Con was walking towards me, looking like he'd been hauled out of a river.

'Oh my God, Con,' I hissed. 'What have you done?!'

It was all I could say to him. Through my disbelief and outrage I kept trying to remember that this wasn't Con's fault, but I couldn't get past the fact that Leo had been busting a gut to save him and had quite possibly given his own life as a result.

Con was led to a police car.

'Bloody idiot,' Danny said, shaking his head. He was sitting on the dripping steps of the fire-escape.

I watched as the police officer put his hand on Con's head to guide him on to the back seat, but I couldn't bear to see any more. I turned away when they drove off.

The remaining officers stopped me and asked questions. I gave them an edited version of the truth and made sure they knew Con should be on suicide watch. An officer spoke into his radio and confirmed with me that, because he was so drunk, Con would be spending the rest of the night in a cell under supervision.

The ambulance had taken Leo to A&E at St Luke's, but I knew they wouldn't let me see him. I considered waiting in a corridor at the hospital for the rest of the night, but in the end I rang for a cab to take me home instead.

By the time I got back, night was starting to peel away from the sky, leaving a low band of orange like a smouldering fire, on the horizon. My bedding was in a heap on the floor. I dragged it onto the bed and got in fully clothed and sopping wet. I buried my face in the pillow and wept. Great surging sobs rose from deep within me.

Leo couldn't die. He'd been brave and heroic. He'd been prepared to risk his life for Con. The sobbing left me shivering and I knew I had to take off my wet clothes. I pulled on my crumpled pyjamas and curled into a foetal position.

More than anything, I wanted to sleep. No, that's not true. More than anything, I wanted to wake up and find the horrors of the last few hours had merely been another nightmare.

I was up at six the following morning, ringing the hospital. Leo was in a coma in intensive care. There were no visitors allowed outside the family and I sincerely hoped that Kim and Felicity would have put their grievances aside to be there for him.

Meanwhile, I got dressed and was waiting outside the police station near Waterloo when it opened at 9am. Con was being released, but the police wanted to see him later for questioning. I grabbed his wrist as he came towards me.

'My place. Now,' I instructed. We waited for a cab. He no longer looked like someone I wanted to associate with. His hair was filthy, trailing in his bleary eyes and he smelt of disinfectant. I didn't want to be anywhere near him, but I had a job to do.

'I tried to give a statement,' he said, 'but they wouldn't accept it. Said I was too drunk.' He wiped his nose with his sleeve. 'How's Hansson?'

'Not at all good,' I said.

'It wasn't my fault.'

'Of course it was your bloody fault! He was only up there because of you. He was trying to save you!'

'Whatever…'

'I'm going to have to do the procedure myself.' He let me pull him along by his sleeve like a dawdling child. 'I've seen all Leo's notes. He was waiting for a special drug to arrive from Seattle. I should be able to do what needs to be done. I just need to get into his office. Or his cottage. I'm not sure where his notes are.'

'Doesn't exactly sound promising,' he snorted.

'You haven't *exactly* been helping,' I retorted.

I had to remind myself again that this wasn't the Con I knew. I was seeing a distorted version of him, through frosted glass. I did, however, want to get one thing straight with him. 'For the record, Leo and I were never lovers and I don't want to talk about it ever again.'

When we got back to my flat, I made toast. I wasn't hungry, but I couldn't remember the last time I'd eaten properly. Con tucked in heartily. As I pushed the marmalade-coated slice around my plate, I wondered how the hell we were going to carry out the next stage. I couldn't reverse Con's false memories without Leo's notes and the drug from America. I might be able to gain access to Leo's office, but with him in a coma, where would the package end up? In the post room? On Lian's desk? Sent back to Seattle? In the blink of an eye, everything had gone hopelessly wrong.

But I had to start somewhere. Con agreed to spend the day with Danny, so I went straight to the hospital to find Lian.

A bundle of tissues was scrunched up on her desk and she was trying to hold a conversation on the phone with one of Leo's patients.

'You've heard…' she said, as she put down the handset.

'Yes. It's terrible news.' I didn't want her to know that I'd been there when Leo had fallen; she'd only ask questions and it would waste time.

'Such a wonderful man. So dedicated,' she said between sniffs. 'We've all got to hope he's going to pull through.'

I went round to her chair and put my arm on her shoulder, scouring her desk for the morning's post. There was no small parcel.

'I know this is a difficult time, but we were working together on a few patients. They'd had surgery with Dr Hansson and then been passed on to me for psychological support.' She nodded. 'I may have left some notes in his office. Would it be okay for me to take a quick look? Dr Hansson might have squirreled them away somewhere – with it being confidential.'

'I don't see why not. I'll come and help.' She got to her feet.

'No, no,' I almost pushed her back into her chair. 'I don't want to take up your time. You'll have important people you need to contact, I'm sure.'

She sank down again. 'Yes, I suppose so,' she said, scrolling mindlessly through her contacts list.

She handed me the keys. 'I'll join you when I've made a few calls,' she insisted.

The blinds were down, so I flicked on the light. Leo's office smelt of freshly cut paper and the vestiges of his expensive musky aftershave. It captured him so perfectly that I half expected him to slide out from behind the door and ask what had kept me.

We'd been here in his office when we'd discussed the reversal procedure. His notes had been strewn across his desk. It was bare now, except for the photo of his wife, an old-fashioned leather ink blotter and a gold fountain pen in a holder. Leo wasn't a man to use a biro.

I swiftly unlocked his desk and filing cabinet. I was sure the notes wouldn't be labelled, certainly not with anything useful, like *Flashback Reversal Method*. All I knew was there'd be a blue file and a green one; each about a centimetre thick.

I pulled out folder after folder, flipped through box-files one after the next and drew a complete blank. The notes were handwritten, so it wasn't going to be on his computer. I shouldn't have been surprised that I couldn't find them. Leo knew the police were crawling around and it wouldn't have taken them long to link the notes with the suicides if they ever got their hands on them. They'd be tucked away somewhere safe. But where?

I sensed movement behind me. 'Any luck?' said Lian, she was clutching a pile of envelopes.

'No. Must be somewhere else.'

They must be at his cottage. Out of harm's way. How I was going to get in and find them was another matter altogether.

Lian put the bundle down on Leo's desk. 'Post has just arrived,' she said wearily. She ignored me and began sifting through, making a pile for Leo, a pile for herself. I didn't move. I was staring at the desk, watching her stack four parcels beside Leo's letters.

Just as she finished, her phone rang and she scuttled away to answer it. I didn't hesitate. I lunged at the packages, scanning them as quickly as I could.

My luck was in. I snatched the parcel postmarked Seattle and stuffed it into my bag. Then I slipped out of Leo's office and used the keys to get into the medical supply store. I grabbed a handful of hypodermic needles. When Lian returned to Leo's office I was switching off the light and holding out the keys.

'Do you have a list to show which consultants saw which patient?' I asked, as I followed her into her room. I'd already seen the list that Debbie kept on file, but there was one question I'd omitted to ask.

Lian flipped through files on her desk and pulled one out. As I'd thought, the list Debbie had given me was a photocopy and Lian's sheets were the originals.

'Whose signature is this?' I asked, pointing to the scribble beside each of Terry Masters' entries. Leo had seen Jane, Jake and Con for their injuries, but never Terry.

She gave it a glance. 'I've no idea. Must have been a locum.'

'Is there any way I could find out who it was?'

The surgeon who had seen Terry, could have become involved with the others too. That person could be the missing link.

She snatched the folder out of my reach in a way that suggested she hadn't time for such insignificant matters. 'Debbie has the list of current locums,' she muttered. 'You should be able to track them down from there.'

There was something odd about the locum's signature. 'Let me look again,' I said, reaching out. I thought we might be in for a tug of war, but reluctantly she let me have the file.

I slid the original form under the angle-poise lamp to get a closer look, then held the sheet above the lamp, so that the light was shining up through the paper. I could now see what the problem was.

The original signature had been covered with a discreet layer of correction fluid. There was another one written over the top. I checked all the entries beside Terry's name and they were all the same. Each one had been very carefully altered; undetectable to the naked eye.

'The signature's been changed,' I said, musing out loud, inviting Lian to lean over and look.

She cleared her throat and looked away.

'Did you know about this?' I asked gently.

She opened her mouth, then closed it. 'Did someone fake the signature, Lian?' Again, softly without accusation.

Her shock over Leo's critical state had dislodged her cast-iron guard. She jerked upright. 'Why are you doing this?' she whispered.

I spoke the unspeakable words. 'Did Dr Hansson alter it so he wouldn't be connected with Terry Masters?'

'No. It wasn't him,' she protested. She gulped as if she was short of breath. 'It was *me.* I wanted to protect him. Dr Hansson has been under such pressure lately – what with his wife...then these suicides...' She grabbed my arm. 'I talked him into it. It was stupid, I know. But after the first two deaths he had a bad feeling. He was worried about his job, like you. He was concerned the hospital would mount a full investigation and find him... wanting.'

'Wanting?'

'Yes – he's been a bit off form in surgery, lately. He hasn't been himself. I mean, it's understandable...' She made a grab for the incriminating page. 'Please don't tell anyone. It doesn't matter now, does it? I mean Terry's dead. It's no one's fault.'

The possible repercussions bounced around inside my head. Leo *had* been the common factor at the hospital. All four patients: Jane, Jake, Terry and Con had seen him exclusively for their injuries. Did this cover-up put Leo in the frame or had he simply been worried about his job?

'I'll take this,' I said, holding the sheet out of her reach. 'But I promise I won't take it any further until I've...spoken to Leo.'

I left her staring into space, chewing a nail.

Before I went anywhere else, I stood in the stairwell and made a call to Imogen. She was about to give a seminar, but she said she could spare me a few minutes.

I told her Leo had fallen from the roof and was in intensive care.

'Oh, how awful,' she said. 'Is he going to make it?'

'It's in the lap of the gods.'

I closed my eyes and told her the next bit.

'Hold on…' she said. There was horror in her voice. 'You're going to attempt this procedure *yourself*?'

'I have no choice.'

'That's a tall order, Sam.'

'It's for Con.'

'You shouldn't be experimenting with this on your own. You need a neuroscientist to be working at this level. The damage it could cause doesn't bear thinking about.'

She was absolutely right, of course; I hated the idea that I was stepping in like some kind of omnipotent saviour. Nevertheless, a life was at stake and I didn't feel like I had any choice.

'It's like I'm up against a time-bomb here,' I said. 'Con has made two attempts to kill himself already. He's terribly unstable. No other professional would dare come on board with me while the whole thing is being investigated by the police. It could be weeks before Con gets the process reversed. You see my problem?'

She sighed. 'I'm not happy, but – just be really careful, okay?'

'I will.'

I thanked her for not disowning me, took a deep breath and strode round to intensive care to see if there was any news about Leo. No change. As I returned to my office, Debbie came running to meet me in the corridor. She was grim-faced.

'It's not Con, is it?'

She shook her head. 'There are two men waiting for you in your office.'

'Police?'

'No…' Her frozen look told me everything I needed to know.

She abandoned me at the door and I walked gingerly inside.

'Dr Samantha Willerby?' asked an officer in uniform. I spotted the word *Security* on his epaulette.

'Yes.'

In unison, they hooked their hands under my shoulders and almost lifted me off the floor. 'We are escorting you from the building, Dr Willerby,' said the taller one. 'We're under strict instructions not to allow you inside the hospital premises during your period of suspension.' His voice was deadpan, as though he could do this job in his sleep.

The two guards took me right out as far as the pavement.

'Why wasn't I told about this?' I said, pulling down my sleeves, once they'd let go.

'You should have had a letter in the post,' came the reply.

I clicked my tongue. Checking my post had gone by the wayside in the mania of the last few days. The smaller guard held his hand open. 'Keys and pass, please.'

Chapter 36

I went straight to the Young Vic to find Con. He was on stage taking some students through their lines for a new production of *Much Ado about Nothing*. Danny was in the wings, marking up the stage directions.

'Thank you so much for watching him,' I said, patting his shoulder.

We both looked over at Con who was waving his arms, like a conductor, in front of a group of teenagers. His untamed hair shimmied from side to side when he shouted. He was a formidable presence; upright, confident, charismatic. It was the first thing that had attracted me to him. Was his possessiveness so bad? If it was the only snag in our relationship, once the flashbacks had been dealt with, then we were doing pretty well, weren't we?

Except, deep down, I knew it wasn't the only snag.

'He's been less subdued today,' Danny said, sliding his pencil behind his ear.

I sank down onto a stool beside him. The whole place smelt of chalk; it crept into my throat, my eyes. 'I'm suspended from the hospital,' I said flatly. 'Not allowed inside the building.'

'Shit!' He drew in his chin sharply. 'For how long?'

'I've no idea. Until the suicides have been fully investigated and I'm cleared. It could be weeks.'

Danny let out a little snort of outrage. 'But none of this is your fault. Con told me about it.'

'I know. They've got a bloody cheek. Talk about innocent until proven guilty.'

A thought lodged in my head. Perhaps this was Professor Schneider's doing, to get me out of the way.

A burst of applause erupted from the stage and I watched Con take mock bows in front of his group. He was loving the limelight. He strode jauntily over to join us.

'Hiya – good day?' he called out.

'No – not really. I've been suspended from the hospital.'

He pulled me to him, planted a kiss in my hair. 'Well – never mind. It won't be for long, I'm sure.' I couldn't believe his insensitivity. Danny caught me nipping my lips together. 'Anyway, that's good, isn't it?' Con carried on. 'It means you can spend more time with me.'

I drew away, but didn't say anything. It struck me that I could tell Con every single thing about me and he would never really know who I was. He'd never grasp what made me tick. It left me with a sinking feeling.

Con climbed the stairs ahead of me when we got to my flat. He stopped abruptly on the landing. I drew alongside him. At first, I thought heaps of rubbish had been left outside my door, until I realised one of the items was a blue suitcase. In the midst of the heap, something moved.

'What are you doing here?' I said with dismay. 'Why aren't you at Linden Manor?'

'I couldn't bear it,' she said, getting to her feet.

Con hugged her. 'Hi, babe,' he said cheerfully.

We went inside. I had one hell of a headache coming on.

'You can't stay here…' I was about to say her name, but didn't know whether she was currently calling herself Mimi or Miranda. 'You have to go back for your own safety.'

Con stepped between us. 'Can't she stay and catch her breath?'

'You! In the kitchen,' I said. I had no surplus energy for niceties. I ushered him against the fridge and shut the door. 'You don't know what she did to my mother's face. We don't know what she did to escape. She's a danger to herself…and others.'

'We're all a danger to ourselves and others,' he said flippantly.

'Yours is temporary,' I pointed out. 'Miranda has had her craziness for a lifetime.'

'She was doing so well.'

I was shouting now. 'Well, that's what mental illness is like. It comes and goes. That's why we've got to be so careful. I'm in enough trouble as it is at the hospital.'

I sat down and motioned for him to do the same.

'We're nearly there, Con. I just need to get Leo's files and then I can take you through the process.' I put the package with the drug we needed on the table and patted it. 'I've got what we were waiting for.'

'Hang on – you're seriously going to strap me to a chair and stick needles in me with some mind-bending drug that's going to strip away all—'

'Sounds great,' said Miranda, barging in. 'Can I have a go?'

'It's not a game, Miranda.' I took a chance on the name and she didn't flinch.

'But what if I've got bad memories I want to remove?' she queried.

I wanted to slam my hand on the table and tell her that Mum, Dad and I were the ones with the bad memories – after all her years of outrageous behaviour, but I managed to stop myself. 'No – this is different,' I said wearily.

'Have you got a flash-gun like they use in *Men in Black*?' She stuck a finger in her mouth and began sucking it like a toddler.

'No, Miranda.' I put my hand over the package. 'This is for a very specific condition and you don't have it.'

'Is this about those patients who died? The ones with the hallucinations?'

I hadn't realised she'd picked up so much information while she'd been around us. I glanced at Con and he looked away, confirming my hunch that he may have played a part in that.

'Do the memories have to be recent?' she said sombrely.

'I don't think so,' interjected Con. 'Just very clear.'

'Oh – they're clear, all right,' she said.

'Listen, Miranda. Let's talk about your memories another time. I need to use this special method urgently – just with Con. You shouldn't know about it. Until I can give him the treatment, Con's in danger if you mention it to anyone.'

She giggled.

I sat down and sank my head onto my folded arms. The headache had set up a punishing rhythm of its own throughout my entire body; my temples, my lower back – even my teeth. I felt like a whole jungle tribe were thwacking drums and jangling bells inside my veins.

There was still one serious drawback to my plan. I had no idea how I was going to get the notes from Leo's cottage.

Before long, Con and Miranda were playing card games in the sitting room like old friends. I heard Con cry out in mock complaint.

'Aces again! That's not fair,' he said. 'Are you cheating?'

I laughed wryly to myself. Whenever things weren't going his way, Con immediately assumed he was being deceived.

I watched from the doorway, desperately wishing I could join them. I ached for this to be over and for the three of us to laugh, joke and poke fun at each other. More than anything, it would have been nice to spend some private time with Miranda, but no doubt she would be snatched away again at any moment.

I turned my attention instead to Leo's cottage. I remembered the trademark Banham keyhole on the front door. A sturdy five-lever lock. I was hardly going to be able to slide a credit card inside the doorframe and be rewarded with an instant *open sesame*. I tried to remember if Leo had a burglar alarm. I couldn't recall seeing a number pad anywhere in his hallway. That was a vague plus-point in the sea of negatives.

What about the back of the property? I'd been in the kitchen and could bring up images of French windows leading to a tiny patio, but there was no back gate, as far as I could recall, just a high brick wall.

I ran through all the options I could think of, no matter how ridiculous they sounded. Con could climb the back wall and break in; he was a natural risk-taker. Right now, however, he was changeable and volatile. Too unreliable.

There was Danny – I ruled him out immediately. It wasn't even fair to consider him. Who did that leave? I started running through everyone I could think of and suddenly I had it. It was so obvious, I didn't know why I hadn't thought of it before.

I picked up my phone and made a call to Lian.

'You're suspended,' she said accusingly. News travelled fast.

'I know, but this isn't a hospital matter directly.'

I told her what I needed. One simple thing.

She was reluctant at first, so I was forced to switch on the charm. 'I'm sure Dr Hansson would be grateful – he does seem to think rather highly of you.'

'Well…' she said, sounding smug and making me wait. 'No more favours after this one, okay?' I could hear how much she was enjoying occupying the moral high ground. I wrote down the number she gave me and thanked her through gritted teeth.

I made the call straight away. The phone rang and rang and I was about to give up, when a female voice with a refined accent came on the line.

'Felicity Hansson speaking…'

I almost leaped up with joy, but reined myself in. I needed to get this next part absolutely right.

'Hi, Felicity – it's Sam Willerby. We met at your Mum's funeral. I work with your father at St Luke's Hospital.' She didn't say anything. 'I'm so very sorry about what's happened to him.'

'Right…' she said inconclusively.

'Listen, I know this isn't a good time, but there's something I need to ask you.' Again, nothing was coming back. 'I think your father has some research papers we were working on together at his cottage. They're confidential and it's imperative that I get hold of them. Have you been over there, recently?'

'No. I've never been to my Dad's new place. And I don't have a key.'

Those last six words hit me like a steel wrecking ball. My vision went hazy.

'No key?' I said in a whisper. My neck barely felt strong enough to hold my head up any more.

That was that. No key. No notes. No way to save Con. My mind was whirling with such confusion and despair that I barely registered she was speaking again.

'Sorry?' I said with a croak.

'I said, we always used to leave one with a neighbour, but—'

'Really?' I swallowed. 'Can I ask you to help me?'

'I'm not sure I—'

'Please,' I interrupted. 'It's very important – one of your father's patients could die.'

I let her think about it. In the silence I could feel my world slowly splitting into pieces.

'What do you need me to do?' she said eventually.

I sank against the kitchen wall. 'Could you get over to Holland Park by about seven o'clock? Have you got his address?'

'Yes. He gave it to me at the funeral.'

We agreed to meet at his cottage and take it from there.

I left Con and Miranda in charge of each other. It was like leaving two sticks of dynamite with lit fuses, but I didn't have many other options. I only hoped the authorities didn't track her down before I got back. Apart from the furore that would cause, I didn't want Con to be left on his own.

I walked under the mew's archway at the entrance to the cobbled cul-de-sac and spotted her straight away. She seemed younger than when I'd seen her at the funeral and more fragile; trying to hold herself together, trying hard to be strong, just like her father. I noticed for the first time how very beautiful she was, real supermodel looks, with straight blonde hair shimmering like gold thread and Leo's soft charcoal eyes.

'I've been next door. Dad hasn't changed his lifelong habits.' She held up a key.

I pressed my hands together in a silent moment of gratitude.

We went inside. It was around twenty-two degrees outside, but inside it felt cold, damp and two-dimensional without Leo.

'I'm so sorry about your father.' She had the same sleep-deprived grey moons under her eyes that I had. 'He's a wonderful man.'

'Everyone says that,' she said neutrally.

'How long has he lived here?'

'Months – since Mum went into hospital. He gave up on the big house.' She took in the décor. 'I can't believe I've never been here.'

I followed her into the sitting room. 'He never invited you?' I asked.

Her throat snagged on her reply. 'He was always too busy.'

'He *does* think the world of you and Kim – he really does. He knows he's got plenty of ground to make up.'

'He said that?' She twisted her hands together.

I nodded. 'He feels terrible about the way things have turned out. I think he'd do anything to have his time with you again.'

She stared curiously into my face like she was debating whether or not to believe me.

The clock on the mantelpiece chimed and she shuddered.

'Do you know where these notes are?' she said. We both seemed uncomfortable being there without Leo. My eyes skimmed the shelves, but I could see nothing the size of the files I was looking for.

'It's all confidential,' I replied. 'Your father might have put them somewhere safe.'

Felicity turned her back on me. I thought at first she was looking around the room, but it occurred to me she was, in fact, stalling. She looked like she was about to change her mind and ask me to leave.

'I'm not sure we should be—'

'It's lifesaving work, Felicity. I wouldn't ask unless it was crucial,' I explained. 'I've got at least one patient waiting, depending on it.'

She gave a brief nod as if she'd silently agreed something with herself.

'I know Dad had the safe brought over from our family home. He might keep files in there. It'll probably be in the cellar – if there is one.' She went back into the hall and snapped open a sloping door under the stairs. She ducked inside and found the light switch. 'Yes – it's here. I'll bet he kept the same combination.'

Moments later she joined me, holding an armful of folders. We went into the kitchen and she laid them on the table.

'Any good?' she said.

I spotted a blue and a green file lying next to each other and slid them out.

'This is what I'm looking for,' I said, recognising the first few sheets.

'What's it about?'

'Oh...psychology stuff.'

The side of her mouth crept up. 'I'm training to be a doctor.' I heard Leo's pride in her tone. It reminded me of that first time I'd bumped into him and how I'd concluded in about five seconds that he was the most arrogant man I'd ever come across. 'Let me see.'

I had to let her take a look, dread crawling up my legs like a swarm of ants.

She laughed. 'Gobbledegook to me. I know Dad likes probing the hidden depths of the human psyche even though he's a plastic surgeon, not a psychologist.' It was the first time she had referred to him with any degree of tenderness.

'You're fond of him...'

'I'm very *angry* with him,' she said bitterly. 'About everything. His sole drive in life was to be respected, to be a luminary. He got involved in his work and made a lot of money. The key to everything...'

She sniffed and turned away, as a glassy tear dribbled down her cheek.

'Have you been to see him?' I asked softly.

She stiffened. 'Yes. As soon as I heard. He looked dreadful. Grey and so still. Like part of him had already gone...'

'He was trying to save a man's life,' I said. 'I was there when he fell.'

'I didn't know that.' She took my hand and led me back into the sitting room. 'Tell me what happened.'

I told her in as much detail as I could. Once I'd finished, she sat staring at the soggy tissue scrunched in her palm. 'He's not going to regain consciousness, is he?'

'We don't know yet.'

Her head fell forward. I reached over and she let me hug her.

'You seem close,' she muttered. 'Are you the one who chose the necklace for Kim?'

I nodded.

'Will you be honest with me?' She looked up, her eyes red-rimmed. 'Are you and my dad…?'

'No. Absolutely not,' I assured her, before she could get the words out. 'I think very highly of him, but it hasn't gone any further.'

'You're good friends, though?'

'I think so – yes.'

'I'm glad.'

Adrenalin was coursing through me like a water main about to rupture by the time I got home, but all was well. Con and Miranda had ordered a takeaway and left a plateful in the oven for me. Miranda put it on the kitchen table. She seemed remarkably normal after the outburst with my mother, but I was still mystified over what had brought on such an extreme attack.

'I'm sorry I've been such a useless sister to you,' she said unexpectedly. 'I've seen a lot of things more clearly recently and…I want…I hope things can be better between us.'

Flashes of compassion from her like this made me see how much Miranda was worth fighting for.

I ate properly for the first time in ages and spent the next hour running through Leo's notes, making sure I was absolutely clear about the reversal process. I was no longer allowed inside the hospital, so we would have to carry it out right here, in my flat. Fortunately, it looked possible to erase a small bank of memories without any specialist medical equipment, other than a syringe.

Con had drunk at least one glass of wine and I was too exhausted to attempt it that night. I told him we'd do it first thing in the morning.

After that, Con tuned up my old guitar and began strumming through some old Paul Simon songs. We all joined in. I had to hold back tears, thinking first about Leo in intensive care, then the three of us sitting together like a family. Miranda would soon be carted off and Con – well, I might be about to cure him or kill him – I had no way of knowing which way it would go. If I didn't act, it was only a matter of time before another flashback caught him unawares and his suicidal impulses got the better of him.

Miranda knew the drill, pulling the spare duvet out of the airing cupboard and draping it over the sofa. She went to bed first and Con started to undress in my room. I got into bed quickly, hoping he wouldn't see me shivering. I was desperate to sleep, but terrified to close my eyes in case more of the hellish images came for me again.

I was grateful for his warm body. For the familiarity of it, but I wasn't in the mood for anything else. I wasn't sure, with Con, if I ever would be again.

My feelings for him had slumped down another notch, even before Leo had fallen off the roof. I knew the false memories were making Con act out of character, but his perpetual suspicion that I was being unfaithful had been simmering long before then. Con had been exciting and dynamic at the start, but having met Leo, I could see there were too many holes in our relationship.

Con stroked my back and pushed closer.

'Not tonight, Con.' I said. 'I'm knackered and we've got a big day ahead.'

There was an uncomfortable silence and he turned over with a grunt.

Chapter 37

When the alarm went off, I felt the warmth of Con's body snuggling into my back – and for five seconds, I forgot everything. Then it hit me. Leo was in a coma with his life in the balance. And saving Con was all down to me.

I hated the idea of messing with Con's mind, but the only alternative was to abandon him to his suicidal compulsions. That would be tantamount to letting him wander into an enclosure of crocodiles – he wouldn't stand a chance for long. It was entirely in my hands. Hands that were shaking before I'd even got out of bed.

I didn't remember any disturbing dreams during the night, but I must have been crying, because my eyes were puffy, my lids like shiny slugs.

Miranda was already in the kitchen pouring orange juice. 'You look like shit,' she said, never one to mince her words.

'Cheers,' I sniffed.

Fears started escalating inside my head. What were my chances of getting this procedure right? Of Leo coming out of his coma? Of my own sanity surviving in one piece?

The room shifted to the right all of a sudden and I sat down. I just had to hold it together for another hour or so. Ironically, Con had slept peacefully, for once. He rolled into the kitchen wanting a glass of milk. I suggested he shouldn't have anything except water until we'd finished the process. He grumbled something and sloped into the bathroom.

I opened my laptop and started writing a letter to Linden Manor Residential Care Home. I told them I was Miranda's sister and, in my medical opinion as a Clinical Psychologist, suggested Miranda be removed from the secure ward and returned to the open unit where she'd spent the last few years. I left it in an envelope by the front door.

Before I did anything else, I rang Dina, my psychotherapist, to make an emergency appointment. I'd meant to get around to it earlier. I hadn't seen her in years, but she'd made it clear that her door was always open to me. She didn't have any spaces for three weeks, but offered to fit me in on her day off, on Sunday.

'That's incredibly kind,' I said, touched by her generosity.

'I know you well enough to recognise this is a crisis, Sam. I can hear it in your voice.'

I looked at the clock as I put the phone down; it was eight-thirty. I couldn't put this off any longer.

Miranda was going to stay in the kitchen. She was under strict instructions not to disturb us unless I called for her. I left her my mobile, unplugged the mainline phone and disconnected the doorbell.

I ran through the procedure again in my mind. I'd briefed Con that at exactly the right moment, he had to bring his disturbing memories forcefully into his consciousness – he needed to see them, feel them, conjure up all the sounds and smells, with every ounce of energy in his body.

I'd played several relaxation discs to Con earlier, and he preferred the one with sounds of the ocean, so I set it up. He told me he'd done meditation classes at the theatre and it came easily to him, so that, at least, was something in our favour.

I filled the syringe with the right amount of *tronocept* and laid out my notes, then washed my hands for the fourth time. I was feeling hot and prickly all over.

Con strolled into the bedroom and laid down. I smoothed his hair on the pillow as he got comfy.

'Okay,' I said, trying to hide my anxiety. 'We're ready. I've led relaxation and guided imagery before. It's not that different.'

In fact, it was as different as sugar was from salt, but the last thing I wanted was for Con to be alarmed. I needed him to be in a super-relaxed state if any of this was going to work.

'I'm more worried about that needle,' he said, drawing back as though it was a venomous snake. 'Have you done this before?'

'Of course,' I said dismissively. A friend who had diabetes let me administer her injection once, when I was in my teens. Hardly a level of experience likely to set Con's mind at rest, but it wasn't a lie.

I pressed play and the soft, rippling sounds began. Con's breathing slowed a little. The gentle rush of the water changed subtly, getting slower and steadier and Con's eyes stopped fluttering. I waited. There was no sound other than the soothing rhythm of waves rolling onto a beach. *Roll and splash…roll and splash.*

I watched his chest rise and fall, waiting for the moment when it slowed right down. When his mouth fell open, I began reading out Leo's instructions from the green folder, following everything to the letter. I felt my own heartbeat thumping away as the ocean waves swirled around us. If Con was at one end of the stress scale, I was certainly at the other.

He appeared to shudder when I inserted the needle, but I continued reading and he didn't stir. I pressed the plunger and instructed him to relive the tortuous memories in as much detail as he could. He squirmed and moaned, but didn't open his eyes.

Around two minutes passed before I reached the final section:

…and when you wake up you will have forgotten every single harrowing image relating to the fire on the Underground. You will have no more flashbacks or nightmares. You will feel relaxed and at peace and forget everything we've done here.

I counted down slowly from ten to one, guiding him back to the here and now. The recording stopped.

Silence.

Con didn't move. I leant over him tentatively. He didn't seem to be breathing. I grabbed a mirror and held it above his mouth. Suddenly he twitched and sighed loudly.

'What time is it?' he muttered blearily, as if he'd been asleep for hours.

I quickly pushed the syringe and the notes under the bed.

'Nearly half-nine.'

'Blimey – it's late. Why didn't you wake me? Has Danny called?'

'No, he hasn't.' I willed my voice to stay flat, matter-of-fact.

'I'm starving.' He got out of bed and went to the kitchen.

I rang Imogen straight away.

'I think I've done it,' I whispered.

'Well done, girl. How are you holding up?'

'I'm okay,' I said. 'Just coping hour by hour, right now.'

I didn't dare tell her I might have to call on her as a last resort, if my own nightmares came back. I had enough of the reversal drug left to do the procedure on myself, if it came to that.

Miranda put her head round the door. 'All done?'

I nodded cautiously.

'Before I forget,' she said, 'you had a call on your mobile.'

She handed me the phone. It was the hospital number. I sat on the edge of the bed and listened to the message without thinking. It would be about the suspension; the police investigation.

'I knew you'd want to know, Sam,' came Debbie's voice. 'Dr Hansson died during the night.'

I slid to the floor, breathing fast. There had to be a mistake.

Debbie's recorded voice went on. 'He didn't regain consciousness.' *No. No. It can't be true.*

Miranda was still standing in the doorway. She came over and crouched down to hold me as I sat spread-eagled on the carpet. 'Is it that plastic surgeon?'

I nodded.

I rang Debbie's number immediately.

'It was good of you to call,' I croaked. I had to draw on all my reserves to push the words out. 'What happened?'

'His internal injuries were too severe in the end, Sam. He passed away at around five this morning. Everyone here is still in shock.'

I'd been so certain he would come round. This was too cruel.

'I'd like to see him, if I can.'

'Hold on,' she said. There was a rustle followed by a murmur as she spoke to someone. 'I'm sorry, but it looks like it's family only,' she said. Her tone was warm, but the words themselves were wrapped in barbed wire.

'Okay,' I said. 'I understand.'

I let the phone fall from my hand.

'You really liked him?' Miranda asked, her gaze soft and sad.

'He was a very special person,' I muttered. I got up and wandered blindly around the room.

Con came in pulling on a clean T-shirt.

'What's going on?' he asked, yawning. I stared at him unable to speak. The realisation of what had happened was slowly dripping into my brain. Any chance to see Leo, to speak to him ever again had been snatched away. He'd gone.

'Has someone died – or something?' he said jovially.

I had no words.

Miranda gave me a pained look and led him into the kitchen. 'I'll get the toast on,' I heard her say to him.

'What's wrong with *her*?' came Con's voice as I closed the bedroom door.

I climbed into bed and pulled the covers over my head. I wanted to block everything out. I'd lost him. It was too much to take in.

After a restless hour, I emerged and took a shower. Miranda and Con were playing dominoes in the kitchen. He seemed relaxed and playful; the fraught splintering around his eyes had gone. I asked him how he felt.

'Me? I'm fine.' He tried to put his arm round me, but I ducked away. 'Miranda told me that surgeon bloke died. She said he was in an accident…'

He narrowed his eyes, seemingly unaware of the full picture.

'He had a terrible fall,' I said tentatively, watching his face for signs of recognition about being on the roof, but nothing came.

I didn't say any more. Con must have lost additional memories during the reversal process, but it was a small price to pay.

Miranda got up and held my face in her hands. It was a tender and heartfelt gesture.

'They won't let me see him,' I whispered. I wanted to dissolve there and then, but if I let go, I feared never pulling everything back together again.

Con turned around. 'You doing laundry today?' he said, having a stretch. 'You couldn't slip my jeans in could you? They're filthy.'

Miranda gave me a wink. It looked like Con was on the way back to being his old self, but there was one thing I knew I had to try which would be the ultimate test. I went into the bedroom and came back with the paperback I'd hidden under the bed.

'Con, have you seen this?'

He tutted. 'You showed me that a few days ago. It's not my cup of tea.'

'But do you recognise the story at all?'

He told hold of the book, flicked it over to the back, then opened it at the first page. 'No.'

'What about page seventy-three?'

He swung his weight on to one hip and indulged me. 'Right, page seventy-three.' He started reading out loud in a lacklustre voice:

Lee turned to Robbie. 'Can you smell that?' he said. 'It's smoke.'

The train lurched to a stop in the tunnel. For a second, it seemed like everything was silent, then all hell broke loose. Everyone was on their feet, screaming, as smoke started billowing into the carriage…

He tossed the book on the table. 'A load of rubbish, Sam,' he said. 'I hate these melodramatic things. I don't know why you're showing me it, again.' He went towards the window, his mind on something else. 'Fancy getting some fresh air?' he said.

'Yeah – soon,' I said. I'd need to keep an eye on him for a few days to make sure, but the early signs were promising.

'I'm going back to Linden Manor,' Miranda announced. 'I've decided.'

Another tremor of loss. Even though I found her erratic behaviour so unmanageable, I'd started to warm to the idea of getting to know her all over again.

'You're doing the right thing,' I said, trying to be adult and sensible, when all I wanted was to beg her to stay for a while.

Once she'd packed up her stuff, I pressed the envelope I'd left by the door into her hand. 'I'll see you soon,' I said. I meant it.

Danny came over shortly afterwards for Con. He'd agreed to spend time with him, just in case things hadn't gone as smoothly as we'd all hoped.

Once they left, I was at a total loose end. My flat was too quiet and I was on high alert thinking there was something I should be doing. Somewhere I ought to be. Not having work or any plans meant too much time to think about Leo. With every moment that passed the hollow ache claimed another part of me. I had so much to process emotionally about him, about Con and the suicides – with dismay, confusion and grief all wrapped up, fighting for air.

I couldn't help feeling concerned for Leo's daughters too, left as orphans in such a short space of time. Not least, I was scared that my own disturbing visions were still around the next corner, ready to pounce now my guard was down.

Con came back late to spend the night. He thought his luck was in as we got ready for bed but, for me, having him there was more about making sure the memory reversal hadn't left him with any nasty side effects.

As I climbed into bed beside him, I told him I felt sick – it was true – but I didn't tell him why. He sighed and huffed in response.

Even with his protective presence beside me, I was too frightened to close my eyes. I needed to sleep, but the darkness that kept slipping its arms around me was neither warm nor inviting. It kept trying to snatch me away to dingy festering places. I tried to soothe myself with pictures of Leo's face, his words reassuring me, but all I could find was an image of his twisted fallen body.

I'd never felt so alone.

I woke at around 9am with my cheek sticking to a newspaper and a crick in my neck. I must have got up in the night and fallen asleep in the kitchen, never making it back to bed.

A croaky rendition of *Come Fly With Me* was coming from the bathroom. Con bounced in with wet hair, boisterous and raring to go.

'I've already been out for a run,' he said, 'unlike some lazy tykes!' He squeezed me hard and kissed my forehead.

The old Con was back all right. I asked him if he'd slept well and he said 'never better' as if things hadn't ever been different.

The phone rang before I could check how much newsprint was smeared over my face.

'I thought you would have rung by now.' It was my mother.

'I'm sorry, Mum, I've been a bit—'

'I'm fine. Nice of you to ask.'

'I'm sorry, I—'

She ploughed on as if I hadn't spoken.

'I'll be scarred for life,' she said. 'Anyway. Look, the reason I'm ringing is to tell you that as far as anyone is concerned and I mean *anyone* – that includes Aunty Lorna and Uncle Jim – I was attacked by a dog, you understand. A savage dog. We're keeping *that girl* out of it. Okay?'

I squeezed the word out. 'Fine.'

I wanted to ask why Miranda had gone for her like that – there had to be a reason, but I knew I'd get nothing out of her.

'Anyway, I just wanted to make that clear. Oh, and your father wants to talk to you, too. I've got to go. We've got a WI meeting tonight and I'm needed.'

With that, I was abruptly passed on.

'Hi, sweetheart,' he said. I heard their front door shut in the background.

'How's Mum's face? How is she doing?'

'Oh, she'd all right. Still absolutely fuming. She's too humiliated to admit it was Miranda, so I've got to go along with this "mad dog" story.' He tutted. 'That's all she seems to care about.'

'What happened? What made Miranda react like that?'

'Honestly…I don't know. Moira said something to her in the hall, I know what – then the next thing, Miranda flew at her. Moira won't talk about it. In fact, she's removed the few family photographs we still had left around the house and put them in the loft. There are just pictures of the three of us, now. There's no sign that Miranda is part of our family at all, anymore.'

'That's awful! Why didn't you stop her?'

He sighed heavily. 'I've got to live with your mother, Sam.'

He had a point.

'It's not easy,' he went on. 'She doesn't know I've been in close contact with your sister all the time she's been in care.'

I'd often wondered about the quality of my parents' marriage; my mother so self-obsessed and demanding, my father always in the shadows and in her eyes 'weak and ineffectual'.

'Moira's got a holiday booked with Lorna in a couple of days' time. I'll be glad of the break, to be honest.'

I was tempted to say he was better off without her for good, but caught myself just in time.

'Moira's been in such a foul mood and *I* can't seem to do anything right, either…'

I gave him the chance to let off steam and took the opportunity to join in. We both railed against my mother, homing in on the appalling way she'd always treated Miranda. It was good to give vent to the tornado raging inside me that was really about Leo's death.

'I'm not blameless,' Dad insisted. 'I allowed Moira to get away with treating Miranda so callously all these years.'

'We *both* stood by,' I said, acutely aware that I'd let Mum poison my mind to her, when I should have known better.

'Right now, I'm more concerned about Miranda than anyone else,' he said. 'The care home said she ran off again, but she went back of her own accord.' Another weary sigh. 'I'm going over to see her today. She said she's hoping you'll visit her, too…'

'I will…very soon,' I said.

'She feels terrible about what happened between you. She said she'd give anything to have her little sister back.'

I bit my lip. I couldn't speak.

'Sam?'

'Sorry Dad. I've had a tough week.'

'That boyfriend of yours okay?'

'Yes. Much better, I think.' Con had given me no cause for concern whatsoever in the past twenty-four hours.

'Ah, well, that's all right, then.'

Dad didn't know about my suspension, Leo's death or my own precarious sanity. I told him I had to go. I couldn't face explanations.

Con went back to his flat that afternoon. He wanted to see the Saturday matinee at the theatre and he took me at my word when I said I needed to be alone.

I left it as late as I could before going to bed that night. I was beyond tired, by then – dizzy, disoriented, wiped out. I took twice the stipulated dose of sleeping tablets, praying for a tiny piece of oblivion.

Even so, shortly after I hit the pillow the demons claimed me again. For no apparent reason, I was forced into my fiercest nocturnal battle yet. I awoke with all my bedding on the floor, my pyjamas soaking in sweat, my heart clanging inside my ribcage. I felt like I'd been dragged across the Sahara without water, made to stumble over rocks on a barren moon and dropped back amongst hostile outcasts in pitch darkness.

Then, still in my dreams, blinding lights came on and I had to witness brutal events that seemed to be caused entirely by me, and me alone. I saw Jake, falling like a broken branch from the bridge; watched as his face was crushed under the front wheel of the number forty-six bus. I saw Jane, her legs caught in reeds sucking her down in the fast-flowing river; heard her lungs fill with water. Then there was Terry inside an industrial waste bin, his open eyes pressed against the carcass of a rotting fish, a family of rats taking chunks out of his ankle. I saw the needle sticking out of his arm like a giant insect.

When I woke, it didn't stop. I felt to blame for Leo's death too. For dragging him into the situation that ultimately killed him. For causing his daughters, having already lost their mother, to be without both parents. I felt like every terrible thing that had happened was my fault.

I went to the bathroom and poured cold water into the sink, letting more and more gush in until it was filled to the top. I stared at it and gripped both taps, seized by the thought that there could still be other affected people out there. I knew of only four – but there could easily be more.

For a split second, I hated the world and all the evil and brutality within it. It wasn't a place I wanted to belong to any more.

Without taking a breath, I pressed my face under the surface of the water. Bubbles gurgled by my ears. I stayed under, my nostrils burning, my cheeks ready to burst.

Don't do this.

Was that Leo's voice, calling to me from some faraway place?

I came up for air, hungrily sucking it in, my shoulders heaving. I buried my face in the towel. I wasn't ready to give up. I had an appointment with my therapist in three hours' time. All I had to do was hang on until then.

When the time eventually came, I spent the entire session in tears. I told Dina everything.

'You've been through hell and back,' she said, when my tragic story finally drew to a close. 'I'd say you're suffering from extreme stress – nothing more sinister than that.'

I wanted to hug her. Leo was the only one until now who'd offered me this level of empathy at any point during this entire ordeal – and he'd gone. Only now did I see how much I was still struggling to cope with.

'You need a break, take some time to catch up with old friends,' she said, as the session ended. 'Be with people you trust.'

I felt uplifted when I left and decided to catch a train to East Grinstead to surprise Miranda. On the way, I rang Hannah and invited her out to dinner.

'My shout,' I insisted. We fixed a date.

Then I called Stephanie, an old friend from school, to invite her for a drink and catch-up in the luxury Oxo Tower Restaurant next weekend. I even stopped at a newsagent's on the station and bought thank-you cards for Imogen and Dina, scribbled in them hastily and dropped them in the post box.

I was almost starting to feel myself again.

Chapter 38

My phone rang as I stepped into a taxi at East Grinstead station. Linden Manor was ten minutes away, the driver said, so I took the call.

'I found more of Dad's psychology notes.' Felicity's voice sounded brittle. 'I thought you should know.'

I took a deep breath. I thought I'd already got everything Leo had been working on.

'I haven't read them in detail,' she continued, 'but there's another file. Looks like the same kind of material as the notes you took – stuff about memory research – only old stuff. It doesn't mean anything to me.'

Anything linked to the false memory research was gold dust. If nothing else, it might point to who was responsible.

'Can I take a look at them?'

A hiccup of silence. 'There's just one thing. Dad put a note in big letters at the front: "Confidential – these notes must be destroyed without being read" – I'm not sure if I should be handing them over to anyone.'

I couldn't afford to let this slip through my fingers. 'The notes could be very important,' I stressed.

'I know.' Her voice dropped in volume. 'I don't want to shred them and then find out they were part of some ground-breaking research.'

The wheels crackled on the gravel as the taxi driver took me through the imposing gates of the Manor and up the long sweeping drive.

'How about I take a quick look at them to help you decide?' I suggested.

'Maybe that's the best thing. You'll be able to make sense of them.'

We arranged to meet in Hyde Park, a couple of days later.

Linden Manor was regal and impressive from the front; the kind of place the National Trust would salivate over. Georgian, with a Palladian entrance, it boasted a frieze of Greek figures running under the edge of the roof. The facade was dominated by rows of sash windows, but when I looked closely, I noticed every one of them had bars on the inside.

I climbed the broad stone steps and walked inside, welcomed by the pungent smell of lilies. A nurse asked for identification and signed me in, before leading me through a series of corridors to a large room. Net curtains billowed in the breeze from the open windows, like sails on a ship.

Miranda was in the far corner, adding touches to an oil painting. There was no one else there and she hadn't seen me. I stood inside the door and watched her. She took a few steps back from the canvas, bent her knees and darted around getting different viewpoints of the picture. I realised there was so much about my sister I didn't know. I didn't recognise her movements for a start; the way she dabbed the palette knife onto the canvas, tipped her head to one side, tapped her middle finger on her lip in contemplation.

For around twelve years she'd been a ghost – a whited-out figure in my life. Even before that, I hadn't wanted to know her. Miranda had been a disruptive child – that was never in question – but I hadn't persisted in asking why. When she'd been diagnosed with schizophrenia, Mum had said it explained everything, but I should have followed up my doubts. I should never have let my mother make up my mind for me. I was convinced now, more than ever, that the story she had force-fed me for years contained strategic omissions.

Miranda turned and saw me. Her unbridled delight made we want to cry before we'd even exchanged a word. I gave her an enveloping hug and asked how she was doing.

'I'm good. Your letter helped. I'm getting an early assessment from the psychiatrist, but they're already letting me use this room again.'

I took a step towards the painting.

'It's not finished,' she said. As if that would make any difference. It was chaotic, savage, smudged in orange, red and purple. I didn't pretend to know what it was or what it meant.

'Do you have a title for it?' I wanted to sound interested.

'Degradation,' she said softly.

I couldn't tell whether she wanted me to ask more. She looked at it again, rubbed the knife on an oily rag and left it on the table. 'Let's go for coffee.' she said. 'We can sit in the grounds. You haven't been here before, have you?'

'No.' My voice was sodden with shame. In the two years since she'd moved there, I'd not visited once.

We went into a large library and she poured from a stainless steel coffee pot on a table in the corner. The cups jiggled in their saucers as we carried them outside. We strolled down stone steps to a gravel walkway and continued down to the next level; a large expanse of freshly mown lawn, with cows dotted across the rolling fields in the distance.

A woman in her pyjamas was standing holding one arm up in the air, next to a bird bath. From time to time she stamped her foot and let rip with an expletive at the top of her voice, 'Bastard… gobshite…arsehole…'

The edges of my heart curled up at the thought of Miranda living in a place like this.

A nurse bustled over. 'Come on, Nancy, how about we have another go at hunt the thimble?'

We carried on across the grass.

'There used to be a lake here,' Miranda said, 'but it was too dangerous in a place like this. Now there's just a fountain,' she pointed to a walled garden on the far side, 'but people still try to drown themselves.'

There was an unoccupied bench beside a sprawling cedar of Lebanon, so we sat and sipped, not speaking for a while.

There was no sound except for a pair of squabbling blackbirds and a distant tractor.

'Thank you for coming,' she said eventually. Miranda seemed to be back to her adult self; the 'little girl' tucked away for the time being.

'I really wanted to.'

For a moment, I thought of Leo. There was no way now that he could ever make things right with his family, but I could still do something about mine.

She cupped her hand over mine. It felt cold. 'How are you feeling after the doctor died?' she asked.

'I'm going to miss him – terribly. It's such a dreadful waste. He had such a sharp mind – and more than a few sensible things to say about you, as it happens.'

'About me? Like what?'

'That I should ask questions I ought to have asked a long time ago.'

Her eyes flickered over my face before she dropped her head. 'He's right. But I want to ask *you* a question first.' She finished her coffee, tucked the cup and saucer under the bench and turned to me. 'What's the worst thing you remember about Mum…when you were little?'

'The worst thing?' It was a strange question. I puffed out my cheeks. 'I don't know. Putting relentless pressure on me to get good grades? Being hard and angry when I didn't? Being harsh and intolerant about…everything?'

'I asked you that question when you were ten years old and when you answered in the same kind of way, I knew.'

'Knew what? Miranda, what are you saying?'

She looked into the distance. 'That I was the only one.'

I felt a violent juddering in my abdomen.

Miranda spat the words out. 'It was our nasty little secret. I hated her. I hated you for escaping it. I hated myself for being chosen, for being too weak to stop it.'

I couldn't move. I felt like I was standing on the hard shoulder of a busy motorway with a truck heading straight for me, blaring its horn.

My mother?

I tried to keep my voice smooth. 'Are you saying she..?'

She nodded. 'I've been trying to tell you,' she continued. 'For a long time.'

A tiny sound escaped my lips. I must have looked lost because Miranda put her arm around me as though I was the injured party. I squashed my face into her neck, tried to hide in her chiffon scarf.

'I was seven when it started. She told me it was the best way to control a "wayward child".'

Without warning, the memory I'd had recently flooded into my mind, in 3D this time. The one with Miranda coming out of Mum and Dad's bedroom in her nightdress, trailing a towel behind her. The memory I'd always felt strange about.

Then I remembered Leo's words: *Have you ever considered that Miranda might be broken inside?*

My stomach jerked with a sharp convulsion and I threw my head forward. I gagged, but nothing came up. Miranda rubbed my back and I tried to swallow gulps of air.

'My God,' I whispered.

'She locked us in the bathroom together – and sometimes when everyone was out, we'd be in her bedroom. She…made me do things…' She tried to sound matter of fact. 'That's why I paint,' she went on. 'Memories too painful to remember are locked away inside – it's the only way I can let them out safely.'

She paints, doesn't she? That's what Leo had said. *Maybe the answer's there.*

My mother had sexually abused my older sister.

I was trying to let Miranda's revelation soak into my mind, but my thoughts were misfiring in all directions. No wonder Miranda had gone off the rails. No wonder she'd had tantrums and manic outbursts – always worse in the school holidays. Her behaviour was the only tool she'd had at her disposal. She was trying to fight back and none of us saw it.

Your mother's arms should be the safest place on earth.

I tugged her wrists. 'I knew something was badly wrong. In these past few weeks, I knew you were trying to tell me something. I'm so sorry.'

She wriggled free and scooped a strand of hair away from my eye. 'You can't mind-read, Sam – I just couldn't say the words.'

'Why didn't anyone see? Why did no one pick it up?'

'When I was about thirteen, I told a child psychologist. It got passed on to Dr Millais, you know, our family doctor, but nothing ever happened. No one believed me.' Her eyes were locked wide, innocent, fixed on mine. '*You* do though…don't you?'

My voice broke. 'Of course, I do! I'm, I'm…devastated. I don't know what to say. How could she?'

'You're the only person I've told since then,' she said. 'That's quite nice, after all this time, don't you think?'

I was deeply shocked, crushed and humbled all in one.

'I've never had sex with anyone,' she went on in a neutral tone. I saw her hands twitch and she sat on them. 'I've never been able to…do it…properly. She's made me into a freak.'

I sat squeezing her arm, blinking frantically.

'Dad never knew?'

'He's blind as a bat.'

All at once, the territory of my life didn't look the same any more. The idyllic scene in front of me – the cows grazing passively, the breeze caressing the leaves – became surreal. It was out of focus, distorted around the edges with a jagged black smudge down the middle: my doe-eyed, devious mother. That abominable, callous woman.

Miranda had spent her life being persecuted. She'd been living with a knife in her back the whole time and none of us had seen it. I should have asked more questions, seen the signs, paid more attention to that little voice inside me that told me her illness was more than a random pathology.

I looked over at her. She was calm, taking it all in her stride, perhaps even a little apologetic for upsetting me. I stood and swept her up in my arms, held her tight and sobbed into her collar.

'I'm so sorry, I'm so sorry,' I babbled, over and over.

She guided me back down on to the bench and rocked me, soothed me, pressed a tissue tenderly under my eyes. 'Bet you didn't expect this when you set out,' she said.

I laughed. Too loudly.

'What do you want to do about it?' I asked.

She shrugged. 'What I've always done. Get on with it. Avoid her.'

'How can I help?'

'Just be there – understand.' She met my eyes. 'Believe me.'

'I *do* believe you. Thank you for telling me.'

I pressed my open hand against hers, palm to palm and noticed the differences in size and shape – like children do. Like sisters do.

'I'm sorry it's taken me so long,' she said.

'Don't apologise. For what it's worth, I think owning up is a sign of your recovery. Attacking Mum was part of moving forward, too, although I know most people won't see it that way.'

I could understand exactly why Miranda saw taking a chunk out of my mother's cheek as finally asserting herself, finally saying 'no' after all this time. Defending herself in a way that her child-self never could.

'She said something to you, didn't she…at the house, before you attacked her?'

She nodded and looked away. I let the silence run its course between us. She picked up a leaf and twirled the stem. 'I moved in with Con to get back at you, you know,' she said. 'I was still blaming you for being the one she never touched and I was also angry that you had something special that I didn't.'

'Ah, is that why?'

She must have spent most of her life being secretly furious with me, wanting to punish me at every turn – hence the broken toys, the hostility, the withdrawal when she went into care. It explained a lot.

She grimaced. 'Are you cross with me?'

'No,' I replied honestly. 'I can understand why you would want to hurt me…'

'It's going to rain,' she said, looking out towards the horizon where murky clouds were gathering in numbers, ready to close in on us.

I wanted to turn the conversation back to her.

'Do you have good professional people to talk to here?' I asked.

She shrugged.

'Will you tell them what you've just told me? Explore your feelings about it, until I can see you again?'

A hardened glaze skimmed over her eyes. 'I'll think about it.'

'It might even help your cause for getting out of here, if you take your recovery into your own hands.'

'I suppose so.'

Another silence. I knew there was more to come.

A buzzing insect tried to settle on her face and she batted it away with the back of her hand. 'It wasn't just Mum turning up, out of the blue, that freaked me out. You were right,' she went on, meeting my eyes. 'She said something.'

I held my breath.

'She stroked my face and said: "Mamma make it all better, Mims?" Just like she used to…when…before she…'

She cried then for the first time; tiny little chokes. 'I wasn't going to take it any more,' she spluttered. 'She'd tormented me for long enough.'

I sat with her, holding her until the tears subsided. We both took deep breaths and looked out across the horizon. Cows nuzzled the grass, a thrush made off with a worm. Life out there seemed so ordinary.

She put her arm around me and we sat a while longer, talking in a way I realised was entirely new, before walking back arm in arm through the French windows. She went back to her painting with her head held high.

I left feeling like I'd finally found her.

Chapter 39

The phone was ringing. I got out of bed and stared at the handset, contemplating what fresh piece of information I was about to hear that would throw my life upside down once more. Just before the answerphone took over, I grabbed the receiver.

'It's Debbie,' came the voice. 'From St Luke's.'

I was tentative in my response, fearful that the police investigation might have taken a turn for the worse.

'It's the shortest suspension I've ever heard of,' she said.

'Sorry?'

'You're back. If you want to be – that is. Someone very high up must have put in a good word for you,' she said. 'Normally this kind of thing drags on for months.'

I did a little skip across the room. 'When?'

'Today if you like. I can book you patients from noon if you're ready?'

'Yes please. I'll be there.'

I pulled on a black pencil skirt, an ivory silk shirt and my best Karen Millen jacket, ate some underdone toast and grabbed my briefcase. I was so ecstatic, anyone watching might think I'd just won a cruise around the Caribbean.

I was going back to what I did best.

Debbie was leaning over the photocopier in her office, when I found her, poking the end of a paper clip into a slot at the side.

'That's not going to do it any good,' I whispered, creeping up behind her.

She gasped and shot round.

'Hey, you,' she said, blowing up her fringe with her breath. 'Glad to have you back.'

She snapped open the front of the machine and started randomly pressing buttons.

I elbowed her out of the way. 'Woah – this has got to last us another twenty-five years,' I said. 'Looks like the paper's got stuck.' I leaned across and teased out the rogue sheet, then fanned through the remaining pile in the tray and clipped it back in. I pressed the green button and the next page came through sharp and clean.

'I hate people like you,' she huffed, offering me a custard cream.

I left her and spent the morning checking my emails; mostly reminders about training days and new NHS proposals, and catching up on paperwork. It didn't take long, however, for the exhilaration of my reinstatement to slip behind a cloud. Even though I'd known Leo for such a short time, the hospital felt a different place without him; hollow and soulless.

On the way back from the canteen after lunch, I wondered how Lian was coping. I had a few minutes spare before my first appointment, so I took a diversion to the Burns and Plastic Surgery Unit to find her. There was a new name on the board for that day's surgery: Dr Frank Benson. It said *locum* in brackets after his name. I tapped on Lian's door.

'Come in.'

Another woman was standing behind the desk – she had thin colourless hair, loose skin under her chin, and wore flat lace-up shoes.

'Oh, sorry, I was looking for Lian Moore,' I said. 'Is she here today?'

'I'm afraid not. I'm her replacement, Maureen Shipman.' Her greeting was charmless. 'You are?'

She strode towards me holding out her hand, formality in every step. She wouldn't have looked out of place in a girl's public school brandishing a whistle, overseeing a hockey match. Her grip was firm and manly.

I explained who I was and backed out of the door with apologies for disturbing her.

I popped in to see Debbie again on my way back. 'I've just been down to Lian's office,' I told her. 'There's some battleaxe in her place saying Lian's gone. Is she on holiday or something?'

'No. She's left for good. Gone to Bradford, I think. She was so loyal to Dr Hansson, I'm not sure she wanted to stick around after what happened.'

It didn't surprise me. I'd seen the glint in her eye and the swish of her skirt every time Leo was within flirting distance.

'They offered her a transfer to Professor Schneider's office, but she said no.'

That didn't surprise me either. Bradford or Professor Schneider. No contest.

'Anyway, the professor might not be here much longer, either.' It was a throwaway line and she quickly clapped her hand over her mouth. 'Oh, heck – you won't say anything, will you?'

I shook my head. 'Where's he going?'

Her voice dropped to an almost inaudible whisper. 'He's got a brain tumour. That's the reason for his sudden absences. Apparently, he's been frantically trying to find his own treatment for it. His wife is divorcing him but she doesn't actually know how ill he is. I only found out because I overheard him on the phone to his solicitor. You mustn't say anything. Promise?'

I crossed my heart. It explained a lot. Not only his disappearances, but his distractedness and changeable moods. *And* the EEG machine in his office.

She patted my arm. 'Listen – it looks like your suspension was re-evaluated and the board decided it was premature. I gather that as long as the police don't find anything untoward, you're in the clear.' She reached over to her desk and handed me an envelope. 'Here's your confirmation from the Central Board of Medicine – I wanted to give it to you in person.' I slipped it under my arm. 'I wish I had friends like yours,' she added with a smile.

'By the way, I meant to give you a copy of this ages ago.' She put a glossy brochure on the desk in front of me. It had a photo of Leo on the front.

'I know it's terribly sad now, but Dr Hansson won the *Remmington Award* this year for contributions to surgical science. He took a keen interest in psychology too, apparently. There's a feature about him in here. Thought you might be interested.'

'Sure. Thank you,' I muttered, suddenly choked at the sight of Leo's lined, craggy face. 'I'll give it a read, later.' I said, tucking it under my arm. I took another custard cream and went back to my office.

My first patient was Aaqil, the Asian man stabbed after a family funeral. He was alive! I was so glad to see him. He was still in a fragile state, but keen to start sessions.

'They offered me someone else, but I wanted to see you,' he said.

I could have thrown my arms around him. At the end of the consultation he looked a different person; his chest was broader, plumped up with optimism. 'I knew this was going to help,' he said. 'Thank you.'

It was great to be behind the wheel again, as it were. Though my brain and body were aching for a holiday, I knew I was back where I truly belonged. By the time my final patient left the room that day, I was getting into my stride.

When the doorbell rang before breakfast the next morning I thought it must be Con. I'd been avoiding him; working towards telling him we needed to sit down and have a serious talk, but I couldn't face it yet.

I stood still behind the sitting room door and thought about not answering, but Mahler was playing on the radio and I knew it would be audible from the landing. In any case, knowing Con, he'd keep his finger on the bell until I let him in.

I gave in and opened the door to the last person I expected to see.

'Don't just stand there with your mouth open,' she said, a headscarf hanging loosely over her face. 'The least you can do is invite me in.'

I stood back without acknowledging her and watched her drag an ominous overnight bag onto the rug in the hall.

'I've had a hellish journey…and these stairs are so steep…I thought you could have come down for my bag, but the buzzer isn't working.'

Already everything was someone else's fault.

'Is this all there is to it?' continued my mother, walking into every room uninvited. 'A one-bedroomed flat. Bit on the poky side.'

'It suits me perfectly.' I blocked her path. 'Dad said you had a holiday with Lorna booked. What happened?'

She dropped her head. 'Yes, well – that didn't quite work out. After the shock of…*this*,' she cautiously touched her cheek, 'and being rushed to hospital, I must have got the dates mixed up. '

'So why are you here and not at home?' Something serious must have happened for her to end up at my flat.

'Why the hostility? Aren't you just a bit pleased to see your dear mother?'

'Listen - I've got to get to work.' I said. No way was I playing happy families now. I stood with my hands on my hips. 'What's going on?'

'Well…when I told your father I wasn't going away after all, we had…a bit of a row. He had the audacity to say he was looking forward to a week without me. He even had a go at me about that sister of yours…'

I twisted my mouth, hiding the smile. *Good on you, Dad.*

She sighed. 'Tea would be nice…'

I boiled a kettle, poured her a cup and left it on the ledge in the hall. Then I walked past her and finished emptying the washing machine. She took the tea into the sitting room and began flicking through my books. I folded the last towel and stood in the doorway, watching her.

She shook her head. 'Little bit tacky, darling, a bookshelf made with bricks.' She pulled out a thick volume and browsed the opening pages. 'This library book is overdue,' she said, handing it to me.

The light from the window fell across her face and I noticed the scar on her cheek. It was the same shade as her lipstick with intervals of white stretched skin between the stitches, making it look like my sister's teeth were still embedded in it.

'I went to see Miranda,' I said.

'Is she still insisting on using that ridiculous name?'

'Mum!' I protested.

'We all know Mimi's got serious problems – just look at *me*. I'm disfigured for life.' She fiddled with the scarf, trying to get it to cover the wound. 'And by my own daughter no less. Such a wicked child. Hard to believe we're the same flesh and blood.'

'You've got a nerve,' I snapped.

'Why are you on your high horse?'

'She told me,' I said, pinning my eyes on hers.

'Told you what? What nonsense is it now?'

My tongue wouldn't form the words properly. 'You…t-took advantage…' I stuttered. 'You forced her into…' I stopped and started again. 'You *molested* her. That's what you did.'

She clicked her tongue as if I'd accused her of squeezing the toothpaste tube in the middle. 'Not all that business again.' She sounded bored. 'Don't tell me you're tempted to believe her?' She threw her eyes up and plumped herself down onto the sofa.

I was caught unawares. My mother's dismissal came across as entirely uncontrived. I didn't know what to think. Was she one step ahead of the game? Was she so clever that she'd pre-empted this accusation, knowing it would come, one day?

'I might not have been the perfect parent,' she conceded. 'I've never been all that maternal, but I took good care of both of you. I loved you, nurtured you, encouraged you.' Her words were underpinned by an earnest tremor. 'I've got my faults. Maybe I pushed the two of you too hard at times, but I knew you were bright, capable. I wanted the very best for you. But I never laid an inappropriate finger on either of you. I can't imagine the kind of mother who could do such a thing.'

'You never touched her?'

She bolted upright. 'Not like *that.* What do you take me for? You didn't see the half it, Sam. She hated me from the day she came into this world. She did nasty, despicable things you never knew about...'

'Like what?' I was still standing with my arms folded.

'You really want to know?' She patted the sofa beside her.

I stayed where I was. 'I want the truth. That's all I've ever wanted.'

She sat back. 'Mimi, sadly, is unhinged. Always has been. When she was old enough, she used to collect rabbit droppings and put them in my face cream. She tore holes in my dresses, stole money from my purse. I caught her once, spitting in my coffee. She was a very sick little girl. She claimed I was touching her back then, she even told our GP.'

I was flummoxed. This wasn't what I was expecting. I felt like I was slowly sinking. I needed to get a more reliable person's side of the story.

'If that's true, you won't mind me calling Dad.'

She waved her hand, unconcerned. 'Go ahead – but don't tell him I'm here. He thinks I've gone to Guernsey on my own.'

I picked up the phone and punched in his number, watching her for signs she might be backtracking. She went back to looking at my books, unperturbed.

He answered with a weary sigh. I took a deep breath.

'Hi, Dad, it's just a quick call. This is going to sound left-field,' I said, 'but I wanted to ask you something...about Miranda.'

'Of course, what is it?'

I had to dive straight in. 'When she was younger did she ever make an accusation...of abuse of any kind?'

He was quiet and I could tell it didn't come as a shock. The silence was a considered one, where he was trying to find the right words.

'I'm afraid it did come to that at one point,' he said. 'She was seeing a child psychologist who put silly ideas into her head. Miranda was thirteen, I think. Claimed she could remember being abused at home.' He carried on in his matter-of-fact tone. 'The therapist told Dr Millais and she took it seriously, of course. We all had to go to various meetings and Miranda had to have a physical examination. It wasn't pleasant. It was your mother she accused. As you can imagine, it all came to nothing. Just another of Miranda's attempts to shock everyone.'

Unease coiled up my spine. I shifted from one foot to the other, losing the certainty I'd had before.

My father was speaking again before I had the chance to gather my thoughts. 'I'm finally getting some peace and quiet without Moira,' he said.

I had my stare fixed on her as I spoke, raising my voice. 'She'll be in a much better mood after her break, Dad. She'll be grateful for the way you've been running around after her, I'm sure.' My mother was flicking through the *Radio Times* now, pretending not to listen.

As soon as I ended the call, I gently slipped the magazine out of her hands.

'Mum – look at me.' I got close enough so that she was forced to make eye contact.

I had to know for sure.

'What did you say to Miranda,' I said, 'the day she attacked you?'

'Nothing!' It was crisp and too fast. I kept my eyes on hers, refusing to let her end it there. She gently dabbed at her corrugated skin with her fingertips. 'I merely reached out to stroke her face and this is what I got.'

'No, you said something to her.'

'I'm telling you, I did *not* say a word.'

I knew for a fact she was lying. Dad and Miranda had both told me, independently, that she'd said something. My ears filled with a roaring sound that made real life seem a long way away.

To any outsider it might have looked like we'd reached a stalemate. Who would people believe? The word of a disturbed woman with a history of schizophrenia and attention-seeking or the assurances of her caring, doting mother who only ever wanted the best for her. Miranda had never stood a chance in any public arena in the past, and she wouldn't now.

But for me, it was clear-cut. My mother was a well-practised liar. She'd been doing it for years.

I tried one final time. 'Mum – did you abuse Miranda? Sexually abuse her as a child?'

'Absolutely not. Don't be ridiculous.'

Nothing changed on her face, not one single muscle shifted or dropped, except for the slightest flicker of an eyelid. It was barely perceptible and had I not been scrutinising her face with an experienced eye, I would have missed it. But I'd seen it before. Just once or twice – when my mother had felt trapped or had something to hide. It told me, loud and clear, everything I needed to know.

Leo had been right. Miranda was telling the truth. I knew it in my bones. She'd told me her secret, not in a fit of spite or to shock me, but as part of our deepening relationship. It was a sign of her recovery. I knew enough about psychology to recognise that much. Besides, I had another way of finding out for sure – I'd go after work. I should have done it earlier, as soon as Leo mentioned it.

'I've got patients,' I said. 'I need to get to the hospital.'

I picked up my briefcase and was pulling on my jacket, when I realised my mother was speaking. She'd followed me into the hall. '…if that would be all right?'

'What?' I snapped.

She casually brushed bits of fluff from her skirt on to the floor. 'Just for a couple of nights.'

My eyes snapped wide. 'Stay here?'

She sniffed. 'I wouldn't ask – only your father seems to have forgotten to transfer the usual amount into my account this month…I don't have a penny.'

He really was punishing her.

'You know what I think?' I said, snarling at her. 'I think you blighted Miranda's life. You resorted to…*that*…because she wasn't the child you'd hoped for. Perhaps if you'd owned up to it, things may have been different…but I can't have a relationship with you, not like this.'

No way was I having this woman in my home any longer than I had to. I grabbed her arm and pulled her towards the door. 'You're throwing me out? After all I've done for you?'

'This isn't about me – it's about Miranda.'

A look of outrage took hold of her face. 'So – what if I admitted to…those things your sister said…would that make any difference?'

'You can't have it both ways, Mum. You either come clean or you don't.'

I squashed her handbag against her stomach and opened the front door, easing her overnight bag over the threshold with my foot.

'You don't understand what a nightmare she was – that girl – I had to control her. I was at the end of my tether—'

She dragged her feet towards the top of the stairs, her head bowed, like a bag lady. I felt not one ounce of pity for her as I slammed the door.

I counted to fifty and left.

Chapter 40

Camden felt like it was just coming alive when I got there, after work. I wove through a mix of office workers and hippie types half my age holding pints of beer in plastic glasses. Passing vintage clothes stalls, jewellery stands and paperbacks spilling out of boxes onto the cobbles, I arrived at the lock area. A rich aroma of Moroccan spices followed me as I eased through curtains of wafting silk scarves until I reached the main door.

Outside the gallery, a saxophone quartet was playing raucously and inside the foyer, a mime artist – male or female, I couldn't tell which – had a group of children transfixed. I walked straight to the main gallery, dropping a fiver into the collecting box and picking up a brochure from the desk on the way.

The majority of the paintings in the main room were Miranda's and since I'd visited last time, several more had a red spot on the title card indicating a sale. I was cross with myself for not looking properly at the pictures that first time, for not stopping to take them in from a therapeutic, analytical point of view.

I'd worked with patients using art materials before and seen how images could reveal what was impossible to put into words. Here was my tormented sister – my own flesh and blood – and I hadn't even considered using these skills with her until now. I started on the right and read every title, scrutinised every painting.

'She's been trying to tell us, all along…' I muttered to myself. It was all here. I'd been utterly blind.

I stood back, allowing the images to speak to me. Instead of vague abstract shapes, this time, identifiable forms began to emerge from the splashes and rough brushwork. I could make out disfigured breasts, a distorted womb, scar tissue and torn female genitalia, dominated by the colours of fresh and dried blood. Nothing there was male – the symbolism was all female. In conjunction with the pictures, the titles brought everything into focus: *Birthright, The Invader, Chosen, Child in the Night,* moving on in intensity until I found the most savage painting with a ripped canvas, entitled, *Mal Salope* (which I later translated into *Evil Bitch*).

I recalled Leo's words: *She paints, doesn't she? Maybe the answer's there.*

I felt like I was inside a lift where the cable has snapped, leaving me plummeting fast. *Why, oh, why hadn't I seen this earlier? Why hadn't I talked to her? Asked questions? Realised what was going on?*

I'd turned my back on my sister for years when she needed me. I'd spurned her when she was a victim of *incest* – there was no other word for it. A crime that had been hidden under the pretence of normal family life. I felt as appalled with myself as I was with my mother.

I stuffed the brochure into my pocket – the titles themselves felt like irrefutable evidence – and staggered out for some much-needed fresh air.

In the thirty minutes or so since I'd been inside, it had started to pour down. The area had cleared of people, and stallholders had brought out make-shift covers; tarpaulin and plastic sheets to cover their wares like shrouds for the dead. Suddenly, everything looked cheap and pitiful.

Someone had left a bloodhound tied up to a large barrel and he had started howling. I felt like lying down in the expanding puddle beside him and letting the rain wash over me in some kind of improvised purgation ceremony. I stood in the puddle instead, allowing the water to creep over the edge of my sandals and seep under my toes.

Could Miranda ever forgive me?

The dog looked at me guardedly and sniffed at my trousers. He didn't bark or bare his teeth, so I perched on the edge of the barrel, both of us getting drenched. Soon, the dog laid his muzzle on my leg, resignation in his big brown eyes, and stopped howling.

Time passed and eventually a man with dreadlocks down to his waist came along to claim the dog. The bloodhound was ecstatic to see him, slobbering white spume onto his cuffs. I smiled at them both – at the purity of their bond – and headed to the Tube.

The showers were over by the time I got to Hyde Park to meet Felicity. As I waited, I watched tourists avoid the skaters, who twisted and dodged around them perilously on the busy footpaths. I watched dogs chasing Frisbees, groups of children pretending to be Wayne Rooney. Everyone seemed to be joyful.

Felicity tapped me on the shoulder from behind and offered me a lemon cupcake.

'I don't fancy it now,' she said, holding the bag open for me.

I took the sticky lump, holding it awkwardly in my hand. Seeing her again seemed to highlight Leo's absence. I couldn't stomach it either.

We took a stroll around the lake and I asked how she was coping. She'd lost both parents in a matter of days.

'I don't know, yet,' she said.

We stopped by the water's edge and I broke off half the unwanted cake and handed it to her. In unspoken kinship, we crumbled it and tossed it to the birds.

She dusted off her hands. 'By the way, I found this when I was looking through my father's files.' She handed me a small sealed envelope with my name on the front.

I slipped out the single sheet:

I suggest you get the painting insured. It's an Absil. Just a little back-up for you and your sister, should you ever need it.

It must refer to the painting Leo gave me.

I held it out so she could read it. 'Have you ever heard of a painter called Absil?' I asked her.

'Hughes Absil?'

'Not sure. He painted a lonely boat drifting down the canal in Venice.'

'Oh, I *love* that picture. Yes – Dad said he'd given you something special. It's worth a fortune.'

I pictured it on my bedroom wall above the bed. 'I didn't realise,' I said.

She kicked crumbs into the water.

I turned to meet her eyes. 'You've been through such a lot,' I said. 'I might be speaking out of turn, but if you wanted to see a counsellor, I could help you find someone…'

She nipped her lips together in a pinched smile. 'I don't want therapy.'

I nodded. We stopped short as a group of geese took flight in front of us.

'Let me know if you change your mind. I can recommend good people.'

She dropped her head. 'Thanks, but I don't think so. I don't like the idea of paying someone to try to understand me.'

I gave her a wry smile and we walked for a while, in silence.

'Can I ask you a question?' I said. She nodded. 'Your father called himself *Dr* Hansson at the hospital, but he's a surgeon. I mean, aren't most surgeons called *Mister*?'

'Good question. Dad always preferred a title. I think it made him feel more important in the eyes of the public. Sometimes people think that because you're 'Mr' Smith or whatever, you're not properly qualified. That was Dad's pride.' She laughed. 'Oh – and alongside all his surgical training, he had a PhD in psychology. But, no doubt, you knew that.'

I couldn't help but smile. A PhD? Leo had managed to keep that particular achievement from me.

'I'd better go,' she said. She pulled a bulky plastic carrier bag from her rucksack. 'Here are the files. I hope they mean something.'

She made a brave attempt at a smile and I hugged her. 'If they're significant, let me have them back and I'll pass them on to the hospital – otherwise, shred the lot, like Dad said.'

Part of me wanted to offer to keep in touch, but I had the feeling it would be too painful for both of us.

As soon as I got back, I tipped the contents of the carrier bag onto the kitchen table, then rang for a pizza. I needed something to take my mind off Miranda's revelation and wading through Leo's notes might do the trick.

I glanced at my lava lamp and remembered Miranda's childlike delight with it. I brushed against the apron on the back of the kitchen door. She'd been the last one to wear it. I felt a lump in the pocket and pulled out a lip-gloss she'd left behind. I unscrewed the top and took in the smell of it. It was like bubble gum and made me smile. She was everywhere. Everything I did, every movement I made, she was there with me. And so was the abuse. It was heartbreaking.

I turned to the pile of papers. Just as Felicity had said, written in large letters across the front were the words: *Confidential – these notes must be DESTROYED without being read* in large letters. It certainly wasn't ambiguous.

I hesitated before I peeled away the covering sheet, feeling like I was breaking his trust. These notes weren't intended for me, but Felicity had agreed I was the best person to check them over and ultimately that set my mind at rest. His secrets were safe with me. I'd take a quick look, that's all. They were the last link I had to him, even though they could be a pile of meaningless scribbles.

I flicked through the loose sheets and discovered that they were interspersed with thinner pages, sheets torn from notebooks and even newspaper clippings. A sheet of cream watermarked paper caught my eye straight away. It had St Luke's Hospital NHS Trust logo at the top and underneath it, my name in capitals.

My cheeks began to tingle as I started reading. It was a glowing report of my work and career, completely exonerating me from any connection with the suicides. There were statements from people I recognised from St Luke's and my previous posts, continuing on to a second page.

Leo was the one who'd got me reinstated at St Luke's, just before he died. He must have gone to considerable effort to track down upstanding members of the medical profession who'd worked with me over the years and invite them to support me. It was addressed to the Central Board of Medicine, with a copy to the police and another to Professor Schneider. No wonder I'd been invited back to work so quickly.

Tears blurred my vision turning Leo's flamboyant signature at the bottom into a grey wobbly blob. I pressed the letter to my chest and silently thanked him for it. I wiped my eyes with my sleeve and went back to the notes.

A past I had no inkling about started to open up before me. The notes went back decades. Leo had spent his early years in Sweden. There were press clippings referring to various successes and awards given to his parents. His mother was the well-known historian, Erika Berg, and his father, Ulf Hansson, was an acclaimed biophysics professor. High achievers indeed.

As I read the next batch of pages an unsettling feeling began to crawl over me. I read the gist of it again. *No, no, this can't be right.* There were details of experiments. False memory experiments. Dozens of them, just like the one I'd found in the medical journal, only these were dated twenty-five years ago and involved different methods. They all had Leo's name on them.

Twenty-five years ago. Leo had been working on this stuff. He had received awards in Sweden for mind-control, for persuading volunteers to believe certain things. For creating *false memories.*

My head was spinning. I couldn't believe it.

Of course – Felicity had said her father had a PhD in psychology and Debbie had mentioned something when she gave me the magazine recently. What did she say? Something about Leo winning the *Remmington Award* last year. I tutted to myself. That was an award for *psychology,* not surgery! How had I missed it?

Two other names cropped up: Professor Frederick Kane, a neuro-psychiatrist and Dr Denise McRay, a neuro-scientist, as well as names I recognised: Dr Clara Warner and Professor Hune.

All of them had been working in the false memory field. No wonder he'd found experts to help so quickly.

Leo's research centred on the Kings Cross fire in 1987. It appeared that he had treated victims for burns at St Cuthbert's, a hospital near Farringdon, where he'd worked at the time. The records showed he'd seen a number of survivors in the hours immediately following the disaster. Then he'd given them follow-up treatment for trauma.

I had to fight my trepidation as I gripped each sheet. Could the kind, understanding Leo really have committed the recent horrors at St Luke's? I waited for the shock to burst up my spine.

Leo had used less sophisticated memory implantation techniques back then on victims of the fire, but as I continued to read, another side to it emerged. Instead of inflicting harrowing memories, he'd done the exact opposite. He had created false *positive* memories to aid the victims' recovery. He'd been genuinely helping them.

Nevertheless, a bad taste coated my tongue. *Why hadn't Leo mentioned any of this? Why hadn't he said he'd been studying false memories all those years ago?*

I pressed my hand to my chest and read on. Leo had added further handwritten notes, dated 1989, about how he'd stopped his research that year, because he believed ultimately that in spite of the benefits, what he'd been doing was unethical. He gave instructions stating that none of this work should ever be made available either to the medical authorities or the public. It made sense. If patients got to hear about his ground-breaking ideas, the sessions would be worthless. No one would trust their memories after they'd had a consultation with Leo; they'd know any new thought or belief could be fake. I turned the last page. That was it.

Leo had been messing with people's minds years ago, for certain – but he'd done it with every good intention; in order to save their sanity.

It was almost 11pm and pitch black outside. I got up to draw the curtains. I decided to call it a day and try to sleep. I'd written the names of all the specialists involved on a scrap of paper. My job for tomorrow would be to look them up and see if I could get one step nearer to finding out who was responsible for the deaths of my patients.

Con rang early the next morning. He sounded exuberant; said he was dying to get his hands on me.

'Con – I've got to get to work.' I was pulling on my skirt with my free hand, struggling to do up the zip, between sips of black coffee.

'I'll come and meet you for lunch,' he said, 'Perhaps you could pull a sicky for the afternoon…I've got *plans* for us.' His voice dropped an octave. 'We could go back to your place…and I could…'

'Con – let's meet tomorrow, instead,' I said brusquely. 'We need to talk.'

'You're making me wait until tomorrow…what about today? We can talk, if you like, but then we can touch…and kiss and…' There was a time when I would have melted at his words, but not now.

'Tomorrow,' I insisted. How could he misinterpret the chill in my voice? It was well below zero. I couldn't keep on stringing him along.

That evening, I focused on the mystery mind-twister. I'd Googled the four names I'd found in Leo's notes, but it hadn't got me anywhere. No one in their right mind was going to list 'implanting traumatic false memories' as a skill on their CV. They were all based in universities abroad with no direct way of getting in touch.

I called Imogen. She didn't know the names, but suggested I contact a colleague she knew in New York, Dr Francis Peach. I owed it to Jane, Jake and Terry to give it one last go, so as soon as we ended the call I punched out an email to him and pressed send.

I propped my elbow on the table and sank my chin into my hand. No new patients had come to me with the distorted story about the fire, but it didn't mean there weren't any. A maniac was still at large, possibly still preying on patients at St Luke's, but the trail had gone cold.

I rearranged my appointments the following afternoon and made my way over to Ham House near Richmond. I didn't want Con to come to the flat, so I'd suggested somewhere neutral; there was less chance of a scene that way.

He looked grumpy as he walked towards me.

'I didn't know I'd have to pay to get in,' he said. 'I told them I was in a costume drama they filmed here,' he added, as though that ought to have granted him free entry.

His strop was short-lived. 'Hey – before you say anything, I've got some fantastic news.' He grabbed both my hands and blew a loud kiss into them. 'I've got a call-back for another movie – it's due straight after we finish *Machine on Mars*.'

'That's great news,' I said, trying to stir up some enthusiasm. My mind was on one thing only: saying what I had to say – and leaving. Unfortunately, Con was now brimming with excitement and I wasn't going to escape that easily.

'It's not my usual choice,' he said. 'A disaster movie, believe it or not? I wasn't interested at first, but Danny persuaded me to do the audition. When I read the script, something clicked. I could really step into the part. It's all panic and hysteria. Not me at all.'

I couldn't help but smile. Con hadn't mentioned the flashbacks or any suicidal thoughts since the reversal process. It looked like the horror had been completely wiped out of his memory bank.

'Sometimes we don't know what we're capable of,' I said.

He explained more about the film, how, if he got the part, he'd have to go straight on to Mexico after the filming in Arizona.

'Listen, Con. It's probably good timing that this has come along when it has. I'm really happy for you – and I think it's absolutely the right thing for us.'

'What do you mean?' he said cautiously.

'Well – I've been giving things a lot of thought. And…I think we should go our separate ways.'

He got to his feet and looked like he was going to storm off without another word. But, he spun round, brought his hands to his hips, then, as if all the outrage had seeped out of him, sank back down again.

'Yeah, whatever.' He hunched forward on the bench. 'I've been doing a fair bit of navel-gazing myself, actually,' he said. 'And I've come to the conclusion that…our relationship feels too much of a struggle.'

Okay – so now he knew the writing was on the wall, he wanted to turn it round so *he* was doing the dumping. That was fine by me.

'Right…' I said.

'A relationship is about discovering the other person,' he pointed out. 'It's a journey. Building trust and respect along the way. You don't seem to want to commit. That's why I was afraid to tell you…'

'Afraid to tell me what?'

Prickles went up my spine.

'All those times I had to rush away – it wasn't about the theatre.'

I shuffled forward on the bench. 'Go on…'

'I have a brother.'

'What?' He'd told me he had only a sister.

'Tim. He's going to jail.' He examined his trainers. 'He got himself in a real mess. Dealing hard drugs. He was on the run at first, then he was arrested. He finally pleaded guilty last week.'

I hitched closer to him. 'Con – why didn't you tell me?'

He dropped his head, his hair hiding his face. 'I don't know. It's not very glamorous, is it? I thought you'd go off me – find it too much of…an embarrassment…'

'You think I'm that superficial? Con, you really don't know me at all, do you?'

I got to my feet. I wanted to stop there. I didn't want to open up a whole new conversation about Tim.

All of a sudden, there didn't seem much more to say.

He grabbed my hand and pulled me down again.

'You *were* seeing him – that surgeon – weren't you?' Not again.

I couldn't bring myself to argue with him, so I folded my arms and said nothing. As time had gone on, I couldn't deny I'd developed strong feelings for Leo, but we'd never crossed the line. Nor would I have done without telling Con first.

He read my silence as guilt. He bent down and ripped a clump of turf from the ground. 'I knew it.'

I sat back. Once again we were poles apart. I really didn't want us to end like this.

'I'm going now,' I said, hitching to the front of the bench. 'I really hope everything goes well with the filming and it all turns out for you.'

He muttered something I couldn't hear and flopped against the back of the bench. He'd turned his face towards the sun and closed his eyes, shutting me out.

I stood more resolutely this time, and squeezed his knee as I walked past him, heading for the main gate.

Chapter 41

I met Hannah that evening and we went for a long walk along the Thames before settling into a gastro-pub near Tower Bridge. Unlike Imogen, Hannah wasn't a team player. She was impetuous and disorganised, but with flashes of inspiration and downright genius at times. If she hadn't been a psychotherapist, she could have easily been a wedding planner or even a TV producer.

We ordered a bottle of red – I've no idea what type, but it was full-bodied and slipped down a treat – and shared a plate of nachos with salsa and sour cream.

I poured my heart out about Leo and Con. The more my inhibitions melted away, the more distraught I felt about losing any chance of a future with Leo.

Hannah was usually loud and gregarious, never one to let a party fizzle out, but on this occasion she listened, she understood and asked sensitive questions, until my eyelids began to droop. A thick fog of extreme exhaustion settled on me shortly afterwards.

She was one of those annoying people who never flagged and she had to nudge me twice to keep me awake. She called me a cab before 10pm to take me home. Apparently, I'd started to snore.

I felt strangely serene when I got back to my flat. My life felt like it had reached a tipping point where things could only get better. It was probably something to do with the alcohol, but I wanted to believe this tortuous phase was behind me now.

I opened my laptop and found a return email from Dr Peach, Imogen's contact in New York. One line gripped my attention:

...suffice to say, I am familiar with the research involving the 'parrot in the bedroom' scenario and while I am unable to reveal the source until The Jeffersen Prize is announced, I can confirm the author is female and not based at a London institution.

I sat back, mulling it over. So, whoever was conducting up-to-date false memory research wasn't Leo or anyone else at St Luke's. It was as though a blockage in my lungs had suddenly dissolved and I could breathe properly again.

I sent a silent thank you towards the heavens.

Maybe it was time to go to the police. I had no one to protect any more, although I knew they wouldn't be happy that I'd taken so long to speak out. I would have to get my story straight and be prepared for the worst, but if that led to them finding the bastard, it would be worth it. I made the decision then and there; I'd call them tomorrow.

All that was left was a decision about Leo's notes. They were in the original carrier bag, hanging behind my bedroom door. I wanted to keep the letter he'd written about me, but I didn't see the value in keeping anything else. There was nothing there that the medical world needed to know about. I made the decision to tell Felicity and shred the papers at work the next day – and that would be that.

In my intoxicated state, I snatched at my dressing gown on the back of the door and managed to rip the plastic bag, scattering the contents onto the floor. I bent down to collect Leo's notes together and spotted a loose envelope I hadn't seen before. It had sticky tape on the side and must have been secured inside one of the folders. The words, *Dr Sam Willerby – Private & Confidential* were written on the front in Leo's handwriting. I snapped my finger along the gummed edge and a USB stick fell out.

With it was a photograph. I recognised the silver necklace with the opal around the girl's neck. On the back it said, *I know you didn't choose this, Dad, but it's perfect.*

I brought my hand to my mouth.

There was a sticky note attached to the USB stick. *I owe you this,* was all it said. I brought my laptop into my bedroom and plugged in the stick. There was only one document, an audio file, so I downloaded it and clicked play. I certainly couldn't leave this until tomorrow.

'I'll get straight to the point because I haven't got much time.' It was Leo's voice. He sounded hoarse and strained. I sat on the bed and pulled my knees up to my chest, hugging a pillow.

He cleared his throat. 'I've made a dreadful, dreadful mistake,' he continued. 'And I know it's going to ruin everything between us. I will try to explain and hope at the end of it, you might have a shred of understanding.' His breath sounded laboured.

I didn't understand. Leo must have made this recording in hospital. Had he come out of his coma at some point?

'They left my wife to die. They walked away when they could have saved her.'

What was he talking about?

'There were potential bone-marrow donors for my wife – and none of them came forward. I tried to coerce them at first, but it didn't work.'

I clicked pause and staggered to the kitchen sink to pour myself a glass of water. Then I threw it away and poured myself half a glass of brandy instead. I came back and clicked play, drawing away sharply as if I'd detonated a bomb.

'I was desperate to find a donor,' he said. 'I ran secret tests and, out of hundreds, I finally found four patients who were a match – right here in the hospital – but they wouldn't help.' His voice faltered. 'Jane, Jake, Terry and Conrad were all tissue-matches for her, but none of them could be persuaded to donate their stem cells. I pleaded, but *not one* of them would give Helena a chance.'

His throat rasped. 'By then, I knew Helena was dying and there was no way back. I was upset. To the point where I found myself standing on the clifftops at Dover, thinking about jumping off. But I changed my mind and came back.'

My mind whirred trying to take it all in.

'I resorted to false memory methods I'd first explored years ago. I knew all about recent advances in optogenetics. I thought I could get those who were tissue matches to change their minds by instilling memories that would invoke shame and guilt.

'I spoke to experts to check the finer points of the procedure long before you and I talked about it, but I didn't tell them why I was interested. The process involved technical know-how, but it could be carried out in a hospital setting, using scalp electrodes fed back to a bio-amp with a serial cable.'

I pressed the pillow to my mouth in disbelief.

'I thought the false memories would trigger a desire to help. I thought it would make them come forward, but it didn't work. Instead, they turned the guilt on themselves and…you know the outcome…'

His voice was hoarse now.

'I knew inflicting the false memories was cruel, but I never dreamt it would lead where it did. I just wanted them to feel overwhelming compassion and respond by presenting themselves as donors. But it didn't have that effect. That was so incredibly short-sighted of me. I didn't want them to *die* – I only wanted them to come forward…'

Leo *was* the killer!

I felt my faith in him curl up inside me and shrink to a crisp. 'Leo – how could you do such a thing?' I whispered.

A yawning chasm opened up between us, pushing us away from each other. I was on one side and he was on the other. Divided by far more than life and death.

'I wanted you to hear it from me,' his voice went on.

'I arranged unnecessary "check-ups" for those four patients after the normal treatment for their injuries. Then I went to work implanting the false images. You were right about that novel – the one you tracked down. My God – you are clever! I borrowed scenes where innocent victims were trapped and panicking, but I added one important element: the oppressive guilt – memories where each of them ignored innocent people crying out…'

I slapped my hands over my ears, appalled, locked in my own bewilderment. Leo was right here, speaking to me in the room while inside I was silently screaming at him. He said he hadn't meant for the patients to die – hadn't meant for it to go as far as causing their suicides. But was that a lie, as well?

'It only took around forty minutes, involving electric shocks and bright lights activated at intervals as I read out passages from the book. None of them had any idea what had happened once they came round.

'I was useless in the face of my wife's illness. I felt guilty that it was her, not me, who was dying. Helena didn't deserve it. I was so *desperate*. Can you understand that? I was powerless to do anything about it. I'm a surgeon, for Christ's sake. I'm used to making everything better.'

And playing God..!

I didn't know whether to yell or burst into tears. I sank to the bed and hammered my fists into the mattress. More than anything I was bitterly disappointed that this man I admired so much had sunk so low.

Why had he gone to all this trouble to tell me this?

'It's only a matter of time before you work everything out. You knew the patients weren't genuine survivors of the Liverpool Street fire. You're a smart woman – the novel, the fake signature in Terry's records. You were piecing it all together.'

There was a hiatus and I wondered if the recording had finished. Then his voice, barely there, resumed. 'I was the one who left the lead in the bookcase in your office. I was taping your sessions to see how the patients were responding.'

I shook my head.

'There were only ever four of them and you're not affected, by the way. Any nightmares you're still having are purely down to stress. I know I should be punished, but there's not much time left for that. Is death punishment enough? I wish things had been different. I think you know what I mean…'

There was a click, followed by a prolonged hiss.

I couldn't move. Nothing was solid any more. Then came an overwhelming surge of despair; an acute sense of loneliness and I sat up.

Everything looked the same; the fluffy bunny Con had won at a funfair on the laundry basket, the coat hanger sticking out from behind the chest of drawers. The half-drunk mug of cold coffee on the carpet waiting to be kicked over. It was as if everything in the flat was mocking me, every item was staring at me with its barefaced normality.

But everything had changed.

Leo had betrayed me.

My thoughts were charging around too fast. I had to tell the police. Didn't I? If I didn't explain what I knew, wasn't I some kind of accessory to the deaths of my patients? Could I be charged for failing to report a crime? Then again, had any crime actually been committed?

I stood and screamed at the audio file on my laptop; a thin white bar across the screen, like a flat line on an ICU monitor.

'Tell me you weren't in your right mind, Leo! Tell me it wasn't you who did this terrible thing!'

Why wasn't he here, standing in front of me, so he could explain everything? The audio file was defiantly silent.

I wanted to despise him, but all I could feel was a devastating sadness. I finished the last dregs of the brandy, crawled into bed and closed my eyes. But my mind was still alert. I went over and over the facts, trying to work out what I should do next. There had been three suicides, but had there been a crime? Death by proxy? Would that stand up in court? Con wasn't a credible witness – he couldn't remember a thing.

I thought of Leo, angry and hurt. He'd taken secret tissue samples and run tests and found that those four individuals were potential donors. When they'd refused to help, he'd implanted false memories in their minds to make them come forward. This decent man had seriously lost his moral bearings under the weight of his grief. But, he'd tried to redeem himself, eager to reverse what he'd done to Con. He'd died trying to save him. That had to stand for something. Didn't it?

I stayed up most of the night, playing the recording again and again. I wished I'd known he'd briefly come out of his coma. How long had he been conscious? Long enough for this and, now I thought about it, long enough to take steps to make sure I was reinstated from my suspension, too.

I wished someone had let me know. I could have seen him. I had so many questions stored up inside, but perhaps that's what he couldn't face.

By the time dawn was oozing through the cracks in my curtains, I was convinced. Leo had certainly committed a grave sin – he had tampered with people's free will, but he *hadn't* known his methods would have had such dire consequences.

That part hadn't been deliberate, I felt sure of it – or maybe that was just what I wanted to believe.

I made up my mind. I'd wouldn't go to the police. There was no need to ruin Leo's name or drag his daughters through an ignominious scandal – they'd suffered enough. It was over – Leo said there were no more than four victims. He was dead. Surely, he'd paid his price.

As for Leo's USB stick, I wanted to keep it, for the time being at least. Even though the content was hard to hear, I couldn't part with his voice just yet.

I propped the photograph of Kim on the mantelpiece and dragged myself to the kitchen to make a strong coffee.

Chapter 42

25 September

The car jerks to a halt. My hands make ten-to-two on the steering wheel, but I have no idea what the time is.

I switch off the engine. Tiny spots of rain spatter the windscreen, gradually coating it with liquid fog and I marvel at the way each drop looks like it is heading straight for me and then is caught, just before it reaches my face, by the intervening glass.

I get out and begin the ascent, following the narrow winding path, but it's not steep like the first time. The rain spits, pricking my cheeks; the wind is fierce, pressing my trousers against my legs as if I'm under water. Just like before. Only now it's no struggle.

I have all the time in the world.

The air is crystal clear with a mossy undertone and there is a vague aroma of freshly caught fish. With every breath I feel renewed, emancipated, expansive.

Being back here in Stockholm, where my life began, is like completing a perfect circle.

I cast my mind back to St Luke's. When those four patients turned their backs, I had to do something. It was devious and against all my better judgement, but I never wanted them to die – Sam must know that, surely – it wasn't meant to go that far.

Some might say staging my own death was a cop-out, but I'd got myself into a tight corner in the end. I couldn't risk carrying out the reversal on Con and then turning round to find my wrists in handcuffs. Sam was smart – she would have worked it out sooner or later, but I wouldn't have left unless I'd known one thing for sure. That everything had been set up so she could carry on without me. She didn't need me anymore. And I was forced to run – I had no choice. I could never have been sure that Sam would understand.

I head towards the rocky outcrop, soaking up the view across the lake – it's breathtaking. Islands are dotted here and there on the horizon, like broken chunks of tarmac, stretching north-west towards Norway, towards other worlds.

The fall from the roof came at the right time. It looked worse than it was; I had a broken rib and internal bruising, that's all. I turned it to my advantage – into my escape route.

I understand how hospitals work and Lian helped everything along even though she knew I wasn't taking her with me. I made it clear my feelings weren't the same. How could they be? Helena is still the blood running through my veins.

Leaving Felicity and Kim was the hardest thing about my entire plan – and so soon after their mother's death. After I was seen at A&E, Lian made sure I had a private room and that my daughters were my only visitors. She made sure they arrived at the right time and applied clever make-up to make me look like I was at death's door. Having to lie there, frozen and mute, while they leant over me, weeping, nearly destroyed me.

Then it was a matter of Lian finding a corpse of similar age and build, and swapping toe tags at the right time. An admin 'mix up' we engineered meant I was sent for cremation, before the coroner got to hear about the death and by then I was reduced to dust.

I stare out over the sheen of untroubled water. The sun will set here in a couple of hours.

In the long run, my demise will be better for everyone. Felicity and Kim always thought I was a useless father. They'll get the money from both properties and can do what they want with their lives. Best for them to start again with a clean slate; there is too much ground to make up.

Then there's Sam. She intrigues me in so many ways; calm on the surface, but complex and troubled underneath. We are both made the same. If things had been different, who knows what might have happened between us.

I come across a pool and pick up a smooth stone. I skim it across the water and it kisses the surface six times before taking a final dive into the depths.

Sam has probably told everyone about my misdemeanours by now – only 'Dr Leo Hansson' is dead and the story is over. Such a shame she is too morally squeaky-clean to be let into this final secret. Maybe she could have been part of it, but we are all making sacrifices.

The outcome is I live and breathe. Not as before, but with a new name, Anders Olsson. I've still got the off-shore account and I'm free to take my place in the world again, only here, no one knows who I am. My forged papers mean I'm no longer a plastic surgeon. Or a closet psychologist. I can leave all that behind me and start something new. I've no idea what that will be, but I will do my utmost to make a difference.

I wait until the minute hand on my watch reaches 4.30pm precisely before turning back. I'll return to my apartment via the indoor market at Östermalms Saluhall. Stop for a coffee at that cinnamon bakery Helena loved when we came here, years ago.

I get into the car, lay my jacket carefully on the back seat and wait a minute before starting the engine. My mind rewinds to the day I climbed the cliffs in Dover. My other life. I was in shreds then, trying to find a way out. Now, I don't need gravity to claim me. I am a new man. With a new beginning.

I adjust the gold cufflinks in my crisp shirtsleeves and flip the key in the ignition.

THE END

About the Author

A. J. Waines is a number one bestselling author, topping the UK and Australian Amazon Charts in two consecutive years, with ***Girl on a Train***. The author was a psychotherapist for fifteen years, during which time she worked with ex-offenders from high-security institutions, gaining a rare insight into abnormal psychology. She is now a full-time novelist with publishing deals in UK, France, Germany, Norway, Hungary and Canada (audiobooks).

Her fourth novel, ***No Longer Safe*** sold over 30,000 copies in the first month, in twelve countries worldwide. In 2016 and 2017, the author was ranked in the Top 10 UK Authors on Amazon KDP (Kindle Direct Publishing).

A. J. Waines lives in Hampshire, UK, with her husband.

Find out more at **www.ajwaines.co.uk**. She's also on **Twitter** (@ AJWaines), **Facebook** and you can sign up for her **Newsletter** at http://eepurl.com/bamGuL

Lightning Source UK Ltd.
Milton Keynes UK
UKHW012323150920
369943UK00001B/186

9 781912 604692